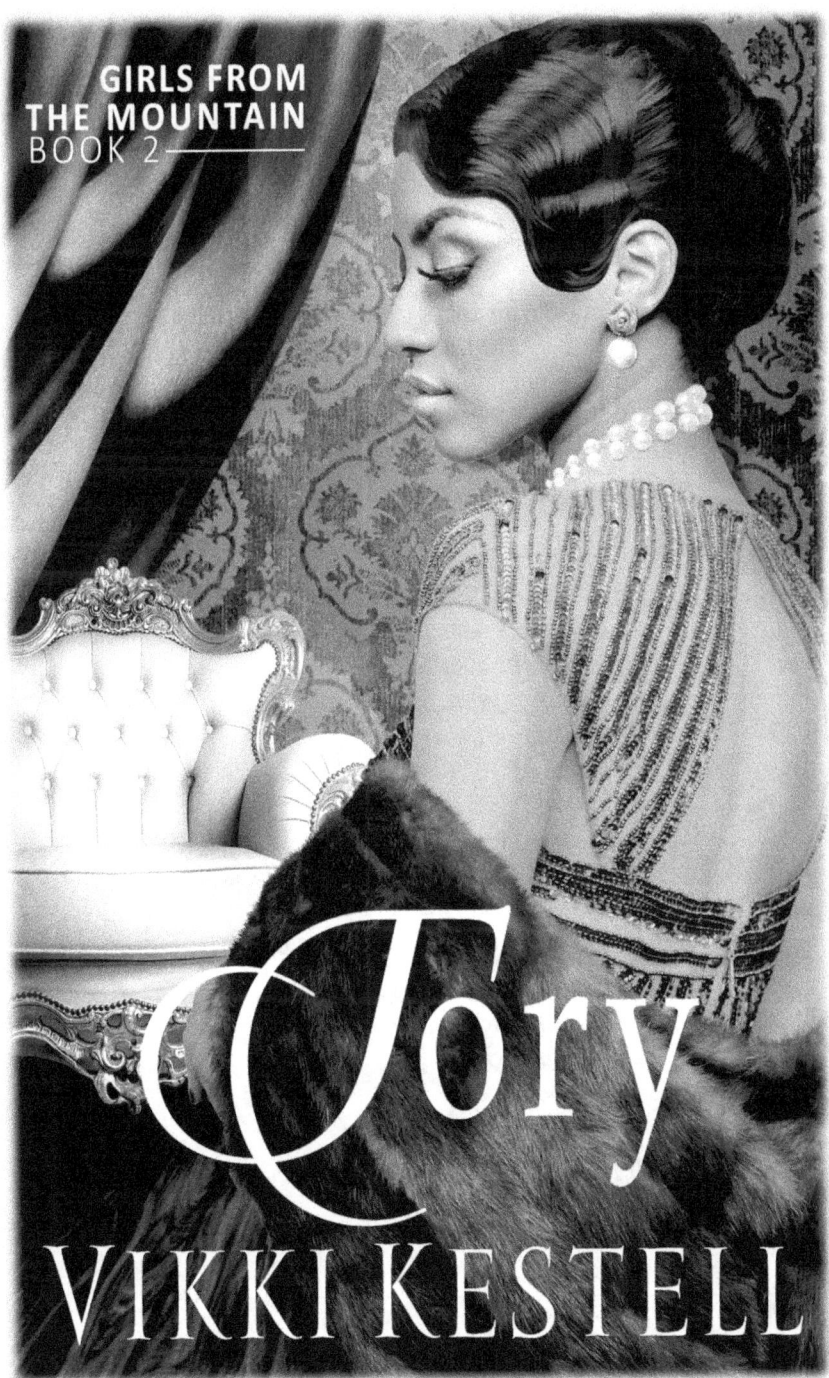

GIRLS FROM
THE MOUNTAIN
BOOK 2 ———

Tory

VIKKI KESTELL

*Faith-Filled
Fiction*™

www.faith-filledfiction.com | www.vikkikestell.com

Girls from the Mountain, Book 2
Vikki Kestell

BOOKS BY VIKKI KESTELL

GIRLS FROM THE MOUNTAIN
Book 1: *Tabitha*
Book 2: *Tory*
Book 3: *Sarah Redeemed*

A PRAIRIE HERITAGE
Book 1: *A Rose Blooms Twice*
Book 2: *Wild Heart on the Prairie*
Book 3: *Joy on This Mountain*
Book 4: *The Captive Within*
Book 5: *Stolen*
Book 6: *Lost Are Found*
Book 7: *All God's Promises*
Book 8: *The Heart of Joy—A Short Story* (eBook only)

LAYNIE PORTLAND
Book 1: *Laynie Portland, Spy Rising—The Prequel*
Book 2: *Laynie Portland, Retired Spy*
Book 3: *Laynie Portland, Renegade Spy*
Book 4: *Laynie Portland, Spy Resurrected*

NANOSTEALTH
Book 1: *Stealthy Steps*
Book 2: *Stealth Power*
Book 3: *Stealth Retribution*
Book 4: *Deep State Stealth* (2019 Selah Award Winner)

Girls from the Mountain, Book 2
Vikki Kestell

Victoria Washington—sophisticated and elegant, owner of Victoria's House of Fashion, designer of haute couture gowns for the wealthy and elite of Denver, a brilliant and successful businesswoman in her own right.

Tory, as she is known to her friends, is also a supporter of Palmer House—a most extraordinary refuge for young women rescued from prostitution. Deceived, kidnapped, and beaten into submission, the girls of Palmer House had been held captive in Corinth, the little mountain village above Denver, forced into an occupation not of their own choosing, until freed by the combined efforts of U.S. Marshals and Pinkerton detectives. Through no fault of her own, Tory *was* one of those girls—also rescued from a life of shame and degradation.

And Tory's past hides more than one dark secret: She was born in the Deep South to Adeline Washington—a negress, the daughter and granddaughter of slaves, and the "kept" woman of a wealthy, married, white man. Tory's mixed blood, her illegitimate birth, and the shame of her exploitation follow her down the mountain and haunt her, even to the cusp of her success.

What will happen when those who hate Tory expose her secrets? Will her business and reputation survive the scandals? Or are the rumors a cover for a more sinister plot? Is Tory's life also in danger? And, if so, why?

GIRLS FROM THE MOUNTAIN
    Book 1: *Tabitha*
    Book 2: *Tory*
    Book 3: *Sarah Redeemed*

GIRLS FROM THE MOUNTAIN

The full stories of a select group of women introduced in the little mountain village of Corinth or later at Palmer House in Denver, the mile-high city (hence the series title, **Girls from the Mountain**).

Tabitha, *Tory*, and *Sarah Redeemed* are three such stories—the testimonies of fallen women redeemed by God's amazing grace, led out of darkness to become lights in this sinful world. Each book can be read as a standalone volume but having already read **A Prairie Heritage** may increase your enjoyment.

తురు**❋**తురు

DENVER, 1909

Joy was thoughtful. "You said something just now... You called them *girls from the mountain*. I rather like that."

"Certainly less degrading than 'former prostitutes.'" Grant smiled his endearing half-smile.

"Perhaps that is how we should refer to them from now on. Of course, when the Lord gives us women from Denver, the phrase will no longer apply."

"Denver is surrounded by mountains. I don't see a problem with it. It could be our own little code for the young ladies of Palmer House."

Joy nodded. "I like that."

—An Excerpt from *The Captive Within*

Acknowledgements

Many thanks to my esteemed teammates,
Cheryl Adkins and **Greg McCann**,
who give selflessly of themselves
to make each new book the most effective
instrument of God's grace possible.
I love and appreciate you.

Additional thanks
to my wonderful launch team!
**Cindy, Deborah, Emily, Jessica,
LuAnn, Mary Ellen, Patricia,
Rita, Sharon,** and **Sharyn.**
Your insights have helped make *Tory*
a blessing to many hearts.

Cover Design

Vikki Kestell

To My Readers

This book is a work of fiction,
what I term Faith-Filled Fiction™.
While the characters and events are fiction,
they are situated within the historical record.
To God be the glory.

Scripture Quotations

The King James Version (KJV)
Public Domain

AUTHOR'S NOTE

I have attempted to craft this story within the historical frame of reference. We learn from history, whether it was kind or harsh, right or wrong, and it is important that we maintain an authentic and accurate picture of our past.

As an author, I dare not (and should not) alter or moderate historical/cultural facts (such as ugly, offensive, and racially disparaging designations) to fit present-day sensibilities. A truthful recounting of our history shows us how far we've grown—or deteriorated—as a society. As George Santayana wrote, "Those who cannot remember the past are condemned to repeat it."

I beg your forgiveness if aspects of Tory's experiences are painful to read.

—Vikki Kestell

$\mathscr{P}$ROLOGUE

DENVER, COLORADO
FEBRUARY 1911

Victoria Washington entered the ballroom to enthusiastic acclaim. She wore a gown of her own design for the fashion parade—a lovely, beaded creation that sparkled and shimmered along her slim figure as she moved. The light glinting from the amber beads infused her gleaming caramel skin with rich fire. The mahogany fox stole draped about her arms was the perfect accent.

Tory circulated among a throng of guests, the cream of Denver society. She thanked them for coming to view her spring lineup and accepted their accolades while wearing a small smile—an expression that projected confidence and satisfaction, but it was a smile that gave nothing away. Particularly her fear.

Near the end of the reception, Tory retired from the crowd and stood near a watermarked silk curtain overhanging a cozy nook. From her vantage point in the room, Tory studied her guests and patrons—the wealthy and pampered of Denver.

Without turning her head, Tory swept her eyes across the room, searching. Searching for that one individual in the crowd Mr. O'Dell had insisted would attend her event: the unknown someone who had proven himself determined to destroy her reputation and her business.

The same person who had already made one attempt on her life.

I am poised on the brink of success in this city while this man plots to harm me—but why? I do not understand. And will the reasons matter if he succeeds in ruining me?

Tory exhaled to calm her nerves. The "why" was unimportant at the moment and must wait for an answer.

Mr. O'Dell believes this man—whomever he is—will be here, that my event presents him with a favorable time and opportunity to strike, neither of which he will pass over.

"He is likely here already," Tory breathed, "waiting, biding his time."

She blinked as a thought occurred to her. *It must be a person with great personal animosity in his heart toward me—so it must be someone from my past.*

Someone from my past . . .

PART 1:
LOUISIANA

CHAPTER 1

But thou, O Lord,
art a shield for me; my glory,
and the lifter up of mine head.
Psalm 3:3

APRIL 1901

The hours following dawn promised balmy skies and warming temperatures. The trees of the orchard flowered and dropped their blossoms; the mingled fragrances of lilac, honeysuckle, and wild wisteria saturated the heavy, moist air.

On any ordinary morning this lovely, Tory would pursue her studies for three hours under the watchful eyes of her *mère*, Adeline. When Tory had completed her lessons to her mother's satisfaction, the two of them would wander the grounds of Sugar Tree for an hour.

Not this morning. No, this day was far too significant for school work or frivolous pleasures, and Tory gave no thought to engaging in ladylike outdoor play.

Ladylike outdoor play.

Tory giggled aloud. Adeline also allowed Tory forty minutes of unsupervised play time each afternoon—and she expected Tory to amuse herself in the proper manner of a genteel young lady, such as dressing her dolls or some similar sedate pastime. Tory almost always used those forty minutes to run wild through their orchard, racing along the lip of the bluff, glimpsing the shimmer of the river to their south, flying as fast as her long legs could carry her.

She would run until her lungs caught fire—and she would keep running, pushing herself faster and faster as the fire spread throughout her entire body and a second burst of energy fueled her forward. Afterward, Tory would bathe her face at the pump in the courtyard behind the house, tidy her hair and dress, and wait, her hands folded demurely in her lap, on the bench near the garden's fountain for her *mère* to call her to tea.

Adeline, never the wiser, usually remarked, "The fresh air does you much good, Victoria."

Tory smiled. No, she would not be "playing" today.

She scrutinized her white kid gloves. The gloves' tiny pearl buttons ran along the inside of her slender wrists. The gloves were so tight that the buttoned closure pinched her wrists' tender skin. Tory worried that her long, tapered fingers might burst the seams at the gloves' tips, for she hadn't had a new pair of gloves in more than a year, and her hands—indeed, her entire frame—had shot up since last spring.

Tory's stomach growled. The small portion of mush and half slice of toast she was allowed for breakfast never satisfied her for long. She grimaced—it was not as though food at Sugar Tree was scarce! This morning Tory had eyed with longing the plate of sausages and eggs intended for her mother. Adeline, however, admonished her daughter at every meal to curb her hunger just as she restrained hers.

"A Southern woman curtails her appetite," Adeline murmured. "She must not allow her figure to suffer from overindulgence."

It was a discipline Adeline practiced and intended to instill in her daughter: Whatever food was placed before Adeline, she ate no more than five bites of it. Adeline expected the same restraint in Tory. The girl received a full bowl of mush swimming in cream and two slices of buttered toast but, under Adeline's watchful eye, Tory ate the allowed half a slice of toast and five bites of mush.

The remains were removed from the table—and Tory imagined the servants gobbling them down.

I know I would.

The remembrance of hot, juicy sausages brought on further complaints from Tory's deprived belly, and her dark brows knotted.

Tory suspected that Adeline's resolve in curtailing her daughter's appetite was, in part, to slow Tory's unprecedented growth. However, the limits put upon Tory's eating were in vain: Her body grew of its own will until Tory looked to be all long arms and gangly legs. As a consequence of her height, Tory was often thought to be older than she actually was.

I am but ten years old, yet my chin is as high as Sassy's great-granddaughter's—and she is thirteen.

Tory pulled her mouth into a solemn moue as she pondered this phenomenon, and her wide-set chocolate-brown eyes grew thoughtful. The fact that Tory was tall for her age presented a number of difficulties. For example, the hem of Tory's skirts, according to her mother's well-thumbed fashion magazines, should have ended somewhere around mid-calf.

The girl was knowledgeable of fashion for her age: She studied each precious periodical with more care than did her mother.

Tory knew that knee-length hemlines had been appropriate for her *last* year when she was nine. However, Tory was ten now, and she had grown—and yet she was wearing the same dress she had worn on a similar day the previous spring.

Tory tried to swallow down her concern. *Will he notice how ill my dress fits me? Will he remark on it?*

Four times a year, the household spun itself into a frenzy of cleaning and cooking for today's visitor. Four times a year, *Maman* fretted over her own toilet and appearance—leaving nothing to chance and no detail undone. And four times a year, Adeline expected Tory to deliver a flawless presentation before today's guest.

Tory sighed and examined her hands, looking for offending smudges. Finding the gloves to be spotless, she smoothed the gossamer folds of her dress. She dared not blemish or stain the delicate fabric—such a *faux pas* could ruin the day. As she touched the fabric, Tory willed the voluminous skirts to, at the least, cover her knees. Yes, their visitor was exacting, but Adeline Washington was more so—and Tory wanted to please her mother.

Tory gave the gloves one last tug, hoping to stretch them even the tiniest bit and relieve the pressure the gloves' tight seams exerted upon her fingertips. The gloves did not move even a smidge.

Now that she was primped and ready, Tory would wait at a drawing room window for their guest to arrive. She spent the time with one of her mother's fashion magazines propped before her, a pad of paper on her lap. Tory generally sketched whatever caught her eye, but what captured her interest the most were the women pictured within the pages of the magazines and their lovely apparel. Tory had filled a folio with her fashion sketches—many pages bearing her own improvements or changes, even if her artistry was immature.

Every few minutes, Tory would tear her attention from her sketch pad and peer between the curtains, looking for their visitor to appear. Monsieur Declouette always arrived midmorning upon his magnificent dappled bay, *Victorieux*. Tory loved the spectacle of Monsieur Declouette galloping up the long, graveled drive, his tall, upright figure one with his horse. *Victorieux* would toss his head and prance in high spirits as his master reined him in.

In past years, the groom would take Monsieur Declouette's steed, the butler would announce the visitor, and Tory's mother, Adeline, would receive him in the parlor. Monsieur Declouette and Adeline would take tea and visit for the space of an hour before Adeline summoned Tory.

And in past years, Tory's governess, Miss La Forge, would oversee her dress, hair, and other preparations. Once Monsieur Declouette had arrived, Miss La Forge would wait with Tory in the library that served as their school room until Tory's mother rang the delicate silver bell in the parlor.

At the sound of the bell, Tory would walk—with great decorum—to the parlor and knock upon the door. Tory's mother would answer, "Come," in her low, sweet voice, and Tory would enter the room, closing the door behind her.

Tory, with her hands clasped before her, would offer her mother a kiss on each cheek. Then she would greet their visitor.

Tory would approach his chair and sink into a deep curtsy. "*Bonjour*, Monsieur Declouette." She always spoke her greeting in French, and he answered her in the same.

"*Bonjour*, Victoria. Come. Let me have a look at you."

Tory would stand before him, and he would run his eyes over her and comment upon her appearance and how well she was turned out. Then, at his request, Tory would recite poetry, play on the tiny pianoforte, and offer examples of her schoolwork for his examination. She particularly liked showing him her sketches.

"Victoria has a gift, Adeline," Monsieur Declouette once remarked, "a keen sense of style and fashion. Why, soon her drawings will be every whit as good as those found in newspapers and magazines."

"Thank you, Henri. Yes, she has a lovely hand," Adeline had replied, and Tory had beamed with pleasure and pride.

Before she was dismissed, Monsieur Declouette would put a number of questions to her, after which he would present her with a gift—a book, a card of ribbons, or some such trinket.

The questions Monsieur Declouette asked varied, but the routine did not. The formal ritual was long established.

After a private luncheon, Adeline and Monsieur Declouette would climb the stairs and retire to Adeline's chambers for an hour. Adeline described this recess as "a rest" before Monsieur Declouette took his leave for the ride back to his home in the city proper.

Tory was not allowed upstairs while Monsieur Declouette "rested," so she entertained herself in the schoolroom or, if the weather permitted, out-of-doors to walk the garden or orchard paths with her sketch pad until something caught her eye.

When Adeline and their guest descended the stairs, Tory would again, from behind the drawing room curtains, observe as Monsieur

Declouette mounted *Victorieux* and galloped away. He would return in another three or four months, always sending a letter in advance to announce the date of his next visit.

In a manner Tory did not comprehend, she and her mother were dependent upon Henri Declouette. Since Tory's *mère* had hinted at their dependence (through exhortations for Tory to do her best not to disappoint the gentleman), Tory had drawn her own conclusions. She understood that their large, comfortable home and the orchards and grounds around them had belonged to Monsieur Declouette's late mother. Tory assumed that he had inherited the house and grounds. She also supposed that the funds to manage the household came from him—although, of late, the amount seemed to be far less than what was needed.

Tory had never gone without new gloves and a new wardrobe in years gone by, and Tory knew her mother was worried.

Monsieur Declouette had missed his visit in December. Christmas was generally merry because of the wealth of presents and cheer Monsieur Declouette customarily brought with him during his late December visit. But, this past December, he had sent a note conveying his regrets. The note had accompanied two small, inconsequential gifts in his stead, one for Adeline and one for Tory.

Tory was not privy to the contents of his note but, after reading it, Adeline had taken to her bed with a sick headache for two days. The holiday had been dismal.

Tory understood that Monsieur Declouette's visit today, the first in seven months, was of great consequence. It would not do for Tory to appear before him in any state other than one of ladylike perfection.

"So, are ye ready, Miss Tory?"

Startled out of her thoughts, Tory jumped a little. "Yes, Sassy."

"Well, let me look at ye." The house's cook, Sassy Brown, had shortened Victoria to Tory, and the girl rather liked the diminutive. Sassy inspected Tory; her wizened black eyes, surrounded by a wealth of ebony creases, missed nothing. No detail escaped her perusal.

"*Quoi?* Ye have no color in your cheeks, child. As always."

Tory raised her face but did not respond while Sassy pinched both of Tory's cheeks repeatedly to coax a flush into her caramel-toned skin.

Tory believed her mother to be the most beautiful woman in the world—and herself to be but a pale and inferior copy of her mother's splendor. Tory's abnormal height and ungainly figure were the subjects of regular discussion among the servants, as was her "color."

Tory's complexion was not the sooty coal-black that Sassy, Sassy's granddaughter Venus, or her great-granddaughter Ellen possessed, nor was it her mother's glowing, inky brilliance. No, Tory's skin gleamed with bronze undertones, and her eyes had a wide, curious cant to them, hinting of indigenous or exotic blood.

Tory's hair also came under continual comment. Adeline kept her own raven tresses oiled and wound in sleek, elegant coils: Every lock gleamed in midnight beauty. Tory's hair was not her mother's purest black but a deep brown. Worse, frizzy, unruly strands shot with perplexing gold peppered Tory's dusky tresses.

Miss La Forge had once spent hours plucking those telltale threads the morning of a visit from Monsieur Declouette. The scorned strands had only grown back. Another time, Miss La Forge had buttoned an apron over Tory's dress and applied bootblack to her curls. Afterward, following Monsieur Declouette's departure, Miss La Forge had stripped Tory and scrubbed the blacking from her hair lest it stain Tory's sheets or clothing.

Tory understood that she was different, although she did not understand why she was different or, more importantly, why those differences mattered. Tory wanted to understand, but she felt uncomfortable asking her *mère*, and it was too late to ask Miss La Forge. Months ago, Tory's governess had packed her belongings and quietly departed.

Of course, Tory had demanded the reason.

"I was constrained to let her go," Adeline had answered. "It was not my desire to dismiss her, but we must economize, Victoria."

Gone with Miss La Forge were the butler, the maids, and the groom—gone with Tory's pony, *Fantaisie*, and *Maman's* horse, *Chevallier*. Of what had once been a staff of nine, Sassy alone remained. She cooked and tended the green garden, while her granddaughter and great-granddaughter came twice weekly to clean.

Tory, with no maid to assist her as she was accustomed, had dressed herself this morning. Afterward, Tory's mother had come to her room and done her daughter's hair in oiled, painstaking ringlets.

Sassy's gruff voice drew Tory out of her thoughts. "Be doing your best now. We be riding the same train as ye."

Tory did not know how to answer Sassy; she did not understand what she meant by "We be riding the same train as ye."

Instead, she asked, "Am I presentable?" Somehow the question meant more, implied more than those three words should have.

"*Oui*. Ye will do. Go now, and watch for our guest as ye do. But have a care to sit still and not be undoing your mother's efforts w' your hair."

"Yes, Sassy."

Tory, too nervous to sketch, waited an hour before her sharp ears picked up the sound of approaching hoofbeats. With her face hidden behind the drawing room curtains, Tory peered through a crack in the panels. There he was! Monsieur Declouette stood in his stirrups as he rounded the bend in the drive at a full gallop. Then, unlike the usual grand flourish of his arrival, he slowed his horse and walked *Victorieux* the remaining distance to the house.

Victorieux did not care for the sedate pace. He jingled his tack and pulled at his bit. Monsieur Declouette paid him little mind and, with his chin dropped down upon his chest, Tory thought he appeared preoccupied. Reflective. Perhaps . . . melancholy?

When man and steed reached the house's front entrance, Monsieur Declouette dismounted. In the absence of a groom, he tied *Victorieux*'s bridle to the ornate hitching post himself—and something clenched in Tory's chest.

Monsieur Declouette loved his horse and spared no effort or expense for his care: Even in the absence of a groom, Tory knew he would not leave *Victorieux* saddled after the heat of a long ride. That is, unless . . . unless he did not mean to stay long?

With no butler to respond to the heavy knocker falling upon the door, Tory expected Sassy to answer. She was startled to hear her *mère's* step in the stone entryway.

Tory crept to the drawing room doorway and listened.

"Henri! Oh, my love, I am overjoyed to see you at last!"

Tory's eyes widened.

"Good morning, Adeline."

In comparison to Adeline's ardent welcome, Monsieur Declouette's greeting fell flat, and the pressure in Tory's chest swelled. She heard little more as her mother and Monsieur Declouette turned into the parlor and closed the door.

Tory's anxiety increased. A desire—no, *a need*—to hear the details of her mother and Monsieur Declouette's conversation gripped Tory. For a long moment, she debated within herself. Then, she stepped out of the drawing room, tiptoed down the hall toward the rear of the house, and slipped out the door closest to the outdoor kitchen.

In a flash, she flew across the grass to the path that rounded the side of the house. She followed the path until she neared the parlor.

The parlor had six French windows, three on the front of the house and three on the side. The windows were tall and narrow, their frames stretching from a foot above the parlor floor to within a foot of the high ceiling. Two parlor windows, one front and one side, were opened outward to allow the gentle breeze to circulate through the room.

Disobeying every stricture and code of conduct her mother had impressed upon her as far back as she could recall, Tory crept toward the nearest open window. A yellow climber rose flowered along the house's stone foundation and beneath the open casement. Tory eyed the lush bush and its many long, thorny tendrils, knowing those spiky barbs would spell disaster for the delicate fabric of her dress.

She could hear her mother and Monsieur Declouette speaking in low, earnest tones; Tory strained closer, but could not make out the words. Then a knock sounded upon the parlor door, interrupting the conversation: Sassy delivering the tea tray. Tory glanced again at the window—so near, but so unapproachable—and elected a wild course of action.

While Sassy arranged the tea items, Tory fumbled with the buttons on her dress. Undoing all of them took longer than she wanted, but soon she was able to skim it over her narrow hips, drop the garment to the garden path, and step out of it. Clad in her chemise and bloomers, Tory picked up the dress and spread out its length beside the path to minimize wrinkles.

Then, with her spotless gloves to protect her hands, Tory crouched down, pulled back a long, trailing rose bough, and crept closer to the window. She had to wind her way through many thorny branches that scratched and pulled at her gloves, her underclothes, her bare arms, and the wealth of ringlets her mother had painstakingly wound into her hair before she crouched beneath the parlor window.

When her fingers touched the warm stones of the house's foundation, Tory unbent her knees and eased herself upright until she could peek over the window sill and take in the scene before her. Sassy had closed the parlor door behind her, and Tory saw her mother in profile—serene, the epitome of grace—pouring Monsieur Declouette's tea, adding the sugar he took in it, and handing him his cup. Monsieur Declouette sat nearer the window; his back and shoulder turned toward Tory.

Tory withdrew to the side of the window where she could listen without being seen. The next words Tory heard came from her mother. Tory frowned as Adeline spoke: Her mother sounded nervous.

Uncertain. Out of character.

"We have a crab salad for our luncheon today, Henri. Fresh greens, the first of the season. Quite refreshing."

"I do apologize, Adeline, but I will not be staying for lunch."

"Henri? But you always take lunch with me!"

"I am sorry, but no, I cannot. I must . . . I must speak to you and depart immediately after." He hesitated and added, "Adeline, what I say will, no doubt, distress you."

"Henri! No, please!"

Tory heard her mother's tea cup rattle against her saucer as she set it on the table before her. It was, for Tory, another indication of how shaken her mother was.

A lady's every action is graceful and measured; she makes no sound other than the gentle conversation of a refined mind.

"Adeline, do not make this more difficult than it already is. I am not a callous man, an unfeeling man; I came in person to say what needs to be said. After all we have meant to each other, I did not want to . . . break this news to you through the impersonal lines of a letter."

"Do not speak; please, I beg you, Henri—do not destroy my heart!" Adeline's cry ended on a sob.

Tory's heart thundered against her ribs, and she began to tremble. She had never seen or heard her mother—always composed and self-possessed—in the throes of emotional agony. Being witness to her distress was like the ground shaking beneath Tory's feet.

A gentlewoman does not yield to discomfiture or strong emotion. She manages herself at all times.

"Adeline, my dear Adeline! I have never heard you thus! But you *must* listen, my darling, for it cannot be helped. My circumstances have altered dramatically, and our . . . arrangement cannot go on as it has these past twelve years. Please. You must hear me."

Several moments of silence passed before he muttered, "The family businesses are in difficulties—mysterious difficulties. At present, I can scarcely maintain my obligations."

"Henri, I love you! Please—"

"Pray, do not interrupt, Adeline. I wish to be clear, and I must finish. My son goes to university in the fall—and I will be hard pressed to pay his school fees. My daughter, Yvonne, will be a *débutante* this season, and I must be able to buy her wardrobe and provide a dowry for her.

"Adeline, when you and I met, I confided to you that Marguerite and Bastiann were lovers, that my *wife* had betrayed me with my *brother*. Although they have been most circumspect, their *affaire* has strengthened rather than waned over time.

"Until of late, Bastiann had shown little regard for the workings of our family's dealings. As long as he received his allowance and dividends on time, he was content for me to shoulder the burdens and day-to-day responsibilities of our several enterprises.

"However, he has, over the past eight months, ingratiated himself into the confidences of some senior employees. His interest concerns me—as do his probing questions to my accountant. I believe he has sown his own funds here and there, seeking to buy or foment disloyalty between me and my employees regarding my management and leadership.

"I now suspect Marguerite and Bastiann of working together to overthrow me. As I said, income from the businesses has, inexplicably, dwindled. At the same time, I believe Bastiann looks to disclose my . . . relationship with you and the monies I've diverted to keep you. What better way to disgrace me than to blame my inability to provide for my family on my 'immoral' expenditures?

"Bastiann knows that as long as I pay his allowance and dividends on time, the money from the businesses is mine to do with as I please, but that would not hold back the scathing rebuke of society should I fail in my family obligations. I believe he and Marguerite intend to charge me with financial malfeasance and adultery in the court of public opinion—all while hiding behind their own façade of self-righteous injury. Marguerite will don the airs of the aggrieved party while keeping her own wrongdoing a secret."

It was as if Adeline had not heard Monsieur Declouette's long explanation, as if she had stopped listening at a point many sentences past. She interrupted his account, her voice rising.

"*Daughter?* You must be able to provide for your *daughter? Victoria is your daughter, too*, Henri! I have done as you asked: I have kept Victoria sheltered from the community and society around us; I have raised her in the manner you wished me to. What of her?"

A Southern woman of good breeding never raises her voice.

Tory felt her arms and legs chill and grow heavy, her body turn to stone.

"You have done well with Victoria, Adeline. If you continue your attention to her education and training, surely she will . . . find someone appropriate."

"*Find* someone appropriate? How? How will I find a worthy husband for her without your support? With no father to claim her and without a dollar to her name, who of any worth would have her? Henri! You promised! You promised to care for her! No! No! I cannot bear this!"

Tory's mother was shaking. Sobbing.

A lady of culture does not weep in the company of others.

Tory found herself weeping with her mother.

"Adeline, it is not like you to make a scene."

All Tory could hear were her mother's wrenching sobs and the echoing words, "Victoria is your daughter, too!"

Heedless of thorns and the ache that had turned her limbs to lead, Tory pushed her way through the long, trailing branches, back out onto the garden path. She grabbed up her frock from the grass and ran across the front of the house, up onto the porch, and through the entrance.

Tory burst into the parlor. The perfect ringlets Adeline had coaxed into her hair were snarled with stickers and bits of leaves. Tory's arms and shoulders were scratched and bleeding. Her chemise was torn and stained.

Adeline and Monsieur Declouette stared at her in astonishment.

"*Mon Dieu!*" Henri Declouette exclaimed. The words were tinged with disgust or amazement—Tory did not know which.

"Victoria!" Adeline admonished—but her admonishment was whispered.

Tory did not care. In her state of undress and dishevelment, she threw her frock to the parlor floor and pointed at Monsieur Declouette.

"Is it true? Are you my father?" she demanded.

The man Tory had admired, had revered, shook his head—not in denial, but in guilt. He licked his lips and glanced at Tory's mother.

Tory stamped her foot as only a child can do. "Are you my father?" she repeated.

When he would not answer, Tory, still pointing at him, turned to her mother. "Is this man my father?"

"Yes. Yes, he is." Tory's *Maman* began to gasp, as if she could not catch her breath.

"Adeline! You were never to tell her! Not even when she was grown!"

"And you were never to abandon us. You promised, Henri. You made a vow to me before Victoria was born that you would care for us. Always."

"I am sorry. I cannot do more, Adeline."

Adeline struggled to put some semblance of order to the chaos engulfing her. "Henri. You cannot leave me; you cannot abandon Victoria. You-you signed a contract with my mother, remember? I have it still. You cannot break such a sacred document. It is as binding as marriage."

Monsieur Declouette frowned. "Oh, Adeline, Adeline. We are entering a new century and *plaçage* died nearly one hundred years ago at the turn of the *last* century. I agreed to the arcane conditions your mother insisted upon in order to assuage *her* conscience—but such an arrangement has no legal standing, has had no basis in society for decades."

Here Henri Declouette paused. "Besides . . ."

He hesitated as though he knew he was taking a step that could not be walked back, was uttering an insult that could not be retracted.

"Besides . . . you are not a light-skinned quadroon, Adeline. You are not less than one-sixteenth negro, as *plaçage* dictated. You are a full-blooded negress, the child of negros. Your grandparents were born into slavery, as were your parents. This cannot be disputed."

Tory's eyes darted from her mother to . . . this man and back, hearing the words and straining to grasp their deeper implications. *Maman's parents and grandparents were slaves?*

"Society has changed, Adeline. Common law unions between white and negro are no longer winked at or even tolerated—they are illegal. The public stigmas dividing us could not be stronger or our *mésalliance* more taboo than it is now."

He gazed out the open window as he spoke. "Please understand: Bastiann watches my every move. It is why I did not come at Christmas. He purposes to blame our business woes upon my mismanagement and the funds with which I have supported you. If my *affaire* with you becomes public knowledge, Marguerite will accuse me of adultery without appearing to have soiled her own hands in doing so. She—the 'righteous' and injured party—will be justified in demanding a divorce, and Bastiann will go to court to wrest the family businesses from my control."

He turned back to Adeline. "You must perceive how tenuous my situation is. I have risked everything to come here today—and I can never return. If I hope to survive Marguerite and Bastiann's snare, I must sever all ties with you."

Adeline whispered, "But . . . but where will Victoria and I go? What will we do?" She was breaking, shattering, as was every foundation, every sure thing in Tory's life.

"Go? You need not go. I gave you this house, my mother's house. It came to me when she died. You have the deed; Sugar Tree is yours. But I cannot send you any further money, nor can I return here ever again."

He patted his breast pocket, reached inside, and drew out a photograph. "I regret that I must return your gift, Adeline; however, it is too risky for me to keep." He stared at the image. "I-I . . . would treasure it, could I retain it safely."

He placed the photograph on the tea table between himself and Adeline, and Tory glimpsed the picture: a likeness of her mother, taken some years before.

Then, as though he had not destroyed two lives, he stood and began to draw on his gloves.

Tory glanced at her mother, but Adeline seemed stunned. Frozen. Unable to move or speak. A shell of the woman Tory knew.

The icy cold that had swept over Tory dissolved and fell away. In its place surged a hot and powerful rage, an anger she had not known could exist.

She advanced on Monsieur Declouette and, standing within inches of him, she screamed, "You, Monsieur Declouette, are a horrible, deceitful, dishonorable scoundrel! You are *not* a gentleman and you are *not* my father! You have hurt my mother, and I hate you! Do you hear me? I hate you! I hate you! I hate you!"

She did not know she was hitting him, pummeling his chest with her fists, until he caught her hands in his and restrained her against his chest. His vest smelled of mint and cherrywood tobacco. She struggled and shrieked and tried to break free, but he held her fast until, after many minutes, her rage faltered, and she, exhausted and limp, slumped in his arms.

Monsieur Declouette stroked her cheek again and again. "Ah, my poor poppet. I am sorry to have wounded you so."

Tory did not believe his words or the tenderness of his touch: They were as false as he was. As her *father* was. She submitted to him because he was stronger than she was, and she had no strength left to fight him.

When her sobs quieted, he released her. "Good bye, Victoria. Good bye, Adeline."

Tory heard the heavy door of the front entrance close behind him. She left the parlor and wandered upstairs, leaving Adeline crumpled on the parlor carpet, weeping softly.

Tory went to her bedroom, stripped off her torn and soiled underclothes, and crawled into her bed. She wanted to sleep, to escape the turmoil in her heart. But long after Monsieur Declouette was gone and before slumber took her, Tory smelled the cherrywood tobacco of his vest and felt the gentle caress of *her father's* hand upon her cheek.

CHAPTER 2

S ugar Tree, Tory's home, sat upon a low alluvial bluff deposited by an ancient course of the Mississippi river. The five acres atop the ridge belonged to the house, and the raised wedge of property formed a natural levee against seasonal or storm flooding.

Not many plots in the Mississippi basin could boast of a rise like that upon which Sugar Tree sat: The northern side of the bluff faced Lake Pontchartrain, several miles distant; the other sides sloped down toward fertile bottom land interspersed with swampy bayous, eventually reaching the banks of the river's present course.

The house's drive, lined with Southern sugar maples, wound its way down the bluff and intersected a dirt track. The track ran westward into farming country and roughly east toward the nearest market village. From the village, the track meandered to the southeast where it joined the old Metairie Ridge road leading to town—the bustling city of New Orleans.

According to Sassy Brown, much of the land around them had once been part of the Sugar Tree plantation owned by Monsieur Declouette's mother, her father before her, and his father before him. Generations of Sassy's family had served Monsieur Declouette's mother and her family— before the war as their property and after the war as paid servants. The war (which Sassy could recall in great detail and which she said Southern white people referred to as the "War of Northern Aggression") had decimated the South—killing off a generation of its young men, stealing its dignity and traditions, stripping it of its wealth.

Reconstruction had been the final blow to Southern white aristocracy. According to Sassy, Monsieur Declouette's maternal great-grandfather had sold off his plantation, piece by piece, to keep ahead of exorbitant Reconstruction taxes. He had carved off bits of Sugar Tree until all that remained was the house and the raised strip of land surrounding it.

What Sassy did not speak of was how the war had set thousands of negroes free from their slavery—and how the newly freed men and women no more knew how to survive in the free society they entered than that society knew how to receive them. Many on both sides fell back on what was familiar and "comfortable," the master and servant model, which reinforced the racial divide.

As years passed, that divide was further fortified by pride, bitterness, and increasingly stringent laws that segregated blacks and whites into distinct classes, one below, the other above.

In short—and despite the care Tory's mother took to educate her and ensure that she grew up as a lady—Tory was ignorant of life beyond Sugar Tree. In the ten years of Tory's short childhood, she had never left Sugar Tree land, had never glimpsed what lay outside its boundaries. She knew that the outskirts of New Orleans began several miles or more south and east of them, but she knew nothing of the city or its surrounds. What she knew of the world she had learned from the many books she devoured.

During the years that Monsieur Declouette had sent adequate funds for Adeline to manage the household, servants had run the errands and done the marketing in the nearby village, or taken a wagon to fetch whatever Adeline or Tory needed from town. The gardener had husbanded the green garden and fruit trees; another man had tended a flock of chickens and a number of sheep and cows—enough to keep them in eggs, meat, and milk. What the tiny estate produced above the requirements of the house was taken to market in the village for cash money or for barter.

Tory's acquaintances were the negroes who staffed the house and grounds of Sugar Tree. Their white neighbors did not ascend the winding drive to come calling, nor did Tory interact with their children or have friends her age. The sole white people with whom she had personal contact were her governess, Miss La Forge, and Monsieur Declouette.

She did not perceive that she and her mother, living in relative wealth and ease under Mr. Declouette's protection, experienced the world differently than did most of their race. She was unaware that Adeline's mother had leveraged her daughter's natural beauty to lift her above the rest of her family, how Adeline's parents had worked themselves into early graves to educate their daughter and place her where she would attract the attentions of a wealthy patron.

When Monsieur Declouette had reduced the amount of money he sent, Adeline had been forced to let the majority of the staff go. She had leaned upon Sassy Brown and on Venus and Ellen (who lived but a mile west of them) to keep house and make the most of what the land could provide. When bills came due, Adeline had them sell off livestock rather than suffer the indignity of bill collectors at her door.

Despite their reduced income, Adeline had maintained—had insisted upon—a façade of gentility. It was as though Adeline had deluded herself into believing that Monsieur Declouette would, someday, acknowledge Adeline as his companion and Tory as his daughter and that Monsieur Declouette's world would, eventually, accept her as their equal.

With Henri Declouette's announcement, Adeline's façade crumbled to dust. She had no money—none at all—to pay wages, to buy what the house and land could not provide. She had nothing to maintain the carefully crafted delusion.

Overnight, life at Sugar Tree changed.

When expectations of wages dissolved, Venus and Ellen abandoned them. Tory thought Sassy would go with them, but the old woman did not. All Adeline could offer the old woman in exchange for her service was her board and a share of whatever food they had. For her own reasons, Sassy remained at Sugar Tree and retained her sleeping quarters in the lean-to behind the outdoor kitchen. Sassy may have been slowing down with age, but she did what she could from morning to evening and continued to eke out three meals a day from whatever food was available.

"Told ye t' have a care. Told ye we was all riding the same train," Sassy grumbled to Tory. "Now your *mère* ain't got two nickels to her name. She cain't pay me . . . but I might as well stay on as not. I got no place else to go 'cept my granddaughter and her sharecroppin' husband's leaky hovel—and they got no room for me nor food to feed 'nother mouth."

Tory said nothing in response to Sassy's complaints. She did not see how *her* actions—however precipitous they may have been—had anything to do with her mother's penniless state. Had not Monsieur Declouette planned to break off his attachment to Adeline before he arrived?

In the weeks following Monsieur Declouette's final, disastrous visit, Adeline attempted to adapt to their straitened circumstances. She closed off large sections of the house—the library, dining room, and the entire second floor. She and Tory lugged their bedframes and mattresses downstairs and set them up in the drawing room. Mother and daughter lived, ate, and slept in two rooms—the parlor and, across the hallway, the drawing room.

The most severe adjustment was to Adeline and Tory's daily routine. Each morning, Adeline and Tory dressed in their most serviceable clothing and went out to the green garden to plant, weed, and harvest what it produced. The garden was where she and Tory, under Sassy's direction, spent the cool of the day.

For those first weeks, Adeline tried hard to acclimate to the many changes while retaining her dignity, but beneath her calm exterior, her heart was broken. She followed Sassy's lead and did what needed to be done, although her mind and thoughts were often elsewhere. In her mother's distraction, Tory fell more and more under Sassy Brown's supervision—but she did not mind much.

If truth be told, Tory reveled in the hours she spent out-of-doors and in the arduous work Sassy insisted she do.

"If ye don't hoe your rows each day, the weeds'll be taking the green garden, missy, and the garden is most all we have. Ye've never sit down t' table with naught to eat, but I have. 'Tis not pleasant t' have an empty belly and naught t' fill it." Sassy wagged her bandana-wrapped head. "Ye'll likely find out soon enow."

Never got to eat my fill when we did *have food.* Tory cast her eyes down so they would not reveal her angry, contrary thoughts.

Tory learned to feed and water their rooster and half-dozen chickens, to gather their eggs, and to milk the lone cow. Under Sassy's stern instruction, Tory skimmed and strained the milk, churned butter, kneaded bread, and picked over beans, chickpeas, and other garden produce.

Tory also learned to clean. With no maids to tidy up after them or wash their clothes, Adeline and Tory had to assume the household tasks.

Tory's normal, healthy appetite spiked under the unfamiliar physical activity and became a ravening need. Tory was shooting up, her growth adding to her cravings. Although Adeline frowned at Tory's hunger complaints, she did not object to the larger portions Sassy served the girl—not that they were "large" portions but certainly more than what Sassy served herself or Adeline.

It still wasn't enough. Tory was always hungry. If she had a moment of free time, she would forage among the garden thinnings and sneak early or unripe produce, sometimes paying with a belly ache or loose bowels.

The house's greatest need was for fresh meat. Adeline had sold off most of the stock, but kept the chickens for eggs and the cow for milk. At least milk was plentiful and they enjoyed an egg twice a week. Still, their lack of meat meant the green garden and what it produced was their primary source of food.

So needy were they for meat, that Sassy taught Tory how to set snares to catch the rabbits, squirrels, mice, and voles that plundered their garden. Tory disposed of the mice and voles and handed the rabbits and squirrels over to Sassy to stew.

Sassy skinned and cooked the first three rabbits caught in Tory's snares; the fourth rabbit was young and still small, so Sassy did not kill it. Instead, she helped Tory to repair an old hutch to keep the young rabbit. "If we trap a mating pair, we can be breeding them," Sassy insisted, "feeding them from the garden thinnings. In a few weeks, the female will bear a litter and, soon after that, we'll have meat on our plates, regular like."

Adeline insisted on one remnant of their previous lifestyle: Tory's lessons, even if they were shortened or infrequent. During the heat of each day, Tory spent two hours in the parlor at her books. Adeline no longer supervised Tory while she studied; instead, she set Tory's lessons, went on to other chores, and checked her work at the end of the short school period.

This arrangement suited Tory. She sped through her lessons and used the remaining minutes to sketch, copying the mannequins in the now-outdated fashion magazines, telling herself, "Someday, I will dress as these women; someday I will create beautiful gowns and fashions."

~*~

September arrived and, with it, Tory's eleventh birthday. Unlike every prior birthday of Tory's short life, Monsieur Declouette sent no gift. True to his warning, five months had trickled by without note or letter.

In the hot outdoor kitchen, Sassy, Adeline, and Tory were putting up muscadine juice and jellies. Two cauldrons steamed and bubbled on the wood-burning stove. Adeline stirred them while Sassy and Tory picked over the grapes, mounding the acceptable ones on a cloth for the next batch.

Even with the door and windows open, the heat in the kitchen was oppressive. Dark red juice stained their hands and aprons; the kerchiefs they bound around their heads did little to stem the sweat that trickled down their faces and soiled their scalp and hair.

Although Louisiana enjoyed a long growing season, the three of them were picking and canning as much of the produce as they could manage against the wet, colder months. Tory longed to gorge herself on what they were putting up for winter, but Sassy was more determined than Adeline had been to keep Tory's appetite on short shrift.

"Ye'll thank me soon enow when the cold rains come, I dare think," Sassy said. "Ye have enough t' eat t' keep body and soul together—and enow 'tis good as a feast."

Tory glowered at Sassy's back. "Well, I'm *hungry*."

"Tory." Adeline's one-word rebuke was gentle but firm. "You may thin the carrots if you wish something more to eat."

Tory pulled and ate young carrots most every day, but they were poor fare for a growing girl. However, Tory wasn't blind; her mother, too, was suffering from self-imposed deprivation. As hard as she worked, she ate no more than she had before, and Tory noticed the plump curves of her mother's cheeks sharpening, the waistband of her dress slackening.

Tory spied a split grape and a lone ant crawling on it. She pinched the ant and, turning her head a little, slipped the grape into her mouth. It was warm, soft, and overripe. Tory sucked on its sweet pulp and swallowed the skin without moving her jaws.

"This be the last o' the grapes," Sassy announced. "Winesaps be next."

Tory's ears perked up. At her first opportunity, she would revisit the grape vines and glean what their picking had missed.

"How many apple trees?" Adeline asked. Her question was heavy with weariness, but Tory enjoyed the picking. She was brave enough and physically able to climb the tall ladder and harvest fruit out of reach of pickers on the ground. Furthermore, hidden by tree boughs, Tory often ate her fill of whatever fruit hung around her.

Tory's ever-hungry stomach lurched.

"Hello! Anyone in the house? Anyone at home?" A man's deep voice. A stranger. The voice continued calling as the unknown visitor wandered down the side of the house.

Sassy and Tory's mother exchanged surprised glances.

"See who it is, please, Sassy," Adeline asked.

Sassy wiped her hands on her apron and left the kitchen. Tory and her mother heard Sassy speaking near the back door, then opening the door and ushering the man inside.

Adeline scrubbed at her stained fingers. "Tory, run to the drawing room and lay out my green day dress. You know the one. Wash your hands well beforehand."

"Who is it, *Maman?* Who has come?"

"I do not know, but Sassy has shown him to the parlor. Oh, my hands! Why can I not remove these stains?"

A lady's hands reflect a life of gentility. A gentlewoman's hands are always clean and soft.

Tory ran to the back of the house and went inside. As she crept down the long hallway toward the front of the house, she met Sassy returning from the parlor where, presumably, she had installed the visitor.

"Where ye going, child?"

"To lay out *Maman's* green dress."

"Ah. *Bien.*" Although Sassy *said,* "Good," her expression did not signal "good."

"Who is it, Sassy? Who is the man?"

"Not now, child. I need t' prepare your mother."

Prepare my mother?

Tory went to the drawing room that served as her and her mother's shared bedchamber. She washed her hands in the wash basin and dried them on the hand towel. Conscious of her own stained fingers, Tory drew on an old pair of her mother's gloves and, with care, removed her mother's green day dress from her cedar chest.

She spread the summer dress, with its short, puffed sleeves, upon Adeline's bed and, with the edge of her gloved hand, worked the creases out of the delicate fabric. Thinking also of her mother's grape-stained hands, Tory searched for and found a pair of crocheted gloves and placed them near the dress.

They will hide the stains, she decided.

She was cleaning Adeline's comb and brush when her mother entered the drawing room. Tory glanced up and was startled by the pallor of Adeline's ebony face.

"*Maman!* Are you ill?"

"No. I am all right, Tory. I am all right."

But Tory sensed that Adeline was telling herself to be "all right," rather than responding to Tory's concerns.

Adeline had stripped off her apron and head scarf in the kitchen and left them there; now she fumbled with the buttons and ties of her simple housedress. Her fingers trembled and could not work the buttons through their fastenings. Tory stood behind her and helped until the dress slipped from Adeline's thin shoulders to the floor.

Tory went to the bed, lifted the green dress, and held it for Adeline to step into it.

"Thank you, *ma chère*."

Tory heard Sassy returning to the parlor. "Is Sassy serving tea?" They had precious little of it to spare.

"Yes. She must buy me time . . . to fix my hair."

Tory nodded. Her mother's beautiful raven hair was tangled and dirty. "Sit down, *Maman*, and allow me to brush it out for you."

Tory dipped her fingers in a jar of sweet, oily pomade and rubbed them together. She ran her fingers through Adeline's wavy hair until Tory was able run a comb through the curls and tangles. Then, with a few rhythmic strokes of the brush, Tory felt her mother's stress bleed away. In the mirror, Tory saw Adeline's eyelids sink closed, watched her lips move.

To whom is she speaking?

For a moment, Tory wondered if her *mère* was praying, then she discarded the notion.

We do not pray in our home, she reasoned. *Sassy Brown said so.* "*Prayers be worthless in a house of sin,*" Sassy had said.

Tory didn't know what sin was, but it did not sound like a good thing. Nevertheless, Tory knew Sassy prayed, although she kept it to herself, her lips often moving without sound. Prayer was a mystery to Tory—as was the God to whom Sassy bent her head.

Tory combed Adeline's hair into a simple, elegant chignon at the base of her mother's neck and secured it with a pair of carved tortoiseshell combs. Adeline's neck was long and slender and gleamed like the polished black onyx paperweight that sat upon *Maman's* writing desk.

"*Très bien*, Victoria. Your hands have learned new skills."

Tory smiled upon her mother with adoration. "I learned by watching you, *Maman*."

Adeline rewarded Tory with a kiss on her forehead before she stood and studied her preparations in the mirror. "It must serve. I cannot delay longer."

She walked toward the door, then turned back. "Remain here, Victoria," she commanded, "until I know what he wants of me."

Who? What who *wants of you?* Tory wondered.

Adeline had no sooner crossed the hallway and entered the parlor, than Tory tiptoed after her to the parlor door and placed her ear upon the wood.

She heard her mother from the center of the room. "*Bonjour, Monsieur*. I am Adeline Washington. To what do I owe this . . . unexpected visit?"

The man snorted a laugh of sardonic surprise. "Why, do you not know who I am?"

"As you announced yourself to my housekeeper, I may presume that you are Monsieur Bastiann Declouette, younger brother to Monsieur Henri Declouette."

"Very good. And despite your veneer of refinement, you are the n****r tart my brother has kept on the side these many years."

Tory didn't understand some of the man's words, but she knew by his tone that they held no goodwill. And that anyone should speak to her mother with such disrespect, such contempt? She simmered in rising fury. Waited for her *mère* to answer. To put this uncouth man, *this boor*, in his place.

She was not disappointed.

Her mother's gentle but firm reply was, "Monsieur Declouette, your behavior is unbecoming of a gentleman. Unless you have legitimate business with me, I bid you good day."

"You bid me good—" Again, that sharp bark of surprised laughter. "My, my. You give yourself great airs—for a whore."

Adeline did not answer; instead, the bell calling for a servant rang out. Tory frowned. The single servant on the property was Sassy. Would she hear? But even if she came, what could an old woman do against the strength of a man?

Tory's hands balled themselves in to fists—so tightly that her nails began to cut her palms.

Apparently—and perhaps Adeline had counted on such good fortune—Bastiann Declouette had no knowledge of Sugar Tree's staffing levels, and Tory heard him mutter,

"No matter, no matter! I shall go. I wished to set eyes on you for myself before Marguerite takes Henri to court next month. She is suing him for divorce, you know. My testimony may be required."

He did not mention that Henri's health, under the stress of the struggling family businesses, was suffering. Bastiann did not allude to the heart condition Henri's doctor had diagnosed nor to the fact that Marguerite, in anticipation of gaining more from Henri's death than through divorce, had rescinded her threat to take her husband to court. Bastiann, anticipating that Sugar Tree would come to him at Henri's death, had ridden out of the city to stake his claim ahead of time.

He liked what he saw in the house's current tenant. Oh, yes. He liked it very much.

Tory expected her mother to maintain her reserve: *A gentlewoman does not argue or raise her voice—*

She was taken aback when Adeline retorted, "I am surprised Henri did not sue for divorce himself, considering that his wife's adultery with you came first, Monsieur Declouette."

A moment of deathlike silence ensued. Then Tory heard the crack of an open hand upon flesh, followed by an involuntary cry of pain.

Did he hit my Maman?

Tory burst into the parlor. Adeline was cringing away from the man who had attacked her—a man too similar in appearance to Henri Declouette not to be his brother.

"How dare you strike my mother!" Tory screamed, her hands clenched at her sides. "Get out! Get out of our house at once!"

Bastiann Declouette, hand upraised, stared at Tory as though she were an apparition. He may have resembled Henri Declouette in height, build, and facial characteristics, but the resemblance ended when Bastiann sneered, "Well! And what have we here?"

He looked from Adeline to Tory and back and smirked. *"Your* daughter, certainly, but Henri's, too, unless I miss my mark. Like in manner; the same imperious attitude. And a pretty little morsel, indeed. No wonder he fought so hard to conceal you."

He grabbed Adeline by the arm and pulled her close to him until his mouth was inches from her face. Tory saw the way his fingers dug into the soft skin of her mother's upper arm, how Adeline leaned back, away from his hot breath, until she was almost bent in half.

"Know this: Henri will not be able to protect you forever, my dear. The day is coming when I will strip him of every family asset he manages, every dollar of personal wealth he has accrued. *Your* house? This house and all that is in it belongs in *our family*. I will return soon to put you out into the gutter like the trash you are."

Tory blinked as her mind worked to rescue her mother. She was possessed with the idea that they needed a manservant to save Adeline from this monster, this *Bastiann Declouette.* But they had no manservant! Only Sassy Brown.

However, *he*, this intruder, did not know that.

Tory began shouting, "Mr. Brown! Mr. Brown! Come at once!"

Startled, Bastiann Declouette released his hold on Adeline and strode toward the door. As he passed near Tory, he slowed, looked her up and down, and smiled. Tory didn't know what the smile meant, what it portended, but it froze her to the marrow of her bones.

The front door slammed shut behind Bastiann Declouette, and Tory ran to her mother. Adeline enfolded Tory in her arms, and they held each other as though the world was ending, until Sassy, out of breath, stood in the doorway.

"Be he gone?"

The drama had taken a few minutes, no more, to unfold.

"Yes," whispered Adeline.

Sobbing, Tory broke from her mother's embrace and ran to the front entrance. She thrust home the strong lock that secured the entrance and leaned against the door's solid wood surface.

CHAPTER 3

Despite the shock of Bastiann Declouette's news and threats, Tory was surprised to discover her mother in good spirits the following day. When she arose from her bed, she found Adeline in the parlor, dusting, smiling to herself, and humming under her breath.

A Southern woman does not fidget, scratch, or hum, Victoria.

"Good morning, *Maman*. What are you doing?"

Adeline snapped out of her reverie. "Oh! Oh my, Victoria. You quite startled me."

"I am sorry, *Maman*, but you were . . . humming."

"Was I? Um, well, I should not have been. Are you ready for breakfast?"

Adeline was quick to sweep Tory's questions aside, but her good humor persisted. Days later, Tory ventured again.

"*Maman?* You seem happy, but are you not afraid of that man . . . who hurt you? He said Monsieur Declouette's wife was divorcing him and that Monsieur Declouette would lose everything. That man, Bastiann Declouette, said he would take Sugar Tree from us."

The prospect of leaving Sugar Tree haunted Tory. Where else in the world could they go?

"I am not afraid of him, Tory. He does not know, but I hold the deed to Sugar Tree. And besides, if Marguerite does secure a divorce from Henri, then that could mean . . ."

Her voice trailed off.

"What, *Maman?* What could it mean?"

Adeline studied her daughter, already tall, healthy, and strong, on the cusp of womanhood. "Perhaps it is time for you to understand certain things, Tory, particularly if . . .

"If what, *Maman?*"

Adeline drew Tory to a settee and they sat together, Adeline holding both of Tory's hands in hers. "My darling, if Monsieur Declouette—your father—if Henri's wife divorces him and he has nowhere else to go, I cannot but hope he will come to us."

Tory's eyes widened. "Here? To live?"

"Oh, yes, Tory! Would that not be wonderful? We could . . . we could be a family, *ma chère*. He could be the father to you he promised he would be before you were born."

Tory had an immediate and intense aversion to the idyllic picture Adeline painted. As she allowed Adeline's words to sink in, Tory's aversion increased and ran to revulsion. Not a girl who often answered back or gave her opinion, in this instance Tory's response was sharp. Cutting.

"That man shall never be my father."

Adeline stilled and drew back, her joyous expression crushed. "Victoria, you cannot mean that."

"*Non, Maman*. Not one word you speak on his behalf will change my mind. Monsieur Declouette is nothing to me—he is less than nothing. I do not wish to ever again see his face."

Mother and daughter studied the other, and Adeline, seeing the obdurate lines of Tory's young mouth, so like the father she despised, looked away. She did not object when Tory quitted the room.

~*~

Eight months passed, and spring arrived again. Tory was grateful that the chilly winds and rains of winter were giving way to warmer nights. The climate in Louisiana always boasted of significant precipitation, but December and January had been particularly wet and the nights cold. The house had grown dank, and the two rooms Adeline and Tory shared had been difficult to keep dry.

In early December, Adeline had suffered a cold that began first in her head, then settled in her chest. The cold refused to improve, and the coughing and congestion had kept Adeline confined to her bed or the sofa in the parlor for several weeks.

Sassy, also, had not done well in the cooler, wetter weather. Although she never shirked her duties or missed preparing a meal, Sassy seemed to creep through each day and disappear into her room each afternoon.

"Is Sassy unwell, *Maman?*" Tory had asked her mother.

"She is old, Tory, and tires easily. We cannot expect her to do as much as she once could."

It was during the weeks while Adeline was ill and Tory waited on her, that Tory ventured to seek the answers to the questions her awakening young mind had begun to ask.

"*Maman?*"

Adeline opened her tired eyes. "Yes?"

"*Maman*, how is it that you . . . how did you meet Monsieur Declouette?"

Adeline closed her eyes and sighed. "Is that all you wish to know? Surely you wish to understand how the daughter of two poor, colored house servants could acquire the culture and social graces to become mistress of Sugar Tree?"

"Yes, *Maman*. All of these things."

With her eyes still closed, Adeline tried to explain. "My parents had nothing. They had no hope for bettering their lives, but they wished for so much more for me.

"My mother found me a position with an elderly white woman. She was not wealthy, but she had been once. She could not afford a more suitable companion, so she chose me. I was to fetch and carry for her. Sit for hours and listen to her prattle. Read to her. In exchange for my room and board. I was eleven years old, Victoria. Your age."

Tory held a glass to Adeline's lips. "*Oui, Maman?*"

"My mother charged me to learn all I could from the white woman: How to to sit, stand, eat, and speak. How to act as a white woman. My employer gave me her worn, outdated clothes, and I remade them. I became comfortable in my role.

"After four years, the old woman passed away. I was fifteen. I could not . . . go back to the life of my parents. I no longer belonged there. Another white woman and her husband hired me to watch their children, so I moved into their home.

"In the autumn, the couple I worked for had guests in for the weekend. I was on my way to the kitchen to fetch the children's bedtime milk when I encountered your father in the upstairs passageway. We began to talk. He . . . asked to see me again. We met at the park where I often took the children. While the children played, Henri and I grew to know each other.

"He was unhappy in his marriage, and his wife was unfaithful to him. We fell in love. Two months later, he brought me here, to Sugar Tree."

Tory mulled over everything her mother had told her. It was all foreign to her. In particular, she could not fathom the ramifications of Adeline learning "how to act like a white woman."

How was a white woman different than a black one?

~*~

March and April were warmer and drier, and Adeline seemed to shake her illness, enough to help Tory (under Sassy's imperious supervision) plant the garden and begin the labor of the long growing season all over again.

Adeline may have been ill and weak through the winter, but her expectations of Tory's schoolwork never wavered, even when spring arrived. She required Tory to study for two hours each afternoon, use her French and Italian while they labored in the garden, and practice the pianoforte each evening.

These skills seemed disconnected from Tory's present life and circumstances, and they rankled on her—until she recalled what her mother had said: *My parents had nothing. They had no hope for bettering their lives, but they wished for so much more for me.*

She realized Adeline wished better for her daughter, too.

With grudging but dogged determination, Tory focused on her studies.

On a sunny afternoon in May, Tory was in the parlor, her head bent over her lessons. Adeline had set Tory's assignments and left her to help Sassy in the outside kitchen. Tory looked up at the sound of hoofbeats upon the graveled lane. She ran to the windows and peeked through the curtains—carefully, so that she did not stir them.

Bastiann Declouette.

Tory's heart pounded. She knew her mother was in the kitchen, unprepared for visitors. How could she warn Adeline?

I will not answer the door, she thought, turning from the window. *I will run to the kitchen and tell Maman who is knocking.*

But Bastiann Declouette did not knock; he thrust open the unlocked door. The weighty wood slammed against the opposing wall from the force of his entrance, and she heard his hobnailed boots screech on the stone floor.

Then . . . silence.

Tory imagined the man standing in the foyer. She could sense his powerful, seething anger—and she had no avenue of escape.

"WHERE ARE YOU, WHORE?"

When he roared, Tory jumped.

Before she had fully formed the decision, Tory ducked behind the old damask drapes. She pressed her back against the wall and let the drapes settle around her.

"WHERE ARE YOU?" Bastiann threw open the parlor door and sauntered inside.

Tory felt the oppressive force of his presence in the room as he wandered about, cursing under his breath. She also recognized the soft patter of her mother's footsteps as she entered the parlor.

"You again!" she exclaimed.

"Yes. I came personally to deliver the happy news: My brother, Henri, *is dead*."

"No!" Adeline screamed. "No, you are lying!"

"Ah, but I am not, I assure you. Henri was thrown from his horse early yesterday morning. He was not well—had not been well for some time—but he took it into his head to race *Victorieux* through the woods near his house, even though he had not ridden for months because of his ill health. *Victorieux* returned to his stall without Henri and was discovered when the groom arose that morning. Henri was not found until midday. The fool had broken his neck."

Adeline sank to the floor, groaning. "No, no, no! No, Henri! Henri, my love!"

Bastiann observed her with a sneer. "You will pack your things and depart this house immediately."

Adeline did not react at first. Finally, she sniffed. "What do you say?"

"You heard me. You will pack and leave within the week."

Adeline gathered herself. Stood. Calm, but resolute. "No, I will not. This house is mine. Henri gave it to me."

Bastiann drew back. "You lie, whore."

"I do not lie. Henri deeded this house to me more than eleven years ago—prior to the birth of his *daughter*."

Grinding his teeth, Bastiann said, "You cannot prove that. Your claim will not stand in court."

"It will. I have the deed. It is here." Adeline stumbled to her little desk and removed a ledger. From between its back cover and the last page, she withdrew an envelope, which she opened. She unfolded the deed and held it up. "It is as I said. Sugar Tree belongs to me. You may not take it from me—nor may you ever set foot on this land again. It is mine."

A few seconds passed. Then, in a reasonable voice, Bastiann answered, "If I am wrong, I shall trouble you no further. May I examine the deed?" He walked toward her.

Bastiann's rage seemed to have subsided, so Tory parted the drapes a little and peeked out.

She saw as Adeline, eager to prove her claim, held it out to him—at the last instant perceiving her error. Bastiann grabbed the paper from her grasp and turned away. His eyes ran down the sheet and stopped at the seal affixed to his brother's signature.

"Give it back to me," Adeline whispered.

But, holding the deed in both hands, Bastiann tore it in two, tore it again, ripped the pieces into smaller bits and let them flutter to the floor.

"I will return in one week with the parish sheriff. If you remain here, he will arrest you for trespassing." Bastiann glanced around. "And if anything of value is missing when I return, I shall have the sheriff and his dogs hunt you down." He leered at Adeline. "And he has exceptionally good dogs, I assure you."

Adeline did not answer him in look or word. She stared at the shreds of paper on the carpet, the remains of her deed to Sugar Tree—her solitary security in the world. She seemed dazed.

Tory saw something in Bastiann's manner shift. His mouth widened, then twisted into an ugly smile, and he edged closer to Adeline. When she seemed to take no notice, he snaked an arm around her waist and drew her to his chest. With his other hand, he rubbed her bare arm, then began unfastening the buttons at the front of her bodice.

Tory jumped from behind the drapes and ran to her mother's side. "Stop that! Stop it, I say!"

She scrabbled for the man's hand, but her efforts did not deter him. He swept Tory aside—then, tired of fumbling with the many buttons, he grabbed the bodice of Adeline's dress and ripped it away, exposing her chemise.

With a scream of outrage, Tory flew at Bastiann Declouette, scratching his neck, his hands, his face, pounding him with her fists. Bastiann released Adeline and took Tory by her neck. She screamed louder and fought him, but he shook her until she could not breathe.

"I would have your mother, little half-breed," he snarled. Then Bastiann's eyes swept over Tory. "But perhaps I will have the daughter before."

Adeline woke from her stupor; she fell to her knees before Bastiann and pleaded, "No! No, please! You may take me—I will submit to you— only please do not ruin my beautiful daughter! She is but a child. *A child*."

Bastiann grinned. "She looks older than she is; I will have you both. No better way to spit upon my brother's grave than to have his whore and his half-caste pickaninny, too" he answered.

"Ye mus' kill me first," Sassy shouted, "'fore ye'll defile my babies over my dead body."

Tory's frantic screams had reached Sassy out in the kitchen; the woman wielded a cleaver in one gnarled hand and a butcher knife in the other.

Bastiann eyed Sassy with derision—and a measure of disquiet. "Old woman, do you know the penalty for striking a white man?"

"Oh, I'll cut ye t' bits and hang with a glad heart an' a smile 'pon my lips, I will," Sassy snarled. She sliced the air with the cleaver and advanced, knife swinging, in Bastiann's direction. He cringed at her strokes and stepped back.

At that moment, Tory experienced a strange, vivid insight. *Why, this man, he is full of himself, but in his heart, he is a coward. A bully.*

Sassy gestured again with the knife. "Get ye gone, ye devil! Go!"

Bastiann Declouette cursed, but he released Tory, and she dropped to the floor next to Adeline. With one angry eye fixed on Sassy, Declouette adjusted his suitcoat and shot the cuffs of his dress shirt.

"No need t' put on sech haughty airs," Sassy goaded him. "We know what ye are—and 'tis not th' gentleman ye pretend at." Keeping the knife tip extended toward him, she edged farther into the parlor so she was not blocking egress from the room; she pointed to the doorway with the cleaver. "Ye know th' way out. Go."

He growled at her and moved toward the door. When he reached it, he turned to face them. "Do not doubt me: I will return in seven days with the sheriff . . . or perhaps I will employ my own men—men I can trust to keep their mouths shut. Should I find you here, no one will stop me from having my way with my brother's whore—" he pointed at Adeline and then at Tory "—or his bastard child."

Sassy swept aside the drapes and watched until Bastiann Declouette and his horse rounded the bend in the drive. Only then did she lay her weapons upon a shelf and attend to Adeline.

Tory was urging Adeline to stand. "Come, *Maman.* Let me help you. Lean on me."

It took both Sassy and Tory to bring Adeline to her feet. Her head lolled, and her eyes did not focus as Tory and Sassy led her to the drawing room.

"What brought that devil man here again?" Sassy asked Tory as they undressed Adeline and put her to bed. "What did he want?"

Tory pressed her lips together before speaking. "To tell my *mère* that Monsieur Henri Declouette has died."

"*Mon Dieu!* Ah, but this is most unwelcome news."

"Bastiann Declouette said we must leave Sugar Tree, but *Maman* showed him our deed. He grabbed the deed from her hand and tore it to tiny pieces. Then he . . ." Tory choked on the words.

"*Non, non, ma petite chère.* No more. No more." Sassy took Tory in her arms and held her a moment. "Let us leave your *mère* t' recover, eh?"

Tory pulled in her chin. "I shall stay with her."

"*Non.* She will sleep and recover from th' shock. I will find something t' cook ye. Something sweet, perhaps, yes? Come."

With a last worried glance at her mother, Tory allowed Sassy to pull her away.

~*~

When Tory went to bed that evening, Adeline was still sleeping. Hours later, in the deep night, Tory woke to the rustle of bedclothes and the uneasy squeak of bedsprings. She rose, lit the lamp, and found Adeline tossing in distress.

"*Maman? Maman?* Are you having a bad dream? *Maman?*" When Adeline did not respond, Tory placed her hand on her mother's cheek.

Adeline's skin was scorching hot to the touch.

"*Quoi? Maman!*"

"Victoria . . . so hot."

Over the next hour, Adeline alternated between throwing off the bedclothes and shivering uncontrollably. When she shivered, Tory piled blankets and quilts on her; when Adeline flung them off, Tory soaked a clean cloth in water and sponged Adeline's face. Even through the damp cloth, she could feel heat radiating from her *mère's* skin.

Her mother's groans became panted words and garbled, incomplete thoughts. "Henri . . . Come back . . . no . . . my love . . ."

Adeline continued to moan and thrash, so Tory filled a glass with water and tried to awaken her to drink. She tried cajoling, even speaking sternly to her *mère*, but nothing would induce Adeline to drink. Tory became truly alarmed when even shaking Adeline's arm did not rouse her.

Tory slipped on her shoes and, clad only in her nightgown, raced down the hall to the back door. She slipped the lock and ran across the yard to Sassy's lean-to.

She had to knock continuously before she heard Sassy's irritated, "*Oui?* Who is it?"

"It is Victoria. Please come, Sassy! *Maman* is sick; I do not know what to do."

Tory heard Sassy's sigh and heavy breathing as she climbed from her bed and shuffled to the door. A moment later, it opened.

"What is wrong with her, child?"

"Fever. She is awfully hot and-and-and I cannot wake her, Sassy."

"*Ce n'est pas bon.* I will come. Go back to her and wait for me. I must gather some things."

Tory returned to the drawing room and found her mother mumbling incoherently. By the time Sassy entered the drawing room, Tory was beside herself.

"Shush," Sassy commanded. She bent over Adeline's fretful form and placed her hand on Adeline's forehead, her cheek, the side of her throat.

"*Mon Dieu!* She is on fire."

Tory quaked with worry. "What are we to do, Sassy?"

"Go to the pump," Sassy commanded. "Pump water into the trough until it runs cold. Fill a clean bucket and bring it to me."

All that long night until morning, Sassy and Tory bathed Adeline's feverish body. They soaked rags and cloths in cool water and placed them on Adeline—on her face, under her arms, along her legs, and upon her chest and belly. When Adeline's fever warmed the rags, Sassy and Tory rinsed them in the bucket and reapplied them. After many applications, their heated rags warmed the water in the bucket, and Sassy sent Tory to pump more.

Sassy also ordered Tory to build a fire in the kitchen stove and heat water. The old woman drew crushed leaves from a bag, brewed a strong tea, and tried to induce Adeline to drink it. She stopped trying when she managed to get a sip into Adeline's mouth, but Adeline was unable to swallow. Instead, she choked and gagged until Sassy lifted her up and let the tea dribble onto the bed clothes.

Morning was dawning when Tory, for the fifth time, pumped a fresh bucket of water. She was grateful for the rising sun: The shadowed drawing room held terrors her young heart could not face.

Through two more days and nights, Sassy and Tory covered Adeline with cool cloths, but Adeline did not respond to their attempts to break her fever. Their efforts to wake Adeline and coax her into taking any kind of drink were fruitless. In her delirium, Adeline babbled nonsense and struggled against Sassy and Tory's ministrations.

Tory was weary, so weary, but she knew Sassy was more so. The old woman was near to falling down. Finally, without a word, Sassy collapsed on a chair. Her head nodded on her breast, and she dropped off to sleep.

Tory hovered near her mother's bed, dread her nearest companion. Tory's every sensibility was tuned to the small sounds in the room. She identified Sassy's soft snores and monitored for any change in her mother's condition.

You must get well, Maman, she pleaded. *You must!*

Something deep in her heart suggested that she call out to the heavens. *But Sassy Brown said prayers are worthless in a house of sin.*

The idea persisted; however, Tory did not even know to whom she might pray. In all of her education, she had received no religious training.

An hour later, Adeline drifted into what Tory hoped was a deep and healing sleep. She stopped thrashing and became quiet. Somewhat reassured, Tory laid herself down next to Adeline's bed.

I will rest a few moments, she told herself. Exhausted beyond her strength, she slept.

She did not know how long she slept; when she woke, shadows were long, the day was approaching evening. Sassy had not wakened . . . but something had changed.

Tory listened. Sassy's even whiffling breaths were as they had been. *Maman?*

Tory struggled to her feet and approached her mother's side. Tory gasped. Adeline's eyes were open, but her face had fallen in on itself. Her beautiful, glossy skin seemed to have shrunk and fused to the bones underlying it.

"Maman? Maman!"

Adeline's chest rose and fell in quick, fluttering movements.

And then it moved not at all.

CHAPTER 4

Sassy, shedding her own tears, washed Adeline's body and dressed it in Adeline's pretty green summer dress. Tory had wanted to assist, but Sassy had refused her offer, had sent her from the house. "*Non*, child. You remember your *Maman* as she was, eh?"

Tory wandered without aim through the orchard, alternately crying and fighting off bouts of terror that left her gasping for air. *Oh, Maman! I didn't want you to go! Why did you leave me? What will I do without you? What will become of me?*

A while later, Sassy called her to the house. "We must have help now, child, to bury your sweet *mère*."

Sassy could neither read nor write—and could form but few letters—but her granddaughter could read a little, so Sassy dictated a note for Tory to compose. In shaking hand, Tory scrawled, "We have suffered a death. We beg ye deliver this note to Venus Marjon. Venus, come help us bury Miss Adeline."

On the front of the folded note, Tory scribbled a few simple directions to Venus' house as Sassy told them to her. With no frame of reference, the directions meant nothing to Tory. When she finished the note, Sassy told her, "Walk to the end of the drive and stand there. Give the paper to the first body t' drive or walk by going the direction the sun sets. Tell them who 'tis for. Venus' shack be not far from the road. Most who pass Sugar Tree will know it. White or colored, they will not refuse ye in your time of need."

Late that afternoon, Venus brought her husband and his brother to dig the grave. Tory watched as the men sweated and shoveled out a long, narrow hollow under the branches of a tree in the little orchard where the grass grew high and the soil was soft. When they had finished, Tory led them into the house.

As they entered the drawing room, Tory saw that Adeline's mattress and bed clothes were gone, her bed nothing but a bare frame. Sassy and Venus had wound Adeline's body in a clean sheet, all but the tops of her shoulders and her head, and laid her upon Tory's bed. Another sheet lay beneath her.

Adeline's face had softened and, even in death, Tory thought her mother still the most beautiful woman she had ever seen. Tory stroked her mother's cool, stiff cheeks and placed a kiss on her brow, hoping—begging!—that somehow Adeline would awaken.

Venus' husband moved to finish twining the sheet about Adeline—but when he wound the fabric across Adeline's face, hiding it from Tory forever, her heart shattered.

"No! Stop! Stop! *Maman! Maman!* Do not hide my *Maman* from me!"

Sassy and Venus enfolded Tory in gentle arms and led her outside. Moments later, the men, holding the corners of the sheet beneath Adeline's body, emerged from the house. Sassy, Tory, and Venus followed them to the grave.

The ceremony was brief and wrenching. Later, all Tory could recall was the moment they lowered her *mère* into the deep hole and Venus' brother-in-law asked God's mercy on Adeline's soul.

When they began to shovel the dirt in upon Adeline, Tory screamed and tried to bolt. She wanted to run as far and as fast as she could to escape the horror, but Sassy held firm to her. The old woman whispered again and again, "Courage, Miss Tory, courage. Act as your *mère* would expect of ye."

Tory descended into a stupor and remained so until the men finished mounding the dirt over Adeline, until they and Venus departed. Until Sassy led Tory away.

Sassy did not return Tory to the house; instead, they walked in the direction of Sassy's lean-to. Their pace slowed, and Sassy's steps began to falter, until she leaned upon Tory's arm and the girl supported her. Tory realized that Sassy was worn down with grief and exhaustion, likely more than Tory was.

When they entered the lean-to, Tory helped Sassy to her bed. As Tory unbent and looked around at the bare room, Sassy reached out and took her hand.

"Sit, Miss Tory." Her voice was breathless. Fragile.

Tory obeyed her.

"Ye know how I loved your *mère*. Served with her grandmother in the old days, helped your *mère* be borned, I did," Sassy whispered. Her old voice rasped and quivered in her throat.

"Adeline's mother, your grandmother, said she'd never seen such a beautiful babe, and she were right. Said she were destined for great things—and mayhap she were, but . . . I dinna think being a white man's kept woman were the greatness she meant."

A white man's kept woman. The words, dirty and obscene, screamed at Tory.

"Monsieur Declouette mayhap loved your *mère* and treated her with dignity for more'n twelve year gone by but, in the end, he failed her. Broke his promises, he did. They all do, when they's backs agin the wall."

She sucked air for a few moments. "But . . . for all his failings, Monsieur Declouette were a gentleman in this: Never would he lay a hand t' a woman or violate her. Ah, but *his brother*," Sassy spat the words with uncharacteristic venom, "*his brother* seen your *mère* as a piece of property t' be used as he wished, and . . . and I seen how he looked at ye also, girl."

"At me?" Tory denied what Sassy asserted—although, in some terrifying, unknown manner, she knew what Sassy meant.

"*Oui*, child. At ye, bein' not yet twelve year old. Ye are tall for your age and anyone can be seeing' the woman ye will blossom into, give a year or so."

Sassy struggled and gulped a ragged breath. "Bastiann Declouette promised to return in a week, but I do not trust him to wait that long. So listen t' old Sassy now and do as I say: Get ye away from here quick as ye can, Miss Tory, afore that man comes back an' puts his hands on ye."

That man. Tory shuddered.

"But . . . but where shall I go, Sassy? I-I have never been off Sugar Tree land. What will I do? How will I live?"

Sassy struggled to breathe. "I . . . cannot say, child, but go, go quick. At first light. Walk ye down the drive 'til it reach the track. Turn east, facing the sunrise. The track will take ye through the village an' on t' the Metairie Road. Follow it t' town. Mayhap there ye will find work t' keep body and soul together. 'Tis a long walk—nine or ten miles—but ye can do it. Heed me, Tory—and beware Bastiann Declouette. I, too, will leave tomorrow."

"W-what will you do, Sassy? Where will you go?"

"Venus will come for me early in the morning."

"Could I . . . could I not come with you?"

Sassy did not speak for a moment. When she did, her voice was low with regret. "I must say *non, ma chère*. To place such a young woman in front of Venus' man . . . *non*. He is not one to be trusted, that one, and he knows I have the measure of him. That is why he likes me little enow."

She scrabbled for Tory's hand and clasped it to her breast. "Ye have learnin' and a gentlewoman's manner about ye, Miss Tory. Ye speak and write well and can do figgers in ye head. Present yeself in the city t' a shop owner of good repute . . . Someone, a kind soul, will take ye on, but ye cannot trust Bastiann Declouette. Ye must go straight off. I will pray . . . pray . . . for . . ."

"For me? You will pray for me?"

"Shou . . . shoulda tole ye 'bout Je . . . sus . . . though your *mère* say no. Shoulda tole ye . . . anyways. I . . . will pray . . ."

Though she gripped Tory's hand, Sassy stopped speaking and her breathing slowed to the soft shuffle Tory knew. Sassy had fallen asleep.

She is more exhausted than I. Rest will do her good, restore her energy, Tory told herself, although she was puzzled by Sassy's last words.

Should have told me about Jesus? Who is he?

Without disturbing Sassy's slumber, Tory extricated her fingers and crept outside. She wandered into the orchard, toward her mother's grave, hoping some sense of Adeline lingered there. All she found was the mounded earth the men had piled upon Adeline's lifeless body. The mound was hidden by the tall grass of the orchard and would, in a matter of days or weeks, be lost in it.

"Oh, *Maman!* Why did you leave me?"

Tory crumpled under a peach tree not far from the grave. There she sobbed her heart out until she had exhausted herself. Shuddering with grief and fatigue, Tory leaned back against the old tree and stared up into the branches. The blossoms had faded and fallen from the tree and the new-green leaves were unfolding, stretching toward the sun, filling the spaces between the boughs. Tory knew that if she looked closely, she would find tiny nubs growing where the blossoms had been.

I will not be here when the fruit trees ripen this year, she realized. *I must do as Sassy says and abandon Sugar Tree.*

She pushed herself to standing and gripped the tree's trunk, unsteady on her feet. After a few moments, she felt better, and went toward the house. The pump near the kitchen drew her attention. A sudden, raging thirst came on her.

I have had nothing to eat or drink since . . . But she couldn't remember. Everything about the past four or five days—Bastiann Declouette's news of his brother's death, his threats, Adeline's collapse and sickness, the long hours of caring for her, her death and burial—all of it blurred before Tory's eyes. She had lost track of time.

Her overpowering thirst drew her out of the confusion. Tory pumped water into the trough. Her thirst was so insistent, so compelling, that she knelt beside the pump and drank as water gushed from it. Tory gulped the water, drank her fill, then drank more. When she finished, her belly sloshed within her, and another appetite, digging at her with painful claws, made itself known.

I will eat later, she told herself, even as the world whirled around her when she stood.

She went into the house and walked down the long hallway. Her footsteps echoing on the parquet floor emphasized how alone Tory was in the house.

When she stood before the drawing room door, she did not put her hand on the knob. Instead, she waited, envisioning her mother on the other side, imagining life as it had been before Monsieur Declouette stopped sending money.

What would her *mère* be doing?

Tory, thinking it was afternoon, nodded to herself. "Why, *Maman* is dressing for tea, of course. Venus has set out the tea things in the parlor, and *Maman* has chosen her blue tea dress today. *Maman* is so beautiful in blue! And what shall I wear? But I must have a new dress, mustn't I? All of mine are much too short." Tory mentally paged through her sketchbook until she found the right design. "Yes, this one, I think, cut from deep yellow, like the yellow of crocuses and buttercups."

Tory smiled and opened the door. "Come to tea, *Maman*. It is all prepared, and Sassy has made a lovely lemon sponge cake. Your favorite, *Maman*—"

It was no longer afternoon. Evening shadows had fallen, and Adeline's bed, stripped of its mattress and coverings, testified to her death. Tory swallowed down the bile that rose in her throat. On wooden, unfeeling legs, she stumbled to her own bed and threw herself on it. An untapped reserve of tears poured from her eyes, and Tory sobbed until sleep took her.

~*~

Tory's thirst woke her in the earliest morning hours while the sky was dark. She rose and poured a glass of water from the pitcher. It was warm and stale, but she drank it down. The roar of her empty stomach answered the water. She ignored it.

Resolve had settled in her heart while she slept: Bastiann Declouette had given them one week to vacate Sugar Tree. Tory would weep no more tears until she had gotten safely away from Sugar Tree, far from the reach of that man.

Tory moved a chair to Adeline's wardrobe and climbed up on it. She reached for the brocade carpetbag atop the ornate chest and pulled it down, set it upon the chair. Then Tory emptied the wardrobe and chests, piling the garments on her bed.

What must I take? Sassy said to ask for work in a shop. What shall I wear to convince a proprietor to take me on? I must be as smart as I can be.

Tory chewed her lip; her clothing choices were scarce. Adeline had made over a few of her older garments for Tory's work dresses, but they were stained from long hours in the garden or the kitchen. "These will not do, and yet I am not grown enough to wear *Maman's* dresses, and most are too fine for shop work besides."

Tory studied her work dresses again. The skirts were in better shape than the cuffs and bodices. She held up one of her mother's unstained blouses. "Perhaps . . ."

She stepped into her best work dress then slipped the blouse over her dress and adjusted it until the sleeves covered the worn, stained cuffs of her dress. The bodice of the blouse fit her ill, but the sleeve length was passable.

Tory fetched her sewing kit and stitched a quick, four-inch basting seam down the back of the blouse. She slipped the garment over her head a second time and nodded at the improvement. She could not waste time now completing the job; she would finish it later. She found and packed another blouse and two dresses into the bag, tucking her sewing kit beside them.

"What more?" She did not really know what a shop looked like or how a shop maid might dress, but she knew how Venus and Ellen had dressed when they had served them in past years.

The maids had worn immaculate aprons over simple black dresses.

"So, I must have a black dress, *non?* Yet I do not own one."

Tory chewed on her thumb. What had become of the maids' dresses when Adeline dismissed them?

Tory lit a candle and wandered toward the back of the house and opened the walk-in closet where the brooms, mops, and cleaning supplies were kept. She held up the candle and spied, at the back of the closet, the hooks where the maids had hung their black dresses—one for Venus and one for Ellen.

"Surely, I am nearly Ellen's size?" Tory exclaimed. She grabbed up the garment and examined it. Then she held it to herself. "A little long, but I will re-hem it. And I must have an apron, too."

Another hook held a number of aprons. They were not in the best of shape; as the money had dwindled, so had the house's standards. Tory studied each apron and selected the best of the lot, a plain, white garment, unstained except for a sizable scorch mark at the hem.

Venus wore this one, and it is longer than I need. I will shorten it, Tory decided, *to remove the burn.*

She returned to the drawing room, folded the dress and apron into her bag, and added Adeline's best apron—a lovely, frilled affair. "Perhaps I will appear in a more presentable light wearing a fashionable apron."

Then Tory gathered her mother's jewelry into a small velvet bag and packed Adeline's dresser set—comb, brush, and mirror. "I will carry away these things that were yours, *Maman,* but I have no image of you to keep my heart from forgetting your face—"

Tory hesitated. What had become of the photograph of Adeline that Monsieur Declouette had returned to her? She rummaged through Adeline's drawers but found nothing.

Did Maman hide the photograph so she would not be reminded of Monsieur Declouette? Perhaps she destroyed it?

Tory again opened Adeline's jewelry box, now empty, and stared at it. She ran her fingers around the side and across the bottom of the box. Tory's fingertips found a slight rise under the stiff brocade lining. She scrabbled with the edge of the fabric and prized it up. There, under the lining, she found what she sought: the image of a younger Adeline, even more beautiful than Tory recalled.

Adeline's luminous eyes stared into Tory's as though she were speaking to her daughter. Comforted, Tory pressed the photograph to her lips. Then she turned it over—and comprehended why her mother had been loath to destroy it—but also why it had pained her so much that she had hidden it.

Tory traced the inscription on the back. "For Henri, my only love and the father of Victoria, my greatest joy."

I was Maman's greatest joy? The words warmed Tory's heart and infused her with courage.

"I will not disappoint you, *Maman.*"

Tory drew the stiff brocade lining from the jewelry box and folded it in half. She placed the photograph within its protective sleeve and laid the lining flat on the bottom of the carpet bag.

Tory finished sorting and packing and surveyed the room before closing her bag. The corner of her sketchpad—forgotten for many days— peeked from beneath a dress Tory had tossed aside.

"My sketches! My fashions!" She grabbed up the pad and a few pencils, slid them, too, beneath the clothing to the bottom of her bag. Then, feeling the urgency of the coming day, Tory gripped the bag and her cloak and ran through the house and out the back door to the kitchen.

She searched through the food stuffs and found nearly a full loaf of bread wrapped in a tea towel in the bread drawer. Sassy had not baked in nearly a week, and the loaf was beginning to mold. Tory did not care. She pinched away the moldy edges and tossed them aside. Then she tore off a hunk of the bread and stuffed it into her mouth.

Nothing had ever tasted so good! The hunger Tory had been denying roared to life, and she ate with greedy abandon—until she realized she had to make the loaf last. She wrapped the remains of the loaf in the towel and tucked it into her bag, adding a cloth bag of dried apple slices to her meager supplies, and filling her pocket with shelled pecans.

Tory knew she could not take away any of the jars of produce lining the shelves; her bag had already grown heavy. "But I do need water," she whispered.

She found a small empty jar with a good lid. This she filled at the pump, then drank as much water as she could hold, refilling the jar when she was replete.

"It is enough," she said aloud. Taking up her bag and cloak, Tory walked with determined steps around the house and down the curved drive with its row of sugar maple sentinels.

Today she would step onto the road toward town; she would go where her feet had never trod and see sights her eyes had never seen.

The first traces of dawn were breaking when Tory reached the first bend in the drive. She turned and stared through the shadows toward the stately house, the only home she had ever known.

"Goodbye. I shall see you no more." With tears choking her, Tory added, "*Au revoir, Maman.*"

CHAPTER 5

As Sassy had commanded her, Tory followed the narrow dirt track leading east from Sugar Tree. She was frightened, her heart ached, and she longed to run home, home to the safety and comfort of her mère's arms. Each time she was tempted to turn tail, the awful image of that mound of freshly turned dirt in the orchard rose before her eyes.

Maman is dead, she told herself. *She is no longer there. Even Sassy has gone away by now. Sugar Tree is empty, but Bastiann Declouette will come.*

She was haunted by the image of the man with his hands digging into Adeline's arm. Hurting her. Bruising her. She shuddered when she recalled how Bastiann had turned away from Adeline, had taken Tory by the throat and shaken her.

I must not be near Sugar Tree when that man makes good his promise to return in seven days!

Tory's despairing tears were frequent, but she forced herself to keep going. There could be no going back to Sugar Tree. Not ever.

At first the track Tory walked traced the lower edge of the bluff, then its path wound away to the east where it widened. Tory passed slender plots of cotton, corn, sorghum, tobacco, and sugar cane planted between fingers of creek and bayou; she glimpsed the occasional house through the fields and orchards, some distant, others not far. As she walked, Sassy's words echoed in her heart.

Ye have learnin' and a gentlewoman's manner about ye, Miss Tory. Ye speak well and can write and do figgers in ye head. Present yeself in the city to a shop owner of good repute . . . Someone will take ye on, but ye must go.

The girl nodded, switched the short strap of the carpet bag to her other shoulder. "I will find the best part of the city and apply at the shops there. Someone *will* take me on."

The rest of Sassy's advice—her dangling, unfinished sentence—came back to Tory.

I will pray . . . pray . . . for . . .

Tory wondered aloud, "Was Sassy saying she would pray for me? Does prayer matter? And to whom does one pray?"

"*Shou . . . shoulda tole ye 'bout Je . . . sus . . . though your mère say no. Shoulda tole ye . . . anyways. I . . . will pray . . .*"

Tory again wondered, *Who is this Jesus Sassy spoke of?*

Tory skirted the little market village and kept walking. It was late morning now, and Tory's stomach felt both empty and alive at the same time. It grumbled, rumbled, and roared at her, demanding she respond. She was thirsty, too.

Tory had bobbed her head to a few carts or walkers headed in the opposite direction, but the lane seemed deserted at present. She stepped off the road into the shade of a bamboo stand and swung her bag through the grass to scare off any snakes that might be lurking nearby. Then she dug in her bag, pulling out the bread and jar of water. She gnawed on a chunk of bread and a handful of pecans and washed them down with sips from the jar.

It was not enough, not by half. Biting her lip, she returned the jar and the heel of the loaf to her bag, and fished out the sack of apple chips. She took but one, then closed her bag, thinking to break off little pieces of dried apple and suck on them as she walked.

She had risen to continue on her way when she heard—then saw—a carriage and several riders racing toward her. She stepped back into the shadows of the bamboo stand to avoid being trampled. When they had passed, she trod on, coughing on the dust their passage had thrown up.

Perhaps two hours later, she came to a junction where her primitive track emptied into a wider road with a well-used, graveled surface. A sign on the opposite side of the road pointed right and read, "New Orleans: 3 Miles."

Tory shouldered her load and started in the direction the sign pointed. Right away, she noticed the increase in houses, barns, and shacks along the road. There were more of them and closer together. She encountered more people, too, some who paid her no mind and others who stared with curiosity. Tory averted her eyes and walked straight on.

An hour later, Tory reached the outskirts of the city proper—and she saw something she had read about or seen sketches of in magazines: an automobile. She heard the mechanical novelty before she saw it, and she fled to the side of the road as it whizzed by, kicking up choking dust in its wake.

"What a noisy, dirty thing," Tory pronounced. She kept walking, but she was growing wearier as the sun mounted higher. It had passed its zenith before Tory knew she was near the city.

The girl kept a tight grip upon her bag, but it became difficult at times to make headway through the throngs of people. *People!* People everywhere, pushing, shoving, shouting, moving. And that was but along *the sides* of the road, which had widened considerably.

Traffic *in* the road terrified her as horse and wagon, man and cart, motorcar, and even motorized trucks sped at inconceivable speeds this way and that. What terrified her most was the seeming nonchalance of people as they dodged in and out of the traffic, coming so close to death or dismemberment.

Tory was overwhelmed. Her head pounded and her breath came in quick agitated gasps. *Oh! If I could just get away from this crowd, if I could find a place in the shade to sit a moment . . .*

Ahead was an open-air market and even denser throngs of people. Tory could not stand it. When she spied a lane intersecting the busier road, she turned to the side, threw herself across the flow of the crowd, and struggled until she reached the lane.

She raced up the lane into a narrow band of shade thrown by tall trees overtopping the stone wall of a residence. Gulping for air, Tory sank to the ground and leaned her back against the wall. Even here, groups of chattering people walked by her, most aiming for the road she had just left.

Tory was very thirsty. She planted her bag between her legs and retrieved the jar of water. Little remained. She drained the jar into her mouth and let the water sit there until it was warm before she swallowed it. When her stomach lurched and growled, she glanced at the remaining crust of bread and the apple chips. She had finished the pecans along the way, and she was too parched to eat bread or suck on dried apple; her tongue seemed thick and sticky in her mouth.

I must find more water.

That was when Tory realized that, in addition to desiring water, she was hearing it—hearing water trickling, bubbling, and falling somewhere close. She struggled to her feet and followed the wall, listening for the particular plinking sounds that flowing water makes.

It is a fountain close by, behind this wall! Surely, there must be a gate in this wall and someone I could speak to who would, perhaps, allow me to fill my jar.

The lane led up a mild slope. Tory followed the lane, walking close to the wall to remain in the shade of the trees on the other side of the stone barrier.

Tory came to a break in the wall, to a drive that led up to a two-story house shaded by magnolia and live oak trees. Halfway up the drive, she spotted what she sought most desperately: A tall pineapple fountain. Its three tiers, carved from weathered stone and topped with ornamental stone fruit, rose from a base embedded in the lawn. Water cascaded and splashed from tier to tier, pooling in its wide bottom well.

Between Tory and her goal, where the drive met the wall, stood an imposing gate, cast from iron. She peered through the gate's narrow bars. The water called to her; she could almost feel its cool, misting spray on her hot skin, taste its liquid refreshment. She craned her neck, searching for a gardener but, other than the sharp cry of a peahen, the grounds beyond the gate felt empty.

Surely the owners would not begrudge her a simple drink of water?

Tory, holding her empty jar, looked around. Across the lane, a little downhill, she saw a line of thick shrubs. She waited until the last pedestrians on the lane had passed before she jogged to the shrubs. With another glance to see if anyone was watching, she pushed her bag deep into the undergrowth. Then she crossed back to the gate, stared at the fountain a moment, and—glad for her thin body—squeezed through the bars.

She wasted no time, but raced up the drive to the three-tiered fountain and dipped her jar into its lowest well. She drank the jar's contents down, refilled it, and drank again. Then she filled the jar and screwed down the lid.

Tory felt much better for sating her thirst and was taking in the shadowed beauty of the house and its grounds when an angry male voice shouted, "Hey! You n****r! Get your filthy black hands out of our water!"

The shouted words so startled Tory that she almost dropped her precious jar. A man—the gardener, judging from his clothing and hat—jogged toward her, brandishing a set of loppers and shouting, "Get out of here, scum!"

Tory ran for the gate. She squeezed through and fled downhill, rounding the curve in the wall before stopping. Her heart thundered in her throat, but she smiled and hugged the jar to her chest.

~*~

Bastiann Declouette and five men for whose discretion Bastiann would pay (and pay well) halted at the foot of Sugar Tree's winding drive. They had departed the city in the early morning. Ten miles later, they arrived at the foot of Sugar Tree's drive.

Bastiann's prized chestnut stallion pranced with nervous energy; three of the men who accompanied Bastiann were also mounted. The fourth drove a closed carriage, while the fifth rode beside him up top.

Bastiann addressed the men in a soft voice that did not disturb the quiet of the countryside. "Listen well. The estate at the top of this drive belonged to my grandmother, then my brother. At his death, it fell to me. Due notice to vacate the house and land was served to the current occupants a week ago."

He did not mention that only five of the seven days had passed.

He lifted his hand and pointed up the drive. "Exercise care: You are to take nothing from the house nor damage any property, but you *will* search every room and every outbuilding and round up anyone on the premises.

"I wish to deliver a message to whomever you find trespassing on the estate, and I leave it to you to ensure that they receive my message—with these exceptions: The negress living in the house and her daughter are mine; you are not to harm them. When you find the woman and the girl, put them in the carriage and keep them there—even if you must tie them up."

The dominant male in the crew spewed a long stream of tobacco onto the crushed rock lining the drive. "Cain't we have a bit o' fun with the women first?"

Bastiann bared his teeth in a cruel smile. "Well, I don't know, Mr. Crump. What value do you place on your life? Is a little sport with a woman worth that much?"

The men attempted to laugh off his questions, but under Bastiann's unwavering gaze, their chuckles fell flat. The men averted their eyes and shifted uneasily.

Bastiann murmured, "I have made myself clear, have I not? However, I am not one to withhold the reward of work done well. If you find women other than the negress and her daughter, I care not what you do with them—but only after you have secured what I have come for."

Not waiting for their response, Bastiann wheeled his horse about and started up the sloping drive. His hired men followed in silence.

The moment Bastiann walked his stallion into the house's courtyard, he sensed he had come too late. The house seemed—it *felt*—empty. Vacant. Gesturing for his men to surround and enter the house, Bastiann kept his seat and waited. Twenty minutes later, they returned, as silent as they had gone.

"No one in the house, Mr. Declouette," Crump said. "No one out back in the kitchen, the lean-to, or the stable."

Bastiann cursed under his breath. "Wait for me here." He dismounted, handed his reins to Crump, and walked through the open front entrance. He looked first in the parlor. The room had a cluttered, lived-in feeling. He glanced around, then crossed the hall to the drawing room.

It had been converted to a bedroom, and the disarray, the open wardrobe and scattered clothing, bespoke a hurried departure. One bedframe, stripped of its mattress and linens, caught his eye, and he frowned.

He wandered upstairs from room to room and realized the upper part of the house had not been disturbed for weeks, perhaps months. He returned to the drawing room and stared, first at the bare bedstead and then at the painting of his grandmother upon the drawing room wall.

Where have you gone, Adeline? Who has helped you and where have you taken refuge?

Bastiann was angry that the woman had escaped him and, frustrated, he grabbed the bedstead and overturned it, hurling the empty frame against the wall.

With a modicum of his ire expended, he retraced his steps, closed the front entrance behind him, and retrieved his horse. Just then, one of the mounted men returned to the courtyard.

"Any sign of them?"

"No, sir; did find what I b'lieve is a fresh grave."

"A grave!" Bastiann recalled the stripped bed and stared at his hands with horror. "Whose?"

The man shrugged. "Someone cobbled t'gether a cross outta scrap wood, scratched coupl'a letters on it. Cain't rightly make 'em out."

"Show me."

Bastiann mounted his horse and followed the man around the house and out into the orchard. The unpruned, overgrown branches tore at his fine clothes; he soon dismounted and followed his guide on foot.

Hidden in the tall grass between two trees, he spied the mounded dirt. The mound was already beginning to settle, and the slapdash cross listed to one side. He yanked it from the earth, surprised to find it longer and more deeply planted than he had expected. The pieces of wood, a dry tree limb broken to about three feet in length and its crosspiece, a weathered slat likely ripped from a low fence, were bound together with baling wire.

Someone had scratched what could have been a shaky "A" into the slat followed by other scratches. He traced the second letter, down, up, down, up . . . "W," Bastiann whispered. "A. W. Adeline Washington."

Aggrieved—not at the woman's untimely death, but that his sport had escaped him—Bastiann ground his teeth and hurled the makeshift cross to the ground.

So, Henri's whore is dead, but someone packed to leave in a hurry, presumably my brother's bastard brat.

Fuming, he walked back to his horse and returned to the courtyard. "We are finished here," he told the men. "Follow me back to town. I will pay you there."

❧ ✳ ❧

$\mathcal{C}$HAPTER 6

T ory leaned around the bend in the wall and peeked up the lane. No one had emerged from the gated drive. She waited a little longer before fetching her bag from the shrubs. Feeling much better for her drink, she ate the last of the bread and decided to brave the crowds.

Where the people go, I will find shops and stores—and a source of water for travelers?

Although dreading the stifling press of the crowd, Tory realized that she had to endure the open-air market. Both water and work had to be nearby. She reached the intersection of the lane and the market-going throng, and let them carry her along until they arrived at a trampled dirt-and-grass field.

The marketplace was worse than Tory had imagined: wagons and booths of fruits and vegetables; cages of chickens and pigs, crafted wares, hanging meat blanketed with bloated flies. The glut of market vendors and goers joined in a cacophony of shouts and a melee of demanding, pressing, shoving bodies.

The cloying closeness of so many people was far worse than the noise: Tory could not bear it. Again, she pushed her way to the edge of the throng, out of the densest of it.

She shuddered. There would be no work for her in this raucous chaos.

Pushing on, Tory came to another intersection, this time of two cobblestone streets, one leading away from the market, the second street running perpendicular to the first. Tory's hands were stiff and sore from clutching her bag so tightly. She pulled it up into her arms, hugging it, and walked forward, away from the marketplace.

Tory wandered for an hour, passing other turns, but keeping to worn stone streets. The occasional home became commonplace, the houses growing thicker, closer together, until they were a wall of side-by-side, dirty hovels crammed against each other. Soon the "residential area" gave way to businesses of the seedier sort: disreputable boarding houses, motorcar repair shops, bars, and rowdy gaming dens. If this was the business center of the city, Tory would find no work here!

The afternoon grew toward evening, yet she had found nothing to give her hope of a place to sleep or a job to be had. And she was so tired. She knew she had to reconcile her expectations to the facts at hand and whispered to herself, "I should find somewhere safe to spend the night."

She did not add the word, "outside," but it clamored in her mind.

She studied two dark storefronts as she passed them. One of them had a sign that read, "Wheel and Axle Repairs." The other building looked vacant. A narrow passage ran between the buildings. Looking around first to see if anyone were watching her, Tory shouldered her bag and crept into the shadowed space between the two buildings.

Within seconds she could no longer see the way ahead. She reached out one hand and felt for the rough planks on her right. She kept inching forward. After what felt like a lifetime in the close confines of that black corridor, Tory came to its end. The two stores were built back-to-back against another structure that spanned the narrow passage.

When her hands encountered cold, moist brick, Tory realized she had gone as far as she could. She looked up and, as her eyes adjusted to the shadows, she realized that the eaves above her overlapped.

I shall be sheltered here should it rain during the night.

Tory pulled her cloak about her shoulders, huddled against the damp brick wall, and slept.

~*~

Tory emerged from the dank passage into the light of a new morning. She felt as sticky and clammy as the bricks where she had slept.

"The city *must* have proper, established shops where—"

An imp of a boy grabbed Tory's bag with such speed that Tory might have lost everything had she not had a firm grip on its handle. When he pulled, the bag jerked out of Tory's hand, but its sudden release caused the boy to stumble. Then he was up and running.

"Stop!" Tory shouted. Then, "*Maman!*" The photograph of Adeline!

With no other thought than to retrieve her mother's photograph, Tory gave chase. The boy was fast; Tory was faster—her legs were longer and stronger. She was on him in moments.

"Stop! Thief!" she cried, grabbing hold of his shirt.

He glanced back, obviously surprised, but he did not stop. Instead, he kept moving forward while trying to shake her off.

Tory acted purely on instinct: She leapt upon the boy's back and wrapped her lanky legs around his chest, twined her long arms about his neck. The child ran between buildings, down alleyways, occasionally pausing to buck her off.

"Git off'n me!" he screeched in outrage.

"No! You give me my bag!" Tory clung to his back like a tick to a dog. He tried to peel Tory's arms from his neck, but she squeezed them tighter; the more he swung himself to throw her off, the harder she held to him until he came to a standstill between two brick buildings. He backed into one of the walls and attempted to scrape Tory against it.

Tory responded by biting his ear. She hadn't thought to do it; the act was an impulse, a means to protect what was hers.

"*Yeowww!*"

"Let go of my bag!" Tory screamed.

He did. When the bag fell from his hand, Tory, with a parting cuff to the boy's head, dropped to the ground and grabbed the bag's handle. She clutched the bag to her chest and stared with defiance at the boy.

"You are a thief!"

The boy, perhaps the same age as Tory but shorter, snarled at her. His hair was dirty and matted, his face and clothes no better.

"Whatcha got in there?"

"What I have is not your business."

He eyed it again. "You got food?"

Tory looked closer, noting now how thin he was. How desperate he seemed. "Why? Are you hungry?"

"What if'n I am?"

The only food she had left were a few handfuls of apple chips, but she had a thought. "Do you know where I might find a public pump? Water to drink?"

His expression sharpened. "Mayhap. What'll ya give t' know?"

Tory nodded slowly. "I see. A bargain." Clutching her bag, she said, "All I have to eat are some dried apple chips. I will give you five slices if you show me where I can get water."

He licked his bottom lip once. "Foller me."

He turned and trotted off; Tory followed behind him, keeping her bag clutched in both arms. She was, she admitted, disoriented. She had lost her bearing while giving chase and while riding the boy's back through warren-like passages and alleys—and she fretted that the waif was leading her farther into a maze out of which she would never find her way.

Before long, though, he ducked between two buildings. When Tory caught up with him, he was standing in the alley beside a rusty pump.

"No one cares if ya drink from this. Everybody does."

Tory thought the pump disreputable at best, but it was a source of water, and no one would chase after her with loppers if she filled her jar there. "Thank you."

The boy hovered at her elbow. "Where's m' apple bits?"

"Of course." Tory set her bag between her feet, brought out the sack, and winced at how light it was. She pulled open its draw-string neck. "Hold out your hand, please."

The boy eyed her with suspicion, but offered his hand—a dreadfully dirty one. Tory was loath to count the slices into his grubby palm.

"My, you really ought to wash your hands first, do you not think?"

"You welchin' on ourn deal?" he growled.

"Certainly not!" Tory sniffed with disdain. Arguing with the boy would be unproductive, so Tory reached into the bag, grabbed a handful of chips, and placed five of them in his waiting palm. The moment she counted "five," his fingers closed on them, and he fled away. Tory stared as he disappeared between the buildings.

"My goodness." Tory stuffed the remaining apple slices back into her bag and found her jar. She filled it at the pump, ignored the brackish color of the water, and drank her fill.

~*~

Tory spent five exhausting days walking the narrow, dirty back alleys and avenues of New Orleans, acquainting herself with the layout and commerce of the neighborhood she roamed. She washed her face and hands morning and evening at the rusted, back-alley pump and, despite her wanderings, stayed within range of that pump. She felt tied to the only water source she knew of and dared not stray too far from it.

She was disappointed in the quality of businesses she found. The few merchants, interspersed among bars, gaming houses, and second-hand stores, were as common and rundown as the streets where they sat. Some shops were less than rundown, bordering on squalid. In the back of her mind, Tory harbored a suspicion that she had yet to find the true business center of town. Surely the wealthy of the city would not patronize such common shops?

At first, Tory had interrupted passing pedestrians to ask for directions to a better part of town. Their uncivil and sometimes derisive rebuffs stung her and served to underscore her sense that she was not in the right part of the city. She had also realized how bedraggled her appearance had become and soon stopped asking for guidance.

With her small supply of food long gone, Tory had forced herself to approach the owners of a grocer, a butcher, a diner smelling of rancid grease, a rundown hardware store, three bakeries, and a seedy boarding house, asking for work. At every attempt, the hard-faced shop keepers had shaken their heads.

One such owner had looked Tory up and down in a way that reminded her of Bastiann Declouette. The fine hairs on the back of Tory's neck had prickled and stood on end. She had left the shop abruptly and had run to the end of the block, determined to avoid that street in the future.

After each rejection, Tory struggled against despondency. She was continually hungry now, growing weaker by the day. One of the bakers she had asked for work—perhaps sensing how desperate Tory was—had offered her a half loaf of day-old bread.

That had been yesterday. With hunger pangs tearing at her insides, Tory had ducked into the alley behind the baker's storefront, squatted down between his trash bins, and wolfed the bread in one sitting. Not long afterward, her bowels had given way, leaving Tory craving water and weaker than before.

She had dragged herself through those five long, humid days, walking a little farther afield each time, yet always returning to the rusted pump. Tory's thoughts began to stray; they wandered, without moorings, without anchor—except for the blasted pump.

She had spent long nights hiding from predators, had slept in the shadows where filth accumulated, under molding porches and behind trash heaps. And she had discovered other children like herself, children like the boy who had traded information for apple slices. They wandered the streets as she did, some in twos or threes, but none alone like the boy had been. Like she was.

The children eyed her with the same distrust Tory now turned on them—for she had suffered a close call and was, herself, learning to be wary in order to survive . . .

In addition to the few children she encountered, young gangs roamed the streets, knots of five or more older boys who raced through the alleys, turning over trash bins, stealing from the produce vendors, assaulting lone pedestrians. The gangs were more dangerous at night, for they laid in wait to beat and rob inebriated patrons as they left the bars and gaming halls.

Tory had caught their eye, and they had spotted the bag she carried. Shouting taunts and jeers, they had tried to surround her. Tory's long legs, fueled by terror, had outpaced them, but only just. After an indeterminable distance, the boys had given up, and Tory had collapsed in an alley behind a latrine, sobbing in terror.

As her sixth day on the streets dawned, Tory wrestled with her options and arrived at a difficult conclusion. *If I do not eat, I will die in the gutter like some beggar.*

That morning she went to the pump, washed herself as well as possible and smoothed down her ratted hair. She pulled a clean work dress from her bag and donned it. She also removed a pair of earrings, a pair of lustrous natural pearl drops dangling from fine silver hooks, from the bag holding her mother's jewelry.

It tore at Tory's heart to hold the earrings in her hand and think of selling them. She could see the pearls dangling from her mother's earlobes, their glossy white shimmering against the gleaming ebony of Adeline's long, beautiful neck. Tory nearly put them back in the bag, but stayed her hand, knowing what she must do.

I must sell them, or I will die. Maman would not want me to die.

Her attempts to overcome her grief did not work well. She would sell the earrings as a necessity, but when she left them, she would leave a slice of her heart, also. She consoled herself by imagining what she would buy with the money she received for them. She would return to the baker who had given her the stale bread and buy enough sweet rolls to feast on.

When she had made up her mind, Tory wound her way toward one of the neighborhood's less-seedy pawnbroker's shops. She had read of pawnbroker's shops in a Charles Dickens book Miss La Forge had loaned her. She knew that desperate people parted with their treasures in such places to keep body and soul together.

The bell on the door jangled when Tory entered. Her eyes darted about the shop, taking in the variety of wares for sale—musical instruments, china, crystal, silver-plated tureens and tea sets, clocks of every size, and a glass case of pocket watches and assorted jewelry. It did not escape Tory's mind that every item in the shop had once belonged to someone like her, someone forced to pawn what was precious—and who had not yet returned to reclaim what was theirs.

Tory tried to calm her jittery nerves. At least, as far as she could tell, she was the only customer in the store.

Good.

In response to the jangling bell, the owner shuffled from his back room, parting the curtain that divided shop from workroom. He was a fat man, dressed in fine clothing that had, at one time, fit him better: his unbuttoned suit coat gapped open, and his belly hung over trousers held up by a pair of scarlet suspenders. He looked down at Tory and frowned.

"What do you want?"

Tory's mouth dried up. "I-I wish to sell something."

He sniffed. "Well? What is it?"

Tory pulled the earrings from her pocket and held them out for inspection. The man's eyes widened. He reached for the earrings. Tory, with Bastiann's trick fresh in her mind, jerked her hand back. She picked out one of the earrings and allowed him to take it.

The man pulled a magnifying glass from a drawer and studied the dangling pearl through slitted eyes. "Where did you get these? Did you steal them?"

"Certainly not!" Tory was indignant. "They are—were—my mother's."

"Your mother's, you say?" He pursed his lips and laid the earring on the glass countertop. "Let me see the other."

Tory retrieved the first one before laying the second on the counter.

The shopkeeper scrutinized it under the magnifying glass also. "What do you want for the pair?"

Tory's lips parted in surprise. She had not considered the value of the earrings, nor did she have a working knowledge of money and its worth.

"I-I do not know exactly."

A tight smile pulled at the man's mouth—and that was when Tory knew the pawnbroker's shop owner would cheat her. She hardened her own expression: She would not cheapen her mother's memory by allowing the man to take advantage of her.

At least she hoped she would not.

She lifted her chin. "M-make me an offer," she managed, "and perhaps we can come to an agreement."

"Weeeell . . ." he dragged out the word, conveying reluctance and indifference at once. Tory knew it was a sham. She'd seen Venus do the same when money had grown dear and her *mère* had been forced to dicker with Sassy's granddaughter for her services.

Tory waited, as Adeline had, just as calm and indifferent as the shop owner pretended to be. She drew on her recollections of her mother's unflappable demeanor and waited for the shop's owner to make his move.

Please, Maman! Please help me!

The shop keeper hemmed and hawed, then muttered, "I suppose I *could* give you one dollar. That would be stretching it."

Tory did not answer right away; instead, she studied the man. After a full minute, she replied, "Perhaps I will take them across the street and compare offers."

The man reddened. "Two dollars, then."

He edged closer to the counter between them, and Tory, in response, took a step back.

"It would be prudent of me to compare offers," she mumbled.
"Three dollars."

"Five dollars." Tory couldn't believe her ears. She had countered his offer!

As Tory stared at him, her empty belly clenched and gnawed. Her knees quivered and a wave of dizziness swept over her.

What good will five dollars do me if I fall down unconscious? Likely this man would steal Maman's earrings and the rest of her things!

Gritting his teeth in anger, he growled, "Four dollars and no more."

Tory swayed a little as the dizziness passed. "I'll ask the shop keeper across the street to better your offer."

He slammed his hand onto the counter. "All right, you little witch. Five dollars."

Tory nodded. She still suspected him of cheating her, but she could manage no further bargaining. She watched in numb fascination as the man wrote out a claim check, then counted five dollars in wrinkled bills onto the counter's surface.

Tory picked up the claim check and read it. It gave her ninety days to reclaim her property. She knew she would never be able to, but she pocketed the check and placed the earring she held on the counter next to the money. When the man reached for it, she snatched up the bills.

He was angry, perhaps a little humiliated, at being bested by a child. "Go on, now. Get out."

Tory was glad to do as he demanded. She folded the bills, pushed them into the deep recesses of her pocket, and left the shop as fast as her weak legs could carry her. She headed for the bakery, two streets over, scarcely aware of her surroundings, so weak and disoriented was she.

As she cut through an alley to reach the bakery, she smelled the tantalizing odors of cooking food—greasy bacon, potatoes, toast. She was behind one of the seedy boarding houses.

The idea of warm food in her belly nearly drove her mad. She was knocking on the boarding house's rear door before she thought her actions through.

The woman who cracked open the door was sweaty and in a foul mood. "Whatcha wantin'? We don' feed no beggars."

"I'm not begging. I would . . . I would like to buy something to eat. Something warm, like mush or toast."

"You can pay?"

Tory drew herself up. "I can."

The woman didn't believe her. "Let's see, then."

Tory turned to the side, drew out the bills, and selected just one. She stuffed the rest safely down into the pocket, then held up a dollar bill.

The woman's eyes gleamed, and she nodded. "All right, but we don't serve colored in the dining room."

Tory didn't know what that meant, let alone what to think. "Does that mean you will not sell me something to eat?"

"Nay. Set down on the step there. I'll bring ya something. Bacon? Eggs?"

Tory's stomach lurched, but she remembered getting half sick from the bread—what would such rich food do to her? "No, thank you. Just . . . cornmeal mush, if you have it, and toast."

"Got some cooked oats."

"That would be fine, thank you."

The woman left, and Tory sank down on the steps to wait.

Ten minutes later, the woman returned with a chipped bowl upon a cracked plate. The bowl brimmed with thick oatmeal and cream. Two slices of buttered toast lay on the plate.

"Pay first."

Tory handed over the dollar—oblivious of her overpayment to the tune of a hot bath and two days and nights of bed and board. The woman, with a curt nod, handed Tory the plate and closed the door behind her.

Tory sat down, her hands shaking, causing the bowl to rattle on the plate. She inhaled the scent of browned bread and shivered. She bit into the buttered toast, held it in her mouth to savor it, then gobbled down the remainder of the slice. Tory ate the hot cereal in small, slow bites. She didn't care that the oatmeal was lumpy and undercooked—she devoured it. When she had finished the oatmeal, she took the second slice of toast, folded it in half, and put it in her pocket for later.

The influx of food made Tory drowsy—a dangerous state of being for a street urchin. She left the empty bowl and plate on the porch and went in search of a safe place to sleep.

CHAPTER 7

"What nonsense is this? What are you saying?" Bastiann roared. Beside him, his brother's widow, Marguerite, shrank from his bellow.

"As I have clearly stated, Mr. Declouette, Sugar Tree, your grandmother's home and land, does not factor into Mr. Henri Declouette's estate—which is why no mention of it will be found in his will today."

Richard Follinger, Henri Declouette's attorney, had delayed the reading of his client's will for two weeks—much to the chagrin and protests of the grieving widow and her brother-in-law. Follinger had needed time to revisit certain aspects of the will, execute its instructions, and prepare himself to face the outrage those instructions would engender.

Follinger had not even commenced the formal reading before Henri's brother asked about his grandmother's estate. However, the attorney, having served in his profession for more than forty years, was accustomed to the wealthy of New Orleans and their posturing—yes, he was quite inured to their pride, tantrums, and greedy machinations.

And he disliked the deceased's widow and brother on sight.

Follinger sat back and addressed Bastiann Declouette with his most detached air. "Mr. Declouette, I will remind you—once and once only—that I am an officer of the courts of this parish and will tolerate no unseemly behavior in my office or touching any legal proceeding. We shall not continue to the reading of the will until you have gathered yourself and agree to conduct yourself in the manner of a gentleman."

"Please, Bastiann." Marguerite, a petite woman of striking, porcelain beauty, placed a hand upon his arm. "We shall discuss our options regarding Sugar Tree when Mr. Follinger has finished reading Henri's will."

Bastiann brushed off her hand, adjusted his jacket, and replied in a more moderate voice, "Mr. Follinger, our grandmother left Sugar Tree to my brother. By the terms of her will, her estate should—it must—come next to me."

"Yes, yes, I am aware of that stipulation in her will; however, the condition of which you speak applied only if Mr. Henri predeceased *her*. You were to receive Sugar Tree if Mr. Henri died *before* your grandmother's will was executed. Once he received your grandmother's bequest, Mr. Henri was free to do with it as he wished."

"That land has been in our family for five generations," Bastiann snarled. "It is *family* property!"

"Family property? Perhaps, Mr. Declouette. However, once Mr. Henri inherited the estate, he was entitled to do with it as he decided—and he chose to deed it to a party outside the family. And, as said transaction occurred ten years past and is not part of today's proceedings, perhaps we could discuss it at a later date? Er, in private?" He flicked a discreet glance toward Henri's widow.

"Mrs. Declouette is in possession of the facts of her husband's adulterous affair, Mr. Follinger. You need not concern yourself with offending her sensibilities."

Marguerite's plump rosebud mouth shriveled, and she again placed her hand on her brother-in-law's arm—this time less gently. "Your consideration for my feelings is touching, Bastiann."

"Be quiet," Bastiann snarled.

She withdrew her hand from his arm, flounced in her seat, and lapsed into icy silence.

No change of expression altered Follinger's placid mien, but his mind and sharp intuition were at work. *Ah! Unless I miss my guess, the affair between Henri's wife and his brother is not altogether a happy one. Such things seldom endure.*

He flicked a perceptive eye toward Marguerite. *And as to your sensibilities, Mrs. Declouette? I promise they shall be offended further before we conclude this day's business.*

Bastiann composed himself. "Mr. Follinger, pray tell us precisely how my brother disposed of his inheritance from our grandmother?"

Follinger's finely tuned discernment detected more than outrage in the man before him. Was that a hint of anxiety seeping through Bastiann Declouette's otherwise self-possessed demeanor?

"I believe that at the time he took possession of his grandmother's estate, Mr. Henri removed the more important pieces of art from his grandmother's house. Can you verify this, Mrs. Declouette?"

Marguerite stirred herself. "Yes. The paintings, except the one of my husband's grandmother herself, hang in our house, my house. My husband felt his grandmother's portrait should remain where she lived and died."

Follinger nodded. "And I believe that Mr. Henri banked the cash assets of his inheritance at that time?"

"Yes. That is so—although the cash has long since been spent. What remains of his grandmother's estate is the house and land. Sugar Tree."

"I see. Well, I can tell you that Sugar Tree, too, is gone. Henri deeded the house and the five acres upon which it sits to one Adeline Washington."

Marguerite said nothing, but her rosebud mouth again contracted into hard, pinched lines.

She knew about the woman, Follinger saw. *Even knew her name.*

Bastiann lifted his chin. "I am afraid that I have news regarding this Adeline Washington. She has died."

"Oh? You know this how?"

"I and my, er, associates discovered her grave in Sugar Tree's orchard not a week past."

"This is a disturbing report, Mr. Declouette, and must be verified by the authorities. Do you know the cause of Miss Washington's demise?"

"No—but once the authorities ascertain the facts, will the property not return to the family? To me?"

"No, it will not, Mr. Declouette. The deed named Miss Washington's daughter, Victoria, as co-owner."

Marguerite's gasp drew Follinger's attention. *Apparently, she knew of her husband's mistress but not of the woman's child.*

"That whore had a daughter? But, who is the child's fa—"

Bastiann gripped her hand hard, and she clamped her mouth shut.

Follinger, observing with interest the interplay between Bastiann and Marguerite, added, "If Miss Washington has, as you say, Mr. Declouette, passed away, then her daughter, Victoria, is the owner of Sugar Tree by right of survivorship, not inheritance."

Bastiann ground his teeth to contain his temper. He knew that no deed transferring ownership from Henri to Adeline Washington—or to her daughter—could ever be produced. He had made certain of that the day he announced Henri's death to Adeline. With feigned nonchalance, he asked, "In the event that no deed of transfer can be found, what then? How would that affect ownership of Sugar Tree?"

"Oh, the deed was duly recorded with the Jefferson Parish clerk, Mr. Declouette. I submitted it myself and have record of it on file. The transfer of ownership will stand."

Bastiann cursed under his breath.

Mr. Follinger did not allow his smile of satisfaction to reach his lips; he was concerned for the child. "Mr. Declouette, when you visited Sugar Tree and found this grave, did you also see the girl, Victoria?"

"No. The house was abandoned. Empty. I do not know where she is." Inside, he raged. *That darky by-blow has legal right to my family's land?* He wished now that he had canvassed the neighborhood for news of the girl the day he had found the house empty.

"I must report the child's disappearance to the authorities, Mr. Declouette."

Deep in his own thoughts, Bastiann muttered, "I understand."

But Bastiann was not finished—not by half. *The girl is colored. I shall press my claim in court. The right judge—given an appropriate incentive—may rule against her claim, against Henri's madness. In the meantime, I must find the child and make her disappear. Where could she have gone?*

"Shall I proceed with the reading of the will?" Follinger asked.

Marguerite inclined her head. "Yes."

"Very well, let us begin." He drew the will from a drawer, placed it before him on his desk's blotter, and read, "I, Henri Auguste Declouette, being of sound body and mind, do make this last will and testament on this, the eighteenth day of November, the year of our Lord, 1901—"

"Mr. Follinger, please wait. This date cannot be right. Henri wrote his will five years ago. I found a copy in his desk."

Follinger offered Marguerite Declouette his most pacific expression. "Madam, Mr. Declouette came to me last November to rewrite his will. At that time, he revealed to me that you had announced your intention to divorce him? To, er, make public his relationship with Adeline Washington?"

"I-I . . . well, yes; however, we came to an accommodation rather than drag the Declouette name through the disgrace of a public trial. Then Henri became ill in the fall, as you know."

Yes, I know, and you thought you could wait him out, didn't you? That you would do better as a widow than as an aggrieved wife?

"Ah. I think I understand. Your 'accommodation,' nevertheless, does not negate the fact that Mr. Declouette did, indeed, make changes to his will in November of last year. Shall I continue?"

Marguerite's delicate porcelain-and-pink skin had faded to a sickly white, and she could not answer.

"Mrs. Declouette?"

"Go on," Bastiann answered. He, too, was shaken.

Follinger pursed his lips to keep them from twitching.

He read, "I, Henri Auguste Declouette, being of sound body and mind, do make my last will and testament on this, the eighteenth day of November, the year of our Lord, 1901. At the time of this writing, I am a married man, having married Marguerite Eleanor Declouette, *nee* Chartes, on June the sixth of 1879 and with whom I have a son, Devereaux, age seventeen, and a daughter, Yvonne, age fifteen at the time of this writing."

Follinger paused. He desired to watch the faces across from him as he read the next line, but he could not read and observe his audience's reactions concurrently. He suppressed a sigh and resumed.

"On this date, I acknowledge that I have a third child, Victoria Marie Washington, age eleven—"

"No. *No!*"

Follinger continued as if Marguerite had not interrupted, "—Victoria Marie Washington, age eleven, the daughter of Adeline Thérèse Washington of Sugar Tree, Jefferson Parish. I have no other children.

"I have also one brother, Bastiann Jacques Declouette. I have no other blood relations."

He cleared his throat. "To my son, Devereaux, I bequeath the house on Juniper Lane I inherited from my father together with all its furnishings—"

"What? That cannot be! Henri was to leave *me* the house, *our* house! And—"

Follinger stared at her, one brow raised, and repeated, "To my son, Devereaux, I bequeath the house on Juniper Lane I inherited from my father together with all its furnishings, with the single exception denoted in this document. I also bequeath to him the sum of five thousand dollars—"

"Five thousand dollars? Absurd! We do not have five hundred dollars, let alone five thousand!"

"*Ahem.* If I may continue, madam? I also bequeath to him the sum of five thousand dollars with the hopes that he, absent my guiding hand, will apply himself to his studies, find a worthy occupation in life, and grow into a man of good character and reputation. My bequest to Devereaux is to be held in trust by my attorney, Richard Follinger, until Devereaux achieves the age of twenty-one years of age."

"To my daughter, Yvonne, I bequeath the sum of five thousand dollars to be held in trust by my attorney, Richard Follinger, until her marriage or until she achieves the age of twenty-one years of age. I stipulate that she may reside at the house on Juniper Lane until she marries or until such a time as she chooses to leave.

"To my daughter, Victoria, I bequeath the sum of five thousand dollars to be held in trust by my attorney, Richard Follinger, until her marriage or until she achieves the age of twenty-one years of age. I also bequeath to her the painting, *Joseph Reveals Himself to His Brothers*, by Groote van Nierop. The title is apropos, do you not think, given how I have hidden my daughter from her siblings since her birth? This painting presently hangs in my house on Juniper Lane but belonged to my grandmother. The painting will be removed from the house at the time of the reading of this will and held in trust by my attorney, Richard Follinger, until Victoria achieves her majority.

"To Adeline Thérèse Washington, the mother of my daughter, Victoria, I bequeath the sum of one thousand dollars."

Marguerite laughed with bitter humor. "There is no money," she hissed, "not that it matters if the darky whore is dead."

This was when Follinger truly wished he had two sets of eyes, one set with which to read the will, the other to watch the reaction of the individuals seated before him. "The monies for the above bequests are to be drawn from my account at State Bank—"

"We do not bank at this State Bank! Our account is at Orleans First National, Mr. Follinger."

"Madame, pray allow me to continue. All will be clear soon."

He returned his gaze to the will. "The monies for the above bequests are to be drawn from my account at State Bank. This *new* account is established as an unbreakable trust for my children, Richard Follinger co-signatory and trustee. Mr. Follinger is authorized to draw, from this account, funds separate from and in addition to the individual bequests, to pay university expenses and monthly stipends for my children as he deems appropriate.

"At the time of my death, my outstanding debts are to be paid solely from my personal account at Orleans First National, Richard Follinger co-signatory. After my debts have been settled, I bequeath to my wife, Marguerite, the sum of one hundred dollars. Remaining funds from my account at Orleans First National, if any, are to be deposited to the State Bank trust account, managed exclusively by my attorney, Richard Follinger, and divided, equally, among my three children and disbursed in the same manner as their enumerated cash bequests."

Follinger chanced a glance at Marguerite before he continued. She had slumped, moaning incoherently, against Bastiann Declouette's arm. Her brother-in-law, for his part, seemed loath to touch her.

"To my *dear* brother, Bastiann, I leave nothing except the satisfaction of knowing that you will reap what you have sown. You possess your own shares of our family's businesses—the businesses you tried to run into the ground in your efforts to wrest their control from me. I choose this moment to tell you that, at the time of my death, according to my instructions and bearing my power of attorney, Richard Follinger has sold my shares—my majority shares—in every Declouette family company and deposited the resulting funds into the State Bank account to fund the bequests to my children and Adeline Washington.

"You see, Bastiann, I reached an agreement to sell my business interests to those same individuals within our companies whom you bribed or intimidated into doing your bidding. They were only too happy to buy me out and become the majority shareholders. My only stipulation at the point of sale was that the Declouette name be removed from all companies and holdings. The new majority owners look forward to ousting you from the business. You will, of course, receive payment for your shares, however devalued as they may be at present."

Bastiann clenched his fists until the knuckles ached and his nails cut into his palms.

Follinger let the paper drop from his hands. "That concludes the reading of the will. As the terms dictate, I shall call upon you tomorrow, madam, to remove the painting bequeathed to Miss Victoria."

"Do not honor that whore's child by addressing her as 'Miss.'"

Follinger shrugged. "Do you know the painting of which I speak, this *Joseph Reveals Himself to His Brothers*?"

When she remained defiant and silent, Follinger thought better of his initial plan. "I shall feel better if I call upon you this afternoon to retrieve the painting."

He flicked his eyes at Bastiann, real alarm beginning to bloom in his chest. "Hrrmmm. I shall request that the sheriff accompany me for the painting's removal to ensure that the dictates of the will are followed exactly. I should not wish any harm to befall the painting between now and then."

Hate blazed in Marguerite's eyes, and Follinger knew he had been rightly alarmed.

"You may expect me and the sheriff within the hour, Mrs. Declouette." Follinger stood and escorted them out of his offices, relieved to be shut of them.

"John? John!"

"Yes, Uncle?" Follinger's nephew, a young man barely in his twenties, appeared in his uncle's office doorway.

"John, my boy. Please run this message down to the sheriff. I need one of his men to accompany me in an official capacity within the hour."

"Of course, Uncle Richard."

Bastiann Declouette stood on the curb outside Follinger's offices, deep in shock. He had been as stunned as Marguerite to find that Henri had changed his will—not that Bastiann had expected a bequest from his brother—but he had anticipated assuming management of the family business and Marguerite's money. The blow to his expectations was acute.

He slid his eyes toward his sister-in-law. How he detested the woman! He had tired of her years ago but had continued to tolerate her because of his hatred for his brother and his hope that, at Henri's death, he would gain control of Marguerite's inheritance—and power over her under-aged children's inheritances as well.

But Henri had outwitted Marguerite and Bastiann both by selling his share of the business, diverting the monies from the sale to a secret trust for his children, and giving sole control of the trust to his attorney. And Henri had managed—from his grave, no less!—to flaunt his illegitimate child in Marguerite's face.

Bastiann stared down the avenue without seeing. *Henri had to have known that his demise was certain and imminent for him to have taken such steps.*

Marguerite did not interrupt Bastiann's deep contemplation even as her driver helped them into her motorcar. She was trapped in her own rising panic.

Soon everyone will know that Henri fathered a mixed-blood child. My children will know. My friends will know. Society will cast me off, even before it is known that he left me nearly penniless.

Another shocking realization hammered her. *Why, I shall be reduced to living as a tenant in my own home, as a poor relative dependent upon my son's charity!*

Bastiann's fists ached from his clenching them. With the family business and Marguerite and the children's inheritance beyond his reach, his only remaining hope was Sugar Tree—and even that, it seemed, had been wrenched from his grasp.

When a last, desperate idea struck him, he exhaled on his relief. He had thought of a way—a foolproof, legal way—to wrest control of Sugar Tree from Victoria Washington.

Why, of course! The girl is underaged—and as my brother has acknowledged her as his child in his will, no court will refuse to grant me guardianship of my own niece.

He cut a furtive glance toward the doors to Follinger's offices. *This man may control Victoria's inheritance, but he has no legal standing over her guardianship—or over Sugar Tree, for that matter.*

Even as he took his seat beside Marguerite, Bastiann was plotting his next move. *Marguerite would object most strenuously to my taking custody of her husband's illegitimate child and would make my life a living hell. Ah, no matter. I believe the time has arrived for me to cast her off.*

For I must *have Sugar Tree. Without it, without the money I have been offered for the house and land in lieu of my outstanding obligations, the men to whom I am indebted will surely extract their due from my body.*

He nodded. *I will petition the courts to grant me custody of Victoria, then I will set the best detectives on her trail. And no one—no one—will be able to prevent me from taking her.*

CHAPTER 8

Tory woke in the afternoon, steadier for the food she had taken earlier in the day, but needing more. She removed from her pocket the folded slice of toast, now cold and greasy, and ate it with gusto.

When she recalled the money remaining from the sale of her mother's earrings, she pulled out the bills and recounted them. Four dollars! What could she buy with such riches?

She pushed the money down into her pocket and smoothed her dress. Then she headed for the friendly baker to buy his wares. However, when she entered his shop, it was his wife—a sour, prune-mouthed woman—who "greeted" her.

"Ge' out! Ge' out o' here!" she shrieked. "I tole you rabble afore— we don' feed no beggars!" She picked up a rolling pin to punctuate her command.

Tory stood her ground. "I wish to buy something, if you please."

The woman sneered. "Right-o. Th' likes o' you has money!"

"I do have money," Tory insisted. "Please, how many of those rolls will a dollar buy?" She pointed at a plate of sticky buns behind glass.

When the woman caught sight of the bill Tory raised, she lowered her threatening arm. Her eyes shifted to Tory's face and, again, Tory recognized the assessing look. The woman was judging her, figuring out just how much she could gouge the inexperienced girl for.

"Mayhap four or five," the baker's wife decided.

Tory stared at her. *If I am not careful, I will squander what money I have and be forced to sell more of Maman's lovely things. I cannot allow that.*

Tory shifted from one foot to the other, deliberating. "I should like to speak to your husband, please."

"You should like t'—" The woman reddened. "Who d'you think you are, you dirty alley scum?"

Tory flushed. "If you will not call him to me, I shall take my commerce elsewhere—to a merchant who will not endeavor to cheat me."

The woman ogled Tory. She might have been familiar with insults, but she was not accustomed to them being delivered in fine language wielded by a street waif with a mass of wild, tangled hair.

The baker himself chose that moment to leave his ovens and investigate the cause of his wife's ire. "Well, wha' is it, Mrs. Bright? Why're you a-screechin' so?"

He caught sight of Tory. "Oh. You again. I'm afraid we ha' no stale bread of a mornin'. I grinds what's left in th' evenin' and sell't t' a chicken farmer, I do." He added, not in an unkind way, "Now go 'long wi' you, afore you ruin m'missus' good temper." He chuckled at his attempt to lighten the tense mood; but a sideways glance in his wife's direction met with a blistering glower.

He sighed. "I'm sorry, miss, but you mus' be movin' on."

Tory stood taller. "I shall leave as you wish, but I would purchase some of your sweet rolls first, if you please. How many would a dollar buy?" She waved the bill so he could see it.

Before his wife could forestall him, the baker guffawed. "More'n a girl your size could eat in a day, I wager! But, no sense makin' yourself ill, now, is there? Two penny each or six for a dime is our goin' rate. Mayhap three would be enough?"

Tory hesitated, looked down at her dollar bill in confusion. "How much is a dime, please?"

"Bless th' Lord, you don't know money, d'you." He said it as a statement, not a question, then turned to his wife. "Be keepin' your eyes on th' ovens, Mrs. Bright."

With a growl low in her throat, his wife flounced through the curtains into the back of the bakery.

"Not th' sweetest flower in th' bunch, my wife," the baker apologized, "but she's my flower, jus' th' same. Now, see here." He opened a little metal box, grabbed a fistful of change, and spread the coins on the counter. He put his finger on the smallest coin. "This one is a dime. Ten o' 'em t' a dollar," he jutted his chin at her hand, "like you ha' there."

"Six rolls for a dime? But she said—" Tory stopped, loath to finish.

"Well, wha' said she?" he asked with a resigned sigh. Apparently, Baker Bright was familiar enough with his wife's unscrupulous behavior.

"Um . . . she said four, maybe five sweet rolls for a dollar," Tory whispered. She saw how her words affected the little man: Even though he tried to hide it, his face reddened.

"I see," was all he muttered.

Tory sought to distract him. "If you please, could you explain the rest of the coins?"

He sighed again but went through the exchange of pennies, nickels, dimes, quarters, half dollars, silver dollars, and paper dollars until Tory nodded her understanding. Then, tearing off a sheet of waxed paper, he selected three sweet rolls and folded them up in the paper.

"Three rolls a' two cents—two pennies—each. That's bein' six cents. Reg'lar like, I'd take your dollar and be makin' change, givin' you ninety-four cents back: three quarters, one dime, one nickel, and four pennies. Ninety-four cents." He swept the coins back into the box. "Today th' rolls be on me."

He handed the paper package to Tory.

Tory's eyes widened. "But . . . I can pay."

The little baker smiled a wistful smile. "M' wife would ha' cheated you, little miss, sure as rain is wet, an' I'm tha' sorry, I am. Take th' rolls an' be savin' your money. An', if'n I may be s' bold, be careful showin' what you ha'. Many would take 'vantage o' you."

As Tory nodded, the baker had a thought.

"P'raps you would like t' change that dollar bill inta coin? That way, you won't be flauntin' an entire dollar an' temptin' the devil or his kin, so's t' speak."

"You are a kind man," Tory said. Her eyes stung. No one had been kind to her since she left Sugar Tree.

"Now, now. You seem a good sort. Just . . . just be careful like," he cautioned. "This be no' th' best neighborhood in N'Orleans."

Tory left the store, thinking over the baker's last words. *Just as I thought! This is not the best neighborhood in New Orleans. Why, somehow, I must find the better part of town—even if no one will tell me where it is! Perhaps, now that I have a bit of money . . .*

She shouldered her bag and turned into an alley to eat the sweet rolls, her mouth already watering for them.

"Say, you got sump'in t' eat there?"

At the familiar voice, Tory looked behind her. It was the small boy, the boy she had traded apple slices in exchange for water.

Her immediate reaction was to hide the rolls from him and say, "No." But her foray in the city had schooled her somewhat in the ways of the streets: Here, perhaps, was the answer to her quest.

"I have some sweet rolls."

The boy's mouth worked, and Tory understood the hunger cramping his belly. She wished she had a dozen of the rolls, wished she could give him half to ease the ache in his gut.

Now that she had his attention, she added, "When I traded dried apple slices for the location of a public pump, you brought me to this place."

He nodded, but his eyes never left the package she held close to her chest.

"This is a vile and dirty neighborhood without a decent place of work. Do you know better parts of town? Places where wealthy people go to dine or buy fine things? If you lead me to a clean neighborhood with quality shops and stores, I will give you one of my sweet rolls."

"How many you got there?"

"That is not your concern. My offer is for *one* roll."

He grimaced and shifted from foot to foot. "Mebbe I'll take 'em all. Take yer bag, too."

Tory was tired of running and tired of being cheated. She might have been thin, but she stood half a head taller than the boy, and she was wiry. More than that, she was angry, ready to defend what was hers.

She set her jaw and stared him in the eye. "You can try."

He studied her, weighing his chances. Tory did not look away—but he did. Perhaps he was just less determined than she was, or perhaps he was weaker. Tory wondered how long he had been alone on the streets, slowly losing his battle with hunger.

"Ya want me t' take ya where rich people shop?"

"Yes, please. And where there is water, of course."

"Cops don' 'llow beggars 'round that part o' town, 'cause o' th' rich people."

Tory nodded. "I am not a beggar, and I wish to go there."

He sighed. "All right. Foller me."

He was off like a shot, and Tory, getting a better grip on her bag and the package of rolls, ran after him. The boy raced through street and alley, up a slope and down the other side, weaving through a warren of buildings, jumping low fences and walls, the obstacles signaling to Tory that they had left the slum, that the surrounds were improving and they were moving in the right direction.

The fences and walls slowed Tory. She *was* carrying baggage, after all. For a few moments, she lost sight of the boy and worry bloomed in her chest. What if he did not come back—what if she ended up lost in this new and unfamiliar part of the city?

"Are ya coming?" Hands on his narrow hips, the boy reappeared between two buildings.

"Yes. One moment."

He walked now, as though running here might attracted unwanted attention. Tory, when she caught her breath, saw how different were the houses they passed—larger, freshly whitewashed, with tended yards. The scent of flowering shrubs and trees—instead of soot and sewage—filled Tory's nostrils.

The boy took another turn down a wide street. A few blocks later, they emerged together into a plaza, a broad, open square bordered by shops and thronged with well-heeled shoppers.

"Is this good enough?"

Tory nodded. She set her bag between her legs and unwrapped her paper package. The sweet rolls were squished, their sugary glaze stuck to the wrapper. The boy's eyes were glued to the rolls every bit as much as the rolls' sticky sweetness was plastered to the waxed paper.

Tory's heart went out to him. "Say, suppose I give you one, I take one, and we split the last?"

He nodded, a grateful light on his thin face.

Right there, on the side of the crowded plaza, Tory and her guide devoured the rolls. She even tore the paper in half, and they licked all the glaze from the waxy surface.

Tory's fingers and face were a gooey mess. "Where is the pump?"

The boy plunged through the crowd, and Tory had no choice but to follow.

"Pardon me," and "I beg your pardon," she murmured as she tried to keep the boy in sight. Moments later, Tory saw a patch of grass surrounded by a low, cast iron fence, benches fashioned of the same ornate black metal and, nearby, a brick-paved circle. In the center of the circle stood a welcome sight.

"Oh!" Tory rushed toward the polished, well-maintained pump and set her bag between her feet. She rinsed her hands and face, glad to be relieved of their sticky state.

"Thank you. I—" Tory stared all around her, craning her neck in every direction.

Her guide was gone.

She shrugged and delved into her bag to fetch out her jar. Within a few minutes she had sated her thirst, refilled the jar, and tucked it inside her bag. Then, with a tight grip upon the bag's handle, she wandered around the plaza, taking note of the quality and variety of the shops and its pedestrian browsers.

The length of one side of the wide plaza was fronted by a wide boardwalk, the walkway's roof forming a balcony for apartments built above the row of shops. Flower boxes trailed their colorful blooms from the balcony railings, and Tory wandered with slow steps in the shade of the boardwalk.

That raggedy boy has done me a favor, leading me here, Tory admitted. *I must make myself presentable and apply for work in one of these shops. If I could find a safe place to sleep nearby, I would have water to drink and—*

She stopped in her tracks, mouth agape, and stared through the storefront windows of a sizable shop, the last one on the boardwalk. In the window displays Tory saw wire-and-plaster mannequins dressed in exquisite gowns and tasteful daywear. She moved from figure to figure, devouring the details of the designs, admiring the compilation of each ensemble—or criticizing aspects of it.

"No," she whispered. "Not that parasol with a *linen* walking dress," and "the sash on that gown should be a shade brighter to complement the beaded bodice work."

A bell attached to the door of the shop tinkled, and a sharp voice cut into her perusal of the window displays. "Really! How disgraceful— allowing such riffraff entrance to the walkway."

Tory looked up. A short, plump woman and her two companions had exited the shop and were staring askance at her. At first, she was confused: Were they speaking to her?

Tory set her bag down at her feet and, even in her stained work dress, delivered her finest curtsy. "*Bonjour, mesdemoiselles. Pardon,* but do you address me?"

The tallest of the three women looked down her patrician nose at Tory. "Listen to the pickaninny with her put-on airs! No, I was not speaking *to* you, I was speaking *of* you. Coloreds are not allowed on the walkway. Now go along."

Tory's eyes widened, and she blinked in more confusion.

"I said, go along," the woman repeated. Under her breath she muttered, "Insufferable street trash."

Stung, Tory dropped another curtsy and hurried off the boardwalk and into the plaza. She wandered around the fenced, grassy area, trying to gather her wits. She'd heard the terms, street trash and coloreds. But pickaninny? What was that?

Well, I am not *street trash*, she fumed. *And I am not a "pickaninny,"* *whatever that means.* Bastiann Declouette had called her that, too, but Tory did not grasp its meaning—although it was clear he had intended it as an insult.

Tory walked until she calmed. She drank a little more water, refilled her jar, and glanced back toward the boardwalk. That's when she saw the sign attached to the balcony railing above the shop with its wonderful window displays.

Haute Couture
Madame Charlotte Rousseau, Modiste.

Haute couture? Tory fairly vibrated with excitement. High fashion? *This shop. I must find work in* this *shop.*

All that day, Tory walked back and forth in the plaza, inventorying the number and types of stores: florists, confectioners, cafes, jewelers, stationers, cobblers, milliners, and haberdasheries. She always came back to Madame Rousseau's. She studied the shop, its customers, and all others who came and went. In her mind, no other place of employment would do for her.

Her legs and back grew tired, but Tory would not leave. She had to have a plan, a way to ensure that she would make a good first impression. Afternoon shadows lengthened, and Tory remained, her sharp eyes watching. Traffic in the plaza thinned. Still she waited.

From within the shop, a hand slipped between the glass window of the door and the frothy fabric that curtained it. The hand turned the "Open" sign over. The sign then read, "Closed."

Tory's pulse quickened. A last customer, accompanied by her maid, departed. Tory ran her eyes over the woman's maid and made mental note of how the girl was dressed and coiffed.

"*Oui.* Yes, I can be that," Tory whispered. She continued to wait, believing she would know what she waited for when she saw it.

A stern, dignified matron of mature age, dressed in a tasteful but simple suit, strode around the corner from the back of the row of shops. Tory thought she had heard a door close behind the woman. With quick steps, Tory flitted across the way where she had a side view of the rear of the building as well as the front. A younger woman emerged from a door in the back, and trod with quick steps away from the plaza. She was followed by yet another, even younger woman, plainly dressed.

Ah. Madame's workers leave by this back door, as is befitting their station.

Employees were leaving by twos and threes now: three additional mature women and a number of younger women, some in plain work dresses, a few attired much like the last customer's maid. Tory did not stir. Her eyes swept from the rear of the building to the front entrance and back.

For a long while, no one else left the shop. The other stores, too, closed for the day. The plaza emptied, and Tory was alone there. She huddled between two buildings, hoping no one would notice her.

The city had converted the majority of its gas street lights to carbon arc electric lamps, but modernization had not yet reached this plaza. As evening seeped into the air, two men began to light the streetlamps. Tory did not budge as they passed her by. Few backstreets in the city were lit at all, and Tory worried that if she left the plaza, she would be hard-pressed to find somewhere safe to sleep in the dark alleys.

Despite the deepening shadows, something in her heart whispered for her to remain where she was: She did not believe the woman she watched for would use the workers' exit.

After nearly an hour, Tory heard the tinkling bell of the front entrance. A woman stepped out of the shop and onto the shadowed boardwalk. She pulled the door closed behind her, used a key to lock it, then turned to go.

Tory stayed absolutely unmoving; she watched the woman emerge from the boardwalk and step down onto the bricked plaza. The woman was tall and graceful, but she was no longer young or even middle-aged. She carried herself with authority and . . . *presence.* With shadows falling, Tory could not see much more of Madame Rousseau, but she was in awe nonetheless.

I must be ready when she arrives in the morning, Tory told herself, *and I have much work to do before I introduce myself to her.*

For her work, Tory needed light. She glanced up at the flickering streetlamps surrounding the plaza. *Why go anywhere else? Unless a policeman comes along, I can work through the night right here.*

Tory opened her bag, brought out her sewing kit, the black maid's dress Ellen had worn, and Adeline's frilly apron. Both needed to be hemmed to fit Tory.

Tory pulled the black dress on over the dress she wore and, pinning the hem at a few different lengths, finally got it right. She added the apron to ascertain its length, too, adding pins to mark the new hemline.

"I must take up the shoulder straps also," Tory mused, "and I shall hem Venus' apron with the scorched spot while I am at it." She knew she could easily do three hems and the apron straps in a matter of hours. With her cloak around her shoulders to ward off the night chill, Tory worked. As the hours passed, her eyes blurred and her stomach complained.

I should have bought some bread from a street vendor while it was daylight.

The sweet roll she had devoured earlier gave way to an empty belly. Her body had used up what inadequate nourishment it had provided. After so many days of little to eat, her hunger was too deep.

When she finished her work, Tory's hands were numb and her body weary. A light rain began falling. She gathered her things and walked between two buildings, looking for shelter, any dry place to lie down. To hide herself.

After wandering among the buildings, Tory spotted a stoop attached to the rear door of one of the shops. She crept up two steps to the tiny, covered porch and sighed with relief. She rummaged in her bag, pulled out the black dress and apron, and hung them over a railing, smoothing them with her hands.

"You must lose your wrinkles by yourself, my friends," she whispered. "I have no iron here." Perhaps the misting rain would help.

Warning herself not to sleep past daybreak, Tory wrapped herself in her cloak and hunkered down in the corner of the stoop, her head resting against the railing.

CHAPTER 9

An hour before dawn, Tory stirred and rose from the doorway where she had passed the night. Her mouth was dry and parched, and her body weak from hunger.

As she stretched her stiff, aching muscles, she thought, *Today I will find work. I must.*

In the semidarkness, Tory changed out of the soiled dress she had worn for days and into the black maid's dress. With only half its buttons undone, the clean garment slipped over her head and settled over her, telling Tory that she had lost weight. It made buttoning the black dress easier, but the garment hung slack at her waist.

I will tie my apron tighter, she told herself, *after I have washed.*

She walked to the pump in the plaza, took a long drink, and made a thorough job of washing her face, neck, and hands. Then, sucking in her breath, she doused her hair and rinsed away the dust and sweat of days.

When she returned to the stoop where she had spent the night, she pulled out her mother's dresser set to style her hair. That's when she realized . . . *Oh, no! I did not bring the pomade!*

Without the thick, oily pomade, Tory's hair would curl and frizz and refuse to conform to her wishes. The best she could do was attempt to braid it while it was damp and pin it down.

Maman's hair was so beautiful! But Tory knew that, without the pomade, even her mother's hair would have been difficult to smooth or style.

Tory tried to part her hair in the middle, but she could not work the comb through the tangles. Tory used her fingers to pull strands apart as best she could. Knowing the part was uneven, she nevertheless braided each side toward the back, and wound and pinned the braids together at the back of her head. It was the best she could manage, but her mother's mirror spoke the truth: Errant strands and wisps of curl had broken free of the lopsided braids. The overall effect was not what Tory needed this day above all days.

But what else can I do?

Conscious of the passing time, Tory tied on her apron and packed the rest of her things away. She wended her way between buildings until she again entered the plaza and took up a position, not on the boardwalk, but near the steps to it.

She stood still and solemn. Waiting. Quelling anxious thoughts and a hollow stomach. Believing that the woman who was last out the door at night would be first to arrive in the morning to unlock the doors for her workers.

And that moment would provide Tory with an opportunity.

The sun rose, and its long rays touched the plaza. Men arrived to extinguish the gas lamps, and a police officer walking his beat spoke a good morning to them. Tory withdrew into the shadow off the side of Madame Rousseau's shop until he moved on.

When the officer had passed, Tory again crept to where she could watch Madame Rousseau's front entrance—and was horrified to see the woman unlocking the door! Tory had but seconds to act. She raced up the steps onto the boardwalk and stopped beside the tall woman.

Tory tossed her bag into the alcove of the nearest shop window and dropped into a deep genuflection. "*Bonjour, mademoiselle.*"

The woman whom Tory believed to be Madame Rousseau jerked and uttered an oath of surprise.

"*Bonté divine!* What a fright you gave me!"

Tory, holding her curtsy, extended a graceful hand, palm up, and murmured, "I beg pardon, *mademoiselle*. It was not my intention to startle you."

She rose, folded her hands in a demure attitude in front of her apron, and faced the woman. Tory observed the woman's auburn hair—shot with silver—pinned in an ornate and fashionable style and noted the heavily powdered face below. Tired but shrewd eyes peered out from fleshy, powdered folds. Those tired eyes, in turn, swept over Tory, from shoe to crown, taking in all, missing nothing.

"Well, what is it, child?" The woman's mouth was surrounded by fine lines and creases.

"You are Madame Rousseau?"

"Yes, yes. Get on with it."

"*Bien, mademoiselle.* I wish to work for you."

"You wish to . . ." The woman's words trailed off on a scornful sniff as she, for a second time, ran evaluating eyes over Tory.

"*Mademoiselle*, I am well educated, trained in social graces, fashion, and language."

Madame Rousseau's gaze sharpened. "Language, you say?"

"*Je parle trois langues*; I speak three languages," Tory replied.

"*Est-ce vrai?*" Is this true?

"Yes, mademoiselle. English, French, and Italian."

"Italian! And you are fluent?"

Tory switched to Italian. "*Sì, certamente, signorina.*"

For an instant, the woman's powdered cheeks quivered with repressed humor. The moment passed, and her severe demeanor resurfaced. "It has been many years since I warranted the courtesy of 'mademoiselle' or 'signorina.' You will address me as 'Madame.'"

Tory, not entirely deficient in flattery, understood the woman's point, but she had intentionally extended the compliment: *What a gentlewoman speaks, Tory, should always be couched in grace and kindness—even undeserved kindness.*

"*Bien sûr que oui,* Madame." But of course.

"Your French accent is not local."

"My governess, Mademoiselle La Forge, was a native Parisian, Madame."

The powdered brows lifted in no little amazement. "Your *governess?*"

"*Oui,* Madame. Under *Maman* and Mademoiselle La Forge's tutelage I learned language, history, mathematics, music, dance, drawing, poetry, and sewing."

"Sewing?"

"*Oui.* I can baste, seam, and hem by hand with proficiency, Madame."

For a long moment, Madame Rousseau said nothing, but Tory sensed the machinations of a strong mind at work, even as the eyes that— seemingly—missed nothing continued to study Tory. The woman turned her gaze out onto the plaza before asking, "What is your name, child?"

Tory bobbed again. "Victoria Washington, at your service, Madame."

"Hmm. You must understand, Miss Washington: I am no common *modiste,* no ordinary clothier. I am Madame Rousseau, couturière to the city's elite. My fashions are suited only for the most discriminating of taste and style. My maids and fitters must know their place and behave with all deference while assisting my clients."

Tory's mouth dried. It sounded as though the woman intended to take her in. "Certainly, Madame."

The rheumy blue eyes nearly hidden in the powdered folds of skin probed Tory. "Have you other serviceable garments in that carpet bag you, er, *deposited* by my window? Are you able to make and keep yourself presentable? And that hair!"

"As you see, Madame, I am able to make myself quite presentable indeed. A simple mobcap—*une charlotte*—would cover my hair . . . in a suitable manner."

Some intuition had put the words in Tory's mouth. She knew her hair was an issue. It would never conform to Madame Rousseau's expectations without the pomade Tory needed to smooth its natural tendencies.

Madame Rousseau nodded slowly. "You have declared to me that you once had a governess, this Mademoiselle La Forge. Do you, then, have a home, Miss Washington? A family?"

Tory swallowed, looked away, and back. "No longer, Madame."

"You are alone in the world, then?"

Tory couldn't answer. She nodded once. It took all her self-discipline to keep her chin from quivering.

"How long have you been . . . sleeping on the streets?"

"A week, Madame? Perhaps longer?" The days and nights had bled together; Tory was no longer certain of the date.

Madame Rousseau sighed and muttered, "I do not know what I'm thinking, taking in a homeless waif . . . and one from the streets at that." She pressed her wrinkled lips together, then added for Tory's benefit, "However, we have lost our scullery maid. Her absence is taxing my staff, and your arrival is most . . . propitious."

Scullery maid. Tory was familiar with the term: the lowest of the low.

It must do, she whispered in her mind, thinking of the awful places where she had spent recent nights.

"I have but a blanket and a room at the back of the shop. In truth, the room is but a large closet, yet it is what I can offer—that and a cap to cover your . . . hair. You will be charged with the most menial of tasks and will accept whatever is asked of you. However, until you have proven yourself worthy, you will receive no pay."

No pay? Tory's empty stomach roiled. *Ah! But I have four dollars in my pocket. Perhaps it will be enough to feed me until I have proven myself?*

Madame Rousseau continued. "Each morning we receive an order of fresh beignets and an assortment of sweets for our clients. Of course, we serve tea with our refreshments. At the end of each day, you may have the leftover cream and whatever remains of the pastries and treats."

ᴄᴛᴏʀʏ

As though thinking of every possible disadvantage the arrangement might create for her, she added, "You are never to touch our supply of sugar, nor are you to claim the leftovers until the shop has closed—have I made myself clear?"

"*Oui*, Madame. Quite clear."

"And you are to show the deference to my staff that their positions warrant."

Tory curtsied once more. "I will comply, Madame."

Madame cleared her throat. "You have a pretty way about you; it may be that this position taxes your sense of the *apropos*."

Tory, fearing that the woman was changing her mind, replied. "I shall show myself grateful for the opportunity, Madame."

"Hmm. And ready with a pretty answer, too. Very well, then. I will show you where you are to sleep and make your toilet. And I will find you a cap."

Madame Rousseau unlocked the shop door and stepped over the threshold. Tory grabbed her bag and followed the woman into a sumptuous sitting room—a reception area—the entire width of the shop. The room was fitted with fine sofas, settees, chairs, and petite tea tables. A *mélange* of pleasant fragrances tickled Tory's nose.

Her new employer did not pause in the reception area. She parted brocade curtains and led the way down a wide hall past three private showrooms on the left, each with its own number of comfortable seats and a privacy screen in a corner for changing.

Madame Rousseau opened a door at the end of the hall and turned left down a dim passageway. They stopped at an open archway on the right.

"Wait here," Madame Rousseau commanded. "I must unlock the rear entrance to allow my staff in. The workers have tea and biscuits each morning at precisely eight o'clock."

Tea and biscuits? Tory's stomach burbled with enthusiasm.

Madame Rousseau left Tory in the passageway and went through the doorway into a kitchen. A wooden trestle table with benches on both sides and a single chair at one end was the room's centerpiece. Madame walked directly to an exterior door and fitted a key to it. When she opened the rear entrance, nine or more women filed in.

Peeking into the kitchen from beyond the archway, Tory took in the scene. Each woman greeted Madame Rousseau with a brisk curtsy and, "Good morning, Madame."

"Good morning, ladies."

The women went about various tasks with the assurance of long practice: They hung their belongings on hooks along the kitchen wall, tied on aprons they removed from the same hooks, and took seats at the long table while two girls busied themselves heating water for tea and setting the table with cups, saucers, sugar, and creamer. Last of all, one of the girls placed a platter on the table. The platter was stacked with thick, crusty biscuits whose sugared tops sparkled and winked.

Water flooded Tory's mouth. *But I will not eat until this evening—if anything remains of today's refreshments*, she reminded herself. *I must be strong and do without until then.*

Madame Rousseau returned to Tory and pointed farther down the passage with her chin. "Come."

The broad passage ended at yet another door; Madame Rousseau threw open the door and gestured to Tory. As Madame Rousseau had promised, the space behind the door was a wide closet for linens and sundry items. Shelves holding fine tablecloths, napkins, tea towels, and such began at elbow height to Tory and rose to the high ceiling. A faux marble bust (somewhat chipped), a trunk, a few baskets, a tiny tea table with a broken leg, and a dried flower arrangement occupied the floor beneath the shelves. The floor provided ample room for Tory to stretch to her full length—if she shifted things about.

Madame Rousseau drew a faded quilt from an upper shelf and handed it to Tory. "You must make do with this."

"Yes, Madame."

Madame Rousseau pinned Tory with a hard look. "Do not again use the front entrance of my establishment. It is for the exclusive use of my clients. You will come and go through the rear door with the other workers. Do you understand me?"

"*Oui*, Madame. I understand." Tory would have agreed to paint her face green or shave her head, had the woman asked, so desirous was she of pleasing the clothier.

"Leave your things and come meet the others."

Tory deposited the quilt and her bag in the closet, closed the door on them, and followed Madame Rousseau down the hall to the room where the staff gathered for morning tea.

"This is . . ." She frowned at Tory. "What name did you give me, child?"

"Victoria, Madame." Tory could not tear her eyes from the plate of biscuits at the center of the table. She felt weak, and her vision began to swim.

"Ah, yes. As you said." Madame Rousseau addressed her staff. "I will be trying Victoria as scullery maid."

Ten sets of appraising eyes fixed themselves on Tory. All were curious, a few not so friendly.

Madame rattled off names and titles that Tory only partially heard: "Mademoiselle Justine, my principal dresser; Miss Sarasses, assistant dresser; Miss Defoe, head seamstress; Mrs. Horringer, senior seamstress; Pauline, Suzanne, Simone, and Rachael, junior seamstresses; Daphne and Marie, our lady's maids. Marie, you will kindly find Victoria a suitable mobcap."

The women Madame had addressed as "Mademoiselle," "Miss," or "Mrs." seemed to be women of a mature age and seniority. The other employees were young women or mere girls—perhaps apprentices? In Tory's state, the table held a sea of inscrutable faces, unknown and mildly terrifying.

Madame pointed to the opposite end of the hall. "Victoria, the washroom is through there. You will find a dressing area with mirror, water, and soap. Present yourself to me after you have washed and attended to your . . . hair. I expect you to keep your hands and nails in pristine condition at all times. When I have approved your appearance, Marie shall assign you a few tasks, and we shall see how you get on."

The ten women had not moved.

"Marie! The cap, if you please."

A girl perhaps three or four years older than Tory jumped up, curtsied, murmured, "Yes, Madame," and left the table.

Madame Rousseau nodded to the remainder of the group. "Please continue with your tea and biscuits as usual. I apologize for the interruption." Almost as an afterthought, she glanced at Tory. "You may have a cup of tea and something to eat with the others after you wash up, Victoria."

In the washroom, Tory bathed her face and scrubbed her hands and nails until they were raw. All she could see before her eyes were the biscuits waiting on the table. She was trembling when she sank to the bench at the table. One of the women handed her a cup of tea, murmuring something at the same time.

"I beg your pardon?" Tory whispered.

"Cream and sugar are here," the woman repeated, pointing.

When Tory did not respond, two of the older women looked at each other. One of them reached for Tory's cup, dosed it liberally with cream and sugar, stirred it, and set it in front of Tory.

One woman with an inscrutable expression ordered, "Drink up, girl. We have a long day before us."

Tory, lost in a fog of fatigue, lifted the cup and sipped. As the sweet brew hit the back of her throat, Tory sighed—and sucked down the cup's contents. She did not notice the bemused glances exchanged around the table.

Someone took the cup from her hands and refilled it. Added three of the hard shortbread biscuits to her saucer. "Eat, Victoria."

Tory blinked, lifted a biscuit to her lips, and bit down on it. Within moments, she had consumed her second cup of tea and all three biscuits. Energy flowed into her body and her mind began to clear.

The girl, Marie, held out a white cap, spoke to her. "Well, go on, now. Change out of that fancy dress and apron; you don't want to ruin them with the scrubbing and mucking out you will be doing. See me as soon as you are ready."

"Yes, miss." Tory stood, took the mobcap and, with rising strength, found her way back to her "room." As quick as she could, she changed into one of her clean work dresses and the apron she had hemmed to hide the burned spot. The apron was clean but wrinkled. It would have to do.

Tory hung her good black dress and her mother's flounced apron on a nail to the side of the shelves, closed up her carpet bag, and raced to the wash room where she again scrubbed her face and hands. She pulled the cap over her hair, tucked in a few strands of hair, and checked her reflection in the mirror.

The face staring back at Tory startled her: a wide forehead and two huge brown eyes peered out from a pinched face.

How much longer would I have lasted on the streets if Madame had not taken me in? A rush of gratitude coursed through her. *I shall do my best to repay her kindness,* Tory vowed.

And she knew it *was* kindness that had caused Madame Rousseau to take her in.

Tory shivered. But for the couturière's soft heart, Tory would be outside, on the streets of the city, hungry, weak, and failing.

She left the washroom and returned to the kitchen. Five of the workers had dispersed, but the four older women lingered over their tea. Marie, her arms folded across her chest, looked Tory up and down.

"Please," Tory whispered. "Where may I find Madame so she may approve my appearance?"

"Marie will take you," one of older women answered.

Tory curtsied. "Thank you kindly."

"Well, come on then," Marie growled. Under her breath she muttered, "Don't know why I am strapped with the dirty mulatto."

"Marie!" A hand slapped the table in anger.

Tory was starting to distinguish between the older women still seated, was beginning to recognize how their positions in Madame Rousseau's establishment were different—higher—than that of the others. And of the four senior women, the most severe of them stood out in authority and manner.

Marie jerked as the table resonated under the woman's blow. She stared at the floor, her face flushing. "Yes, Mademoiselle Justine."

"I do not tolerate such vile talk. You will apologize—to Victoria and to us all."

Marie flicked a seething glance at Tory. "I apologize."

With wisdom beyond her eleven years, Tory understood that she must not, in any manner, jeopardize her newly formed and fragile position within Madame Rousseau's domain. In particular, she could not afford to make an enemy.

She curtsied low before Marie. "Miss Marie, I am in your hands. You do me great honor to assign me my tasks."

Marie studied Tory through slitted eyes, but Tory remained in her humbled, bent position, chin tucked to her breast, eyes downcast. Finally, Marie sniffed a grudging, "Nicely done. Come with me."

Mademoiselle Justine spoke again. "Marie, please acquaint Victoria with the shop first—the clientele areas versus the workshop, where she may go and not go, how she must behave in each. I would not have her embarrass Madame by her ignorance of our expectations."

"Of course, Mademoiselle Justine."

Tory followed Marie from the kitchen, out into the reception area at the front of the shop. They stood in the center of the room, and Marie recited, as though schooled in what she said, "This is where we receive our patrons and their maids. The shop opens promptly at nine o'clock each morning and closes for the day at six in the evening. The staff takes a thirty-minute recess at noon, during which time the doors are locked. Madame Rousseau and Mademoiselle Justine have the sole keys and only they may lock or unlock the doors."

Tory nodded her understanding. *Mademoiselle Justine is Madame's principal dresser. Before the clients, she is Madame's lieutenant, her second in command.*

She followed Marie into the hall; the girl led her into the first room on the left.

"These are our clients' private showrooms. Only Madame, our dressers, and Madame's lady's maids may enter the reception area or showrooms during shop hours."

She lifted her chin with pride. "Daphne is the senior maid. I am the junior maid. We come and go from the client area during shop hours as Madame, Mademoiselle Justine, or a dresser directs us. We assist the dressers during fittings and see to our clients' comfort, such as serving tea and refreshments.

She studied Tory. "A maid must be properly trained and garbed. The dress and apron you wore this morning might suit a maid's position—but do not aspire to what you cannot hope for."

Her sneer returned. "Even properly clothed, Madame would not train you. *You* will never, under any circumstances, enter this part of Madame's establishment during shop hours—except to see to the washrooms as needed."

Tory nodded and swallowed down Marie's ill will. *I must not care,* she told herself. *I will perform whatever task is given me. I must endear myself to Madame Rousseau and repay her kindness with my devotion.*

Her eyes flitted everywhere, trying to take in the several rooms and what they contained. In each show room Tory noted a round dais with mirrors surrounding it on three sides.

"Please . . . what purpose does the pedestal serve?"

Marie sneered. "Pedestal, eh? In spite of your fancy words, your question betrays your ignorance. *The fitting platform* is where our clients stand while our dressers take their measurements, pin the hems of their garments, and assure a perfect fit."

Tory ignored Marie's taunt. "Ah. I see. Thank you, Miss Marie."

Marie turned on her heel; Tory ran to keep up with her. Before the hall intersected the dim passageway, Marie pointed to a last door on the left. "Our clients' washroom. We are never to use it ourselves—it is for our customers' particular use only. You are to keep it clean and sweet smelling."

Marie opened the door between the hall and passageway, turned right. She passed the employee washroom and opened yet another door. "Be unobtrusive and quiet in all you do and say within these doors," she warned.

They stepped into a broad and open room of vaulted ceiling, polished wooden floor, and many high windows that poured abundant light into the space within. Tory's mouth opened in stunned amazement. She had not surmised—had not so much as suspected—such a vast space was concealed behind the hall opposite the client showrooms.

This, this subdued bustle of design and creation, was the heart of Madame Rousseau, the couturière, the modiste.

Tory's eyes devoured the workroom and its arrangement. She observed a long cutting table, five sewing machines, dozens of wire dressmaking forms, and a wall of shelves burgeoning with bolt after bolt of fabric. Seven of the ten women Tory had met in the kitchen were at work; four occupied machines whose motors generated soft, intermittent whirrs.

Marie nodded at a small older woman. "Miss Defoe is our principal seamstress. She manages the workshop."

Set apart to one side, sat a straight-backed chair upon a carpet. A dark-haired woman Tory remembered from earlier, her head bent, hand-stitched sparkling demi-jewels to the yards of tulle gathered about her.

Marie gestured toward the dark-haired woman and whispered, "Mrs. Horringer does our finest handwork. She is completing the wedding veil of Miss Isobelle Fouche, the fiancé of Mr. Marcel Vivant. Theirs is to be the finest wedding of the year. Her gown is just there."

Marie pointed to the dressmaking form behind Mrs. Horringer. The folds of the silver-white gown glistened in the morning light.

Tory was utterly enthralled.

"Miss Sarasses is our cutter and also a senior seamstress," Marie continued in a quiet voice. She moved with soft steps toward the cutting table and sewing machines.

Tory glanced around, taking in the whole of the workshop. In one corner, she spied a drawing table; it was canted forward, toward Madame Rousseau and Mademoiselle Justine who stood before it, discussing a sketch upon it.

Pulled by an irresistible force, Tory came up behind them and peered between them at the sketch of an evening gown. She was fascinated with what she saw.

"*Ah, comme c'est belle!* Look how beautiful it is!" she whispered.

Startled, Madame Rousseau and Mademoiselle Justine turned toward her, opening a better view to the table. Tory stepped closer to the drawing. Without touching the paper, she traced the dress' form. "But, see? Such simple, elegant lines. Gone is the fuss of an overskirt or inset panels of heavy lace. The lady's figure is shown to perfection—except for this bow upon her bodice. Does that not draw the eye away from the lovely lines of her waist and back?"

She glanced upward—and encountered two implacable expressions. With abrupt realization of what she had done, Tory stumbled back and sank into a curtsy. She began to babble her apologies—entirely in French.

"*Mesdames*, a thousand pardons! I crave your forgiveness for my rude, unacceptable behavior. I apologize most sincerely." *I have ruined everything!* Tory wailed to herself. Tears sprang to her eyes. *They will return me to the streets.*

When no one spoke, Tory dared to look up. She saw Marie first, hovering close by, a self-satisfied smirk on her face. Tory lifted her chin higher, steeling herself for the words of dismissal she knew were coming.

Madame Rousseau and Mademoiselle Justine were looking at each other, not at Tory. And something repressed in their manner made Tory swallow. Were they *laughing* at her?

She frowned. Laughter might be worse than the scathing rebuke she had expected. No, it *was* worse.

Mademoiselle Justine, pursing her lips but not quite able to stop their twitching, arched one brow at Madame Rousseau. "Her French is quite good."

"Alas, she exhibits an unacceptable flair for the dramatic—as we have just witnessed—but, yes, her French is excellent. Her governess was Parisian, I understand."

"Governess!" Mademoiselle Justine's humor was replaced by shock.

"A Miss La Forge."

"What?" Mademoiselle Justine's head swiveled toward Tory. "Miss Lorraine La Forge?"

Tory nodded. "*Oui, mademoiselle.*"

"Ah."

That one word carried significance, but of what, Tory did not know.

"An acquaintance of yours?" Madame Rousseau inquired with interest.

"Yes. Perhaps we shall speak of it later?"

Again, her words signaled hidden meaning.

"As you wish. But now," she leveled her gaze on Tory, "you understand, Victoria, that you are to enter the workroom for specific purposes only—sweeping, cleaning, and any hand work assigned to you. My designs are not to be touched or commented upon." She hesitated. "Although, you make a valid observation regarding the bow."

Mademoiselle Justine was nodding. "Yes. I must say that I agree."

"Remove it then, and we shall evaluate the effect."

"*Oui,* Madame."

Madame Rousseau signaled Marie. "Please consider Victoria's tour complete and set her to her tasks."

"Yes, Madame." Cutting a look of disgust at Tory, she walked toward the workroom door. Tory dropped a quick bob and scampered after her.

"We do not run in my establishment," Madame Rousseau spoke softly to Tory's back.

Tory heard her and turned. "Of course, Madame." Setting a sedate pace, she left the workroom.

"You little brat!" Marie hissed as soon as the workroom door closed. She slapped Tory across the face to punctuate her words.

Tory stepped back, face stinging, eyes tearing. Other than Bastiann Declouette, no one had ever laid a hand upon her.

Marie backed her against the wall and breathed into her face. "Oh, yes, you had best take care, little miss. If you get me into trouble again, I'll do worse than that."

She grabbed Tory by the arm and dragged her to the washroom. "You will clean the water closets each morning and afternoon—and anytime in between if the toilets give off an odor. You will also, after closing time each day, attend to the clients' washroom. However, it must be kept spotless and sweet smelling at all times. When it requires attention, I or Daphne will alert you. You will come and go so no client sees you.

"In addition, you will clean the kitchen each day: Sweep and mop the floors; wash and dry the dishes; polish the silver tea services; wash the tablecloths, napkins, and tea towels and hang them to dry; iron and fold the tablecloths and napkins and restock the linen closet."

A heavy hand pounded upon the rear entrance. "That will be the bakery delivery." Marie glanced at Tory's hands. "You may receive the delivery, but you will not handle our clients' refreshments. After all, you clean the toilets. Do you understand?"

Tory swallowed her indignation. "Yes, Miss Marie."

"Get busy then."

CHAPTER 10

Tory's first day at Madame Rousseau's passed in a blur of activity, punctuated once by a short lunch the staff took as a group. Each woman ate from her own packet of food: bread, cheese, fruit, perhaps a bite of sausage. When Tory saw them unwrap their lunches (modest fare though it was), when she smelled the yeasty bread and spicy meat, she crept into her closet, leaned her head against the coolness of the dark wall, and tried to ignore the gnawing pain in her stomach.

Instead, she contemplated the plates of refreshments Marie and Daphne had arranged in the kitchen and carried to the clients' sitting area that morning. The baker had delivered no less than four dozen beignets and three dozen tiny fruit tarts.

Whatever remains at the end of the day is mine, she told herself again and again. *If anything remains*.

The day was long; the shop remained open until six o'clock in the evening. Near closing time, Tory lingered in the kitchen for Daphne and Marie to bring the last of the tea and refreshment things from the front of the shop. Already most of the staff had departed for the day. Tory believed Madame Rousseau and Mademoiselle Justine lingered in the workroom while Marie and Daphne tidied the front of the shop.

Tory was washing the shop's pretty tea cups when Daphne placed a serving plate on the long table. One beignet and at least five of the little fruit tartlets were left! Tory sighed with relief, and her sigh seemed to echo through all the hollow places in her thin body.

I will eat! she rejoiced.

Moments later, Daphne returned with the day's bundled tablecloths and napkins. She dropped them on the bench beside the table. "Good night, Victoria," Daphne said. She plucked her things from her hook on the wall and sped out the door.

Marie brought the silver service and the last of the tea cups to the kitchen, and Tory, with a surreptitious glance, found that the cream pitcher was empty.

Tory shrugged. *No cream for me, but no matter. I will eat—*

She watched Marie eye the remains of the refreshments, open a cupboard, bring down one of the baker's small boxes, and begin placing the leftover beignets and tarts into it.

"W-what are you doing?" Tory sputtered.

"None of your business, I'm sure," Marie shot back.

A hungry, indignant fire ignited in Tory. "Miss Marie, those are mine. All the remains are my wages."

Marie fisted both hands on her hips. "Since when?"

Tory, determined to claim her dinner, stepped toward her. "Since Madame Rousseau hired me this morning. She said that *all* the remaining refreshments were to be my pay until I have proven myself."

Marie tossed her head and laughed. "Ah, but none will remain, will they? Too bad."

"But they are mine!" Tory insisted. "You have no right to them!"

Marie, half a head taller and many pounds heavier than Tory, gripped Tory by the front of her apron and jerked the girl to within inches of her face. "Listen, you dirty little n****r! Madame put me in charge of you. Unless you want me to give you and your work an unfavorable report, you had better shut your thick lips."

Marie's words drove like a fist into Tory's gut, robbing her of air. She gasped and struggled to breathe, faint from her need for nourishment.

Marie released Tory's apron and, as she did, shoved her onto the edge of the sink. Tory grasped the sink edge and hung on, afraid her legs would give way, more afraid of Marie's threats. What if Madame Rousseau believed Marie? And why would she not?

Tory was torn between her raging hunger and her fear of being tossed into the street.

She said not another word as Marie closed up the baker's box and, grabbing up her shawl from its hook on the wall, announced to whomever might hear, "I'm off now." Then she smirked an aside to Tory: "I *am* glad you are here, Little Miss Hoity-Toity. Daphne and I don't have to stay after and clean anymore, thanks to you." She giggled. "Oh, and *merci* for the treats! I shall enjoy them."

A moment later, she was gone—and, with her, Tory's hope of dinner.

Tory gathered her wits and her waning strength. She needed to wash and dry the silver service and plates, cups, and saucers for the morrow, finish tidying up the kitchen, and wash and hang the dirty linens. With slow, meticulous care, she finished the dishes, then heated more water to wash the linens—five little snowy-white tea tablecloths and three dozen napkins, most barely used.

And wash the tea towels, dishcloths, and my apron after. But I must rise early if I am to iron the clean linens before Madame Rousseau arrives to unlock the shop.

She rinsed and wrung the linens and placed them in a basket. She approached a wide metal bar mounted on the kitchen wall on the other side of the door. Tory grasped the bar and tugged. Four lines spooled out as she drew the bar across the room and fastened it to a hook on the opposite wall. She draped the wet laundry on the clothesline, taking care to smooth the wrinkles out of each item.

Less ironing, she assured herself.

Tory's last task was to examine herself and her work dress in the washroom mirror. She sponged a few spots from her dress sleeves and washed her face. She did nothing with her hair. It would, thankfully, be hidden under the ruffled white cotton cap.

Tory returned to the kitchen, her day done. She drank her fill of water and sank onto the bench in stupefied fatigue.

"Good night, Victoria," Madame Rousseau said. "I am locking you in, but you have all you need, do you not?"

Tory, who had been dozing with folded arms on the table and her face upon her arms, could answer nothing other than, "*Oui*, Madame. *Merci*."

Tory heard Madame's key turn in the front entrance, then she was alone in the shop. Soon night came to the city and also to the shop.

The dark, empty shop was not the pleasant place it had been in daylight, and Tory, feeling the need for something—anything—familiar and comforting, crept into her closet. She dragged her bag toward her and reached inside for its bottom. When her fingers encountered the stiff piece of brocade, Tory drew it out. She could not make out her mother's image in the enfolded photograph, but it was enough for Tory to know it was there. She kissed her mother's picture once, then returned it to her bag.

Tory undressed, hung her dress on a nail and, leaving her chemise on to sleep in, wrapped herself in the quilt Madame Rousseau had given her, and laid down upon the hard, wood floor.

She closed the door—and cracked it open it almost immediately. The complete and utter black within the closet was stifling to both body and mind.

She did not want to cry. After all, how fortunate was she that Madame Rousseau had taken her on and given her a safe place to sleep? She did not want to cry, but she did anyway: The image of the last beignet and remaining tarts teased and tortured her.

I can make it until morning, she reasoned. *Tea and biscuits for all in the morning. I can make it until then.* But her insides burned with acid.

~*~

"I sent for you as soon as I saw them. Of course, I recognized the set—your mother's, I believe?"

Bastiann Declouette held the pearl-drop earrings in his palm—the first concrete evidence he had uncovered proving that Victoria had fled to New Orleans. "Yes. And her mother's before her." He took in the seamy shop within the seamier neighborhood and exercised care that he did not brush up against the dirty edge of the counter. "You have come down in the world, Hugo."

Hugo sputtered. "I have come down? Why, you must mean I've 'come down' since you once brought these very earrings to me as collateral for a loan?" He sniffed. "My present surroundings are but a temporary setback, I assure you."

Bastiann did not wish to be reminded of his own dealings with local loan sharks. He stared at the man. "Not so temporary if you do not curb your gambling impulses, Hugo."

Bastiann enjoyed delivering the occasional insult, the twist of the knife in a lesser man's gut. But then, he despised weakness of any kind, particularly in weak men who could not control their vices—or their women. That he was guilty of the exact weaknesses did not enter his mind. "Tell me about the girl."

Bastiann may have overestimated his power; he should, perhaps, have considered how his insults would be received.

The obsequious shop owner bristled; his hand shot out and plucked the earrings from Bastiann's open palm before Bastiann could react. "I imagine these will fetch a pretty price—in the right market."

Bastiann arched one brow—lifting the mask of cordiality he wore, disclosing the dangerous man beneath. "I am the only market open to you, Hugo. Do not forget yourself—or that the men to whom you owe the most are my . . . business associates."

Bastiann doubted that Hugo's gambling debt to Bastiann's "business associates" exceeded his own—and if Bastiann did not appease those "business associates" soon, his plight would be worse than Hugo's.

Bastiann's precarious position served to heighten his brazen behavior. "Hand over my mother's earrings, Hugo, and tell me all you know of the girl," he snarled.

Hugo stalled. "Why, you must understand, Monsieur Declouette, that I paid dearly for the earrings—twenty-five dollars! And, of course, I sent you word as soon as I realized what I had purchased. I must, at the least, recoup my expenditure."

Bastiann and Hugo engaged in a stare-down that lasted until Bastiann waved a derisive hand at the other man. "Very well. I will compensate you for what you have laid out—on condition that you answer my questions about the girl."

"I agree." Hugo said nothing further, but he waited, wiping at an imaginary speck on the countertop's glass surface with a dingy rag.

Bastiann, with a wry chuckle, withdrew his wallet from inside his breast coat. He slid two bills from the wallet and let them flutter to the countertop.

"This is only twenty dollars, Bastiann," Hugo protested.

"Yes, but you see, I am certain the girl took far less for the pearls, am I right? Ah! I see that I am. Be content, then, Hugo, with what profit you have made today."

Hugo folded his lips together and swept the bills into a drawer beneath the countertop. "What is it you wish to know about the girl?"

"Who was she with? Where is she staying?"

Hugo shrugged. "I saw no one but her. As for where she is staying, how can I say? She carried with her a carpetbag, nice quality, but she appeared worn to a nub. I assumed she needed the money to eat."

"Are you saying she is sleeping in the streets? Around here?" Bastiann shuddered. A young girl, particularly one as striking as Henri's brat, would not last long in this environ. If the gangs did not find her, the pimps would.

She is too fine to waste in that manner. I must locate and retrieve her from this hellhole before she is sullied. Yes. I must save her to gain control of Sugar Tree . . . and to use for my own pleasure.

He would put the word out to the right men, those who were familiar with this low-life neighborhood: Whoever brought him the girl would be handsomely rewarded.

$\mathcal{C}$HAPTER 11

T ory slept hard and awoke muzzy and disoriented. Through the crack of the open closet door, pale light pierced the stuffy dark of the closet. "Oh!" Tory struggled out of her quilt cocoon and sat up. A wave of dizziness swept over her.

She waited until it had eased, then rose to her knees. She was unsteady, but was more concerned that she may have overslept. Dressed only in chemise and bloomers, Tory stumbled down the hall to the kitchen. A clock on the wall declared the morning barely begun: half past six.

Sighing with relief, Tory drank down two glasses of water before using the washroom. She felt all hollow and wobbly, but she went back to her tiny room, drew on her work dress, stockings, and shoes, and returned to the kitchen. She lit the gas range and began heating the kitchen's two irons over the burners.

The sewing room, for the necessity of operating the machines, was wired for electricity, but the remainder of Madame Rousseau's shop did not as yet boast such luxury. She recalled some chatter from yesterday's tea, an anticipation that Madame would soon have electric lights and appliances installed for the remainder of her establishment.

Well, this gas stove is already a luxury to me, she admitted. Sassy Brown's cook stove at Sugar Tree burned wood and was temperamental in the extreme.

Sugar Tree! Had it been only days, perhaps a week and a half, since Tory said goodbye to her mother and her home? Tory had lost all track of time on the streets of the city. A great sob of grief and homesickness bubbled up . . . but she stomped on it. Hard.

Stop this nonsense! You must be strong. Finish the linens before Madame arrives to unlock the shop.

Tory pressed her apron first—taking care not to scorch it as a maid at Sugar Tree had once done—then she tied the apron about her. The strings seemed longer this morning . . . or her midriff thinner. She could not spare the wherewithal to decide which.

Ignoring the fog in her mind, Tory pulled the dried tablecloths and napkins from the clothesline and bent to the ironing. Tory had less practice with an iron than a maid in her position should have had, but she was a fast learner.

She finished the ironing by half past seven and placed the folded articles on the table for Daphne or Marie to take to the reception area. Looking around, Tory decided to put the kettle on for tea. She filled it and set it on the burner, then raced to freshen the washrooms.

She was just finishing the clients' washroom and was holding an armload of cleaning supplies when she heard the grate of a key in the front door. A moment later, Madame Rousseau breezed into the hallway and encountered her.

"Oh! Dear me, child. You startled me. But what are you doing in the front?"

Tory curtsied as best she could—and nearly fell over from the effort. She dropped the bucket she held to grasp the wall. "*Pardon*, Madame. I was freshening the clients' washroom."

"I see."

Madame Rousseau frowned and looked her over. "Are you well, child?"

Tory made a great effort to stand straight and tall, "But of course, Madame."

With a nod, Madame Rousseau passed by Tory, who deposited the supplies in the cleaning closet where they belonged. Then she made a thorough job of washing her hands and face.

The sounds of employees entering the kitchen came to her, including, "Look here! Someone has filled the kettle already and set it to boil. How lovely."

Tory could not wait to sit down to tea and biscuits. She had been up for an hour and a half and what energy she'd garnered from a night's sleep was gone. She checked her appearance a last time and left the washroom to join the others.

Tory had reached the kitchen doorway when things went all wrong.

She stopped—not because she intended to, but because her legs would not respond. They refused to move, to answer her commands. A gray haze intruded. It misted over her eyes, and Tory blinked with sluggish deliberation against its encroachment, against the soft buzzing in her head that grew until it was a great noise engulfing her senses.

Tory did not faint. No, the worn bricks of the kitchen floor opened up and swallowed her whole. She tumbled down. Head cracked on hard brick, but Tory did not feel the injury. She already was senseless when she fell.

"*Miséricorde!*" Mademoiselle Justine was first to react, leaping from her seat at the head of the table. She knelt by Tory's unconscious figure. Blood trickled from her forehead.

"Fetch me a cloth dipped in cool water! *Dépêchez vous!*"

The other employees gathered around Tory, including Miss Defoe, a practical spinster above forty-five years.

She knelt beside Mademoiselle Justine. "Look here. The girl has hit her head on the bricks. Give me the cloth." Miss Defoe held the cloth's cooling moisture to the expanding lump above Tory's left eye. "This wound requires ice. Have we any here?"

"No, Miss Defoe, but I could fetch some from the butcher two streets over," Simone offered.

"Yes, go," Mademoiselle Justine instructed. She looked to Miss Defoe. "But why do you think she fell? Is she ill?"

Marie, from beyond the cluster of concerned women, muttered loud enough for all to hear, "This is the thanks we get—she has likely brought disease into our midst, a contagion contracted from sleeping in the gutters with the unwashed rabble."

Mademoiselle Justine touched Tory's cheek. "I do not perceive a fever." She asked Miss Defoe's opinion. "Do you?"

"No. She has no fever."

Madame Rousseau discovered her well-ordered staff in disarray. "What is this? What is going on?"

"The girl suffered a fainting spell, I believe, and hit her head when she fell," Miss Defoe answered. She swabbed away the trickle of blood from Tory's forehead. "I would attribute her fit to malnourishment. How thin she is!" Miss Defoe lifted Tory's arm, pulled back her dress sleeve, and displayed Tory's stick of an arm. "I question when she last ate."

"You saw how she was at tea yesterday morning," Mrs. Horringer put in, bending down to study Tory's face, "and, now that I think on it, she did not join us for lunch at noon, did she?"

Murmurs of "No," and "I do not recall her at the table," filtered through the little knot clustered around Tory.

"She should have had the remains of yesterday's refreshments for her supper. Daphne, you removed the refreshments. What was left over?" Madame Rousseau asked.

Daphne dropped a curtsy. "Half-dozen tarts and one beignet, Madame."

"Not all that nourishing in her condition, I should say," Miss Defoe remarked, more to herself than to anyone in particular.

Madame Rousseau flushed. "Better, I presumed, than begging for crusts on the street!"

Marie, standing off from the others and chewing the inside of her cheek, caught Madame's attention. When Marie's eyes jittered away under Madame's scrutiny, a tiny suspicion bloomed in that woman's mind.

Just then, Simone returned with a butcher paper package under her arm. "I have ice, Mademoiselle Justine."

"Ah, good. Hand it here, please." Mademoiselle Justine undid the package, and Miss Defoe wrapped a chunk of ice in the damp cloth before holding it to Tory's head. Tory moaned as the cold seeped into her wound.

Madame Rousseau lifted her chin to address the employees standing about. "See here, all the rest of you. Finish up your tea and get on with your tasks—excepting you, Simone. I wish you to go out again to the little café on the corner. Take with you a pannikin with a tight lid and purchase some stout beef broth and a loaf of bread." She held out a few coins and Simone took them.

The remainder of the staff, with the exception of Mademoiselle Justine and Miss Defoe, downed their tea and hurried to their assigned duties. Madame Rousseau, however, singled out Marie with a shrewd eye and observed how the girl had departed the kitchen ahead of the others.

Tory moaned again, drawing Madame Rousseau's attention to her. "The child had already cleaned the washrooms and ironed and folded yesterday's linens when I arrived this morning. I, ah, I may . . . I may have neglected to tell her that we have plenty of linens in the cupboard, that it is necessary to do the washing but once a week."

Miss Defoe, her eyes fixed on Tory, wondered aloud. "At how many years would you place this girl's age?"

Mademoiselle Justine hesitated. "Thirteen? No more than fourteen, surely. She has not bloomed yet."

"I would venture younger—for the same reason—but tall for her age." Miss Defoe addressed Madame Rousseau. "Did she tell you her age, Charlotte?"

"No, but from what she did disclose, I think the child most peculiar. Raised in affluent circumstances, educated, well-bred. Faith, I did not believe the whole of the girl's story, yet her manners served to confirm her tale. By the by, did you intimate, Annette-Francoise, that you knew the girl's governess?"

Mademoiselle Justine cleared her throat. "Yes, I met Lorraine La Forge when she was governess to a wealthy family. Governess, that is, until she suffered a ruinous blow to her reputation. A misconduct, ah, with the gentleman of the house, I believe."

"*Oh.*" Madame Rousseau and Miss Defoe murmured the single word at the same time and with the same clarity of understanding.

"Do you know what became of this Lorraine La Forge?"

"I heard, through a mutual acquaintance, that she had taken a position at a country home outside the city, teaching the daughter . . . of an affluent, unmarried negro woman."

The three women were silent, contemplating possible interpretations of Mademoiselle Justine's simple statement.

After a moment, Madame Rousseau sighed. "Victoria's father must have been quite wealthy."

"And quite white, judging from her complexion," Miss Defoe added under her breath.

"She . . . she did tell me she was alone in the world now. Her mother, at the least, has died."

The three women nodded in unison. Life as an orphan was difficult at best. Life for a motherless mixed-race child?

Madame Rousseau cleared her throat. "Well. It is my decision that we shall not hold the unfortunate circumstances of Victoria's birth or parentage against her," she pronounced. "Perhaps the child will thrive here in my establishment and, when she is grown, find her way in life."

Miss Defoe snorted. "She will not thrive if she does not put some meat on these bones." She stared up at her friend of many years. "And, if I may be so bold, Charlotte, biscuits, tea, and leftover pastries will not sustain a growing body engaged in demanding physical labor."

"I know, I know. Do not chastise me further, Patrice, if you please. I shall make amends." Changing the subject, she added, "But you think her younger than thirteen, do you?"

Tory groaned and reached a hand toward her head, trying to dislodge the cold compress.

"She is coming around. I shall ask her." Miss Defoe leaned over Tory's face. "Victoria, can you open your eyes?"

With another groan, Tory's eyes fluttered.

"Victoria, can you tell us how old are you? Are you twelve? Thirteen?"

"'Leven," Tory mumbled. "My head . . ."

But the women were gaping at each other in consternation. "Eleven!" They breathed the word in concert.

The kitchen door burst open, and Simone reappeared. "The café had no beef broth, Madame, only beef and vegetable soup—very nourishing, they promised me."

"Quite right," Miss Defoe agreed. "And bread?"

"Yes, miss. A fresh loaf."

Tory opened her eyes, then closed them . . . once more, and again, before they remained open. "What . . . why am I . . ."

"You fainted," Miss Defoe supplied. She removed the cloth-wrapped ice and glanced at the lump on Tory's head. "You hit your head when you fell and will have a nice bruise for a week."

Tory, realizing that Madame Rousseau was standing above her, attempted to rise. She fell back as racking waves of nausea swept over her.

Swallowing the bitter bile in her throat, Tory whispered, "*Je suis désolée! Je suis profondément désolée,* Madame!" I am so sorry!

Madame Rousseau's expression was unreadable. "You shall remain in Miss Defoe's care today until she deems you are fit to shift for yourself. In the meantime, we have soup and bread for you to eat."

The woman cleared her throat. "You are to eat every bite of this food before closing time today—a little at a time, since you are disused to a full stomach. Again, I place you in Miss Defoe's care—if that is agreeable with you, Patrice?"

"Yes. I shall take care of her."

Tory again tried to rise; Miss Defoe's hand on Tory's chest prevented her from sitting up. "But I have work—"

"Someone else must take up your responsibilities for the day until you have regained your strength."

"Yes." Madame nodded her agreement. She pursed her lips before venturing, "Tell me, Victoria, when did you last eat?"

Tory, experiencing a sudden and disquieting consciousness of the quandary she was in, did not answer.

"Victoria, I will ask you the same question another way. You will answer me with a yes or no. *Comprenez-vous?*"

"*Oui,* Madame."

"Did refreshments remain last evening when the shop closed?"

Tory's "*Oui,* Madame," came out in a whisper.

"Did you eat them?"

"*Non,* Madame."

"Did someone else take them?"

Marie will tell Madame that my work is deficient! I shall be dismissed, turned out into the street! Tears trickled out of the corners of Tory's eyes; she could not bring herself to answer.

"Victoria, did Marie take the leftover refreshments?"

"You must answer Madame, Victoria," Mademoiselle Justine urged Tory.

Finally, Tory nodded.

Madame Rousseau's mouth tightened further. "I see."

Miss Defoe huffed. "Surely this can wait. I wish to get some of that soup into her while it is hot."

"Yes. Certainly. Come, Mademoiselle Justine. We have clients waiting with only Daphne and Marie to greet them."

When they left, Miss Defoe spoke. "Simone, pour a little of that soup into a bowl and hand it to me. Yes, place the bowl upon a plate with a piece of that bread beside it. Ah, the bread smells good."

"Warm from the oven," Simone told her. She put the plate together and set it on the floor next to Miss Defoe.

"Thank you. You may go now."

"Yes, miss." With a last glance at Tory, Simone departed.

"Let us sit you up now, shall we?" Miss Defoe reached behind Tory and lifted her to sitting.

"Ohhh. Hurts. My head."

"I imagine so. Now, you must take a sip of this soup. Just a taste at first."

Tory opened her eyes and found herself nearly face to face with the severe Miss Defoe—who, upon much closer inspection, was *perhaps* not as severe as Tory had believed her to be. The face so close to hers was spare; the deep vertical lines between her eyes and the downward turn of the corners of her mouth were softer than Tory had thought, more the product of many long hours of labor than a stern disposition. A hint of girlish dimple creased her thin cheeks, and a surprising gentleness had settled in the woman's expression.

"Come, Victoria. Open your mouth." Miss Defoe spooned broth between Tory's teeth.

Tory swallowed it, but her stomach heaved and she gagged. She turned away from a second taste.

"I understand, child. We must keep trying, but allow your stomach to settle between our attempts." Miss Defoe broke off a bite-sized fragment of bread. "Smell this."

Tory inhaled. "Oh! It is . . . heavenly."

She rested against Miss Defoe's shoulder for several minutes until the woman dipped the bread into the soup and urged her to try it. "Just this bite."

The bread, soaked in the beefy broth, melted in Tory's mouth. Without effort, she swallowed. "Umm. It is . . . good."

"Excellent. Another after a minute or two."

Half an hour later, Tory had taken eight bites of bread and broth.

"How are you feeling now, child? Are you in danger of losing what you ate?"

"I do not believe so, but . . . must I not get up soon? I have so much work to do."

Miss Defoe laughed under her breath. "We will manage for a day without you. We had been without a scullery maid for a week before you arrived yesterday morning."

Tory blinked. Had it truly been only yesterday?

"But who—"

A devious twinkle lit Miss Defoe's lined eyes. "Ah, yes." She smothered a small smile. "It is my supposition that our patrons and clients will have to do without the services of Marie this day. She will be . . . otherwise occupied."

CHAPTER 12

When Tory had eaten what she could for the time being and could stand on her own feet, Miss Defoe insisted she try to sleep a while. "Madame has placed you in my care this day, but I also have work to do. Your work will be to sleep. At lunchtime, we shall have you eat more. Tell me, what arrangements has Madame made for you to sleep?"

"At the end of the passageway, in the closet."

Miss Defoe placed her hands on her narrow hips. "So? I must examine this closet."

Tory led her to the closet and showed her the quilt she slept with.

Miss Defoe was not impressed. "Nothing more? No ticking or pillow? What nonsense. I shall not stand for it."

"Please, Miss Defoe, it is all I have. It is warm and safe—that is enough; I am grateful for it."

Miss Defoe, her brows drawn down into an implacable line, answered. "As you say. Sleep here until I return to fetch you out for lunch." She wagged her finger at Tory. "I will tolerate no disobedience in this."

"Yes, miss."

With Miss Defoe's assistance, Tory pulled off her apron and dress. She wrapped herself in the quilt and laid down and, with a satisfied stomach, sleep came easier than she had imagined it would.

Miss Defoe was a woman whose keen mind missed nothing. She had taken in the exquisite quality of Tory's chemise and bloomers, worn thin as they were. With that observation, she accepted *de facto* all Madame Rousseau and Mademoiselle Justine had related regarding Tory's tale of birth and childhood.

Standing near the slightly open door of Tory's "room," Miss Defoe considered Tory's biddable nature, her friendless estate in the world, and Madame Rousseau's declaration that Tory would, in essence, become a ward of her establishment.

In her own no-nonsense manner, she extrapolated upon the situation and, with a firm nod, arrived at a declaration of her own.

~*~

As closing time approached, Miss Defoe allowed Tory to wash up the tea service and tidy the kitchen. Tory went to her tasks with fervent dedication—with Miss Defoe's watchful eye upon her.

The girl was springing back quickly, but Miss Defoe did not linger in the kitchen only to ensure that Tory did not overtax herself. She bid each worker a goodnight and counted them as they departed for the day, adding a "Good evening, Mrs. Horringer," as that woman, too, took her leave.

Ah. Now is the appropriate opportunity, she said to herself.

She went in search of Madame Rousseau and found her with Mademoiselle Justine examining the finishing touches to Miss Isobelle Fouche's wedding dress. Miss Defoe drew near to wait until they finished their conversation—and was bemused to discover that they were speaking, not of the dress, but of Victoria.

"The responsibility is mine, of course. I brought the girl into my shop, Annette-Francoise. I brought her into my shop, and I shall take her into my home."

"Ah, but consider, Charlotte, how the shop requires your undivided attention. A child would, of necessity, diminish your whole-hearted devotion to this establishment. And isn't Madame Rousseau's Haute Couture the child of your heart, the true labor of your lifetime?"

Miss Defoe's brows lifted in astonishment: Mademoiselle Justine's voice had taken on a coaxing, wheedling tone unlike the woman. *Quite* unlike her!

Madame Rousseau lifted her chin, which elevated the tip of her powdered nose a hair above Mademoiselle Justine's. "Ah, but *you*, Annette-Francoise Justine, you who are nearly *five years* my senior, do you think yourself—at your age—to possess the liveliness, the vigor, the *joie de vivre* required to foster a child as intelligent as Victoria?"

It was sweetly said. A barb twice-dipped in chocolate could not have been sweeter.

Mademoiselle Justine sputtered, and the volume of her outraged response increased, keeping pace with her indignation. "Wha—? *At my age?* Why, you barefaced, egotistical—I was not five years your senior on *your* last birthday, no matter what you tell the public. Have you imbibed a magical youth potion? No, my dear, I fear *advancing senility* has affected your mental faculties!"

Madame Rousseau harrumphed and managed to hoist her nose into the air another quarter inch. "Your insults are beneath you, Annette-Francoise. I refuse to respond to them, nor will I tolerate further discussion. The matter is settled."

"Indeed, the matter *is* settled."

Startled out of their argument, Madame Rousseau and Mademoiselle Justine spun round to find Miss Defoe, her arms folded across her breasts—a signal they knew all too well.

Miss Defoe stared them down. "Victoria will come home with me this evening and, if we suit each other, she will continue with me. I am but forty-eight years of age and, of the three of us, I am youngest and best suited to rear her. There can be no contradiction of these facts."

Madame Rousseau's liberal powder did not hide the flush of red rising beneath it. "Patrice Defoe! Why, what gall! What effrontery! What supreme impudence!" she shouted.

Not one to allow a challenge to stand, Mademoiselle Justine jumped in, "I must agree. Patrice Defoe, how dare you! You who possess not a single experience or prerequisite to qualify *you* to raise a girl!"

"Ah, but Charlotte and Annette-Francoise, I once *was* a girl—unlike you two wrinkled old crones. You were not 'born'—you were *hatched*—the both of you, and from cast-off eggs at that. Why, you were halfway to your dotage when I arrived at the orphanage. I was but six years old the day I met the pair of you—ages *ten* and *twelve*, as *I* recall, but both of you already too mature and superior to notice the lowly likes of me. Ah, but I made you notice me, did I not?"

Madame Rousseau snorted. "You, Patrice Defoe, were a pest—you have always been a pest!"

"No, I was *a girl*, while you two were the most supercilious of spinsters six long years before either of you turned eighteen and were thrown out of that hellhole. Why, Charlotte Rousseau, the powder with which you encrust your face is older than I am."

She jutted her chin toward the other women and narrowed her eyes. "Victoria shall come home with me."

Madame Rousseau and Mademoiselle Justine quivered with speechless impotence. Madame opened and closed her mouth, much like a fish sucking water. Both she and Mademoiselle Justine were too affronted to formulate a sufficiently biting riposte.

The standoff, the snarling, hatchet-faced impasse dragged on.

It was Mademoiselle Justine who broke first. She glowered, chewed the inside of her cheek, and clenched her fists—to no avail.

A giggle—accompanied by a hiccup—burbled from her pinched lips.

That tore it. The outrage leveled at Miss Defoe evaporated, and the furious, three-sided argument dissolved into snickers followed by snorts of laughter.

Alone in the kitchen, Tory halted her work as a cascade of cackles echoed from the workshop and down the passageway to her astonished ears.

"Oh, Patrice, what a devilish sharp tongue you hold in your mouth," Madame Rousseau gasped between snickers and guffaws. "How you do not slice yourself bloody is beyond me!"

"I-I-I-I-" Mademoiselle Justine could not catch her breath to agree. Her stutters set the old friends to laughing again. They tittered, sniggered, chuckled, and chortled until the pain of their levity forced them to hold their sides.

"Hush!" Mademoiselle Justine finally managed. "Hush now. Victoria will hear us."

"She will learn soon enough how little of our bark is bite," Miss Defoe sniffed. She fingered the gilt watch face pinned to her bodice and read the time. "My, but I must go. I want that girl bathed before I put her into a clean bed."

The women looked at each other with frank affection and respect. Madame Rousseau spoke next. "I have no doubt Victoria will do well with you, Patrice, but she will need nourishing food and appropriate clothing—expenses you should not bear alone. I must insist on helping to defray the cost of her upkeep."

"Yes. I agree. Victoria will do well with you, Patrice—and I will help also," declared Mademoiselle Justine. "An extra dollar each week will ease the burden you have taken upon yourself."

Miss Defoe's chin quivered. "You are the most generous of women, my dear friends. I shall welcome your assistance."

Madame Rousseau sighed. "Ah, but we three orphans have a soft spot for those we see in straits similar to those we endured, have we not? And I-I confess . . . that I had begun to think the girl would fill a spot in my heart, a place that often, of an evening, feels a bit empty."

Mademoiselle Justine nodded. She tipped her head toward Madame Rousseau. "I comprehend what you imply, Charlotte. Why, look at us: We are three self-made women who scratched and scrabbled our way up from the ranks of poverty, three confirmed spinsters, too old to attract husbands."

She spread open her hands. "Do we have hope of children or family before us? *Non.* It was . . . alluring to look upon that child and wonder, 'what if?' What if I could give Victoria a little of the love and care that is stored up and wasting away in my heart?"

Madame Rousseau took Mademoiselle Justine's outstretched hands and held them between hers. "Well said, Annette-Francoise. Well said. You have put your finger upon it exactly."

They sank into that intimate silence that deep affection permits and remained so for the passing of several minutes before Miss Defoe unfolded her arms. Cleared her throat.

"I shall do my best for Victoria, my friends. But, no doubt, I shall frequently call upon you for your advice. Perhaps our combined wisdom will prevail and we shall make something good of her—this child whom fate has cast upon our barren shores."

~*~

Miss Defoe occupied a small suite of rooms not far from Madame Rousseau's shop. Her apartment, located above a grocer and a barber, featured a tiny veranda overlooking the street. Her landlord let an adjacent apartment to the barber and his wife. Their apartment and Miss Defoe's apartment shared a wall and matching verandas, but separate stairs, on opposite sides of the grocer and barber's shops, led to their rooms.

"I do not live above my means, Victoria," Tory heard as they climbed the narrow steps and Miss Defoe unlocked the door to her home. "Mine is a simple life, but you shall have enough to eat and a clean bed with me. However, since my apartment is small, we shall avoid disagreements by observing a clean and an orderly household."

Tory saw what Miss Defoe meant when she took in the woman's lodgings: The apartment consisted of a tiny sitting room, a tinier kitchen on one wall, a miniscule water closet, and a single, small bedroom. Tory's bed, as it turned out, was a mattress Miss Defoe pulled out from beneath her own bedstead.

"You must make up your bed and slide it under mine first thing each morning. I do not wish to trip over it, nor do I want to be bothered by the unsightly view of an unmade bed."

"Yes, miss. No, miss."

"I will say at the outset, that I prefer plain and forthright speech, Victoria, and I expect the same from you. I am not easily offended; if you have somewhat to say to me, do not beat about the bush. I shall do likewise. It is my belief that if we dispense with unconstructive pretenses, you and I shall get on nicely."

"Yes, miss," Tory answered. She hardly knew what to think of Miss Defoe's offer to take her in; she was too worn down physically to voice any objections or questions.

"In the spirit of candor, then, we must get you a bath. You have kept your hands and face clean enough, but the rest of you grows rank."

Tory bowed her head. "I apologize if I stink, Miss Defoe."

"No apology is needed, Victoria. How could you have done otherwise in your situation?" Miss Defoe patted a straight-backed chair. "You may set that precious bag of yours here and unpack it. When I see what you have, we can determine how many hooks you might need. By the by, how long were you . . . without a place to rest your head?"

Tory placed her bag on the chair as directed and unlatched it. "I-I am not entirely certain, miss. Longer than a week, but not so much as two weeks, I think. I . . . the count of days got away from me."

Miss Defoe did not press her. She presumed that Tory would offer up further details on her homeless experience when she grew accustomed to her new surroundings and had regained her strength and equilibrium.

"I see. Well, then, let me have a look at what you have."

Tory unpacked her few belongings: her other work dresses, some underthings, a nightgown, her mother's black dress and frilly apron. She lifted out her mother's comb, brush, and mirror and laid them on Miss Defoe's bed.

Miss Defoe noted their costliness. "Very pretty."

"They were *Maman's*," Tory whispered.

"Ah." Miss Defoe pursed her lips at the pathos contained in those few whispered syllables. A moment later, she suggested, "Perhaps a place of honor upon my bureau?" She gestured to a weighty set of drawers wedged into the corner between the bedroom door and the room's window.

"Yes. Thank you." Tory laid her mother's tortoiseshell combs and the matching mirror, brush, and comb on the bureau's dresser scarf, stroking the back of the ornate mirror once.

Miss Defoe did not miss the tears that glistened in Tory's eyes. She cleared her throat. "I am glad to see you have comb and brush. Madame Rousseau said your hair was in need of them. When you bathe, we shall wash your hair and, afterward, see what can be done with it."

"Oh!"

"What is it?"

"I did not—that is, *I forgot*—to pack the jar of pomade."

"Pomade? Is this 'jar of pomade' a necessity?"

Tory nodded. "Oh, yes. My hair is difficult to manage without it."

"Hmm. I see." Miss Defoe did *not* see, but she was a woman who knew how to keep an open mind.

Tory again reached inside her bag and hesitated.

"What is it, child? Is the bag empty?"

"No, miss."

Miss Defoe heard a wariness in Tory's voice, a fear that Miss Defoe wished to allay. "I assure you, Victoria, that I have no designs upon your belongings. What is yours, is yours alone."

Tory chewed her lip, hesitant. A little fearful. "I . . . well, you see, Sassy Brown told me to take *Maman's* jewelry. I believe the pieces to be of some value; however, for sentimental reasons, I should not like to part with them—not any of them."

A further loss lurked behind Tory's words. Miss Defoe hoped again that, with time, Tory would choose to share her hurt.

The child needs to grieve. I should like to comfort and help her through her pain.

Miss Defoe folded her arms in that imperious manner Tory now recognized. "You are quite right, Victoria. If the pieces belonged to your mother, then you must keep them safe. I have a spot in mind for them. You may decide if you wish to employ it."

With no little effort, she squeezed her fingers between the bureau and the wall and began to push the heavy dresser from the corner toward the door. When a space of about eight inches had opened between the bureau and the corner, Miss Defoe knelt down. Victoria leaned over her shoulder to see what she was doing.

The woman's fingernails scrabbled against a floorboard. A moment later, one end of a short length of board popped up. Miss Defoe grasped the end and pried the plank from the floor, revealing a shallow hiding place. A small tin box was the hole's sole occupant.

Tory gasped. "How cunning!"

"Yes, thank you. I believe your mother's jewelry will be safely hidden here. What do you think?"

Tory thought for a moment. "If I may know, Miss Defoe, what is in the box?"

Miss Defoe sat back on her heels and Tory, once more, found herself face to face with the woman. In addition to the deep vertical lines above Miss Defoe's nose, Tory noticed the care lines around her pale blue eyes. Those eyes met Tory's and did not blink. More than their physical attributes, Tory discerned the frank honesty staring out from them while they appraised her.

"That insignificant box contains my life's savings, Tory—all I have stored up to keep me in my old age. You see, I trust you. I trust you to not betray my confidence, just as you are considering whether to entrust me with yours."

They gazed into each other's eyes, taking the measure of the other, for a long, solemn moment before Tory nodded. "I shall trust you, Miss Defoe."

"I accept your trust as a sacred duty, Victoria, and declare that you need never fear my intentions toward you."

Tory nodded. She got up, fetched the velvet bag holding her mother's jewelry. Then she dug into her pocket and extracted the money remaining from the sale of Adeline's earrings. She tugged at the drawstring, placed the money inside the bag, and handed it to Miss Defoe.

She watched Miss Defoe tuck the bag next to the tin box and replace the floorboard. Together, they put their backs to the bureau and shoved it into the corner, concealing their secret hidey hole.

"There. That does it. Safe and sound." Miss Defoe opened the bureau's bottom drawer and removed the clothing in it. "This shall be your drawer, Victoria. When we've laundered your underthings, you may fold them and place them in your drawer. And you may tuck your empty carpet bag away under my bed, alongside your pallet."

"Yes, miss." Before Tory fastened the bag's closure, she drew out the stiff, folded brocade holding her mother's image. She placed it on the bottom of her drawer, then slid the bag under Miss Defoe's bed.

Tory had her bath in a tin tub in the living room. Miss Defoe had but a single-burner gas hob, and it had taken three-quarters of an hour to heat enough water to fill the tub with only six inches of blissful heat. Tory sank down into it and remained there until the water began to cool. Then she scrubbed herself all over while Miss Defoe heated more water to wash and rinse Tory's hair and to launder Tory's underthings and mobcap.

It was when Tory removed her mobcap that Miss Defoe began to understand the challenge the girl's hair presented. Out of the corner of her eye, she watched Tory undo the straggling braids and finger comb the tangles. Released from its constraints, Tory's hair stood out all over, a dark, gold-flecked mass of curls, tangles, and frizz.

"Oh, dear." Not much in life was beyond Miss Defoe's abilities and determination; however, when it came to Tory's hair, she acknowledged her limitations. She was unprepared to deal with the task of styling Tory's hair—it dwelled in the realm of the unfamiliar.

"Victoria, ah, where would one purchase a jar of this pomade of which you spoke?"

Tory's brows rose—just as quickly, they bunched together in concentration. "Why, I do not know, Miss Defoe. *Maman* gave the shopping list to our maids once a month. *Maman* and I did not leave Sug—" Tory stopped herself before saying "Sugar Tree." "*Maman* and I did not leave the grounds of our house."

"You and your mother stayed at home? Always? You have never gone shopping?"

"No, miss. I . . . when I set out for town some days back, it was the first time I had ever set foot away from home."

Miss Defoe busied herself soaping Tory's filthy chemise and bloomers. *No wonder the child is so innocent—so naïve. She knows nothing of the world, nothing at all. How she survived on the streets until she came to us, I cannot imagine.* She frowned. *And how will I locate a jar of this miraculous "pomade" of which she speaks?*

The need for pomade became clearer after Miss Defoe had soaped Tory's hair, rinsed it clean, and toweled it dry. Miss Defoe ran her fingers through Tory's thick hair, discovering a texture and resistance she was ill-equipped to address.

This girl's hair will never take a comb without the help of a smoothing oil.

She glanced at her wall clock. "Tory, I am going out for a few minutes. I will only be next door to speak to my neighbor. Dry yourself, put on your nightgown, bail your dirty bath water down the sink, rinse the tub, and hang it out on the veranda, please."

"Yes, miss."

Miss Defoe walked down the steps to the outside and along the walk to another set of steps. By the time she reached the top and knocked, she was winded.

Mrs. Bogg, wife of the barber, answered. "Ah! Good evening, Miss Defoe. So nice to see you. Please do come in."

Miss Defoe sat on the Bogg's divan and sipped a welcome cup of tea. She allowed for the obligatory exchange of niceties before, at the first possible interlude, she managed to ease into her errand.

Mr. Bogg was succinct enough; it was Mrs. Bogg who tended to get on Miss Defoe's nerves. Miss Defoe had little patience for Mrs. Bogg's propensity to rehash and restate the obvious and, in general, talk a thing to death. This evening, however, Miss Defoe needed the Boggs' assistance. She was willing to tolerate a little idiocy in exchange for useful information.

"Mr. and Mrs. Bogg, I wanted to inform you that I have taken on a child. She is employed at Madame Rousseau's shop but is without family, so I am making a home for her with me."

"Why, how commendable," Mrs. Bogg answered. "How old is she? Surely, if she is working she must be in her teens? Quite commendable. What is her name? Yes, how very commendable, Miss Defoe. You are to be commended."

"Hrrmm. Thank you. The girl's name is Victoria, and she is tall for her age. We, too, believed her to be in her early teens; however, it came out today that she is but eleven years old."

"Eleven! Why, just a child! And an orphan? How sad. So, she has no parents?"

Miss Defoe gripped her tea cup. "Yes, she is a child and, as I *said*, parentless. 'Without parents' is what 'orphan' signifies, Mrs. Bogg."

She wondered if Mr. Bogg's lip quivered.

"Why, she is not a teen after all! I'm surprised you let me think her older. Just eleven years old, you say. A child. Commendable of you to take her in, Miss Defoe."

This time, Miss Defoe was convinced that Mr. Bogg's lip spasmed— but he was quick to dab his mouth with a napkin.

Miss Defoe made another clearing sound in her throat, "Hrrmm," before pushing to the point of her visit. "I could use your advice, Mr. Bogg. Victoria has coarse, curly hair that requires the aid of what she calls a pomade. As you are a barber, I wondered if you might know where in the city I could purchase such a pomade."

Mrs. Bogg's brow furrowed in thought. "Coarse and curly hair? A pomade? For a girl?"

Here it was, and Miss Defoe did not shy from it. "Victoria is of mixed parentage. Her hair reflects the natural tendencies of her negro mother."

Mr. Bogg's brows arched in mild surprise; Mrs. Bogg's mouth, however, dropped into a scandalized "o."

"Mixed parentage? Her mother is colored? Is her father not a negro, then?"

Miss Defoe exercised remarkable self-control. *Commendable*, even. "Her mother was negro. Her father was *not* negro. That is what mixed parentage implies."

"But—"

"My dear, please let Miss Defoe speak." Mr. Bogg turned to their visitor. "You are looking for a pomade that negro women apply to their hair? Is that it, Miss Defoe?"

"Yes, that is it."

"I have some pomade in stock that my male customers purchase. If you should like to accompany me downstairs, I shall unlock my shop and show it to you."

"That would be most kind." *And exactly what I was hoping for,* Miss Defoe added to herself.

She returned to Tory shortly and showed the girl her purchase. "Is this what you use on your hair, Victoria?"

Tory looked at the open jar and sniffed it. "Not exactly. This smells . . . different."

"What you mean is that it stinks. I can only assume it was made for men and not women, but it is the best we can hope for at this moment."

Tory nodded. "Thank you." She gathered some on her fingers and massaged it into her hair. Her frizzy tendrils became supple and glossy. Soon she was able to work the comb through her curls, part her hair in the middle, braid it down both sides and twist the sleek braids into a knot at the base of her neck. She pinned the knot in place with her mother's hair combs.

When she examined the result, Tory was satisfied, but she wrinkled her nose at the odor she could not escape.

"I agree. Quite unpleasant—and certain to be remarked upon in Madame's shop. I shall ask Madame to allow me to go out during the morning and find a jar with a more . . . agreeable scent."

Just then, Tory's stomach lurched and growled.

"I apologize, Miss Defoe."

"No, it is I who should apologize. I was so focused upon your bath that I neglected our dinner. We must eat; however, it is late. I shall cook some eggs and a bit of ham."

Tory sucked in a breath. She had not had an egg or any meat in weeks!

They sat down at the tiny table and Miss Defoe spooned a large portion of scrambled eggs onto Tory's plate along with a slice of fried ham. Between their plates, Tory's benefactress set a rounded loaf of bread. She tore off a piece and placed it on Tory's plate also.

"Eat, now, child—but if you feel your stomach filling up, leave what remains on your plate. I do not want you sickening from eating too much at a sitting."

Tory devoured all her eggs with bites of bread between. She could feel Miss Defoe's eyes on her and tried to slow down, but could not. The soft eggs were too good.

It wasn't until she began to fork ham into her mouth that she experienced what Miss Defoe had warned her of—a sudden sense that if she swallowed one more bite, her stomach would rebel.

Sleep tugged at her with abrupt insistence. She laid her fork on her plate and closed her eyes. When she opened them, Miss Defoe was watching her.

"Please, may I be excused?"

"Yes. You may ready yourself for bed now. In the future, you will clear off the table and clean up after meals, but this one time, I will do so."

"Thank you, Miss Defoe."

Minutes later, Tory crawled into the trundle bed and dropped into dreamless sleep.

CHAPTER 13

When Madame's employees lined up at the rear door of the shop in the morning, they were surprised to see Tory and Miss Defoe arrive together. Tory wore a clean apron from Miss Defoe's closet; her hair was smooth and lustrous, not a strand out of place. She held the freshly laundered mobcap, ready to return it to Madame.

As good as her word, Miss Defoe left the shop midmorning and returned with a jar Tory recognized.

"Why, this is exactly like the jar *Maman* had!"

"I am pleased, Victoria. It, um, smells much better."

Tory grinned at the implied humor, and the corners of Miss Defoe's mouth twitched—just a little.

Nothing was said or announced; however, the staff soon recognized that Tory's status had risen. Tory's position as scullery maid had not changed—she attended to cleaning duties as assigned—but Miss Defoe's guardianship of Tory became apparent: When the staff sat down to tea and biscuits, Tory sat beside Miss Defoe; when Miss Defoe unpacked her lunch, she served Tory as well as herself. At the end of the day, they left together.

Marie, observant of Tory's newly elevated and protected status, made no comment, and Tory was too busy working and attending to Miss Defoe's maxims to notice the frequent glares the older girl shot in her direction.

~*~

A week passed. Miss Defoe made certain that Tory ate three healthy meals a day, and Tory needed no coaxing to consume whatever was placed before her.

"She has the appetite of a starving jackal," Miss Defoe, with wide eyes, confided to Mademoiselle Justine. "She leaves nothing uneaten at any meal—and stares about with ravening eyes, looking for more."

"I should, perhaps, allow another quarter dollar per week for groceries?"

Miss Defoe did not argue the point. "If you please."

~*~

Under Miss Defoe's watchful eye, Tory grew adept at her scullery tasks and was able to complete them with time to spare. In the afternoons, Miss Defoe set her to basting.

When Tory had stitched several simple, straight seams to the head seamstress' exacting standards, Miss Defoe had her sit with Mrs. Horringer, adding tiny seed pearls to Miss Isobelle Fouche's wedding veil.

Mrs. Horringer was demanding and the hand-stitching tedious. Tory's neck, from bending over her work, grew tired and stiff.

"You are doing fine, but do sit up, girl. Hold your work out in front of you a little more. 'Twill be less strain."

"Yes, ma'am."

Tory's life settled into a rhythm after that. She and Mrs. Horringer finished the beadwork on Miss Fouche's veil, and the delighted bride—accompanied by her mother, the groom's mother, the groom's grandmother, two aunts, five bridal attendants, and a number of their personal maids—arrived for the final fittings of the bride's gown and her attendants' dresses.

The fitting was an event of such magnitude that Madame Rousseau closed the shop early that day to accommodate the wedding party and their demands. Daphne and Marie served an afternoon high tea to rival New Orleans' most notable tea room; Mrs. Horringer, pencil and tiny notebook in her hands, accompanied Mademoiselle Justine and Miss Sarasses during the fittings.

At the end of the month, when the furor of the wedding was successfully concluded, Miss Defoe bought lengths of black worsted wool and deep blue cotton. She and Tory remained after hours in the shop's workroom to cut and baste new work dresses for Tory.

"We shall allow for plenty of hem in your dresses, Victoria," Miss Defoe pronounced, "so we can let down the length of your skirts as needed."

She taught Tory to operate the sewing machines, how to guide the top thread through the machine and adjust the tension, how to wind the bobbins correctly and properly set the filled bobbins into their slot in the lower part of the mechanism. She showed Tory how to place the pinned seam under the presser foot, lower the needle onto the basting line, and ease the sewing head into action.

After two weeks of evening labor, Tory had three new black and two navy work dresses. She wore them proudly, knowing she was dressed as properly as Daphne or Marie. In addition, she and Miss Defoe had, by trial and error, mastered the combined art of pomade and braiding to produce beautifully smooth ropes of braided hair that Tory coiled and pinned at the nape of her neck.

"Your hair is quite satisfactory today," Madame Rousseau remarked. "I had not noticed before, but your braids have lovely gold flecks."

Tory was astounded. "Do you . . . do you really think they are lovely?"

Madame Rousseau wagged her finger. "Modesty does not ask for compliments, my girl."

"I am sorry. I only meant . . . you see, Miss La Forge used to pull out the gold hairs. Once she used boot black to hide them."

Madame Rousseau blinked, trying to make sense of what Tory said. "To hide them?"

Tory hung her head in shame and nodded.

"So . . ." Madame did not finish her thought, but she went her way, chewing on this mystery. Later, she recounted the conversation to her friends.

Mademoiselle Justine asked, "Could it be that Tory's colored family regarded her white blood with as much disgrace as many white people view her negro blood?

Miss Defoe's struck a fierce pose, her arms strapped across her breasts. She snapped her answer: "Stuff and nonsense! Ashamed of a child's hair? Well, I never!"

"Well, you must agree that my suggestion is possible, Patrice."

"Yes, Annette-Francoise! I am not so dim as to misunderstand your argument. What I meant was that such attempts to dispute or alter *facts* is stuff and nonsense. She is not responsible for her parents' choices, nor should she be made ashamed of them—or her hair."

"Ah. I take your point. Yes, I grant you that."

Madame chuckled, but it was an ironic chuckle combined with ire. "How many small, ugly people enter our shop every day, Patrice, their mouths dripping with small, ugly pontifications? Unfortunately, we cannot beat ugliness from a person's heart, not even with a stick, can we? But I tell you this: Within my house, I shall tolerate no diminution of Tory's worth and value because of her mixed blood. Here, she shall rise or fall on her own merits, not the choices or faults of others."

"Agreed," Mademoiselle Justine echoed.

"As it should be," Miss Defoe sniffed.

~*~

With Miss Defoe's regular, nourishing meals, Tory regained her health; under the woman's watchful eye, Tory learned. The spinster set exacting standards for Tory in her work, appearance, and manner, and Tory thrived in the woman's care.

Through the remainder of spring and the hot, humid summer, Tory raced to complete her daily scullery duties so she could spend the afternoon in the workroom. In this way, she absorbed the hidden, backroom workings of a house of fashion. She studied Madame's designs whenever the opportunity presented itself and loved seeing the sketches brought to life. Tory felt honored to baste, press, trim threads, or even sweep up the workroom.

As Tory became proficient at simple sewing tasks, Miss Defoe, a master seamstress, added to the girl's knowledge and skills.

"The child is flourishing in your care, Patrice," Madame Rousseau acknowledged. "You are teaching her well, too."

"Her love for fashion is uncanny, Charlotte. It is as though she was born to this life." Miss Defoe then hemmed and hawed, unlike herself.

Madame frowned. "What is it, Patrice? You are twitching like a sleeping dog's hind leg."

"And I have the sharp tongue? How you betray your common, vulgar roots, Charlotte." Miss Defoe harrumphed and folded her arms. "It is only that . . . that Victoria has told me she aspires to be a great couturière someday. She has set her heart upon it. Her every spare moment—and I grant her few of those, mind you—is spent sketching and drawing fashions she has seen or made up herself."

The two women fell into a troubled silence together before Madame Rousseau muttered, "I suppose we should attempt to lower her expectations."

Miss Defoe snorted in anger. "No, we should not! I will train her to be an excellent seamstress. She shall, at the least, own a worthy skill with which to make her way in the world—but I cannot countenance destroying her dream. The world will do so soon enough."

Madame Rousseau sighed and acquiesced. "As you wish, Patrice."

CHAPTER 14

On the third Sunday in September, Madame Rousseau and Mademoiselle Justine crowded into Miss Defoe's little apartment to celebrate Tory's twelfth birthday.

Tory and Miss Defoe prepared a festive meal, and their two guests brought with them a small chocolate cake spread with thick frosting and toasted slivered almonds. Before they sliced and served the cake, Miss Defoe placed a shiny gold box, a few inches square, on the table in front of Tory.

"What is this?" Tory asked. She was already brimming with gratitude, overwhelmed with the kindness and generosity of her patrons—her unconventional surrogate family.

Miss Defoe cleared her throat. "It is your birthday present, of course. You may open it."

The three women had discussed the gift at length, bickered over its selection for hours, and fought for who would contribute the greatest amount toward it. In the end, Miss Defoe's practicality won out—but not without consideration over what gift might hold the most meaning for Tory.

"We shall settle upon the item, agree to its cost, and divide the expense evenly among us," she declared. "I shall approve nothing expensive or ostentatious, of course. The present must be simple, as befitting a child of her age and station in life."

Mademoiselle Justine had pursed her lips in concentration. "A child of her age. Hmm."

"A child? Have you looked at her lately? Really looked?" This from Madame Rousseau. "With plenty of food, she has filled out—and I declare she has grown an entire inch in the past four months!"

"Nearer two inches," Miss Defoe had whispered. "Her father must have been a tall man. She has let down all her hems, and . . ."

"And what?"

"She is budding out. All the signs of nascent womanhood are there. I am afraid to look away for fear I shall turn back and find her a grown woman, not a child."

The three friends had fallen silent, each considering the implications of Tory's emerging womanhood.

In the space of four months, Tory had become so much more than a charitable project for them, greater than any philanthropic endeavor. She had woven herself into the fabric of their lives and hearts as a vine entwines itself about post and trellis. And like a vine, she was stretching toward the sunlight.

Each of the women—for the simple joys Tory lent their lives—wanted the girl to remain dependent upon them. They grieved a little that she could not stay a child forever. How long would she need those who had acted the part of prop and lattice?

Miss Defoe had broken into their self-reflection when she placed a card of stiff brocade before them.

"What is this, Patrice?" Madame Rousseau asked.

Miss Defoe unfolded the card and revealed the photograph within—the image of a striking young woman.

Madame Rousseau reached for it; Mademoiselle Justine leaned over her arm and the two women studied the woman's glossy-black skin and hair, gazed into her luminous eyes.

"I believe this is Victoria's mother. Her name was Adeline. Read the inscription on the back."

Madame turned over the photograph. "For Henri, my only love and the father of Victoria, my greatest joy," she read aloud. She turned back to the image "Yes. I think we can be assured that this is Victoria's mother. Victoria is very like her."

Mademoiselle Justine nodded her agreement. "And yet, I sense Victoria will outshine her mother's loveliness."

Miss Defoe sighed. "I agree. Victoria describes her mother as the most beautiful woman in the world, but her view of herself has been damaged. She does not see herself objectively as we do. Victoria will outgrow this coltish phase and likely stun us all. Her eyes, their slant and the gold in their depths . . . are mesmerizing. She will be tall and comely." She cleared her throat. "We must be vigilant, for her sake."

Madame Rousseau's powdered face had drawn down into grim lines. "Indeed. We must be on our guard against any man seeking to take advantage of our girl. But you brought this photograph for a purpose, Patrice. Did you not?"

"Yes. This subject of a suitable birthday gift kept me awake on my bed last night. I wished to give her something memorable—but what do we know of suitable gifts for a girl on the cusp of womanhood? I was, finally, drifting off to sleep when the idea came to me . . ."

Now, weeks later, the three women waited for Tory to open the little gilt box she stared at.

"What is it, please?" she whispered.

Tickled, the women covered their mouths and laughed into their hands.

"Why, silly girl! Birthday gifts are to be surprises—the nicest kind of surprises," Mademoiselle Justine answered.

"That is so," Madame Rousseau interrupted. "You must open your gift to discover what is hidden within."

Tory was beside herself. "Thank you. Thank you so much."

"But you have not opened it," Miss Defoe reminded her. "Go on, now."

Tory sniffed back her emotions and fiddled with the gold box. The lid lifted off and, nestled within folds of softest cotton, lay an oval-shaped locket, a rose carved from ivory upon its face.

"Oh, my! It is so beautiful." Tory lifted the locket by its chain—a chain made to be stronger than, perhaps, fashion dictated. "You are all so kind."

"Victoria."

"Yes, ma'am?" Tory lifted damp eyes to Miss Defoe's.

"You will find a tiny clasp on the locket's side."

"A clasp?" Tory bent her head and studied the locket, discovered it was hinged, and found the clasp of which Miss Defoe spoke.

Tory pressed the clasp and, with a "click" it released and the locket unfolded like a miniscule book. Tory encountered her mother's loving reflection staring out at her.

She burst into tears.

"*Maman!* Oh, *Maman!*" She pressed the locket to her heart and wept.

The dribbling eyes of Tory's three protectors met over the girl's head. The women could only nod what they were thinking: *Ah, yes. We chose rightly. Well done.*

After the cake had been shared around and their guests prepared to depart, Miss Defoe *hrrmmed* to draw Tory's attention. "Now, Victoria, we recommend that you wear this locket tucked into the neckline of your work dresses. To protect it."

"Of course! I shall care for and treasure it always. Thank you . . . all of you." She hesitated before, in a faint voice, she added, "When *Maman* died, Sassy Brown told me to leave our home and come to town. She said a kind shop keeper would give me a job, and she said . . . she said she would pray to Jesus for me."

She glanced with shy fondness at her benefactors. "I-I do not know who Jesus is but, many times, I think that Sassy Brown's prayers must have brought me to you."

Madame Rousseau smiled through tight lips. "Hmm. I am afraid that even should any of the three of us aspire to a religious persuasion, nothing of our lives would commend us to God, Victoria. It was likely that fate brought you to us."

Tory raised her eyes to Madame Rousseau's. "Whether God or fate, I am profoundly grateful."

She fastened the chain about her neck and found it to be long enough that she could open the locket and see her mother's face with little difficulty. "How did you do this? How did you put my mother's likeness within the locket?"

"Our Patrice did it, Victoria. She borrowed the photograph you keep in your drawer. You showed it to her once, do you remember?"

Miss Defoe nodded at Tory. "I took it to a good photographer who photographed the picture, thus making a copy. The photographer printed and cut the copy, trimmed your mother's face to fit the locket, and set it behind the glass in the locket—but it is a gift from all of us."

"I do not know how to thank you."

"Wear it with joy, Victoria, to keep your *Maman* close. Let her nearness comfort you."

Tory slipped the locket into her dress and felt where it stopped near her heart. "I shall. Always. I promise."

~*~

In the spring of the following year, Tory had completed her morning chores and taken up her sewing when Mademoiselle Justine rushed into the workroom. "Victoria! Come, child! Madame needs you most urgently."

Tory sprang to her feet, assuming an unfortunate "accident" needed her attention. "Should I bring cleaning supplies?"

"*Non, non*! No. See, here is Marie. Marie, take off your apron and give it to Victoria. Quickly, now."

Tory's eyes widened even as Marie's expression boiled with humiliation.

Mademoiselle Justine stripped off Tory's work apron and threw Marie's fine one over Tory's shoulders. "Here. Let me tie the bow in back for you." She whirled Tory about to study her, picked up her hands and made sure Tory's nails were clean and trimmed.

"Well enough. Now, come with me."

Tory, casting a glance back at the astonishment of the workroom, followed Mademoiselle Justine down the hallway toward the reception area.

"What am I to do, Mademoiselle? What does Madame wish of me?"

"You shall see. Hurry."

She parted the curtains and led Tory into the reception area. There, Madame Rousseau waited upon a longtime customer and the matriarch of the Vivant family, old Mrs. Vivant. Seated with her upon a crushed velvet settee was a companion of similar years. To her left sat a much younger woman.

Victoria curtsied first to Madame and then to the clients, keeping her chin tucked to her breast.

"Ah, Victoria. This is Mrs. Vivant. Her cousin, Signora Bellini, is from Milan. Signora Bellini and her granddaughter speak only Italian. As Mrs. Vivant insists that her Italian has grown rusty, I assured her that you would be able to serve as interpreter."

Tory swallowed. Within the powdered folds of skin around Madame Rousseau's eyes, she saw hope and trepidation warring. Tory realized, *Madame has staked the success of this moment upon my having said I was fluent in Italian!*

"Of course, Madame. It would be my pleasure."

She curtsied again to the clients and addressed herself to the elder of Mrs. Vivant's companions. "*Buongiorno signora,*" she greeted her. Then, casting her eyes down and continuing in Italian, she asked, "How may I be of assistance?"

For the next two hours, Tory conversed with the two Italian women, conveying their wishes to Mrs. Vivant, Madame Rousseau, and Mademoiselle Justine, serving tea and cake to the clients, and generally smoothing the way to a satisfactory order of three walking dresses and an evening gown for Signora Bellini's granddaughter.

By the time the clients departed, Victoria was exhausted. She had used every speck of her *mère's* wisdom and instruction to accommodate the clients' needs and desires, in particular, those of old Signora Bellini, who was growing hard of hearing. Tory had nearly shouted her answers in the old woman's ears.

The following day at lunch, while the staff was gathered for their brief noonday meal, Madame Rousseau praised Tory. "You did well yesterday, Victoria. Our clients were delighted, and I am pleased. They will be returning for Miss Bellini's fitting in a week."

She coughed to ensure she had everyone's attention. "I have decided to promote Victoria to lady's maid, half-time. Of course, the scullery work must be done. Therefore, you will work by Mademoiselle Justine's side each morning and return to your other duties in the afternoons."

She nodded to Marie. "Marie, you will alternate with Victoria. Mornings as scullery, afternoons with Mademoiselle Justine."

Mademoiselle Justine and Miss Defoe smiled their approval, and the staff added a smattering of applause. Everyone congratulated Tory. Everyone except Marie. The young woman's expression was stiff. Brittle. Tory squirmed in her seat and cut a glance toward Marie.

She shivered at the hatred sparkling in the maid's eyes.

~*~

"Victoria, please serve tea to our clients."

Tory curtsied. "*Oui*, Mademoiselle." She had been assisting in the reception area for several months and was growing more comfortable in her new role.

She brewed the tea, arranged beignets on a plate, and prepared a tray. She carried the tray to the reception area, and placed it upon a low table before two women, a mother and daughter who, Tory had been told, were preparing for the daughter's upcoming wedding.

The mother, a tiny but still beautiful woman of middle age, addressed Madame Rousseau. "Mr. Richard Follinger, attorney, administers my daughter's trust fund. His office is on Court Street. You may send the bill for my daughter's gown and trousseau to him."

"Cream or sugar, madam?"

"Just cream. For both of us."

Tory smiled and nodded while taking in the unnatural puffiness marring the woman's lovely skin—a sign, Mademoiselle Justine had whispered to Tory only yesterday, of a lady who drew to excess upon the liquid courage and the temporary comfort alcohol afforded.

The woman took a teacup from Tory's hand. As she did, she glanced into Tory's face and faltered, nearly losing her hold on the cup and saucer.

Tory managed to regain her grip on them both before they tipped and spilled. She again placed the cup and saucer in the woman's hand and smiled. "I apologize, madam." She had nothing to apologize for, but Madame Rousseau had taught Tory to smooth away the distress of a social *faux pas* by assuming responsibility for mishaps.

As the woman continued to scrutinize Tory, the cup and saucer in her hands trembled and rattled.

"Mama? Whatever is wrong?" The daughter, perhaps seventeen, took her own cup from Tory and placed it to the side of her chair on one of the little tea tables, to lean toward her mother.

Tory, truly seeing the girl for the first time, stared, blinked, and turned back to the mother, trying to hide her confusion.

The mother did not answer her daughter. Instead, her eyes never leaving Tory, she whispered, "Girl, tell me your name."

Tory was seized by a dread premonition. She stuttered, but felt obligated—no, compelled—to answer.

How could she not?

"V-victoria, madam."

The woman's cup slid from her saucer and fell to the floor, sloshing tea down the skirt of her dress and onto the carpet.

"Mama!"

Mademoiselle Justine, ever vigilant of her customers' needs, excused herself from another client and rushed to Victoria's aid. "Quickly. Fetch Marie," she ordered.

Tory fled from the front of the shop and dispatched Marie to manage the cleanup, but she, herself, did not return. Alarms clanged in Tory's heart. Something about the girl, a hint in the slant of her eyes, the lift of her chin, frightened Tory.

Madame Rousseau and Mademoiselle Justine found her later, in the kitchen, cleaning as if her life depended upon it.

"Upon my word, Victoria! Whatever has happened?" Madame asked. Her powdered brow was creased in concern. "Mrs. Declouette and her daughter left without placing an order. They fled my shop as if pursued by demons!"

"Mrs. D-Declouette?" Tory could not stop shaking. "Mrs. Henri Declouette?"

"Yes, Marguerite Declouette, the widow of Henri Declouette."

Tory's legs gave way; she sank onto a bench and dropped her face into her hands. *No wonder the girl stirred my heart. She has the look of her father. My father. She and I are sisters.*

Madame Rousseau waved a distracted hand to Mademoiselle Justine. "Annette-Francoise, fetch Patrice, please."

"At once."

As soon as Miss Defoe arrived, Madame Rousseau hurried herself and Mademoiselle Justine back to their waiting clients. Madame whispered in Miss Defoe's ear as they passed, "Something has disturbed Victoria. It has to do with Mrs. and Miss Declouette."

At that moment, Madame was glad that she had lost the argument over who would foster Tory; she was grateful her friend had insisted on taking charge of the girl.

Miss Defoe sat down next to Tory. "What is it, child? What has happened?"

"Oh, Miss Defoe! She knew me!"

"Who did? Marguerite Declouette?"

"Yes. She asked my name. When I told her my name was Victoria, she *knew* who I was."

Miss Defoe mulled Tory's words for a minute before the possibility of their meaning came to her: *For Henri, my only love and the father of Victoria, my greatest joy.*

"Are you saying Henri Declouette was your father? Is that it?"

Tory nodded. "I-I perceived the resemblance in Miss Declouette's features, particularly her eyes. They stirred a remembrance in me, but I didn't, right away, attach the resemblance to my memories of her father. His eyes were . . . distinctive."

"Then that must be how Mrs. Declouette knew you, also."

Tory's brow crinkled. "I have his eyes, too?"

"Your eyes possess a wide, noteworthy cant, Victoria, the likely evidence of Cajun-French blood—Arcadian or possibly a Spanish influence. Louisiana bloodlines have been mixed many times since Europeans landed upon this continent."

"I-I always knew I was different, that something was wrong with me, but I did not know what it was. Sassy and Venus clucked over my skin because it wasn't black enough. Miss La Forge fretted because my hair had odd strands of gold in it. All of them frowned at me because I was different, as though different was unsuitable. Inappropriate. *Wrong.*

"I did not even comprehend that I was half white until I was ten . . . when I discovered Henri Declouette was my father. It is his blood in my veins that makes me unacceptable."

Miss Defoe resisted the impulse to pull the girl into her arms and insist—*to vow*—that Victoria was *perfect*, that there was *nothing* wrong with her. She longed to comfort Tory, but she resisted her impulse because, difficult as it would be, Tory would have to meet this challenge alone. She would need to arrive at her own insights: That the ugly prejudices people carried in their hearts could not be easily fixed. That people could not be made to conform to her expectations.

That the world did not work that way.

Miss Defoe, fighting back her indignation, murmured with quiet conviction, "My dear girl, listen to one who cares for you very much: You must accept, here and now, that while those who love you also accept you, the world contains many who will loathe you and never accept you. Even more important than understanding this, you must decide, you must choose—regardless of whether you are loved or hated—you must choose to live an upright life, a life unswayed and unaffected by those who despise you. You must never allow their hate to enter your heart."

It was the most profound thing Tory had heard in her short life.

"I-I will try, Miss Defoe. I will."

"You already succeed, my lamb. You are a humble, gentle soul. We love you, and you are ours. We will allow nothing to ever take you from our hearts and lives."

Then Miss Defoe gave into the yearnings of her soul. She opened her arms, and Tory came to them, sobbing with joy and relief, releasing the hurts of her childhood into Miss Defoe's bosom.

It was a pure, defining moment, binding Tory to her surrogate mother, and Miss Defoe to the daughter of her childless heart, their embrace solidifying their affections forever.

Neither of them had any sense of how soon their attachment would be sundered.

~*~

Bastiann Declouette heard the engine of a motorcar in Sugar Tree's courtyard and, leery of unexpected visitors, threw open the house's front door. He was less than thrilled to find his former paramour alighting from a hired conveyance.

With the execution of Henri's will, Marguerite's financial straits had obliged her to relinquish her own motorcar and live in a much-restricted fashion. And since Bastiann had moved to Sugar Tree, it had been more than a year since they had met. Her unannounced and unwelcome visit—and the expense of a hired car to bring her from town—spoke of either the woman's desperate attempt to reclaim her former relationship with him or a family crisis for which she required his intervention.

He ardently hoped for the latter. He was, after all, uncle to her children, and family crises could be dealt with. Unwanted former lovers, on the other hand, hung about one's neck like the proverbial millstone.

Bastiann snorted. If Marguerite hoped he could alleviate her financial woes, she would be sadly disappointed. His own circumstances were worse than hers.

In the weeks following the reading of Henri's will, while Bastiann had waited for the money from the sale of his shares of the family business, he had been unable to make the rent on his apartment in town. He had been forced to rely upon the grudging hospitality of various acquaintances, spending three or four nights with one before moving to the next.

When the sale of his stocks concluded and he received the proceeds, Bastiann had paid his creditors half the money he possessed. His creditors would have taken everything, every penny—still far less than he owed—but he had promised them Sugar Tree as full payment of his debt when he gained physical custody of Victoria. The desirability of Sugar Tree, its rare location on a bluff above the river, raised the house's value to five times Bastiann's debt; however, his vow to surrender the estate had been Bastiann's only play, the only means of staving off his creditors' ire.

With the remaining half of the stock sale, Bastiann had then parted with a sizeable "gift" as inducement for a certain judge to expedite and approve his application for guardianship over his niece.

After his guardianship was approved, Bastiann had taken up residence at Sugar Tree, the same judge ruling that his presence in the house would prevent looters or squatters from ransacking the estate and ruining its value.

Bastiann had shelled out additional funds to detectives and informants to find Victoria. They had been searching for her for more than a year to no avail—and Bastiann's creditors' latest warning rang in his ears: Find the girl and force the "sale" of the estate to them . . . or else.

The thin stack of bills he carried in his wallet was all he had left, and the length of time remaining for him to locate Victoria was thinner than his wallet.

He managed a tight smile. "Marguerite. To what do I owe the distinction of your presence?"

She glanced over her shoulder at her driver. "Do let me in, Bastiann. I do not wish the driver to report that you kept me waiting on your doorstep."

"Will letting you inside lessen the gossip your visit is certain to provoke?"

"Shut up. I must talk to you—and, I am convinced, you will want to hear what I have to say."

Bastiann opened the door wider, and Marguerite swept inside. He waved her into the parlor. She went directly to the sideboard where he kept his liquor and dumped sherry into an expensive Baccarat wine glass. She gulped half of it in one go, then seated herself.

He was amused by her actions—and the traces of dissipation evident in the sagging lines of her face—but he said nothing, sensing that her visit might possess some merit.

She finished the sherry before she said, "You are yet searching for Henri's bastard, are you not? You wish to find her?"

Bastiann laughed. Marguerite was not often given to crude language. But his brother's widow was correct: The search for Victoria Washington was his last hope. It consumed him.

"I wish to find her, yes."

She turned a calculating eye on him. "What is she worth to you, Bastiann? How much will you give me to tell you where she is?"

Heat rose in Bastiann's face. "You think I will pay you for this information?"

"Ah, but I do."

His first impulse was to choke the breath from this shrew, to throttle her until her bulging eyes begged him *to allow her* to tell what she knew.

How little do you perceive, Marguerite, of how close to the edge I sail, of how desperate grows my plight.

But, other than his mother's pawned pearl earrings, his hired men had uncovered no clues to the girl's whereabouts. Victoria may as well have vanished from the face of the earth—and Bastiann had little time remaining before he must do the same. Either he fled Louisiana or his creditors would ensure that fishermen found his lifeless body floating far down the river.

Bastiann held but a single card in reserve as a hedge should he need to flee Louisiana—those same pearl earrings. He had hidden them well, had inserted them into the backing of the portrait of his grandmother through a near-invisible slit. Said portrait still hung in the drawing room where Adeline Washington had died.

He controlled his frustration and smoothed his expression into bland lines. "I am afraid my cash flow is as dry as yours must be, my dear. I could . . . perhaps . . . see my way to ten or twenty dollars?"

"What? Only twenty?" She studied him. "If you gain control of Victoria, will you, in future, have more?"

Yes, she was as desperate as he.

"Should that happy occurrence be mine, I could agree to, say, a twice-annual allowance of one hundred dollars?" he lied. "For the period of two years only."

She tipped the glass into her mouth and was irritated to find it empty. Bastiann was quick to refill it and return it to her hand. She gulped twice before answering.

"Twenty now, four hundred over the next two years?"

"Agreed—*if*—and only if your information leads to her successful, ah, recovery."

Marguerite stared at her glass, her face haunted. "I saw her. This morning. I came face-to-face with her, Bastiann. She . . . she has Henri's eyes. I knew her at once."

Bastiann could always tell when Marguerite was exaggerating, outright lying—or telling the truth. His heart quickened. "Did you, indeed?" He withdrew his wallet and, gritting his teeth, counted four precious five-dollar bills into her hand. "Pray, tell me where I can find her."

CHAPTER 15

Tory filed through the rear entrance of Madame Rousseau's shop with Miss Defoe and their fellow employees. She was full of health and vitality, ready to meet the challenges of the day—and she carried her precious sketchpad with her.

Today, Miss Defoe had informed her, Madame Rousseau had agreed to look over Tory's sketches after the shop closed for the day. Tory would never have dared presume to ask such a thing, but Miss Defoe's eye had found her designs "promising" and had approached Madame on Tory's behalf.

Humming under her breath, Tory hung her cloak, tucked her sketch pad into an empty kitchen drawer, and filled the kettle for tea. Fifteen minutes later, the staff sat down for morning tea and biscuits.

The shop opened promptly at nine o'clock, and their first clients of the day kept Daphne and Tory busy. Near eleven o'clock, Mademoiselle Justine dispatched Tory to the kitchen to prepare a tray for their latest customers. Tory went to the kitchen, removed the dressy apron she wore when waiting upon clients, and hung it on a hook to keep it spotless while she prepared the tea and refreshments. Under her apron she wore one of her new black dresses; its simple but tasteful style fit Tory well. The fine dress and Tory's height added to the illusion that she was nearer fourteen or fifteen than approaching her thirteenth birthday.

A loud and contentious commotion from the front of the store startled Tory. She crept into the passageway and heard Madame Rousseau's raised protests clash with a man's loud demands for the shop's clients to get out. Miss Defoe was already at the junction of hall and passageway, listening to the disturbance.

The face she turned to Tory frightened the girl, as did her stern command. "Victoria, slip out the rear door and go home. Do not linger—go straight home."

"But why? What is happening?"

"Men have entered the shop, and I heard one of them shout your name. Do as I say: Run home as fast as you can, but hide yourself across the street until I call for you. Darling girl, be brave and quick—do you understand me?"

Tory nodded and ran to the kitchen door. She put one eye to the door's peephole and was dismayed to find two burly males loitering on the stoop. She knew at once that Bastiann Declouette had found her—and that Marguerite Declouette had been the means of her discovery.

She flattened herself against the wall next to the door, screaming inside. *What should I do? What should I do?*

Tory's mind went blank under a wave of terror. She was standing against the wall when the door crashed open. She scrabbled for the door's handle to prevent it from bouncing against her and swinging away, disclosing her. Tory was taller and fuller than she had been when Madame Rousseau had taken her in fifteen months ago, but she was as lean and as lithe as a sapling, easily concealed behind the door.

The men may have seen nothing that aroused their suspicions, but they stood sentry in the kitchen, ostensibly guarding the rear exit against Tory's escape. Almost immediately, Tory heard Miss Defoe enter the kitchen and shout, in her most authoritarian manner, "Who are you men? How dare you break into Madame Rousseau's shop! We keep no money here! Whatever do you want?"

Familiar as she was with Miss Defoe, Tory caught the nervous shrill in the woman's voice—although she was convinced that the strange men facing the imperious Miss Defoe saw only a rock of propriety and decorum, arms folded over her breasts, an austere and formidable force of nature *not* to be lightly dismissed.

"We, uh, we came for the girl."

"The *girl?* Which girl? We employ many girls."

"Guess her name's Victoria Washington."

Miss Defoe's voice hardened. "Oh? What business do you have with her?"

"She's Mr. Bastiann Declouette's niece. The court has 'pointed him as her guardian. We've come t' fetch her."

Miss Defoe's demeanor stiffened further. "And that gives you the authority to break down our doors and terrify helpless women? For shame! Your actions are quite outside the scope of any court order. Why—"

The heavy boots of the men from the front of the store clomped down the hallway, curtailing her tirade. Unbeknownst to Tory, while Miss Defoe was haranguing the men, she had also been maneuvering herself into the kitchen—between the two invaders and the kitchen's back door, waving them, with her last words, toward the passageway.

As soon as she had placed herself between them and the door, Miss Defoe—without turning her head—shouted, "Go! Now!"

Tory bolted from her slot behind the door and flew out the open rear exit, the man's words clanging in her ears: *She's Mr. Bastiann Declouette's niece. The court has 'pointed him as her guardian. We've come t' fetch her.*

One man roared, "There she is!" Both men rushed to follow Tory. That was when Miss Defoe grabbed and slid a bench across their path. The shorter of the men tripped and fell; the other leapt over the bench; as he stumbled and regained his balance, Miss Defoe kicked the back of his leg, sending him to the floor.

These were but temporary impediments at best. Tory's pursuers were up and after her in seconds—but they were precious, vital seconds: Tory knew the plaza, and they did not. She had rounded the corner of a storefront before they set eyes on her. They gave pursuit, one going this way, the second another, but they had lost sight of her, and Tory was away toward home, running like the wind.

Miss Defoe pushed the bench back into its place and sat down hard, her breath coming in gasps, feeling her age in the pounding of her heart in her throat and chest.

Three men herded Madame Rousseau's workshop employees into the kitchen. Two more men, one a sheriff's deputy, followed on their heels. The deputy drove Daphne and Mademoiselle Justine before him and dragged Madame Rousseau into the kitchen by her arm.

The stately woman looked her question to Miss Defoe who lifted one brow a miniscule fraction—to Madame's relief.

Mademoiselle Justine sat down next to Miss Defoe, her back straight, her nose as far in the air as her short neck could manage. Mrs. Horringer put her arm around Miss Sarasses, who was sobbing and holding her wrist. The younger girls, Pauline, Suzanne, Simone, Rachael, Daphne, and Marie, huddled behind the table, as though the senior-most women could protect them from the intruders.

The leader of the invaders paced the kitchen, then stopped and surveyed Madame and her employees. At once, Miss Defoe knew him to be Tory's uncle: tall, wiry of build, a high brow line, and golden-brown eyes set wide with the defining slant so similar to Tory's. There the resemblance ended, for his expression was cold and angry. Heartless.

My girl could not be more different from you, Miss Defoe exulted. She met Bastiann Declouette's gaze with unflinching satisfaction.

He rocked slowly back on his heels, considering her. "Do you know who I am?" he asked softly.

Miss Defoe shrugged, that very Continental lift of one shoulder that denoted "no" and "I could not care less" with equal disdain.

She was unprepared for the clenched fist that struck her face a glancing blow. She slid to the floor, gasping in pain.

A general melee ensued: Mademoiselle Justine cried out and dropped beside Miss Defoe to help her, the huddled girls shrieked and screamed, and Madame Rousseau roared, "Stop this! Stop this at once, you bully! You have no right—"

But Bastiann Declouette's bellow quashed all protest. "SHUT UP! Shut up, you screeching peahens! Unless you wish to see your friend suffer more, you *will* be silent and you *will* cooperate with me."

He looked around to ensure he had the complete attention of the room. "My name is Bastiann Declouette; I am Victoria Washington's uncle, and I hold here a court order granting me legal custody of her. So, no more interference! Now, where is my niece?"

When no one answered, he studied the faces before him: fearful, belligerent, angry, or indignant. All but one. He moderated his expression and voice and, in a long, languid movement, withdrew his wallet from his breast pocket. From the wallet, he extracted the last of his cash and fanned the bills.

"Perhaps I am going about this all wrong? I would be happy to offer an . . . incentive in exchange for helpful information, such as, where Victoria lives?"

He lifted his eyes to that one face, the one whose expression was neither angry nor fearful but shrewd. "You, miss? Do you know where Victoria lives?" He licked his finger and thumb and slid one bill from the sheaf . . . and then another. He held them out toward her.

Marie reached for the two ten-dollar bills—as much money as she would earn in two months. "Victoria lives with *her*." She pointed at Miss Defoe, who remained stupefied, her nose bleeding, her cheek swelling.

When Marie tried to pluck the offered bills from Bastiann's hand, he did not release them.

"See, does it not feel good to do what is right? What is legal?"

"You said—"

"Oh, dear. I am quite sorry." He tipped a sly smile toward the men around him, letting them in on the joke. "But I think it a terrible waste of hard-earned cash to pay for that which I can persuade a gullible girl to give me."

One of his men chuckled. They all grinned.

"You are a liar!" Marie spat.

"And what are you, eh? That you would sell out a friend for money?"

Marie recoiled, slapped with a bitter truth.

Bastiann jerked his head at Miss Defoe. "Take her. Oh. And take that one, too." He pointed at Mademoiselle Justine. "Some leverage, should this one refuse to lead us to her home."

Miss Defoe did not fight the deputy as he dragged her out the back of Madame's shop. She only hoped Tory would do what was necessary when the time came—for Miss Defoe recognized Tory's uncle to be a man desperate enough to manipulate and misuse Tory for his purposes, no matter the outcome. And the wild light in Bastiann Declouette's eyes spoke of other harm that would likely come to Tory should she fall into his hands—harm no child should ever endure, as Patrice Defoe, from her own childhood, knew too intimately.

I cannot allow you to fall into this man's hands, and I shall not hesitate to surrender my life for you, darling girl, Miss Defoe vowed. *I will buy you the time you need, but you must be both wise and ruthless in its use.*

She led the men to her apartment over the grocer's. Keeping her head facing forward, Miss Defoe's eyes scanned back and forth, searching the opposite side of the street for any sign of Tory.

There. Miss Defoe caught the flash of Tory's eyes from behind a shrub on the corner. She gave the girl no sign, and turned to the steps leading up to her apartment.

Ten seconds were all that were needed for Bastiann's men to ascertain that Tory was not hiding in the small apartment. One man yanked the mattress from beneath Miss Defoe's bed then ripped the bed apart, scattering frame, mattress, and linens.

"Where else might she be?" Bastiann Declouette demanded, wrenching her arm.

Miss Defoe allowed her eyes to drift toward the door leading to the veranda. Declouette immediately dragged her to the door, threw it open, and stepped out above the street.

This was the moment Miss Defoe had hoped for. She threw back her head and shouted with all her strength, "RUN, VICTORIA! Do NOT come back! Run! Do NOT—"

Bastiann's hand slapped the words from Miss Defoe's mouth even as he glimpsed the flash of a girl's figure speed from the shrubs at the corner. Shouting for his men to give chase, he attempted to throw Miss Defoe aside—only to find her gripping him with hands made strong by her fervent, tenacious love for Tory.

Bastiann drove his fisted hand into Miss Defoe's stomach. Her fingers released without her permission, and she fell limp at his feet.

"Take this woman into custody, deputy," Bastiann shouted over his shoulder. He ran after his men to pursue Tory.

The deputy left Miss Defoe on the floor. It was many minutes before she regained her breath and was able to sit up. When she got to her feet, he grasped her arm and began forcing her down the stairs.

"Wh-where are you taking me?"

"T' the jail."

"Wh-what have . . . what have I done?" Every breath was an effort, a sharp, pain-filled gasp.

"Interfered in a legal proceeding," the deputy replied. "Harbored a fugitive."

"Victoria . . . no fugitive! One must . . . commit . . . crime . . . to be . . . fugitive."

"Not for me t' decide," the deputy answered. "Tell it t' th' judge."

Tory shivered when she saw Bastiann Declouette drag Miss Defoe onto her veranda. His menacing presence clawed at Tory even from across the street. It was all she could do to remain still, waiting in obedience to Miss Defoe's commands.

Guess her name's Victoria Washington. She's Mr. Bastiann Declouette's niece. The court has 'pointed him as her guardian. We've come t' fetch her.

We've come t' fetch her.

We've come t' fetch her.

At Miss Defoe's shouted warning, Tory bolted from her hiding place across from the apartment and ran as though pursued by the hounds of hell. As she flew, Miss Defoe's shouted warning lent speed to her feet: *RUN, VICTORIA! Do NOT come back! Run! Do NOT—*

Do NOT come back?

Not ever?

Her skirts clutched in her hands, Tory raced through the streets; she fled as fast as her legs could carry her. The lessons she had learned on the streets of New Orleans, fifteen months gone by, steered her between buildings, over fences, through tight cracks, and down alleys. At first, the commotion behind her—Bastiann's men giving chase—spurred her on. But soon she heard only her own breath rasping in and out of her throat and her heart thundering against her ribs.

When Tory collapsed against the back of a building, unable to go any farther without rest, she was disoriented. She had lost her bearings during her headlong escape from Bastiann and his men. Her only confidence at that moment was that she had also lost her hunters—for the time being.

Tory crept out near the front of the building and studied the street. Foot traffic seemed normal. She spotted no men who appeared to be searching.

All Tory wanted was to find her way back to Miss Defoe's apartment and her welcome embrace. *Should I go home? Why would Miss Defoe say, 'do not come back'? Does she mean for me to leave her? To leave Madame Rousseau's employ? Forever? But where would I go?*

Against her better judgment and Miss Defoe's shouted command, Tory decided to return to her familiar neighborhood, only . . . she stared about her, uncertain which way to start. She knew not whether Miss Defoe's apartment lay in the direction of the sunrise or sunset—or, at that moment, which way either of those might be: The sun was high overhead, and she could not distinguish which way it was moving. She had no address for the apartment—although, from Madame Rousseau's establishment, she knew the way.

If I can find Madame's shop, I shall be all right.

She asked people on the street for directions to Madame's shop and followed their either vague or detailed directions as best she could, but she never came upon her goal. She walked for hours without seeing a familiar landmark or street sign.

Have I been going in circles? she wondered.

Twilight was falling. She walked on. Shops were closing for the night, and fewer pedestrians were willing to stop and answer her questions.

A smattering of electric street lights winked on, but the carbon arc lamps were poorly maintained. The short-lived electrodes of a number of lamps had burned out. This neighborhood, it seemed, did not warrant the city's regular attention.

Tory began to panic.

Must I spend the night in a gutter, under a stoop, or curled on a moldy porch? Are Miss Defoe and Madame Rousseau not looking for me? Did Bastiann Declouette speak the truth when he said the court had appointed him my guardian? Can he take me from my friends? From my home with Miss Defoe?

A light rain began to fall. The mist soon became heavy rain and then an uncommon summer sleet. Tory raced down an alley to escape the stinging downpour. She climbed upon a rear porch and huddled, standing up, in its corner to escape the worst of the slushy rain. However, her black worsted dress was already soaked through, and its sodden folds clung to her body. She had lost one of Adeline's tortoiseshell combs as she ran, so the left side of her hair hung down, dripping rain into her collar.

An hour later, the weather shifted; a balmy draft wafted over Tory and she shivered in her drenched dress. *If I spend the night soaking wet, I will sicken. I must walk and let the breeze dry me*, Tory decided.

One street over, she saw lighted storefronts and moved that way, thinking the well-lit area might be safer than the dark. As she walked, she reasoned over her situation and, as painful as her conclusions were, she admitted how true they had to be: *Bastiann Declouette knows where I work and where I live. If he has the court's approval to take me, it will never be safe for me to return to Madame's or to Miss Defoe's. My presence would even place them in jeopardy.*

Tory sucked in a startled, painful breath. *That is what Miss Defoe meant. That is what she meant when she shouted, "Run, Victoria! Do not come back!"* In the same moment, Tory realized that she had, for the second time in her life, lost her home and everyone she loved.

With a sorrowing heart, she drew near her destination. The shouts and raucous singing told her that the lighted storefronts were bars and gambling houses—precisely the type of area Tory knew she should avoid.

She wept as she stumbled away from the brightly lit street, back into the night. *I cannot even return to Miss Defoe's apartment and retrieve Maman's dresser set or her jewelry.* Horrified, Tory recalled her mother's photograph safely held between the stiff, folded brocade that had lined her mother's jewelry box. *No! Maman! I cannot leave the only image I have of you—*

Tory yanked at the chain around her neck. She drew the locket into her hand and pressed the catch on its side. Even in the near-dark, Adeline's luminous eyes stared out at Tory, comforting her.

"Oh, *Maman*," she whispered. "Please tell me what I should do."

But no answer came. Tory was alone and terrified, battered by an urgent question repeating in her thoughts: *Where in this city can I go that Bastiann will not, eventually, find me?*

The answer seemed evident, but it was unthinkable, untenable. "I cannot stay in New Orleans? I must leave? But . . . I do not know where else to go!"

Tory heard soft, quick footfalls behind her. She whirled—almost too late—to see four young men sprinting toward her. She knew what they were; she knew the kind: gangs of homeless street boys who laid in wait to attack and rob the drunken patrons of the saloons and gaming halls. Gangs who preyed upon any woman they found alone.

When they saw she had spotted them, they gave up their attempt to take her unaware. One yelled, "Boyd—git ahead o' her, on her left!"

Another hooted, "Oooo, baby! Cain't wait t' have a taste o' you!"

Tory lifted her damp skirts and flew forward, dodging between two buildings to avoid the smallest boy's attempt to cut her off. She came to an alley and shot left, speeding down the alley's length, mere yards ahead of the gang—only to come up against a high fence stretching across the alley's width. The fence was dense with honeysuckle, forming a barrier she could not avoid or climb over. Trash cans overflowing with refuse barred her way, too.

Panic, fierce and hot, fueled Tory with adrenaline and desperation. Instead of waiting for the gang to converge on her, she grabbed up a metal trash can lid and, screaming with rage, she ran toward the gang. She swung the lid at the boy who arrived first and was satisfied when the metal edge connected with his head and upraised arms, knocking him aside.

His fall made the smallest of gaps, but Tory dashed through it, pushing by an older boy, throwing up the lid between her and his grasping arms. She ran faster than she'd believed she could, but the boys were again a pursuing pack, not far behind.

Up ahead, Tory saw the figure of a man smoking in the alley shadows. Even from a distance, Tory could see the outline of a fedora and overcoat, the glow of his cigarette. Was he a patron of a nearby drinking or gaming house?

Tory, gasping for breath, shouted, "Help me! Please, help me!" and altered her course toward him.

The tip of the man's cigarette glowed brighter, then he said, just loud enough for her to hear, "Get behind me."

Gasping, Tory flung herself behind the man, wondering how he expected to fare against four streetwise thugs. She considered bolting as soon as the gang pounced on the gentleman. Her "protector," however, seemed unconcerned as the gang slowed to a stop to take his measure.

"Hey, old man!" the eldest shouted. "You don' wanna mess wit' us. Give up th' girl, we let you go your way, okay?"

Her would-be benefactor, however, drew down on his cigarette—a long, slow last drag—before flipping the butt away. Tory didn't notice his fingers snake into his coat pocket, but she did see the gleam of metal in his hand when he pulled it out. He trained the revolver on the gang members. "Actually, young punks, you don't want to mess with *me*. Mosey along and find yourself a drunken patsy, like usual, *capisce?*"

The four boys, ranging in age from fourteen to sixteen by Tory's reckoning, backed away, but the eldest couldn't resist flinging a taunt, "You won't always have a gun at th' ready, old man. Me an' m' boys catch you by surprise, we cut you good."

Dirt spat inches from the boy, showering his leg. All bravado gone, he turned tail and ran; the others followed. Fedora Man chuckled and pocketed the revolver. "Okay, kid, I've done my good deed for the day. Now scoot. I have a train to catch."

Tory hadn't seen the suitcase up against the brick wall until Fedora Man picked it up and tipped his hat to her.

"A train? A-are you walking to the station, then?"

"Yup. At a fast trot, too. I, uh, have my own pressing circumstances." With that, he headed up the alley at a rapid clip in the direction Tory had been running when she called out to him.

She caught up to him. "Could I . . . would you mind if I walked with you? Just in case they come back?" Tory had to quick-march to stay abreast of Fedora Man's long strides.

He shrugged. "Makes no never mind to me, s'long as you don't slow me down."

Tory focused on keeping up with him, but she kept glancing behind them and scanning side streets and shadowed alcoves, vigilant in case the street boys were following behind or were ahead, lying in wait. What she did not see was Fedora Man's own shifting eyes and grim-set mouth or that he kept their path to the shadows as often as his route allowed him to.

Truth be told, Fedora Man's hat was pulled low and his face was hidden by the night and the shadow of the hat's brim. If, in that moment, Tory had been asked to describe him, she would have been hard-pressed to do so. She knew the man was tall, well-built, and dressed as a gentle-man, but she had not been able to clearly glimpse his features in the few minutes they had been together.

As they neared a street corner, he, for the first time in their brisk walk, slowed. Then he whispered out of the side of his mouth, "How good are you at playing along?"

"What?"

"I need a favor—and you owe me, yeah?"

"I-I guess I do."

"Then just be calm and, if the situation warrants, smile, got it?" He startled Tory when he looped his free arm in hers. "Act like we're together."

Tory latched on to his arm, but her head began to swivel.

"Stop that. Look up at me."

Tory did. Fedora Man's eyes were shaded by the hat brim, but his mouth was tight with worry.

"You're my, uh, my daughter, got it? What's your name, by the way?"

Tory swallowed. "V-victoria."

"Victoria. Meet your dad, Charles Luchetti. That makes you Victoria Luchetti. We're originally from New York, but we're headed to St. Louis tonight. *Capisce?*"

It was too much for Tory to take in. "*Non capisco, signore.*"

"What? You speak Italian? Incredible. Well, it doesn't matter whether you understand my game or not; just follow my lead, got it?"

His eyes flicked forward and Tory saw three figures waiting in the middle of the street, billy clubs in their hands. Then her rescuer leaned toward her a second time, his manner familiar and comfortable. "Just relax and play along."

Arm in arm, they kept walking. Fedora Man—Charles Luchetti— lifted his hat to the men as they approached them. "Good evening, gentlemen."

He kept walking, pulling Tory with him.

A voice behind them barked, "Hey. Hey, you. Hold up."

Charles turned and, with mild, unconcerned curiosity, asked, "Yes? May I be of assistance?" His diction had altered; it had shifted from a mixture of common and cavalier to genteel and mannered in an instant.

The man who had called to them answered, "Yeah, you can. We're lookin' for somebody." He glanced from Charles to Tory and then fixed on Tory.

Tory started to tremble, but the pressure of Charles' hand clasping her arm was reassuring. Stabilizing.

"Who's the girl?"

"The *girl*," Charles inserted a testy edge to his formal reply, "is my daughter. Please show some respect."

The man snorted. "The darky's your daughter? Yeah, right."

The edge in Charles' voice sharpened. "I am not reluctant to admit that my wife was negro, nor do I take kindly to comments that besmirch our marriage or our child."

The man's thick brows came together as though Charles' fine words were over his head. "Yeah? Well, we don't cotton t' mixed marriages 'round here."

"Then I am happy to report that we were not married 'round here' as you put it. In any event, my wife passed away last year—not that it is your concern. Now, if you please, do not delay us further; we have a train to catch."

One of the man's companions shuffled his feet. "Let it go, Bob. We got a job t' do."

"Yeah. All right." Bob lifted his chin to Charles. "You have a good night."

"You also." Charles' nodded.

He and Tory continued on their walk toward the train depot. They had gone a block when he blew out a breath. "That went well. Thanks for your help."

"Were those men looking for you, then?"

"Most assuredly."

"Why?"

"What's it to you?"

Stung, Tory went silent and they walked on.

They were within sight of the depot, twenty minutes later, when Tory ventured another question. "Are you really going to St. Louis, Mr. Luchetti?"

"Yes; I am relocating to 'the Paris of the West.'"

"Will you . . . will you take me with you?"

Charles stopped, let go her arm, and faced her. For the first time, Tory saw him clearly: dark eyes and brows, a strong jawline, and thin lips. She thought him to be in his early forties—not young but not old, either.

"Well, that brings us to your situation, doesn't it, kiddo? What's an educated, well-mannered—although somewhat bedraggled—young woman such as yourself doing on the wrong side of town at night?"

Tory's jaw jutted forward. "I got caught in the rain."

"No kidding. But that doesn't answer my question or tell me why you want to go to St. Louis."

Tory lifted her nose and stared without blinking, a perfect copy of Miss Defoe. "I want to go to St. Louis because it is not New Orleans."

"So those street thugs aren't the only ones you're running from?"

Tory licked her lips, unsure of how to answer him.

"Ah. Your tell gives you away. Who's chasing you and why?"

Irritated by his brazen manner, Tory threw his own words back at him. "What's it to you?"

He tossed back his head and started to laugh. "My, you are a feisty one, aren't you? And you can run like the wind, I'll give you that—but you're far too young to come along with me. It wouldn't look right. You're what? Fifteen?"

"Sixteen," Tory retorted.

Charles stopped laughing. "You, my dear, are not a day over fifteen." His piercing eyes impaled her. "I'll let you in on a little secret, Victoria: I always know when I'm being lied to. Always. Now, when is your birthday?"

Tory hung her head. "Next month."

"So, you'll be *fifteen* next month."

Tory would be thirteen in September, but she simply nodded her agreement. Charles had convinced himself of her age, and Tory was not going to dispute his conclusion.

"Well, I don't think it a clever idea for a girl of fifteen to travel with me."

Confounded, Tory sucked in her upper lip and chewed on it. "But . . . you see, I need . . . I *need* to get away from this city. I am . . . not safe here."

"Are you in trouble with the law?"

"Certainly not!"

He nodded. "You're telling the truth about that. Okay, let's walk—that train's not going to wait for me and, as I said, I have a pressing need to be on it when it steams out of town." He took her arm again and hurried them on.

"Does that mean you'll take me with you?"

He laughed again, a low rumble in his chest. "How good are you with your hands?"

"What do you mean? I can sew. Even intricate beadwork."

"Sew? What the devil do I need with a seamstress! No, I mean can you handle cards?"

"Cards?"

"Playing cards. Can you shuffle? Deal?"

"I-I am sorry. I do not know what those things are."

He laughed again, louder. "What a babe in the woods. Listen, kiddo, I'm more than flush at the moment, and I'm feeling generous, so I'll buy you a ticket to St. Louis—and who knows? You may again provide cover for me along the way. But I can't promise more than that."

"You will buy me a ticket? Thank you, Mr. Luchetti."

"Call me Charles. A ticket—but that's it. When we disembark, Tory, you're on your own."

"You called me Tory." She was astounded—only Sassy had ever called her that.

"Did I? Sorry. Victoria is a mouthful and puts me in mind of 'her majesty,' that stuffy former monarch from across the pond."

"Tory is fine . . . I was just surprised."

They were approaching the station now, and Tory could see the tangle of tracks and trains within the rail yard. The idling, coal-burning monstrosities were the loudest things Tory had ever heard. They belched soot and steam that mixed in the moist air and rained down upon the train yard and passengers.

It was terrifying.

"What's wrong?"

"I-I have never seen a train."

"You kidding me?"

"N-no."

He chuckled. "By golly, Tory, you're a tonic. Haven't laughed this much in months. Come on; I need to buy our tickets."

A few minutes later, they were seated on the train, Tory next to the window, her eyes wide, taking in everything—the rushing porters and baggage carts, the passengers bidding friends and family goodbye, the sheer numbers of people rushing in all directions, each with their own agenda and destination.

A conductor stopped in the aisle at their seats. Charles handed over their tickets, but the man frowned in Tory's direction.

Forestalling him, Charles inclined his head toward Tory and said, "My daughter."

"Uh, yes sir; a very unusual situation, I'm sure, sir. However, the cars for colored are farther back—"

"You'll make an exception this time, won't you?"

Tory saw a bill appear like magic between Charles' fingertips.

The conductor saw it too. He hesitated, then looked away. At the same time, he palmed the proffered bill.

"Have a good trip, sir."

Five minutes later, the conductor, standing on the platform but holding onto the railing of their car, shouted a last time, "Alllll abooooooard!" The train lurched, then began to ease slowly out of the station; the conductor jumped onto the bottom step and climbed up to the platform between their car and the next.

The train was barely making headway through the station, when another man grabbed the railing and pulled himself onto the steps. Tory sensed Charles stiffen.

"All right, Tory," he whispered, "time to sing for your supper."

Tory *had* missed two meals and could feel the emptiness clear down to her toes. "I cannot boast to a cultured singing voice; I do not think you will care for it. But, will you really buy me supper if I sing?"

Charles sputtered and ran a hand across his mouth. "Kid, you amaze me. No, what I mean is, play along again, right? You're my daughter; I'm your dad."

Tory saw the man at the head of their car and understood. "Oh."

Charles picked up her hand and held it. "Don't look at *him*; look at me and pretend you're listening."

Tory tilted her chin toward Charles and forced herself to ignore the man walking down the car's aisle. Charles said something, and she nodded, as though agreeing.

Charles was talking when the man loomed over them. As though interrupted, Charles looked up. "Yes?"

The man took in the scene, tipped his hat, and continued on. As soon as he left the car, passing to the next, Charles moved into the aisle and stood to the side of their car's door, observing through its window. After a few minutes, the train began to pick up speed and Charles returned, grinning.

"Is he gone?"

"Yep. Jumped off before we cleared the railyards."

Tory was relieved. And hungrier. "Oh, good. Say, were you going buy us something to eat?"

The train was going faster now, rocking side to side.

"Not shy, are you? Well, I, too, as the Brits say, am a mite peckish. The refreshment car is that way." He pointed ahead of them. "I'll go; you best stay put and keep your head down. If our luck holds, they should have sandwiches."

PART 2:
ST. LOUIS,
MISSOURI

CHAPTER 16

AUGUST 1903

As the train steamed into the night, most passengers settled down to sleep. Tory began to nod off, but her benefactor seemed restless. He placed his suitcase on his lap, drew a small packet from his breast pocket and, with long familiarity, emptied the packet's contents into his other hand, closing and returning the empty box to his pocket.

Tory watched, first curious—then fascinated—as Charles shuffled the playing cards, making the deck arc, each card following the others in perfect rhythm, from left hand to right hand and back again. Charles, aware that she was watching, dealt out five cards to three imaginary players and himself.

"Turn those cards over," he said, pointing to one pile.

Tory did. She was unfamiliar with the strange faces on the cards, but many of the cards had numbers, either black or red.

"To win at poker, you must have the highest hand—or convince the other players that you have the highest hand. A specified hierarchy determines the winning hand: royal flush, straight flush, four of a kind, full house, flush, straight, three of a kind, two pair, one pair, and high card. Takes some time and attention to learn all the combinations and their rankings."

Tory nodded. For a while, Charles demonstrated different poker hands and variations on the game. Tory heard, "five-card draw," "five-card stud," "seven-card stud," and other names that indicated which rules would be used.

Charles' explanations droned on. Without realizing it, Tory's eyelids grew heavy and drooped closed. When her head tipped over to rest on Charles' shoulder, he stopped talking, but he gathered the deck and, for another hour, practiced shuffling and dealing.

~*~

The following morning, Tory awoke to the heady scent of hot coffee. She sat up and saw that Charles was holding two cups. He offered her one.

"No, thank you. I do not drink coffee."

He grinned, still holding the cup toward her. "Tea, then?"

"Tea? How did you know?"

"That is my avocation, Tory. I learn people—learn their tendencies, their penchants, their tells."

"What is a 'tell,' please?"

"It is what gives a man's intentions away, a clue to what he is thinking or planning. Could be a twitch, a sniff, the touch of a finger to an ear—mostly unconscious behaviors, like when we met and you licked your lips while you were deciding how to answer my questions. I notice these things."

"How does 'learning people' help you?"

"Well, if I can ascertain ahead of time whether a young lady drinks coffee or tea, then I will buy the right beverage."

Tory frowned. "I do not understand."

"Never mind. Oh, and I bought us some biscuits, too." He handed her the beverage, then pulled a brown paper parcel of shortbread biscuits from his suit pocket and offered them to her.

Tory's smile stretched across her face. "Thank you!"

"When we arrive in St. Louis, it will be late afternoon, close to twilight." He looked her over. "You'd better see if you can do something with that hair."

Automatically, Tory's hand went to her hair. She had forgotten that she'd lost one of her mother's combs. Her fingers detected her hair's disheveled condition, and she grimaced. She pulled out the remaining comb and began finger-combing her wiry hair, pulling it back into as tidy a bun as she could manage without a mirror, pinning it in place with the remaining comb.

As Charles had predicted, the day was nearly spent when they arrived in St. Louis. Charles helped Tory down the steps onto the platform and led her into the station—into a chaotic clash of diverging crowds and shouted departure announcements.

In the center of the station, Charles faced her. "This is where we part, young chick," he murmured.

"I-I . . . yes. Th-thank you for your many kindnesses," Tory stammered. She stared about her, frozen, blinking back tears.

I am so far from home! I do not know what to do or where to go!

Charles watched her, his expression indecipherable. As he picked up his suitcase and turned away, Tory panicked. When he had gone a few steps, she ran to catch up with him. She kept her distance and said nothing for fear he would wheel about and demand that she cease following him.

She trailed him through the bustling station, taking care that she did not lose sight of him in the pressing throng. He wound his way to an exit and stopped outside on the sidewalk to ask directions from a man waiting for a cab.

Then Charles stood on the curb, looking up the street and, for one terrifying moment, Tory thought he was going to hail his own cab—leaving her behind. Instead, he set off on foot, and Tory followed him.

Several blocks later, he squinted up at a lighted sign: Hotel Carlson. He pushed through the swinging door. Tory dithered on the sidewalk, then pushed through after him.

She spied him across the lobby at a counter, speaking to someone. As nonchalantly as she could manage, she wandered along the edge of the lobby, working her way behind him, where she could hear the exchange between Charles and the clerk from a distance of several feet.

"How many nights, sir?" the clerk asked.

"Two, to begin with. I'm new to the city and will be looking for a house."

"A single room, then?"

"Yes; however, I'll need two beds."

"A second bed?" the clerk glanced around. "For another gentleman? A business associate?"

"No, for my daughter."

Charles pivoted on his heel and fixed Tory with a look of . . . amused resignation? Tory—startled that he had known she was following him all along and had given no sign of it—breathed a sigh of relief and joined him at the counter. She tried not to smile, but she could not stop the grin tugging at her mouth.

The clerk looked Tory over, one lip curling. "Sir, this person . . . is your daughter?"

Charles glared at the man, and Tory saw his jaw clench. The clerk noticed it too. He flushed and ran his tongue over his bottom lip.

Why, that man has a tell.

Tory shifted her glance to Charles. He must have read her mind, for his head turned a fraction and the eye facing away from the clerk winked. Tory squirmed. She wanted to giggle in the worst way. Instead, she smoothed her expression into bland lines, taking her cue from Charles, whose countenance did not waver.

"Your key, sir," the clerk murmured.

"Thank you."

When the door to their room closed behind them, Charles dropped his suitcase on his bed and pointed a finger at her. "Sit."

Wary, Tory sat on the edge of the other bed, her eyes jumping around the room. She was unsure of Charles now that they were alone.

"If you are going to stick with me, you have to earn your keep, got it?"

"Yes, sir. I . . . I can cook and clean and mend, Mr. Luchetti."

He snorted. "Good to know. And I already told you not to call me Mr. Luchetti. It's Charles. *Capisce?*"

"Yes, sir."

He put one foot on the bed frame, pulled out a cigarette, and lit it. As the acrid smell of the sulfur match and burning paper hit Tory's nose, she cleared her throat and told herself not to cough.

Charles blew smoke Tory's way. "I will be renting a house as soon as I find one suitable to my purposes. If you are to figure into my strategy, you will need to learn some things and . . ." he looked her over, "you will need some clothes. If you work hard and prove you're worth it, I will buy the clothes you need."

He took another drag. "But let me warn you: If you slack off or have no aptitude for what I teach, I will kick you to the curb. I aim to invest time and money in you, Tory. If you prove to be a bad investment, I will cut you loose. Do I make myself clear?"

"Yes, sir."

"Charles. Call me Charles."

"Yes . . . Charles."

He scratched his jaw, thinking. "We will begin in the morning, so get yourself to bed. Oh. And from now on, you're my *foster* daughter. Daughter of an old friend who passed away, leaving you an orphan."

Seeing the confusion on her face, he added, "Part of the game, Tory, is to never draw too much attention to yourself. Every time I say you're my daughter, it gins up more questions—and we don't want more questions."

Tory's head was spinning. She had no idea what he wanted from her, but at least she had a place to sleep for the night.

"Yes, Charles."

~*~

Their first day in St. Louis was a maelstrom of activity. At breakfast in the hotel dining room, Charles announced, "I cannot take you around in that getup, Tory. Your dress is too plain and, understandably, soiled. We must get you some real clothes today."

Tory swallowed. "I am sorry, Charles."

He shrugged. "The cost of doing business, my dear." However, as they were finishing their meal and Charles was smoking, Tory felt his eyes appraising her.

"What is it?"

"Your hair. Surely something better can be done with it?"

"I must have a jar of pomade . . . to make it behave."

He nodded. "Tell me where to find it."

"I-I am not certain. A barber may be able to tell you."

He tapped out his cigarette in the ashtray. "While I am out, bathe and wash your hair."

Tory did as she had been told; she bathed and washed her hair, sponged the stains from her soiled black worsted, and was dressed in it when Charles returned. He carried the required dressing for her hair, a different brand than Tory was accustomed to, but a welcome sight.

"Deucedly difficult stuff to find. Your suggestion of a barber did help—he pointed me to a pharmacy store. The woman who waited on me there suggested I also buy a large comb. And I picked up some hairpins. All women need hairpins."

He watched as Tory rubbed the oily pomade into her hair, worked it through, and combed out her hair. As usual, she braided the two sides, twined the two braids into a chignon at the base of her neck, and pinned it there.

"Nice," he said, "but too old for you. Too severe. Pull a few tiny strands loose to curl about your neck."

Tory used the comb to tug loose a few wisps.

"Better."

Charles then walked Tory to a ready-to-wear clothing store and, to Tory's indignation, gave her into the hands of a "capable" clerk. "My foster daughter is nearly fifteen and requires a walking ensemble suitable to a young lady of her age and station. I shall expect to see her dressed appropriately when I finish my errands."

"Of course, sir."

When he returned, Tory was fidgeting under the constraints of her first corset. The stiff stays squeezed her breathless and pushed her budding breasts up, producing a conspicuous profile. Tory also wore new bloomers, camisole, stockings, petticoat, and hoop underskirt, over which was buttoned a stylish (although, in Tory's estimation, mediocre) deep-blue walking dress edged with black velvet piping.

Tory had argued with the clerk over the size of the hoop underskirt, insisting that wider hoops had passed out of style, quoting from one of Madame Rousseau's Parisian fashion magazines to make her point.

The clerk, had, at Tory's insistence, fitted her with narrower hoops. "I tell you, miss, the skirt was made for wider hoops; without them, the hem will drag the ground."

"Perhaps not. My height should make up the difference."

Tory had been right. With a sniff, the clerk had pronounced the length "perfect."

"Turn, please," Charles commanded. "And stand up straight. You are going to be a tall woman—do not be shy about it."

As Tory rotated, the swish of her skirt hinted at elegant black walking boots with tall tops and dozens of hooks and buttons. To complete the ensemble, Tory sported baby-blue gloves buttoned at the wrist and a hat that added to her height and the illusion that she was a young woman in her teens. Shopping bags containing additional undergarments, a nightgown, a robe, and her soiled black dress waited nearby.

Charles nodded his approval. "Yes, this will do until we have you in to see a proper dressmaker."

During the hour Tory was being clothed, Charles had not wandered idly but had sought out a reputable tailor and a dressmaker. Now it was Tory who waited through Charles' appointment as the tailor took Charles' measurements and the two men discussed bolt after bolt of suit fabric. When the appointment ended, Charles had ordered two daytime suits and vests, a sleek gray day coat with a complementary charcoal fedora, and two complete suits of evening clothes.

Charles took Tory's arm in his and steered her down two blocks into the dressmaker's shop where Charles informed the owner that he wanted a morning dress, two additional walking dresses, and three evening gowns for Tory. This appointment went better than Tory's visit to the ready-wear shop as Tory—to the dressmaker's initial astonishment and then delight—was able to speak with confidence on current styles and showed herself competent in the selection of fabrics and patterns.

Tory was exhausted when they left the shop, but Charles was not. They next visited a stationer's where Charles perused card stock and typefaces, while Tory, her new boots pinching her feet, stood by until he had ordered a set of cards with his name on them.

Finally, they stopped for lunch at a local bistro, and the food and calm atmosphere revived Tory's flagging energy.

Tory could not help but gape at the money Charles was spending. Compared to Miss Defoe, Charles was a wastrel. Tory, however, made no remark on it: Charles knew what he wanted and his word was law. She went along with his demands although, in the back of her mind, she knew that payment on his "investment" would come due soon enough.

That afternoon, Charles hired a cab that drove them to a St. Louis real estate leasing office. As they neared their destination, Charles, perhaps discerning Tory's thoughts, murmured, "It is important that we present ourselves well when we look at homes, Tory. If you are to be my foster daughter, then you must dress and act the role."

"I understand, Charles."

The leasing agent took them to see three houses. Charles selected the second of the three, a two-story townhome on Crescent Street in the heart of St. Louis. He asked Tory's opinion only after he had made his decision and they were returning to the hotel.

"It is a lovely house, Charles, although it may be much larger than what we need."

"It is exactly the right size, Tory. Once we have purchased furnishings, engaged a housekeeper, and are suitably established, we shall have many guests. And you shall be my hostess."

Tory blurted, "Your hostess! Why, I did not know you were acquainted with so many people in St. Louis, Charles."

His laugh was long and relaxed. "I am acquainted with *no* one in the city at present, Tory, but that will soon change. Inside of a month, we shall be hosting card games one or two—no more than two—evenings a week. These will be exclusive games, by invitation only."

He glanced over to her. "In preparation, we must begin your training. Initially, you will simply make our guests welcome. I will teach you to pour drinks, greet our guests, and see to their comfort. You have the face, manners, and gentility to put our guests at ease, Tory. I wish you to use your Southern charm and grasp of language to create a calm and pleasant experience for our callers."

"And what will you do, Charles?"

"Me? Oh, I shall engage our guests in friendly poker games and endeavor not to fleece them too close to the bone, or they shall go away indignant—and indignant losers generate problems."

"Fleece them?"

"Hmm? Oh, yes. I am, as they say, a card sharp. One of the best, if my many marks are to be given credence."

"Marks? What are they?"

Charles grinned and lit a cigarette. "A mark, Tory, is a patsy, someone easily manipulated, such as a novice poker player. However, I don't bother with the novices. I prefer the jaded and well-heeled. They have money, they play for high stakes, they lose often, and they come back for more. The wealthy care less about the loss if you have granted them the excitement they crave, if you have alleviated their boredom a little and made their pointless lives more palatable."

He sobered. "Mixed within the affluent, however, are those whose means have dried up but who keep up the appearance of wealth, carefully hiding their bankrupt state. These men are dangerous. When they play, they are desperate to win, and desperate men are unpredictable. For such as these, a good hand means they return home with a windfall— conversely, an evening of loss may spell an end to their reputation and social standing."

Tossing his finished cigarette out the window, Charles added, "If you beat such a man, if you embarrass him and deprive him of his standing before his friends, you may be sure he will seek to redress his injury upon you—even when his loss is the fault of his inferior abilities."

"Is . . . is that what happened the evening we met? Those men who were looking for you?"

Charles flushed and nodded. "I had a good setup in New Orleans. I was a regular at games throughout the city and had saved up a sizable nest egg. Sadly, one evening, I picked the wrong man to beat. He may have been flat broke when we finished, but he had connections and political clout—so I fled."

"And then?"

"Then the fellow convinced his 'connections' that I was carrying enough cash to make it worth their while to find me and relieve me of my 'burden.' I knew they were after me, so I rented a cheap room, thinking to lie low a few days then head for St. Louis. I was on my way to the station when I ducked into that alley for a cigarette and you ran up on me. As you well know, I did not shake my pursuers until we got on the train—and they overlooked me while I sat right under their noses."

Tory laughed with him. "I helped you get away, did I not?"

"Yes, you did. That is one reason I let you follow me when we arrived here. However, now, Tory, it is time for you to earn your keep. This evening, after we have dined, we shall commence your training."

His manner shifted again, flashing from jovial to intimidating. "Be aware, my dear, that I shall expect you to show yourself willing and diligent to excel under my tutelage."

"Y-yes, Charles. I shall, of course."

~*~

That night, as Charles had warned her, Tory embarked upon a novel phase in her education. It was after ten o'clock and Tory was exhausted when Charles allowed her to retire. "You have done well this evening, Tory," Charles remarked. "You have a quick mind and some natural talent. I shall endeavor to cultivate both."

"Thank you, Charles."

As she laid her head upon her pillow, cards danced before her eyes and her ears echoed with Charles' instruction:

"No, a full house beats three of a kind, Tory. A full house *has* three of a kind *plus* a pair."

"Never draw to an inside straight, Tory."

"Watch your opponent more than your own hand. He will tell you what he has—or does not have—if you know what to look for."

"Later I will teach you to bluff. Right now, concentrate on learning the game and your opponents' tells."

Tory's fingers twitched in her sleep, shuffling, cutting, dealing, tracking the cards as she dealt them, clumsily palming the bottom card of the deck and dealing it to herself at the right opportunity. She manipulated poker chips, learning from weight and height how many chips were in a stack, what denomination each color represented, how to count the chips and make change.

Her sleep that night was troubled; all her dreams were plagued with Charles' voice and the game he called poker.

CHAPTER 17

"**I** am pleasantly gratified by the maturity of your tastes, Tory." They were at breakfast. Tory's tea cup, halfway to her lips, paused, and Charles continued. "This morning, we shall shop for household fittings. We need not waste funds on new things. The furnishings in our parlor must be tasteful and in good condition, yes, but we will select what we need at auction or the local markets, and you shall assist me, *capisce?*"

"Yes, Charles."

He leaned back in his chair and blew smoke toward a wall. "And, I confess, you have made me curious. Tell me about yourself."

Taken off guard, Tory needed time to gather her thoughts. She sipped her tea, but all she could think was that Charles was cataloging her tells—her expressions, gestures, and delaying actions. Reading her mind.

"We all have our secrets, even you. I can respect that. Perhaps, though, you will answer three questions for me?"

Tory met his gaze over her cup. "I will try."

"All right. You seem to know a great deal about fashion. Did you work for a dressmaker?"

"Yes."

"Yes? That explains the quaint black dress I found you in—but you supply no details, no further insights?" He nodded. "Ah, I see. I shall take it then, that the man you fled New Orleans to escape knew where you worked."

Tory gave the smallest nod she could and looked away.

"Next question, then: Was your father a white man?"

Heat raced up Tory's neck and into her face, but she managed to grind out, "That is not your business, Charles."

He smiled. "Fair enough—and you answered me anyway."

He drew on his cigarette. "Last question—"

"You have already asked three questions."

"No, I asked if you worked in a dressmakers' shop and if your father was a white man. Two questions."

"But you also asked if . . . the man who is after me knew where I worked."

"No, I made a statement. My exact words were, 'I shall take it that the man you fled New Orleans to escape knew where you worked.' You chose to answer a question I did not ask."

Tory glared at him.

Charles chuckled. "Tory, you really are quite wonderful. So naïve and transparent! Yet, so engaging. But, dear girl, I must admonish you: Soon we shall be engaged in serious work. As much as I detest the need, you must lose this childlike innocence and begin to view the world with wiser eyes and act accordingly."

He stubbed out his cigarette. "Third question: What do you carry on the chain about your neck?"

Tory grabbed for her locket as though Charles had tried to rip it from her.

He raised his brows at her fluster. "Your response to my question illustrates my point, Tory. You must train yourself not to react to the unexpected; you must discipline yourself to remain placid and unflappable through any situation."

He leaned toward her, reached across the table, and took her chin in his hand, forcing her to look at him. His expression hardened. "Listen closely, *Victoria*. I care not what you hide on that chain—but I do care about your reaction. It demonstrates a lack of self-control, and self-control is vital to our work. *I must insist* that you improve in this area, Victoria."

Tory was caught in Charles' eyes, unable to look away, taken aback by the mercurial shift in his demeanor. His use of her full name only served to underscore how serious was his warning.

"I-I shall try, Charles."

"Not good enough. You *will* succeed, Victoria. I have no need of you otherwise. Do I make myself clear?"

"Y-yes, Charles."

"See to it then, that you guard yourself. Mentally prepare yourself for anything. *Anything*."

He released her chin, reached for her neckline, and yanked the chain from her neck, snapping it.

Tory—caught between her newborn fear of Charles and the horror of her loss, froze. She did not swallow or flinch; her eyes remained fixed on his.

When a long, charged moment had elapsed, he nodded. "Good, Tory. I am pleased. And I apologize for breaking your chain. I shall fix it myself before we go out."

He held the chain—and her locket—toward her. She slowly reached out her hand, palm up, to receive her treasure. She did not try to take it.

She waited until Charles placed the chain and locket in her hand and folded her fingers around them.

"Yes. Very good," he repeated.

~*~

For the next two weeks, their activity was ongoing and unrelenting. In daytime, they visited auction houses, open-air markets, and second-hand stores, bidding on furniture, art, lamps, carpets, dishes, and kitchen sundries, buying bedding, linens, and drapery. Charles entrusted most of the fitting out of his rented house to Tory's tastes, although he had specific requirements for his gaming tables and chairs.

"We must provide a quality environment for our guests, particularly chairs that allow for comfortable sitting for extended periods."

When the purchased furniture began arriving, they moved to the house and into the second phase of Charles' plans. Tory spent her time organizing and decorating the house; Charles bought a used motorcar and began visiting gaming houses, familiarizing himself with the more prestigious clubs, ingratiating himself into private card games with wealthy players.

He was gone most evenings; when he was home, he drilled Tory in dealing poker. While Charles was out playing cards, Tory spent her evenings altering drapes to fit the house's windows and practicing, hours on end, the card skills and tricks he taught her.

"I shall work you into dealing cards a little at a time," he told her. "We must also perfect our communication."

"Our communication?"

Charles, sitting across the round card table from Tory as she practiced dealing cards, sent subtle signals, some no greater than tapping one poker chip upon another or touching the signet ring on his pinky finger. Under his tutelage, Tory learned to recognize Charles' messages and respond to them, to read his signals as clearly as if he had spoken and to respond with the flick of a finger or the lift of a shoulder.

Three weeks after ordering her new clothes, Charles took Tory to her final fitting at the dressmaker's shop. He insisted on viewing her in each dress before paying for the ensemble.

The day prior had been her thirteenth birthday, but she had not mentioned it to Charles. It was when Tory tried on her first evening gown that she realized how much her body was changing. Had changed. Tory's bare neck, shoulders, and long arms curved gracefully out of a gown that accentuated her slender waist and lifted and emphasized her plump bosom.

Tory saw a woman staring back from her reflection in the mirror. When she observed the dressmaker and Charles' approval, she knew they saw the same thing.

"Your skin is absolutely flawless," the dressmaker gushed, "even if it is, ah, *duskier* than convention dictates. Perhaps a dusting of powder across your shoulders and décolletage?"

Charles nodded. "Yes. Her skin is beautiful—but I must say that commonplace chain she wears day and night quite diminishes the effect."

Tory heard the warning. Before they left the dressmaker's, she slipped off the chain and tucked it and her locket into her stocking. That evening, she stitched a tiny pocket inside her corset, a pocket with a flap secured by a loop and a flat button. She slipped her locket inside and buttoned the flap.

I cannot risk the loss of my locket, Tory thought. *I must hide it where it is not likely to be found and taken from me—even if it means I cannot often look at it.*

That day, Tory stopped thinking of herself as a girl. She became the woman Charles believed her to be, *needed* her to be: of necessity a mature young woman, a woman who had left her childhood behind.

Another two weeks passed. Charles went out most every evening after an early dinner to play cards and returned home late most nights having made money. At breakfast following a prosperous outing, he was jovial, generous, and gregarious.

But, occasionally, Charles lost money. The mornings subsequent to such a loss, Tory found him a different man: irritable, taciturn, unsociable, easily angered.

Tory did not like Charles when he descended into these dark "moods," and, just as she had learned his signals, she learned to perceive the signs of a black temperament and, in those instances, practiced vigilance to avoid the sharp side of his tongue.

She sighed to herself: Since Charles stayed out late most evenings, he would nap in the afternoon to ensure that he was refreshed for his evening foray. His schedule left Tory alone nearly every afternoon and evening, and she had little to keep herself occupied except cooking dinner and drilling herself with a deck of cards and a stack of poker chips. Even the basic housekeeping was relegated to a hired woman who arrived each morning to clean, shop, and prepare a late breakfast.

"When do you anticipate hosting our first party, Charles?"

"Soon. I have my marks in mind, but I must ingratiate myself further into their confidences."

"May I . . . may I have a little money?"

Tory had never asked for anything, and she had no idea how Charles would respond.

"Why? What do you need?"

"I would like to buy a few pencils and a pad of sketching paper."

"You draw?"

She shrugged "I dabble a little."

"I see." He drew his wallet and handed her a five-dollar bill. "Consider this an allowance. Remind me to renew it in a month."

Tory had only once held five dollars in her hands—when she had been so desperate to eat that she had sold her mother's earrings to buy food. She would gladly have gone without the drawing supplies to buy back her mother's pearls. But it was not possible.

"Thank you," she whispered.

He changed the subject. "I have said that you have an aptitude for cards, Tory. I now want you to try your hand at another skill." He withdrew a small, flat case from his other inside breast pocket and unsnapped it. Within the case lay a set of miniature tools—some flat, thin, and of varying lengths, others narrow and cylindrical. A few instruments were bent at their ends in right angles.

Charles beckoned Tory to the pantry door. He opened the door, slipped the skeleton key into the lock, and turned it back and forth, pointing to the locking mechanism, moving out, then in. "This door has a simple lock. The key turns the mechanism that engages the lock. See it work?"

Tory nodded, fascinated.

Charles turned the lock again, but left the door open. "Watch me. I'm going to unlock this door from the inside." He withdrew one of the tools from his kit, poked it into the keyhole, and moved it around. He glanced up. "My pick is touching the mechanism. My task is to move it over, just as the key would."

A moment later, the lock clicked open.

"You may have your art supplies, Tory, but I wish you to spend some of your free time learning how to unlock this door from the inside. I will leave this pick with you."

Tory knew better than to say, "I will try." Instead she answered, "Yes, Charles."

That afternoon while Charles napped, Tory walked to a stationer's where she purchased pencils, sharpener, eraser, and paper. Taking up her packaged supplies, she started home, eager for the evening and Charles' departure, anticipating the few hours of enjoyment her sketching would afford her.

As she wended toward the house on Crescent Street, Tory's thoughts turned to fashion and, inevitably, to Madame's establishment. More than five weeks had elapsed since Charles had purchased a train ticket for her to take her away from the danger in that city. How she longed for Madame Rousseau's busy shop and workroom! She missed helping Mademoiselle Justine wait on customers. More than anything, Tory pined for Miss Defoe. Remembering their last—their only—embrace, Tory's heart grew heavy.

Miss Defoe loved me, and I would have had a happy home with her for many years, had Bastiann Declouette not found me out.

"Excuse me, miss. May I tell you about Jesus?"

Shaken from her despondent self-reflection, Tory's chin jerked up. A young woman with a pale face, plainly dressed but smiling, extended her hand toward Tory. She held out a pamphlet. Automatically, Tory took the pamphlet.

The girl repeated herself, "May I tell you about Jesus? He loves you very much."

Tory frowned and, for reasons inexplicable to herself, she grew angry. "No. And keep away from me."

The girl nodded. "I apologize for disturbing you."

Tory huffed and marched on, but she was disquieted. Disturbed. The mention of Jesus transported her back to that last, awful week at Sugar Tree—Bastiann's threats, Adeline's sudden fever and death, the horror of her burial, and Tory's flight from Sugar Tree. Sassy Brown's weary old face rose in Tory's memory; her parting words rang in Tory's ears.

Shou . . . shoulda tole ye 'bout Je . . . sus . . . though your mère say no. Shoulda tole ye . . . anyways. I . . . will pray . . .

"Jesus? Who is this Jesus?" Overcome, Tory walked faster, attempting to outrun the pain in her heart. She clutched the package of pencils and paper to her breasts. When she arrived home, she climbed the stairs to her room and dropped the load on her bed. Along with the paper-wrapped drawing supplies, a crumpled pamphlet fluttered onto her bed's counterpane.

Tory picked up the paper and scanned through it. Most of what she read made no sense to her.

Is your heart burdened with the cares of this life? Do you long for peace with God? Jesus said, 'Come unto me, all ye that labour and are heavy laden, and I will give you rest. Take my yoke upon you, and learn of me; for I am meek and lowly in heart: and ye shall find rest unto your souls.'

"But who *is* Jesus?" she asked. "I thought he died a long time ago. How could he give me anything today?"

Tory read through the rest of the pamphlet, both irritated and intrigued at the same time. The final paragraphs of the pamphlet struck a chord in her, resonated deep inside in a place for which she had no name or label.

For I know the thoughts that I think toward you, saith the Lord, thoughts of peace, and not of evil, to give you an expected end. Then shall ye call upon me, and ye shall go and pray unto me, and I will hearken unto you. And ye shall seek me, and find me, when ye shall search for me with all your heart.

"Who is this Lord," she wondered aloud, "that he thinks thoughts of peace toward me? What is this 'expected end'? Is that when we die?"

Tory let the pamphlet fall to her coverlet where it lay with her drawing supplies. "I must start dinner before Charles rises from his nap and dresses for the evening." She turned her attention to her purchases and began to plan her evening, anticipating many pleasant hours with her art supplies.

However, when Charles left after dinner and Tory took her supplies to the little desk in her room, she found that the act of sketching clothes only kindled more sorrowful memories of Sugar Tree and painful longing for her lost life in New Orleans. The hurt was too great; she had stifled it too long. She laid her head on her folded arms and wept as she had not allowed herself to do since fleeing New Orleans.

When she had cried her heart out, she dried her face and went to the kitchen to try her hand at opening the pantry lock. Tory worked at the task for an hour. She could feel the tool touching the mechanism, but could not get the latch to turn. Frustrated, she jammed the pick into the lock willy-nilly and twisted it. The mechanism gave, and the latch popped open.

"Oh, my!"

Tory opened the lock five more times with little difficulty. "I just wasn't pushing it in hard enough and turning it like a key," she told herself as she prepared for bed. "I do wish my drawing had been as successful. Tomorrow evening will be better. I will begin again. Perhaps that dress I saw last week . . ."

But the following afternoon and evening went no better. Regardless of what she tried to sketch, the joy and contentment of drawing eluded her. After several days of aimless doodling and unrelenting homesickness, Tory put her sketch pad and pencils away and set her mind solely to the tasks Charles had assigned her—now to include mastering the lock to the house's front door.

My drawing is a distraction. It haunts me. I must put it aside, because I cannot go back. As much as it pains me, I must not look back. It is fruitless to do so.

~*~

The house was ready, and Charles declared Tory adequately prepared to play the part of hostess. He extended a Wednesday evening invitation to a few well-chosen acquaintances, describing the evening as a private party, limited to a small and exclusive circle of players. The response was immediate and enthusiastic, the party a success.

"I wish you to act as the queen of this house, Tory, because—as far as our guests are concerned—in this house you *are* queen. Stand tall and with confidence. Sit with regal presence. In another year or so, I wager you will be taller than most women, perhaps as tall as many men. Your height is an asset. Be proud of it; never slouch or bow your shoulders."

He reminded her to stand straight and tall many more times. Tory always answered, "Yes, Charles." Soon she began to hold herself as he expected.

Charles orchestrated his introductory parties carefully, and he—deliberately—kept his overall winnings low, losing hands or dropping out early, but recouping his losses later. "I must play a conservative game, Tory," he told her, "until I have established a level of trust with our guests."

He was also slow to introduce Tory's role in the parties. At first, she merely greeted their guests, making them welcome and engaging them in bright conversation while plying them with alcohol. Charles hired an experienced bartender to instruct Tory in the art of mixing drinks. The bartender would stay on until Tory was proficient enough to serve drinks on her own. He instructed the bartender and Tory to pour the guests' drinks liberally but to mix the drinks the players bought for Tory at six parts water to a thimbleful of alcohol.

"We want our guests pleasantly mellow, Tory, while you and I remain sharp."

During the first three parties, Tory stood apart from the table, unable to see the players' hands, until a guest looked to her to bring a refill or empty an ashtray. When she approached the table—only at a guest's request—she scanned his hand and, after again stepping back, conveyed the hand to Charles with a series of subtle gestures.

At the fourth such event, Charles asked his guests if Tory might try her hand at dealing for them—playing her off as the novice she actually was. The response had been positive, and Tory had taken her seat at the table. She followed Charles' implicit instructions from earlier that afternoon: "Tonight, you will deal a straight game, Tory—no tricks, no sleight of hand. This is your opportunity to settle your own nerves while you gain our guests' confidence."

When two months of successful Wednesday evening parties had passed, word of the events made the rounds, and other players approached Charles, angling for invitations. After some "reluctance" on his part, Charles added a second party on Saturdays to accommodate additional guests.

As the official hostess of Charles' parties, Tory became a popular fixture. In fact, as the parties' reputations developed, Tory became an unexpected hit. Her quiet manner and fresh-faced beauty won the hearts—and attentions—of their guests.

Charles was delighted. "You, my dear, have become my secret weapon. Our visitors believe you to be seventeen or eighteen and are positively besotted with you. And while they drool over you, I will rob them blind."

It annoyed Tory when Charles gloated. She understood that their goal was to profit from the poker parties, and she did not object to being Charles' shill to charm and retain wealthy players. But she did not appreciate the rough and boorish manner in which Charles referred to his guests and their attentions toward her—ridiculing them and, by the same dint, diminishing her.

She felt cheapened when he spoke to her so, for in addition to becoming proficient at dealing cards, Tory had been forced to adapt to an entirely different and unanticipated challenge: the management of innocent—and sometimes *not* so innocent—flirting.

The gentlemen openly admired Tory—even if she was taller than a few of her admirers. They complimented her exotic eyes, her flawless skin, her figure, dress, and allure. While they vied for her attention and favor, they referred to Tory among themselves as "our young Nubian princess" or (with a suggestion of jealousy) "Charles' dark duchess."

It was during breaks between poker hands that Tory's wits were tested most. The guests, all wealthy men accustomed to getting what they wanted, ran lustful eyes over her body, lingering on her revealing décolletage. Assuming her to be less than "a lady," a few players attempted to maneuver Tory into a corner of the room and put their hands on her.

One sharp and open rebuke from Charles put an end to those incidents. Recitations of the incident percolated through the gaming community with the message that Charles did not tolerate open impropriety toward Tory. However, Charles' protective stance did not prevent the occasional proposition.

"Miss Tory, if I may be so bold, would you care to join me for dinner tomorrow evening and . . . drinks after? I was thinking a private suite at the Ritz Hotel? I would send a car for you . . . and I promise to make it worth your while, say one hundred dollars?"

The money was a fortune in Tory's experience, but she would smile into the man's face and flatter him, while she declined with a simple, "You are too kind; however, I cannot accept your generous invitation. I do not go out with Charles' friends. I am certain you understand."

Tory let her admirers down with grace and tact, but the refusal still stung, and the men usually muttered something along the lines of, "Likes to keep you to himself, does he?" insinuating an intimacy between Tory and Charles that Tory shuddered to contemplate.

Not obtuse or entirely insensible of sexual innuendo, Tory had, more than once, been thankful that Charles had never tried to take advantage of her dependence upon him. He had saved her from assault by four street brutes—yet he himself had never made an indecent move toward her.

When one of Charles' younger guests propositioned Tory and she rebuffed him, he had been angered and snapped this retort: "You do not go out with Charles' friends? Why ever not? You aren't Charles' type, so why should he care?"

His rebuttal had echoed in Tory's thoughts for days. *What does he mean, 'You aren't Charles' type'?*

CHAPTER 18

Marguerite Declouette and her son, Devereaux, were sharing a late breakfast. A delayed start to the day had become their routine after Yvonne had married and departed for her husband's house. Neither Marguerite nor Devereaux rose before ten in the morning.

Devereaux, against the explicit wishes of his father's will, had dropped out of school. He had discovered that, as long as he stayed within the allowance from his trust fund, he need not work. Instead, he dove into a life of dissipation, staying out most nights drinking and carousing with his friends—the perfect picture of spoiled, profligate youth.

Marguerite also retired late of an evening, but for a different reason: She could rarely escape into sleep without first drinking herself into a stupor from the stores in Devereaux's liquor cabinet.

Her son had curtailed her consumption of his drink by locking up all the liquor in the house. Nevertheless, Marguerite managed to cajole certain employees into procuring alcohol for her unquenchable thirst. Little real love existed between the drunkard mother and debauched son, and Marguerite smothered a sly smile. Why, if Devereaux were to take a careful inventory of the expensive little items lying about the house (silver lighters, snuffboxes, and candlesticks or porcelain knick-knacks), he would be staggered to discover how few remained.

Marguerite, her head muzzy and her stomach in revolt, stared at the poached egg and toast on her plate. She wondered how long she could continue her drinking habit before her son found her out.

Then what?

Perhaps a visit to Yvonne in Baton Rouge would be in order—a visit she might need to extend indefinitely.

Devereaux muttered an oath and gave the newspaper in his hand a shake. "Well! Listen here: It is Uncle Bastiann."

"What of him?" she asked, disinterested.

"Why, it seems he is dead."

Marguerite held a hand to her pounding head. "What do you say?"

"Uncle Bastiann was found dead in Grandmother's house."

Marguerite sat up and attempted to clear the fog from her mind. "Devereaux, my dear, do please read the account to me."

His eyes narrowed in ill-disguised contempt, but he replied, "As you wish, Mother. *Bastiann Jacques Declouette, believed dead of strangulation, was found Thursday by a concerned neighbor. Authorities believe Mr. Declouette interrupted a burglary at his home, Sugar Tree, located in Jefferson Parish, approximately ten miles east of New Orleans.*"

"Strangulation! I wonder why the police did not notify us at once?"

"I hesitate to read the remainder of the report, Mother. You do not appear to be in good health or spirits this morning." His words held the undertone of a sneer.

"A mere headache, I assure you, my darling. Do finish the account."

Devereaux sniffed. "It continues, *Authorities believe Mr. Declouette to have been deceased for at least a week prior to the neighbor's discovery—*"

"A week!" Marguerite's stomach tossed uneasily.

"Yes. Quite horrifying to consider, Mother." And Devereaux relished horrifying his mother.

"Yes, terrible." She closed her eyes and willed the nausea down.

"It reads, *Authorities believe Mr. Declouette to have been deceased for at least a week prior to the neighbor's discovery of his body. The police found the house ransacked and all articles of value other than heavy furniture removed from the house.* Who would have done such a thing, Mother? Really, was there that much to steal?"

Marguerite did not answer. Bastiann had as good as told her that his creditors were counting on securing Sugar Tree in payment of his gambling debts—and she had given him the information necessary to locate and take custody of her husband's illegitimate child. He had, evidently, failed on that count. Had his death been the price for his unpaid debts?

Her mind went quickly to another question: Who would now take control of Sugar Tree? Slitting her eyes against the pounding in her head, Marguerite vowed, *I care not—except that the half-caste offspring of my husband's whore never set foot in it again.*

~*~

Life on Crescent Street progressed as Charles had planned. True to his design, he won regularly at their parties and other games he frequented throughout the city—but never so much as to arouse suspicion, nor did he beat an opponent so soundly as to risk anger and reprisal. In this way, Charles' reputation as a superior but fair card player grew. He provided well for himself and Tory and added steadily to his savings—a savings that he carefully salted away in various locations.

"Never put all your eggs in one basket, Tory," he often said.

In his own way, Charles was generous to Tory, buying her new clothes, giving her spending money and taking her to the occasional dinner out and to plays or musicales once or twice a month. Their relationship was an odd mix of parent-child and employer-employee and, for the most part, Charles was as kind to Tory as he was demanding.

When three years had passed in this profitable fashion, he made a munificent gesture for Tory's "eighteenth" birthday, taking her out on the town to celebrate. They dined on premium cuts of steak, fresh asparagus, and iced sherbet; they danced and drank champagne—until Tory was tipsy.

"I am afraid I have had too much to drink," Tory giggled.

"Every girl should experience a grand night out, Tory. You are eighteen, now, although you are easily more mature than your years. I am glad, of course, that you have grown no taller this year—another inch and you would have been as tall as I am!"

Tory, her expression serene, smiled to herself. She had precious few secrets from Charles—one of them her true age. He had been convinced she was nearly fifteen when they met, and she had never disabused him of that fallacy: Today her true age was sixteen.

She remembered her twelfth birthday party, the proud, happy faces of Madame Rousseau, Mademoiselle Justine, and Miss Defoe, the chocolate cake topped with toasted almonds, and the precious gift they had given her.

What would they think of me now? Would they be proud of who I am and what I do? Would Maman be proud? I think not.

The realization saddened Tory.

"What is this?" Charles demanded. "You were happy one moment and despondent the next."

Knowing how astute Charles was, Tory always told him the truth—even if it was a misleading version of it. "I was thinking of another birthday party," she told him, meeting his gaze. "It led me to think of my mother. I still miss her terribly."

She smiled, her mouth lopsided. "Do not fret, Charles. My mood will pass. This evening has been so lovely. Thank you."

Mollified, Charles lit another cigarette. "You are welcome, Tory."

Tory sipped more champagne, her expression placid. *No, Charles. You do not see through me as well as you used to. My thoughts are my own, and I will keep my secrets to myself.*

Indeed, Charles had taught Tory well, and she had taken his lessons to heart: She had grown adept at "learning" people, at fathoming their gestures, words, and nuances. What he did not comprehend was that Tory, after three years as his companion, had become as adroit as he was at discerning the character and behavior of others. She had, quite possibly, surpassed Charles' ability to read others—including Charles himself.

She knew him better than he realized and observed in him the flaws and weaknesses that were gaining ground and to which he was blind.

The many late nights and long hours at the card tables, coupled with little physical exercise, had taken a toll. Charles, entering the last years of his forties, had gained some weight. He had softened and slowed slightly. His regular companions at the gaming tables might not have noticed, but Tory, whose eyes and mind were at their sharpest, watched and took note of those changes: Her mentor was losing his edge; he was growing complacent.

Worse, Charles' ego was expanding with his waistline.

Of course, Tory could not monitor Charles when he played poker away from the house, but it concerned her that when they hosted their "exclusive" games, Charles chose the occasional indiscreet risk over steady, incremental wins—something he would not have done when they arrived in St. Louis, fresh from his near escape in New Orleans. In Tory's estimation, Charles seemed to be relying more upon his cleverness and cunning than on the careful rules he had established to prevent a game from "blowing up," as he put it.

With his flight from New Orleans now years behind him, Charles seemed to have forgotten that one overt or injudicious move resulting in an angered "mark" had the potential to destroy the life he had so painstakingly crafted for them in St. Louis.

Over the three months following Tory's birthday, Charles' behaviors at their hosted card games jangled on her nerves; she began watching him, nudging him gently during the play, distracting their guests when Charles' biting wit stung too deeply, smoothing ruffled tempers when they flared.

Charles may have tended toward indiscretion, but he was not oblivious. Late one Saturday night, after their guests had departed, he rounded on Tory, cursing her. She had known it was coming; she had "handled" him that evening, much as she handled a guest who had imbibed too much drink or whose pride Charles had wounded. Tory had handled *him* before their guests, averting what had been trending toward a heated confrontation between him and another player.

With his expression suffused in anger, he wagged his finger in her face. "You forget your place, *Victoria*. You forget how I picked you up from a filthy alley in the worst part of New Orleans—how I rescued you and made you what you are. Do not *ever again* interject yourself between me and a mark."

Tory withstood the dressing down without change in her demeanor. Inside, however, she was preparing for the inevitable: Soon—not this week or the next, perhaps, but *soon*—Charles would misjudge an opponent and make a mistake of such magnitude that their headlong flight from St. Louis would be required.

Before she retired that evening, she withdrew her locket from its hidden pocket in her corset. Staring at the tiny image of her mother, Tory began to ready herself for that eventuality.

The moment came sooner than she had expected—but its import on her, personally, was nothing she could have anticipated or for which she could have prepared.

~*~

JANUARY 1907

December came and went; a new year moved in. The third Wednesday of the month, they hosted their usual card game, and she greeted the evening's players with the soft, Southern charm to which their guests had grown accustomed and appreciative.

"Good evening, Grayson. You are looking as handsome as ever," Tory murmured. "Come in and shake the damp from your overcoat." St. Louis in late January was rarely snowy, but it was frequently overcast and given to showers.

Taking another man's hat and coat, she added, "I'm delighted to see you, Thomas. You played brilliantly last week! Shall we expect similar cleverness tonight?"

As Tory saw them to the parlor, she mentally reviewed the list of players for that evening—as usual, an even six, when counting Charles: Eugene Morningdale, Grayson Wheeler, Tyrone Barnes, Paul Stokes, and Mitchell Waring.

Mitchell Waring.

She had been disconcerted to find Waring's name on the list. During the last party he had attended, Charles—discounting Tory's signals and warnings—had thoroughly thrashed Waring.

She frowned on the remembrance. It was one thing to beat a man at cards, but Charles had first stripped Waring of his stake, then goaded him into writing a check that, according to rumors, Waring could ill-afford to cover. When Waring lost again, he had stood abruptly, jarring the other players' drinks.

"I say, Waring," Charles had drawled, "I do expect better manners from a gentleman. These are, after all, exclusive games."

It was what Waring replied that had alarmed Tory. "A gentleman? You question me? I can trace my family line back fourteen generations. I doubt you can, Charles Luchetti. Weren't your parents impoverished Italian immigrants? Hardly the pedigree of a *gentleman*."

As Charles began to get up from his seat to respond to the insult, Tory had stood first, obliging the entire table to rise with her—thus diffusing Charles' precipitous move.

She had put a hand on Waring's chest and murmured with an intimate smile, "Oh, my dear Mitchell. I am grieved that your usual luck has deserted you this evening. However, I am certain you will recover—how could you not? You always play brilliantly. Please do not give this evening another thought. It will pass."

Waring's soul had blinked out from his eyes for the briefest moment. "It is not the loss itself, my dear," he'd whispered.

She knew then that he could not cover his forfeitures, that he had overextended himself, perhaps to the point of ruin.

"Do let me see you out." It was the kindest thing Tory could do for him, but the glare of loathing Waring had bent on Charles as he murmured his goodnights to the other players chilled Tory.

Later, she had said to Charles, "I pray you will never invite Mitchell Waring to another of our parties."

Charles had laughed and lit a cigarette. "Waring is a grown man. If he, after he has licked his wounds, solicits another invitation, who am I to deny him? Perhaps I will let him win a little, just to mollify his pride."

Mitchell Waring's pride? It was Charles' pride that worried Tory. He seemed disinclined to heed her concerns of late—and Tory, still stinging from Charles' last tongue lashing, was loath to risk receiving another.

Rightfully uneasy, Tory hoped to find Mitchell reconciled to his last encounter with Charles. However, when she answered the door, she found Mitchell accompanied by an unfamiliar companion. She had difficulty concealing her alarm: The governing rule of their parties was that guests were admitted by invitation only.

"Good evening, Miss Tory. May I introduce my houseguest, Mr. Drake? He arrived unexpectedly from London, and I could not, in good conscience, leave him to his own devices in a strange city, could I? Surely Charles will have no objection to another player?"

Before Tory could answer, the uninvited guest spoke up. "Good evening, Miss Tory. Thank you for receiving me; Mitchell has regaled me with accounts of your beauty and charm. He did not overstate his regard for you."

She studied the stranger, who, if she was not mistaken, carried West Indies blood. His frame was spare and his evening wear impeccable; he combed his black hair straight back from his swarthy forehead. Above his lip he sported a short-cropped mustache.

As he took her hand and bent over it, Tory's apprehension increased. Although the man's manners were faultless, something . . . disturbing had glittered in his eyes.

"Welcome, Mitchell, and it is a pleasure to make your acquaintance, Mr. Drake—"

"Please. I hope you will do me the honor of addressing me by my first name? It is Blair."

"I would be delighted to call you Blair." Tory smiled and turned back to Waring. "Of course, you know the rules, Mitchell. I must leave the decision regarding your guest to Charles' discretion."

"Let us ask him, shall we?" Waring took Tory's arm and steered her out of the foyer into the parlor where Charles and the other players were mingling prior to the start of the game.

Tory did her best to preempt Waring. "Charles?"

Charles turned toward her, and Tory laid a gloved hand below her neck, signaling that the situation was troubling, that she required his assistance. But Charles had already seen the intrusion. Holding a drink in his left hand, he approached.

"Evening, Waring. Glad you could make it. And your companion is?" He appraised Drake, who had, in Tory's estimation, suddenly shrunk in on himself.

Puzzling, Tory thought.

"Blair Drake, at your service, sir. I have only arrived in St. Louis this morning and am staying with Mitchell. Frightfully sorry to put you in an awkward spot. Since my presence goes against the rules, I will not mind sitting out the game. I shall nurse a drink and," he nodded at Tory with a shy smile, "enjoy the view while you chaps enjoy your game."

Every warning instinct in Tory's being jangled. While she dimpled and nodded to acknowledge Drake's compliment, she fingered the center stone of the necklace she wore, signaling, "Beware. Danger."

Charles ignored her.

"Mr. Drake, we would not dream of excluding Mitchell's guest or a newcomer to our fair city. Come, sit. We are about to begin. Are you familiar with the game of poker?"

Drake appeared dubious. "I have heard of it, of course, and had the pleasure of a brief introduction to its intricacies while visiting friends in Baltimore, but, I confess that my usual game is whist."

"Feel free to dabble a little this evening," Charles answered.

"Well, I do have a bit of money with me."

"We shall be happy to include you."

Tory looked from Drake to Charles and back, sensing something "off." Drake's manner had altered from the moment he had greeted her at the door to his introduction to Charles just now, and his assertion of "a brief introduction to its intricacies" rang with hollow sincerity.

Then she slanted her eyes toward Mitchell and grew further concerned: Mitchell Waring's lips twitched as with suppressed gratification.

The game proceeded without interruption or a clear winner for the space of an hour. When the players took their first break, Waring's companion had lost only a little. When the game resumed, however, something in the play altered. Drake began to make subtle moves, raising, doubling down, and bluffing—successfully.

Within a quarter hour, the atmosphere in the room shifted as Drake's abilities "improved" and the competition between him and Charles heated. Halfway through the next hand, when the players threw in cards and asked for replacements, Charles signaled Tory to slip him an ace. She did, and he won the hand and a sizable pot with two pair, aces high.

Seen only by Tory, Charles palmed an ace when he flipped and threw in his winning cards.

In the next hand, the pot grew to an outlandish size, made fat by early bets all around the table. Then, as the stakes increased, players dropped out one by one, first Waring, then three others, leaving only Charles and Drake in contention.

Charles raised; Drake re-raised. The two men stared across the table with open hostility.

The discomfort increased, and Tory glanced around the table. Three players seemed to sense and fidget at the tension between Charles and Drake; only Waring appeared relaxed.

Tory thought him excited but guarded, as though he were keeping his elation hidden. She again signaled "Danger" to Charles. She knew he saw her signal, but his eyes were fastened on Drake's.

"Mr. Drake, I am 'all in.'"

Drake smiled and sat back. "Actually, Mr. Luchetti, you are a cheat."

Time slowed, and the remaining players froze. Tory, unable to look away, saw Charles suppress a cringe of surprise.

"Mr. Drake, you are a guest in this game, yet you make an egregious and unfounded accusation. I could call you out for this."

"Call me out? How quaint. How dated. But I do accuse you, and my charge is neither egregious nor unfounded. *Stop!* Do not move, Mr. Luchetti."

Charles found himself staring into the barrel of a snub-nosed revolver. "How dare you bring a gun into my home!"

"I use it merely to prove my point, Mr. Luchetti. No, do not move: I have now warned you twice. I shall not a third time." Drake pointed his chin at the player next to Charles. "Mr. Morningdale? Please check inside Mr. Luchetti's coat sleeve. Yes, just there."

Eugene Morningdale, one of Charles' regulars, spluttered. "I shall do no such thing! Why, I—"

The veneer slipped from Blair Drake's disguise as he redirected the gun to Morningdale's chest. "I have a bullet for every man in this room, Mr. Morningdale. I am not asking, I am telling you: Reach inside Mr. Luchetti's sleeve and show us what you find there."

Morningdale looked at Charles. Charles' features were carved of white, bloodless stone. Morningdale glanced at Drake's gun and back to Charles. Without further argument, he felt the sleeve of Charles' suitcoat. "What?" He reached two fingers inside and, fumbling a little, retrieved a card and laid it face up on the table.

An ace of diamonds.

"Why, Charles!"

Charles sneered at him. "Shut up, Morningdale. You are a fool, and fools get what they deserve."

Drake waved the gun at Charles. "I repeat my accusation: You, Mr. Luchetti, are a cheat and, for the benefit of your guests who are slow to comprehend, I must expose you and your schemes."

His lips thinned to a sardonic grin. "Your private parties are but an elaborate guise, a front to, at your leisure, strip your 'exclusive guests' of their money. And you do not act alone. Your *precious* 'Miss Tory'? She is your skilled collaborator, dealing deceitfully, signaling you, distracting the other players while you cheat them."

The gaze of every man at the table fixed on Tory; she felt their regard turn from admiration to disgust and loathing. Her breath came in small gasps, and she grew faint.

Drake continued. "You are cunning and *usually* careful, Luchetti. You never appear to win too much or too often but, on occasion, your greed overcomes your good sense. I refer to your ego, Luchetti, your downfall. One such overreach occurred during your last encounter with my friend—my employer—Mitchell Waring."

No one at the table had any doubt what was happening. Mitchell Waring had brought his own card sharp to the party to defeat and expose Charles. Waring's intention was not merely to recoup his losses. No, the payback for Waring would be double: to recover his lost money (split with Drake, of course) and to annihilate Charles.

Charles seethed. "Make your point, Drake. What do you want?"

"Ah, my point. Thank you for reminding me."

Tory did not notice the glittering glance Drake slid in her direction. She had focused all her strength on remaining upright in her chair.

"Perhaps . . . perhaps we should excuse Miss Tory from our deliberations," Drake mused. "Why don't you send her to her room, Luchetti?"

Charles, without looking away from Drake, muttered, "Go to your room, Tory."

Tory tried to stand but could not. Mitchell Waring rose, pulled back her chair, helped her to her feet.

"I am sorry, my dear, but you were part and parcel of this charade."

Tory did not answer. Her worst fears had come to pass. She stumbled up the stairs to her room and closed the door. Locked it. Wondered if the report of a gun would shortly announce Charles' demise.

Downstairs, Drake grinned at Charles. "Don't worry, Luchetti. You are in no danger of my shooting you. I enjoyed this evening too much, old chap. Yes, I quite enjoyed beating you. And I believe I shall enjoy the remainder of this night as well."

To the other players, he commanded, "Take whatever money you have won and get out. Do not bother calling the police—unless you wish the entire city to know how often Luchetti has fleeced you. Consider yourselves lucky to be leaving with what you have."

The glances of the other players skittered around the table, only to come back to the revolver.

Drake laughed. "Go, you lily-livered cowards—before I change my mind."

Morningdale rose first. He scraped his money from the table, stuffed it in his pocket, and skirted the table. The other two players followed him.

When the front door closed and only Charles, Mitchell Waring, and Drake remained, Drake smiled again. "Mitchell, old boy, I should like to renegotiate the terms of our deal."

"What? But I need that money! I—"

"Shut up, Mitchell. You shall take the entire pot, and half of whatever else Mr. Luchetti gives up. I prefer to take my share of the pot in other tender."

Mitchell appeared confused. Charles was not. "You low-down, son of a—"

"Do be careful, old boy. Now, listen closely; here is how this is going to work. Tomorrow, you and your 'Miss Tory,' will leave St. Louis with nothing but your bags and whatever money you have squirreled away that we do not find tonight. Waring here will send hired men tomorrow evening to ensure that you have heeded our 'request.' Do you get me? Or should I say, *capisce?*"

Charles snarled without answering—and Drake discharged his revolver over Charles' shoulder. The mirror above his liquor cabinet exploded; acrid, blue smoke filled the room.

"Do you agree to my terms, Luchetti?"

Charles nodded.

"Ah, good. Now, where else in the house do you keep your funds?"

Charles stirred. "Behind the bar, a loose floorboard. You'll find a strong box."

"Excellent. Get it, Mitchell."

Mitchell Waring had already scooped up Charles' winnings and the money in the pot. He uncovered the strong box and placed it on the table, eager to see its contents. He counted out the cash. "Nearly thirteen hundred dollars."

"Hand me my cut, please."

Drake pocketed the bills. "Now, Mitchell, do find us a bit of rope. I wish to leave Luchetti tied up when we leave. Miss Tory will find him later and undo his bonds."

Ten minutes later, Charles was trussed to his chair.

Drake smoothed his short mustache. "Now, Mitchell, you will wait and watch Luchetti while I extract the remainder of my payment."

"I don't understand, Blair."

"Luchetti does, don't you, old chap?"

The hate burning in Charles' eyes was fearsome.

"What are you talking about, Blair?"

"You shall remain here. I shall be no longer than thirty minutes, perhaps less—depending upon Miss Tory's disposition."

Understanding dawned on Waring. "You do not mean to . . . No, Drake. That is unconscionable!"

Drake snickered. "Conquest is never complete without rape and pillage, is it, Mitchell?" His mouth hardened. "We renegotiated our deal, remember? You kept all the cash on the table, and I said I would take my payment in another form. If you wish to welsh on our deal, I shall demand that you divide the table with me."

Mitchell Waring struggled for a moment, his need for the cash warring over his moral scruples. Finally, he shrugged. "I prefer to keep the money."

"I thought you would."

As Drake ambled to the stairs, Charles shouted, "Tory! Tory, run!"

Upstairs, Tory's head snapped up. She had believed Charles dead following the gunshot. She ran to her door and listened. Footsteps sounded on the stairs, in the hall, ending at her door. She looked around, grabbed her chair, and jammed it under the door handle.

"Open the door, Miss Tory. I have won the pleasure of your favors this evening."

Tory backed away. She was terrified—and looked to her bedroom windows. She tore back the curtains and was unlatching a sash when Drake threw his weight against her bedroom door. The flimsy lock broke. With another shove, the chair she had braced under the door handle splintered, and the door burst open.

"Oh, no, my dear! I cannot allow you to harm yourself."

Drake's arms twined around Tory's waist. She screamed and fought him, but he was much stronger. Within moments he had thrown her to the bed and pinned her.

Tory continued to scream. She fought and raged, but neither did her any good. In the end, Drake had his way.

Twenty minutes later, Drake paused at the bottom of the staircase to adjust his suitcoat and check his tie in a wall mirror.

An ashen-faced Mitchell joined him. "Can we go, now?"

"Yes. I am famished. We should get some dinner, what?"

Mitchell frowned. "I am not hungry."

"Tsk, tsk. Well, let us be on our way." He stopped, as though remembering something. "One moment, if you please."

He went into the parlor and stood before Charles. "Mr. Luchetti, it was my presumption that you and Miss Tory were, ah, intimately acquainted, that the arrangement was longstanding. My enjoyment of her was intended more as an insult to you than to her. However, if it means anything, I did not realize she was a virgin until I took her."

Drake shrugged and sketched a mocking bow. "Please extend my apologies."

CHAPTER 19

Tory could not move. No part of her body responded to her mind's commands. *I must run. Run! Yes, Maman. I must get away from Bastiann, get away from this man, Drake!* Then she remembered it was too late to run, that Drake had come and gone. He had violated her in ways she had not imagined possible. No one had explained these things to her . . . but now she knew for herself what her *mère* and Sassy had feared Bastiann would do.

She lay still and drifted away in her mind. She was a girl again, a child running through the tall grass of the orchard at Sugar Tree, climbing high into the boughs of an apple tree.

Soon Maman will call me back to my lessons, Tory imagined. *I must wash my face at the pump so Maman does not know I have been running in the orchard.*

After I finish my lessons, Sassy will make little strawberry tarts and Maman and I will take our tea in the parlor. We will smile and sip our tea, and I will savor the one bite of tart Maman allows me.

She could hear Adeline's sweet voice, and even feel her smooth, ebony skin beneath her fingertips. *A Southern woman curtails her appetite,* her *mère* murmured. *She must not allow her figure to suffer from overindulgence.*

Oui, Maman.

After a while, Tory slept.

~*~

It was the housekeeper, not Tory, who found Charles tied to a chair in the morning. He had passed the long night in transitory self-flagellation, followed by planning his next moves while waiting for Tory to come down and loose him, then fearing for her life when he heard no sounds from the second floor as the night passed.

"Do not bother with the knots, Mrs. Frye; they are too tight for your fingers to undo. Fetch a sharp knife from the kitchen."

The frightened woman did as Charles demanded. When she had freed him, he sent her home.

Dreading what he would find on the second floor, Charles stretched out his stiff muscles and mounted the stairs. Tory's bedroom door hung askew; the pieces of a chair lay scattered on the planks and carpet of her room.

Tory's form, unclothed and motionless, lay amid the tangled bedclothes. He crept closer.

"Tory?"

Nothing.

"Tory?"

Was that breath? Did she stir?

Tory awoke gradually and shivered with cold. She blinked as Charles pulled the coverlet over her body. "Charles?"

"Yes, my dear, I am here. Are you . . . are you all right, Tory?"

Tory struggled to sit up, and she winced in pain—the horror of the previous night flooding back. "No! No! That man! Is he gone?"

Charles nodded. "Yes, but . . . Tory, I fear we must leave St. Louis. Today. We must make haste to pack what we wish to take with us.

Tory's eyes focused on Charles. "Leave? With you?" Anger and abhorrence filled her. "This is your fault, Charles. All of it. Your pride and ego. You broke your own rules—and *I* have paid the price!"

Charles backed away and folded his arms. Tory watched coldness settle on his expression. "Be it as you say, Tory, my culpability does not change the urgency of our situation. We have until this evening to leave St. Louis. Waring and Drake will send a gang of thugs to check on us; if they find us here, what we suffered last night will be repeated—or worse."

"What *we* suffered?"

Charles, an expression of regret on his face, looked away for a long moment before he replied. "I will set water to heat on the kitchen stove, Tory. I urge you to get up and bathe. Afterward, you must pack. Take whatever you like. You may go with me or you may do as you please. I leave it to you to choose."

He paused at her door. "I intend to sell the car and whatever else I can liquidate this afternoon and take a cab from here to the station to catch the 4:30 westbound train. Waring and Drake stole a portion of my capital, but I have enough hidden away to reestablish us elsewhere. If you decide to come with me, be ready to leave no later than three o'clock."

Tory lay back down, her head spinning, her body aching. She could make no decisions, and the bed seemed to weigh her down, to press in on her aching body.

Forty minutes later, Charles reappeared. "Your bath is ready, Tory."

When Tory did not respond, he pulled back the coverlet, exposing her nakedness to the cool air in her room. He grimaced at the sight of her bruises, then said, "Come, now. Let me help you up."

At first Tory fought him, but she tired quickly, and Charles was insistent. He helped her into her robe, then down the stairs to the kitchen where a steaming tub waited.

"I am leaving the house for an hour or two, so take your leisure—but bear in mind that the clock is ticking. Oh, and you will not be disturbed. I have given Mrs. Frye the day off. She will not return until tomorrow—when she does, she will find us gone."

Only when Tory heard the front door close and lock behind him did she move. Before she felt safe enough to disrobe, she checked the back door. It, too, was locked, but she unlocked and relocked it, twisting the knob to be certain.

She looked around the kitchen and at the steaming tub, wondering why, after three years in this house, every detail seemed strange. Unfamiliar. Foreign.

Finally, she dropped her robe, stepped into the tub, and sank down into the comforting warmth—only to cry out when the heat touched where she was torn.

So. I am a woman now. Soiled. Isn't that what they call a woman who has been ruined?

Tory cleaned herself as best she could, then simply soaked and nodded, falling back into a numb somnambulistic state.

Maman.

Maman?

~*~

The chill of the water as it cooled roused Tory. Struggling through stiffness and pain, she forced herself to climb out, towel off, and put her robe back on. She hurt as she climbed the steep staircase. Once in her room, Tory was tempted to crawl under the covers and fall into the deep sleep that pulled at her.

Charles' warning about the men Waring would send at nightfall made her resist the pull. She grew anxious. *I must pack. Leave. Go, before more men come. But go where? Where can I go where I will be safe?*

Suddenly frantic, Tory searched through her discarded clothing, the dress and underthings Drake had torn from her the night before. When she found her corset, she clasped it to herself, and felt for the secret pocket where she kept her locket.

It was there, safe.

I must dress, must put on my corset to hide and keep my treasure, she told herself.

The corset's ties were broken, and one whalebone stay had snapped in two. Tory opened her sewing kit, took up a pair of sharp shears, and made a slit in the corset. She pulled out the broken stay, then stitched the torn ties together.

"They may never again pull smoothly, but they must do until I can replace them," she whispered.

She patted the secret pocket once more and began to hook herself into the corset, when a crumpled scrap of paper on the floor caught her eye. She stooped and picked it up. It was the pamphlet the pale-faced girl had given her.

Her eyes fell on the wrinkled print.

For I know the thoughts that I think toward you, saith the Lord, thoughts of peace, and not of evil, to give you an expected end. Then shall ye call upon me, and ye shall go and pray unto me, and I will hearken unto you. And ye shall seek me, and find me, when ye shall search for me with all your heart.

Thoughts of peace? Again, the panic struck her. *Where can I go? Where can I hide? What if . . . what if I conceive a child?* Her last thought almost undid the last remnants of her control. Everything about the passage jangled and warred against her present state of mind and body. But something also called to her.

And ye shall seek me, and find me, when ye shall search for me with all your heart.

Without understanding why she did so, Tory grabbed up her scissors and roughly cut out the passage. She folded it in quarters and, unhooking her corset and unbuttoning her locket's hiding place, tucked it inside with her locket. By dint of sheer determination, Tory finished dressing and turned to fixing her disheveled hair.

Looking in the mirror, she marveled that she looked no different than she had the night before as she had prepared for the evening's party. How could she look no different when so much had changed and could never be mended? She pondered the strange phenomenon.

I may look the same, but I see the stain upon my heart. I wonder . . . can anyone else see it?

When she was dressed, she sat on her bed and took inventory of her room. *I must leave here in a matter of hours. I have no money, no friends, no means of travel, no place to go—and Charles demands that I pack?*

Rain pattered on the windows, reminding Tory that it was winter. A harsher reality forced itself on her.

TORY

I have nowhere to go where I would not freeze within hours, let alone days. As much as I loathe him, I must, for now, continue on with Charles.

Resigned, Tory placed an open suitcase on the bed. She laid her cloak, warm gloves, and umbrella on the bed beside the open case. A small trunk waited by her wardrobe. Considering what she needed most, she began to pack.

~*~

When Charles returned, more than three hours later, he found her waiting at the foot of the stairs, her suitcase and trunk ready by the door.

"Have you decided to come with me?"

Tory stirred herself, but did not look at him. "For now."

He nodded. "I have sold the motorcar, collected my funds, and bought our tickets."

"You knew I would come with you?"

He hesitated before answering. "I hoped you would."

Tory chuckled without mirth. "Why? Where are we going?"

"I thought Denver. A fresh start."

When Tory only nodded and did not comment, he added, "I will give up gambling, Tory. Turn over a new leaf. I have enough saved to open a business or, perhaps, buy one. We shall be respectable, you and I."

Respectable? Not I.

She frowned. "You have that much money, even after . . ." Tory did not finish.

"They took my strong box but, as I've often said, I never keep all my eggs in one basket."

Tory sighed. "Denver?"

Charles assumed his usual manner. "Yes. I must pack now. The cab will be here in thirty minutes."

He left her with her own thoughts.

PART 3:
DENVER,
COLORADO

$\mathcal{C}$HAPTER 20

January 1907

C harles and Tory arrived in Denver near noon, two days later. During their journey, Tory had said little, and Charles had not attempted to draw her into conversation. They traveled together but, in spirit, had sat far apart.

As they were steaming into Denver's Union Station, Charles turned toward Tory. "We will find a respectable boarding house to begin with while I scout the city for a business opportunity. When I begin to see some return on my investment, we shall seek a more permanent residence."

He hesitated before speaking again. "I comprehend the grave offense I have caused you, Tory. I do not fault you for holding it against me. However, if we are to continue on together, we should come to some sort of resolution." He sighed. "The silence between us is discouraging."

Tory looked the other way. She could scarcely abide Charles, but she, too, understood—from a practical standpoint—that she had to come to terms with her anger. "I shall look for work in Denver."

"What would you do?"

"I was a fair seamstress; I can become adept with a needle or a machine again."

"Such hard, ordinary work seems . . . beneath you."

She lifted her chin. "I would like to earn my own money and become independent."

Charles nodded, hesitated, then said, "I care about you, Tory, and I am crushed that my choices have hurt you. If I could have stopped . . . if I could have prevented Drake from doing . . . what he did to you, I would have done so. I . . . I would give my life to change what happened."

Tory stared at her gloved hands, not convinced that she believed Charles, uncertain if she could ever trust him again.

Charles choked on his next words. "Tory, you . . . you have grown dear to me these last three years, as though you truly were my daughter. Please . . . please let me take care of you."

Tory still did not answer, but she bobbed her head once, if only slightly.

The train came to a jarring stop, and they disembarked to find a much colder winter than what they had experienced in St. Louis. Tory wrapped her cloak about her body to ward off the freezing wind.

"Go inside the terminal, Tory. I will fetch our bags and your trunk."

Tory heeded Charles and walked directly into the station where, at least, she was out of the wind. Thinking to be of use, she approached a ticket counter. "Pardon me. Could you suggest any clean, respectable boarding houses in the city?"

The ticket man took her measure. "Least expensive but still respectable is the Greenbriar or, if you can afford it, perhaps the Broadmoor Hotel would suit you. Both rent by the week or the month." Without being asked, the man cited the cross streets for both establishments.

Tory took a pencil from her handbag and, on the back of her ticket wrote "Greenbriar" and "Broadmoor" and their locations.

"Thank you. You have been most kind."

"Welcome to Denver, miss."

When Charles found her, she had asked a porter, a conductor, and a woman selling hot coffee their opinions of both places.

"The consensus was that the Broadmoor is cleaner and the food better," Tory reported. "Also, it is located on the edge of the shopping district."

"The Broadmoor it is, then." Charles was pleased that Tory had taken some initiative; he was more pleased that she was speaking to him. It portended, he hoped, a healing of their relationship.

The Broadmoor, a four-story brick edifice with two wings, had small suites available, each with a sitting room and two adjacent bedrooms. Although the rooms were clean, as reported, the establishment had fallen upon lean times. It was evident why the Broadmoor had devolved from a first-class hotel to boarding house: The carpets were worn, the furnishings well used, and the mattresses thin.

After viewing the available suites and choosing one, Charles and Tory returned to the front desk to pay for a month's lodging.

"Good afternoon." Charles looked at the clerk's gold-plated name tag. "Miss Visser, is it?"

"Yes. Mr. Visser is the hotel manager; I am Mr. Visser's sister."

Tory studied Miss Visser. The woman, perhaps in her late thirties, was lean and angular. *Why, everything about this woman is sharp-edged,* Tory thought, *her chin, her nose, her eyes—even her voice.*

"My name is Charles Luchetti. I should like to take Suite 109 for a month, please."

Miss Visser looked from Charles to Tory.

"May I present my foster daughter, Victoria?"

Miss Visser's mouth thinned and she lifted her pointy chin. It was apparent that she did not believe Charles. "One key, then?"

"No, two, if you please."

She handed him his key and placed Tory's key on the counter. "Dinner at six, Mr. Luchetti, Miss Luchetti."

"It is Miss Washington," Tory murmured.

One side of Miss Visser's mouth lifted, but she did not acknowledge Tory's correction.

Charles handed Tory her key. "Thank you kindly." He gestured for the bellman to gather their luggage, then took Tory's elbow and steered her toward their suite.

Tory waited until the door closed behind the bellman to comment. Charles had begun unpacking, hanging his suits in the wardrobe.

"Miss Visser has the wrong impression about us, Charles."

"That is her misfortune." Changing the topic, he added, "I suggest we dress down a little for dinner. The hotel's clientele is, perhaps, not up to our St. Louis standards—and we do not wish to offend or stand out."

At dinner, they were seated at their own little table and discovered the food to be passable, their fellow diners respectable and cordial—and a little nosy. As other boarders approached their table, they welcomed and scrutinized Charles and Tory in equal parts.

With each introduction, Charles answered, "A pleasure to meet you. I am Charles Luchetti; this is my foster daughter, Victoria Washington. We have just arrived in Denver." If their dinner companions asked after the reason for Charles and Tory's move to the city, Charles' answer never varied. "We are looking to settle here and are in search of an investment opportunity. A business, perhaps."

Most of their dining companions made their living in the city; some were clerks; one was a teacher, another an accountant. One gentleman was a supervisor for the railroad. It became clear to Charles that none of their fellow boarders were entrepreneurial in nature.

"I shall have to move in other circles to catch wind of the type of prospect we seek."

"How? What other circles?"

Charles shrugged. "I know of but one means of rubbing shoulders with successful businessmen."

"You said you would give up gambling, Charles."

"I can visit gaming houses and attend card parties without playing."

Tory flushed. "And a fish can sit in a stream without swimming."

"A fish that does not swim soon turns belly up. We cannot live forever without an income, Tory. I have the means of buying into the right venture, but such an opportunity will not drop into my lap. I must seek one out."

Tory pressed her lips together. *And I, too, must find employment, Charles, so that I can, at some point, separate my life from yours.*

That afternoon and the following, Charles and Tory strolled the streets of Denver, acquainting themselves with the city's municipal and cultural centers and its various districts. Charles purchased newspapers and perused the financial sections; Tory searched the employment advertisements.

As they finished breakfast, four days into their stay at the Broadmoor, the hotel manager, George Visser, came alongside their table.

"Good morning, Miss Washington, Mr. Luchetti. I hope I find you both in good health and spirits this morning?"

"You do," Charles answered, dabbing the napkin to his lips.

"I am pleased to hear it. Mr. Luchetti, might I have a word with you when you have finished your meal? At your leisure, sir. Do not rush on my account."

Tory looked at Charles. "I shall be fine. I believe I shall make some inquiries as to local dress shops."

He nodded to Visser. "Shall we say, in fifteen minutes?"

"Excellent. You will find me in my office."

When Tory and Charles concluded their breakfasts, Tory went to their suite to collect her cloak, hat, and gloves. Charles went to the manager's office.

Before Tory stepped outside, she spoke to the doorman. "Pardon me. I know which direction leads to the shopping area; but, in particular, could you direct me to any fine dress shops?"

"Denver offers women's wear mostly in mercantile stores or emporiums. I know of but two dress shops, miss." He pointed down the street. "Turn right at the corner, go three blocks."

"Thank you."

When she returned at lunch time, Tory was discouraged. She had found the shops and stepped inside, only to discover the merchandise to be on par with ready-made garments. When she asked about evening wear, clerks from both dress shops referred her to a modiste who worked out of her home.

"The elite of Denver do not often use her; they prefer to shop back east or abroad," one clerk confided to Tory. "They make month-long pilgrimages to New York, Philadelphia, and Boston, taking in the art, plays, and musicales in the evenings, while shopping during the day. They return to Denver dressed in new finery, whatever is the rage in New York or Paris."

"I see. Thank you for your time and insights."

Tory went to her room, took off her warm outer wear, and checked her hair. She was leaving for the dining room when the door to their suite opened and Charles entered.

"Ah, I was hoping to catch you before you went down for lunch, Tory."

"What did Mr. Visser wish to see you about, Charles?"

"That is precisely what I desire to discuss with you, Tory. Come, sit down and let me explain."

Tory sat in an overstuffed armchair and waited for him to continue.

"Visser heard that I was looking for an investment opportunity. The thing of it is, Tory, he tells me the Broadmoor is for sale."

"For sale? This place?"

"Yes. The owner is retiring and desires to be shed of the responsibilities of management. He wishes to sell to a younger man for a sizeable cash amount down and monthly payments that would fund his retirement."

Then Tory understood. "You are considering buying this hotel?" Her question was tinged with amazement. "Why, what do you know of hotels?"

"A business is a business, Tory. Mr. Visser would stay on to manage the day-to-day operations. My role would be to infuse new life and money into the place."

Charles paced the sitting room, caught up in the idea. "I have the cash payment the owner expects; however, the Broadmoor, if it is to thrive and recapture its former reputation, requires improvements—new carpets, furniture, and plenty of beautifying work—paint, paper, and so on."

He stopped in front of Tory's chair. "Visser and I walked all through the property after we spoke, and I came up with what I believe is a brilliant idea: The hotel has two wings, north and south. If I can convince the owner to take half of the cash payment now, I would use the other half to refit the lobby and the north wing, restoring those rooms to their previous quality.

"I would move all the boarders to the south wing of the hotel and partition the lobby, providing a smaller, separate entrance for the boarders, and designating the greater portion of the lobby to our hotel guests."

Tory was dubious. "You mean to operate the Broadmoor as both a boarding house and hotel?"

"Yes. As the hotel side begins to make money, I would pay off the second half of the down payment. Eventually, of course, I would renovate the south wing also."

He hesitated. "A truly fine hotel needs someone with superior taste to guide the renovations. I would also require a person to keep the books, to monitor income and expenses. You have a good head upon your shoulders, Tory. I thought of you for the job."

"What? Me? What do I know of accounting?"

"You are bright and educated: accounting can be taught. We would hire someone to set up the books properly after which you would maintain them. Additionally, while I oversaw the renovations, you would train the staff and set the right tone for the hotel."

Tory blinked. The idea held some appeal, but the financial side of Charles' scheme seemed thin. "You have no idea what such a makeover would entail, what furnishing four floors would cost. Such quality takes—"

"Quality takes taste and money. I know. I propose we begin with the lobby, dining room, and first floor of the north wing. I would make those renovations my priority and personally oversee the work. As our clientele grew, we would continue to remodel."

"I don't know, Charles."

He rocked back on his heels, nodding. "I have asked Visser to make the offer. If the owner refuses, I have lost nothing."

"And if you sink all you have into this hotel and cannot make a go of it, you will lose everything," Tory shot back.

Charles had a faraway look in his eyes. "I understand the risk."

"And Miss Visser?"

"What about her?"

"Are you blind? Are you insensible to her arch looks and sniffs of disdain whenever I pass the front desk? She believes I am your mistress, Charles. I cannot think how she would take your purchase of the hotel. Why, a single gossip on the premises could ruin you."

"If the owner accepts my offer, we shall move you to your own suite. That should quell any rumors."

"There is also the issue of my color: Miss Visser is a bigot."

"I don't believe I have ever heard you use that word, Tory."

"You shall hear it more in future, if Miss Visser continues her superior, condescending manner."

"I will handle Miss Visser."

"Will you, indeed? I will hold you to it, Charles." Tory cocked her head and studied Charles, knowing he had already decided to buy the hotel. "And my salary?"

She had surprised him, and he took a minute to consider her question. "Room and board, of course."

"Do Visser and his sister live on the premises?"

"I believe they have a suite on the floor above us."

She lifted her chin. "Then my salary shall be something more than Miss Visser's."

"Now, Tory—"

"I *will* be paid for my work, Charles. If this is not acceptable, then I decline your offer."

Charles met her gaze. "Miss Visser receives ten dollars a month in addition to her room and board, but I will not be able to pay you above five dollars a month until the hotel begins to clear a profit. However, I would agree to owe you the difference. In a year, if we are doing well, I should begin to pay you twelve dollars a month and extra to catch up what is owed. Could you agree to that?"

Still underwhelmed at the prospect of Charles buying the hotel, Tory pressed her advantage. "If I agree to your offer, Mr. Visser and his sister must move to the south wing. Permanently. But you and I will take up separate suites on the fourth floor of the north wing. I can put up with carpenters and painters working on the floors below us, but I will not have Miss Visser glaring down her nose at me."

Charles studied Tory for a long, silent moment. Finally, he murmured, "As you wish, Miss Washington."

He left soon after, but Tory remained seated, wondering what she had gotten herself into. Charles believed her to be all of eighteen years old—mature beyond her years, but still only eighteen.

How appalled he would be to discover that I am but sixteen.

Suddenly she laughed. "I am the only one in the world who could disclose the truth to him—and that I will never do."

CHAPTER 21

Charles approached Tory midmorning the next day. "Great news! The owner has agreed to the terms of my offer. I will give him half the cash payment now and the other half in a year—next March, to be exact."

He lit a cigarette and grinned. "We will sign papers this week, but we should plan our first steps now, so that we can begin as soon as the legalities are settled."

"Well, we shall be unable to make any changes until the boarders move. Perhaps today we should choose our new rooms and inform Mr. Visser and his sister that they will be moving all boarders to the south wing, themselves included," Tory suggested.

"Yes. You make a good point. I shall direct Mr. Visser to deliver the news to the boarders."

"I was thinking about the first-floor renovations last evening, Charles, and had an idea. I propose that we combine two sets of rooms into one grand suite—expend more money on carpet, paper, drapes, furnishings, and linens to impress our wealthiest and most discriminating guests."

"A stroke of genius, Tory." He rubbed his hands together as he prepared to find and speak to George Visser. "I must say, I am eager to begin."

When Charles and Tory arrived for dinner that evening, the dining room was abuzz—that is, until they took their seats at their customary table.

"Everyone is staring at us, Charles," Tory murmured.

"Yes. Did you not notice how conversation stopped when we made our entrance? I believe Mr. Visser has been quick to pass along the news."

As dinner drew to a close and Charles lit his after-dinner cigarette, the boarders, one by one, approached Charles and Tory.

"We understand you have purchased the Broadmoor," a factory clerk began, "and intend to bring about improvements. They will certainly be welcomed. I wish you well in these endeavors." He shook Charles' hand and nodded to Tory.

A teacher sidled up to their table. "May I offer my congratulations, Mr. Luchetti? I am convinced the Broadmoor will thrive under your ownership. Of course, it is a hardship to change rooms. I have resided here for more than a year, and—"

"Thank you for your warm wishes," Charles interrupted. "I regret the inconvenience to you, of course, Miss Davies, but the move is necessary. I am certain you would not appreciate the clamor and mess of remodeling going on outside your doors, disturbing your peace at all hours."

"Oh! I had not considered that point. You are right, of course." She bobbed her chin. "Thank you."

Beginning that evening and extending into the following week, Charles received many such overtures and congratulations. The general attitude of the boarders toward Charles and Tory also altered from one of camaraderie to deference as news of Charles' ownership of the hotel settled. Mr. Visser reported that the north-side boarders were selecting their new rooms on the south side of the hotel and preparing to shift their belongings.

Tory felt they were beginning well and that the general reception of the news had been positive with the hotel occupants. All, with the exception of Trudy Visser. She said nothing to either Charles or Tory, but Tory could sense an undercurrent of anger within the woman.

That undercurrent came to the surface when Charles, who had appropriated Mr. Visser's office for himself and moved a second desk into the room for Tory, called a meeting with Visser and his sister to outline the upcoming work.

"As you know, we have decided to remodel the first-floor rooms and hallway of the north wing initially," Charles stated. "While those tasks are underway, we will also commence renovations on the lobby. I have given Miss Washington charge of hotel décor and training of staff. This will be of particular importance when the lobby is partitioned. The smaller, south side will be our boarders' entrance; the larger side will service our hotel guests."

Charles nodded to Mr. Visser's sister. "Miss Visser, when the partition is complete, you will take charge of the desk on the boarders' side of the lobby and work exclusively with them. Miss Washington will apprise you of your duties when the time approaches."

"But Mr. Visser is the hotel manager," Miss Visser spluttered. "I . . . I am not accustomed to taking orders from a . . . *woman*."

What you mean is that you are not accustomed to taking orders from a dark-skinned woman, Tory fumed.

Charles sat back and stared at Miss Visser. "Indeed? Well, as Miss Washington will often speak for me, Miss Visser, you have a choice before you: Either accustom yourself to receiving direction from her or search for new employment. It is, of course, your decision."

Miss Visser slid her eyes toward her brother and received no response from him. He sat, his eyes straight forward, exhibiting no sign of disagreement with Charles.

Miss Visser fidgeted and delayed but, at last, answered Charles. "I understand, sir."

"Good. Now, about the dining room . . ."

~*~

Charles and Tory spent the remainder of the week walking the hotel, making lists and sketching details. On Friday, Charles visited the owner's attorney and put his signature to the purchase paperwork. He returned to the hotel elated.

"Mr. Connally, the previous owner, was as enthusiastic as I was when I outlined our plan. And he was able to recommend a contractor to commence the work."

Tory smiled. Despite her initial misgivings, she appreciated the positive effect the hotel was having on Charles. "I am glad, Charles. I shall be gladder still to see the work underway."

"As will I, Tory. As will I."

"And, with the purchase papers signed, I should like to select my new rooms."

Charles nodded. "As you wish, Tory."

Tory selected a one-bedroom suite at the northwest corner of the fourth floor. The corner afforded her views of the mountains surrounding Denver. Having grown up in Louisiana, snow-capped mountains and endless vistas were a novelty.

"Magnificent," she murmured. She determined to move into the suite that evening and returned to her room to make arrangements.

When the doorman arrived at her new rooms with her scant luggage, Tory thanked him and began to unpack. She had just finished and sat down before the little desk in the sitting room to add to her notes, but could not find her pencils. She pulled the center drawer toward her, hoping to find one, and stared at a little book. The words HOLY BIBLE were stamped on its cover.

"Oh, dear. Someone has forgotten their Bible."

Tory had never handled a Bible. *Somewhere in this book is the passage I keep with my locket.* She picked it up and thumbed through: The pages were thin and the print tiny.

It is so vast. Why, how could one ever find anything? she wondered.

Still unable to find a pencil, Tory picked up the book and took the elevator to the lobby. She walked to the front desk where a young clerk stood on duty.

"Yes, Miss Washington?"

She glanced at his name tag. "Good evening, Mr. Wick. As you know, I have just occupied room 425. I am afraid a previous occupant left their Bible in the desk."

Wick frowned. "I apologize, Miss Washington. It was not left accidentally. A group of traveling salesmen are beginning to leave Bibles in every room they stay in."

"On purpose? Whatever for?"

"I suppose they hope to convert someone by leaving their 'holy' books. I will take it off your hands, miss."

He reached for it, but Tory withdrew the volume. "If I take your meaning, Mr. Wick, this book was left as a gift? To whomever found it?"

"Yes, miss. A nuisance, if you ask me."

"Perhaps, but if it is all the same to you, I may keep it?"

The clerk blinked and drew himself up. "Certainly, miss."

"Thank you."

After securing a pencil from her office, Tory returned to her rooms. She sat at the desk and again thumbed through the Bible, wondering how to find the passage she had cut from the pamphlet.

This is hopeless, she deduced minutes later. Instead, she stopped to read a page that had red print intermixed with the normal black print. She glanced at the top of the page and saw the words, 'John 6.'

"And who is John?" She started at the chapter heading, noting that the passage was marked by sequential numbers. She frowned and read aloud, "After these things Jesus went over the sea of Galilee, which is the sea of Tiberias."

She raced through the fantastic story—barley loaves and fishes miraculously multiplied to feed thousands. Her breath hitched when she read about Jesus walking atop the waves in the midst of a great wind and high seas.

"Impossible!" But she could not stop herself from devouring every word. When she reached verse 40, she stopped.

> *And this is the will of him that sent me,*
> *that everyone which seeth the Son,*
> *and believeth on him,*
> *may have everlasting life:*
> *and I will raise him up at the last day.*

Tory's mouth opened a little. "Everyone which seeth the Son, and believeth on him, may have everlasting life: and I will raise him up at the last day." By then, she had figured out that all the red words were spoken by Jesus and "the Son" referred to him. "But how can anyone *see* Jesus when he lived so long ago?"

Sighing with frustration, she dropped the Bible into the drawer where she had found it.

~*~

On Monday, Charles and Tory met with the contractor and, within a fortnight, the renovation commenced. Tory was involved in all aspects of the work; as Charles was often occupied elsewhere, the foreman became accustomed to finding Tory at her desk and asking direction from her.

As for the rest of Tory's day, it was spent with an accountant who reviewed Mr. Visser's books, established a new set of books for the hotel, and transferred a correct balance from the old books to the new ones. He then tutored Tory in the correct manner of keeping the new books current and correct.

After observing Tory and correcting her mistakes for two days, he announced, "I shall come back next Friday and review your work. If I find errors, we shall amend them together so you might learn from your mistakes."

"Thank you. I shall do my best."

"You shall do well, if your progress to date is any indication," he replied.

~*~

SEPTEMBER 1907

Tory opened the hotel's books and turned them toward Charles. "Do look here, Charles. At present, we are renting all the remodeled first-floor hotel rooms. This is a notable success, but our expenses, including the monthly payment to Mr. Connally, consume all of our income.

"Construction on the second floor of the north wing cannot go forward, and we have saved nothing toward the second half of the cash payment. This leaves us at an impasse. If we do not have more rooms to let, we cannot increase revenue, but without increased revenue, we cannot save for the second half of the cash payment."

She swallowed before adding, "And the payment is due in six months."

Charles looked away, then back. "I must be adding to our coffers."

Tory searched his face—an older face to her eyes, not belonging to the daring and confident man who had rescued her from the streets of New Orleans nearly five years past.

"How?"

"I can still play cards, Tory."

She jumped to her feet. "*No*. You promised—*no more gambling*."

"Circumstances, not good intentions, dictate our paths, Tory. I am, perhaps, not as sharp as I once was but, if I am careful, I can still bring in a steady income until the hotel is solvent. I would not involve you in the games, of course. Your job would be here, helping me to manage the hotel."

Tory stared at him, unspeaking.

Charles pursed his lips. "And I will require a stake if I am to bring in the needed funds."

"You have no money left?"

"Precious little, Tory. I've sunk everything into the hotel."

"Then where—"

"I must borrow from the hotel's accounts."

"But . . ." Tory, who oversaw the accounts and paid the bills, knew they had no margin between their account balance and the bills coming due.

"Decide which bills you can let slip for a few weeks, Tory, and provide me with the cash I need. I will require at least five hundred dollars."

"Five hundred!"

"The games I will seek to join are with players who can afford to lose."

With sinking spirits, Tory nodded. "If you say so, Charles."

Later that day, having tussled with the upcoming bills and chosen which she would allow to lapse into the "past due" category, Tory walked to the bank and withdrew five hundred dollars. Before she left, she carefully noted in the ledgers that the funds were withdrawn at Charles' instruction and that she was giving them directly into his hands. Then she drew up a separate paper.

Tory set the bundled cash and the note on Charles' desk. "Please sign this before you take the money," Tory murmured.

"What is it?"

"A note authorizing me to withdraw the funds at your direction and acknowledging your receipt of them."

Charles snorted. "Not very trusting of you, Tory."

"It has more to do with trust than you think, Charles. You entrusted me with the hotel's finances. Well, I take that commission seriously and insist on managing my responsibilities in a forthright manner."

Charles signed the note without comment and pocketed the money. "I will be out late this evening."

Tory stopped at the door and said, "I wish you good luck."

Tory did not know how late Charles stayed out, but he did not make an appearance at breakfast. When she saw him midmorning, he looked tired but triumphant.

"How did you do?"

"For a first night, as a new face, I played conservatively. Still, I came out a hundred dollars ahead."

Tory released a sigh of relief. "This is not the direction I had hoped we would go, but I am glad of your success."

Three evenings a week after that, Charles left the hotel to play cards. His late nights meant he slept in the following mornings, and Tory found that more and more of the responsibility of the hotel fell on her.

For room, board, and five dollars a month, she complained silently. She did not, however, see a way out of their impasse. Either Charles brought home additional funds, or they would not make the second half of their down payment on the hotel. To that end, she banked every dollar of the winnings he brought home, maintaining his stake at the initial five hundred dollars.

She had started to hope they might make the payment on time when Charles came to her office mid-November and closed the door.

"I will need another stake."

Tory swallowed. "You lost last night?"

"And the night before that."

"But . . . if I withdraw another five hundred dollars, that is half of what we have saved toward the second part of the down payment."

"And we are still five hundred ahead, are we not? Five hundred we would not have had?"

Tory could not argue with him. "I will go to the bank after lunch."

She did not say what was obvious: Barring a miracle, they would not make their March deadline.

~*~

DECEMBER 1907

"I would like the hotel done up right for Christmas, Tory." Charles drew on his cigarette, but the haze of smoke he released did not disguise the dark circles beneath his eyes and the new lines at the corners of his mouth. "We need to entice the holiday revelers, capitalize on the influx of visitors the city will receive through New Year's."

"What did you have in mind?" Tory had stopped presenting the accounts to Charles. He understood how perilously close to losing the hotel they were without seeing the numbers.

"A large decorated tree in the lobby, bows and greenery throughout the lobby and dining room." He waved away the smoke. "I leave it to you to present the old girl in the best possible light."

Changing the subject—as he always seemed to do to avoid any talk of their accounts—he asked, "Have we guests in our large suite?"

"Not at present."

"Hold it back, please. One of my new acquaintances is expecting an old friend, a Mr. Holmes, to visit Denver next week. This acquaintance promised to send Holmes to my hotel."

"Is this . . . guest also a card player?"

"No, but, according to my acquaintance, Mr. Holmes has, in the past year, come into a considerable fortune. I would have him spend it with us rather than elsewhere. My acquaintance also tells me Mr. Holmes may be looking for investment opportunities."

Charles sighed. "More to my point, I hope to persuade Mr. Holmes to invest in the Broadmoor. While I regret the necessity of parting with a share of the Broadmoor's ownership, I would regret the hotel's loss more if we are unable to meet our obligations."

Tory nodded, relieved and glad of Charles' concession to their precarious position. "All right, Charles. I will present the Broadmoor in its most advantageous light and do my best to make Mr. Holmes amenable to your proposition."

~*~

The week before Christmas, the guests Charles expected arrived. Tory had whipped the staff into a flurry of Christmas decorating and had turned out the lobby in exquisite style.

"Tory, may I present Mr. Darius Holmes and his granddaughter, Miss Belinda Holmes?"

Tory inclined her head to a bent, gray-haired gent and his companion, a delicate blonde in her early thirties. Tory stood a head taller than the gentleman and towered over his granddaughter.

Charles looked from their guests to Tory. "And this is my foster daughter, Victoria Washington. She was the daughter of an old and dear friend and, as my foster daughter, I have taken the affectionate liberty of calling her Tory."

"It is my pleasure to meet you, Mr. Holmes and Miss Holmes; welcome to the Broadmoor." Tory smiled and extended her hand to them.

"Delighted, my dear, simply delighted to be here," Mr. Holmes murmured, giving her hand a perfunctory squeeze. His accent confirmed his distinctly Southern origins.

As Tory offered her hand to Miss Holmes, the woman shifted her gaze back to Charles. Tory kept her hand extended a moment before she drew it back to her side, telling herself that Miss Holmes had merely missed her gesture.

"I must say, Miss Washington, the lobby is stunning," Mr. Holmes added. "Festive and breathtaking. Of course, not as breathtaking as you— you are *quite* lovely." He peered up at her with much the same awe as a boy staring through the window of a candy store.

"You flatter me, Mr. Holmes." Tory found that she liked the old gent. "I can hear that you hail from the South, sir. May I ask where you call home?"

"The capital of Mississippi, Miss Washington. Jackson. Have you visited our fair city?"

"No, I confess that I cannot claim that honor." She turned to include his daughter. "By the way, you may be interested to know that we are installing you and Miss Holmes in our best suite, the Broadmoor Regal."

"Excellent! If it lives up to its billing, Belinda and I shall be more than comfortable."

Charles, sensing how well things were going, said, "Tory is responsible for the hotel's décor. The lobby and the Regal suite are her creations. I will allow her to show you to your rooms."

He beamed in Tory's direction. Tory, happy of his pride, lifted her chin and returned his smile with pleasure.

"Ah, that explains it," Miss Holmes murmured, the lilt of her accent as soft and silky as rose petals.

"Yes?" Charles asked.

"I am certain her tastes are as charming as they are *simple*, but I prefer my surroundings to have a certain . . . Continental flair, with the shimmer of crystal and a soupçon of gold, the rich texture of velvet and brocade."

Tory blinked. Miss Holmes had spoken as if she were not standing less than three feet from her, perfectly within earshot.

"And Mr. Luchetti—may I call you Charles?" Miss Holmes blushed. "Oh, do say I might, Mr. Luchetti? You may call me Belinda." Even before Charles responded, she took his arm. "Charles, I hope you will *personally* show us to our rooms?"

As he acquiesced and led her away, Charles seemed flustered. Everything about Miss Holmes bespoke softness and femininity: She stood less in height than her grandfather's shoulder, and her voice was as sweet as nectar, yet she had, with little effort, taken charge of the proceedings.

"My, my, my," Mr. Holmes muttered. "Well, perhaps you would do me the honor, Miss Washington?"

"But of course, Mr. Holmes."

Mr. Holmes offered Tory his arm. As they followed after Charles and Miss Holmes, the woman smiled into Charles' face. "And I must say you have done an admirable thing, *Charles*," she gushed.

"Oh? What might that be?"

"Why raising your dear Tory to from child to womanhood. Think of it: To have given her a home all these years, to have invested your time and talent in her, to have trained her in a skill that enables her to go out into the world and live an independent life? Why, a man who performs such a selfless duty, even when that duty must have been a terrible burden, is to be esteemed."

Miss Holmes smiled again. She glanced back once. When she saw Tory on her grandfather's arm, her smile wilted. As Charles threw open the door of the suite, Miss Holmes rushed to her grandfather's side and dismissed Tory with, "Thank you for looking after Grandpapa, Miss Washington. You have been most kind."

Tory nodded and pivoted on her heel, thinking, *This queen bee warrants prudence. She dips her stinger in honey.*

CHAPTER 22

The Christmas season sped by, the hotel a delightful procession of holiday activities and visitors. The influx of guests provided a layer of padding to the books that Tory hoped would continue into the new year. It did not.

The numbers of guests dropped to a low point as winter set in and visitors to Denver declined. However, Darius and Belinda Holmes tarried at the Broadmoor after Christmas. In fact, Tory was surprised, when she turned the calendar to February, that the Holmes party was still ensconced in the Broadmoor Regal suite.

And Charles, it seemed, had made it his mission to accompany them throughout the city in his ongoing effort to induce Mr. Holmes to invest in the hotel. He and Mr. and Miss Holmes were inseparable through the holidays and beyond.

Tory had been too busy through the holidays to notice Charles pulling away from her. They seldom took meals together of late, yet Charles regularly dined with Mr. Holmes and his daughter. Tory had attempted to join their table once, but Charles had given her a signal they had perfected during the years in St. Louis, a signal that simply meant, "stop," or "no."

Tory, thinking Charles to be close to inducing Mr. Holmes to buy into the hotel, had backed away and made no further efforts to join the threesome. For, in addition to Charles' signal, Tory found it obvious that Belinda Holmes would no more eat with a half-negro woman than she would dine in the gutter.

Staring at the calendar marking the first day of February, Tory's stomach clenched. She had more pressing concerns than Miss Holmes: The note for the second half of the hotel's down payment was due in four weeks.

~*~

By the time the second week of February ended, Tory had grown numb with continual worry and with the distance Charles had put between himself and their financial woes—and between himself and Tory. That morning, she beckoned Charles into her office.

"Charles, are you any closer to securing financing from Mr. Holmes?"

"Ah, Tory. Yes, um, I do wish to apprise you of my progress." He took a seat behind his little-used desk and Tory sat opposite him. Then Charles fiddled with a pencil, chewed his bottom lip, and exhaled.

Tory blinked at Charles' uncharacteristic behavior.

"The thing is—and as I am certain you are aware—if I do not come up with the remainder of the cash payment by the first of next month, the man from whom I purchased the hotel will move to repossess it. I must act quickly to avert this disaster."

"Act quickly? In what way? To do what? I do not . . . I do not understand what you are saying." Tory's heartbeat quickened.

"I have spent a great deal of time with the Holmeses since their arrival in December. I cautiously broached the topic of the Democratic National Convention this July, how the convention will draw upwards of forty thousand conventioneers to Denver—in addition to the fifteen thousand or so convention volunteers. I suggested to the Holmeses how this single event has the possibility of setting the Broadmoor on its feet."

"But only if we pay off the second half of the down payment first."

"Yes, of course, but even paying off the note will not save the Broadmoor." Charles exhaled again and plowed ahead. "We require a large infusion of cash to also finish the renovations before the convention so we can let all of the rooms. Only then would the Broadmoor stand a chance of regaining its previous standing."

Tory's elevated sense of apprehension jumped higher. "And how do you propose to accomplish these lofty aspirations, Charles? Where do you expect to find such money?"

Charles hesitated, then blurted, "I have asked Miss Holmes to marry me."

Tory sputtered, "What? You want to marry *that* woman, Charles? You must be mad! Surely you are joking?"

"I am not joking, Tory. Miss Holmes is her grandfather's sole heir. When Belinda and I marry, Mr. Holmes has agreed to pay the balance of the hotel's debt and provide the funds to fully remodel the north wing."

Tory felt stress bleeding from Charles as if it were blood flowing from a mortal wound.

If Mr. Holmes is going to provide such a large amount of cash—in exchange for Charles sacrificing himself on the altar of matrimony—why is Charles behaving so?

Charles stubbed out his cigarette and immediately lit another. "Tory, changes are coming to the Broadmoor and you must . . . you must ready yourself for the inevitability of such change."

"The inevitability of such change? What change?"

"It, ah, does not suit the future Mrs. Luchetti to have you continue in my employ, Tory."

Tory sat straighter. "Not continue in your employ? Why ever not?"

Charles looked away. "Miss Holmes and I will marry at the end of the month."

"In two weeks, you mean."

"Yes, and I . . . I must insist that you depart before our wedding. She wishes to exercise her own tastes over the hotel and—"

"That woman confuses garish gilt with understated, timeless elegance. Why, she would—"

"I must be clear, Tory. Miss Holmes sees you as an impediment to the hotel's, er, character."

Tory laughed. "*Me*, an impediment to the hotel's *character?*" Then his meaning became clear. "By character you mean my mixed blood. She thinks *my kind* should not represent *her* hotel. She is a bigot, Charles—she and Miss Visser are hand in glove."

Charles sighed. "Perhaps what you say is true, Tory, but Belinda—Miss Holmes—has certain, ah, sensitivities to which I must give due consideration."

"Due consideration? Consider this, Charles: Denver is not Jackson, Mississippi; Denver is not at all like Miss Holmes' precious 'Magnolia State.' How dare she—"

"You make my point for me, Tory. The survival of the hotel is at stake; I, therefore, cannot countenance any clashes between you and . . . my wife."

Tory scoffed. "Your *wife*. Does your future *wife* comprehend what she is getting? A man who prefers other m—"

In one fluid move, Charles stood, reached across his desk, and slapped the rest of Tory's words from her mouth. If Tory's heart had not been so hurt, she might have responded. As it was, she stared at Charles, not believing what he had done, not believing he would throw off their friendship of years in order to save the Broadmoor.

Charles sat back. Looked down and tried to regain his equilibrium. "You would do well to bite your tongue, Victoria."

Tory, her hand still to her face, spit back, "So it is Victoria now. After I have given and given, Charles, you turn me out? All to save your precious hotel?"

"It is not merely the hotel, Tory; it is me. I can no longer make a living at the card table, and I am too old to begin again with nothing. I must stick with the Broadmoor and make it work. And," he paused long enough to make a point, "you have often expressed your desire to be an independent woman."

Tory wanted to scream, to curse. She wanted to hurt Charles, score his face with her fingernails. But she did none of those things. By a supreme effort of her will and with the practice of years of self-effacement, Tory's expression settled to a placid state. Outwardly, she looked calm and unmoved, while within she seethed.

Instead of tossing further invective at him, she asked through numb lips, "Have you an alternative for me?"

"I began seeking suitable employment for you weeks ago, and may be fortunate in that regard."

"Oh?"

"Yes. I have invited a potential employer, a Miss Cleary, to take tea with us this afternoon. Her visit will serve as an interview of sorts."

"An interview? For what sort of employment?"

Charles stubbed out his second cigarette and lit a third. Charles' chain smoking was a nervous habit. Tory knew so from long acquaintance with him. "Miss Cleary, too, runs a guest establishment and requires a polished hostess. You have served the Broadmoor well and possess many admirable skills, Tory: You speak three languages, you play piano, and your sketching is superb. Your social graces would make you a welcome addition to any strata of society."

"But not welcome enough for your soon-to-be *wife* to publicly acknowledge me." The words slipped out before Tory knew they were there.

Charles jaw hardened as did his expression. "You should be grateful to me, Victoria. Remember the gutter from which I pulled you—a girl *of mixed blood and dubious parentage*. Remember that I saved you from being savaged by a gang of street thugs!"

His words were like blades, hurled in quick, deadly succession, but Tory said nothing. She lifted her chin and met Charles' gaze, refusing to be cowed. "You owe me the balance of my salary. I shall expect it before I go."

It was Charles who looked away first. After a moment he said, "I apologize, Tory. After all we have been through together, you deserve better from me." He sighed. "Miss Cleary will arrive at three this afternoon. Please be prepared to receive her."

"I shall be."

~*~

Tory's interview with Miss Cleary went well, although Tory was likely still too incensed to take an accurate measure of her prospective employer. The woman, possibly in her late thirties, was impeccably dressed and mannered, even if her hair seemed a deep and impossible shade of auburn.

They took tea together in Tory's suite, chatting about the weather and recent fashion trends before Tory's guest broached the primary reason for her visit.

"I manage two large and exclusive guest houses where the mountain air is bracing and the views are inspiring, Miss Washington," Miss Cleary explained, "We have a diverse but loyal clientele; my guests come for respite, relaxation, and a brief, transitory escape from the busyness of their lives in the city."

"I see. So, your lodgers come for rest and rejuvenation?"

Miss Cleary dimpled. "Rejuvenation? There you have it."

"Are these guest houses far from Denver?"

"Nearby, I assure you. Just a short jaunt up the mountain."

She dimpled again. "The village of Corinth is lovely year-round, but it is particularly stunning in early fall. The aspens, you know. They change color and set the mountains ablaze in golden fire. The journey from Denver to Corinth by rail is convenient and the destination quite worthwhile."

Tory smiled at the picture Miss Cleary painted.

"Miss Washington, our visitors delight in cultured diversion of an evening, and I am seeking a hostess who can engage in tasteful and refined conversation, discussing art, music, fashion, even politics. I understand that you speak French and Italian?"

"Yes; I am fluent in French; my Italian is good, although a bit rusty from disuse."

"And you play the piano?"

"I am unpracticed of late; a little time before the keys would set me right."

"How lovely to find a young woman of your education and abilities. You are, Miss Washington, precisely what I have been looking for."

"And the train runs regularly? How would I—"

"Miss Washington, if you agreed to work for me, it would be my particular delight to come fetch you myself, even bringing a man to handle your luggage."

Tory sipped her tea and nodded. "May I broach the subject of pay?"

"Certainly. Does fifteen dollars a month—plus room and board, of course—meet with your expectations?"

Tory was pleased, and she nodded. "It does . . . but, perhaps after I take up my duties, we discover that we do not fit?"

"One month's salary at your departure and, at your behest, we would escort you down to Denver."

Tory set her cup on its saucer. "I shall need a little time to consider your offer, Miss Cleary. Two or three days?"

Miss Cleary leaned toward Tory and took her hand in hers. "Please call me Roxanne? I know we shall get on famously."

CHAPTER 23

Soon after breakfast the following day, without knocking or asking permission to enter, Miss Visser threw open the door to Tory's suite. She stood on the suite's threshold and folded her arms across her thin bosom.

"Well, *Tory*, we've come to it at last."

"How dare you barge into my private rooms!"

Miss Visser just smiled. "You are to gather your things, Tory."

Tory stared at Miss Visser, "What do you mean?"

Miss Visser's smile was more of a triumphant smirk. "Since you were slow to accept Miss Cleary's offer of employment yesterday, Mr. Luchetti accepted for you. I am to inform you to pack your belongings."

"But—"

"You have sixty minutes to ready yourself for travel. Be downstairs at the top of the hour. Miss Cleary will call for you and accompany you to your new . . . *employment*."

Tory stood and moved toward the door. "I shall go to Charles for clarification. He will shed light—"

"Mr. Luchetti is away from the Broadmoor at present. Why, you ask? Because he did not wish to see you, Miss Washington. He was specific in that respect. His orders were that you are to pack without delay. If you decline to go with Miss Cleary, you are still required to vacate the premises today."

Tory's eyes blinked rapidly as she absorbed Miss Visser's news. Three salient facts emerged from her statements: First, Charles refused to see her, even to say goodbye. No doubt he did not wish to risk a scene as Tory left the Broadmoor. Second, he did not intend to pay her the wages he owed her.

Tory's breath caught as she grasped with what ease, with such indifference to her feelings—after nearly five years of her undivided loyalty—Charles was able to dismiss her.

Third, Tory must have made a favorable impression upon Miss Cleary for the woman to return so quickly and call for her.

She struggled with something less clear. It niggled as a vague concern in the back of Tory's mind. The sneer with which Miss Visser had uttered the word, "employment," meant something, had sent a discordant jangle down her nerves.

She came to herself. "As you wish, Miss Visser. I shall pack. Please close the door behind you."

Tory's dismissal was as chilly in its formality as she could make it.

"Oh, so proper, so hoity-toity you are! Well, not for long, I reckon." With a laugh that scraped on Tory's spine, Miss Visser slammed the door to Tory's suite.

Tory entered her bedroom, crossed to her wardrobe, pulled her suitcase from the top of it, and laid it open on her bed. She lifted the lid of her trunk. With a glance at the clock on her bureau, she began to sort through her things.

When she finished with her clothes, she went to her desk, emptied it of stationery, pens, and pencils, and placed them in her suitcase. That was when she saw the Bible she had read from only once. With a sniff of anger, she dropped it into the wastebasket.

As the lobby clock chimed the hour, Tory descended the elevator of the Broadmoor for the last time. She was dressed in her best day suit of powder blue velour with matching gloves and hat. Two Broadmoor Hotel porters carried her suitcase and trunk to the lobby.

Tory strode across the lobby; Miss Cleary was already waiting and rose to greet her with a smile.

"Ah, Miss Washington. So lovely to see you looking so well." She looked over Tory's ensemble. "Nice. Very nice, indeed. And are your bags packed and ready to go?"

"Yes. They are there, by the door."

"Excellent. Darrow will load them into the car."

That was when Tory realized Miss Cleary was not alone. A large man, his meaty hands clasped in front of him, waited for Miss Cleary's direction. Miss Cleary was, as she had been yesterday, dressed in an exquisite day ensemble—even if it was, in Tory's estimation, cut a bit too tight in all the "right" places. Darrow, on the other hand, looked uncomfortable and out of place in his black three-piece suit.

Tory eyed him, noting with distaste the perspiration that gleamed upon his upper lip and the way his gaze raked over her. As he lumbered across the lobby to take charge of her luggage, Tory turned to the other woman.

"Miss Cleary—Roxanne—I wish to ask a few additional questions, if I may."

Miss Cleary drew on her gloves and tucked her arm into Tory's in a most companionable manner. "Of course, my dear. However, shall we wait until we have caught our train? I should hate to miss it. We really must arrive in the early afternoon, not the evening. We shall have time enough aboard to discuss whatever you wish."

In step with Miss Cleary, they crossed the lobby threshold to the out-of-doors. A motorcar idled at the curb. The man Miss Cleary called Darrow finished placing her bag and trunk in the motorcar's trunk. He then opened the door to the car's rear seat.

Tory glanced back toward the Broadmoor, wondering if she should wait and try to say goodbye to Charles. *Surely this cannot be the last I shall ever see of him?*

Tory realized that she loved Charles as the foster father he had pretended he was; he had, at least in the main, been good to her since that evening when he had rescued her from the alley gang in New Orleans and taken her on the train with him to St. Louis.

Tory's hesitation caused Miss Cleary to pause with her. "I understand. Change can be difficult, Miss Washington."

"Yes, I-I suppose it can be."

"Please do not fret. You are a treasure, Miss Washington, and I shall take excellent care of you."

Tory was grateful for the older woman's steadying hand upon her arm. "Thank you. You are most kind."

The hired conveyance dropped them at Denver's Union Station, and Darrow set off to check Tory's baggage on the narrow-gauge Denver & Rio Grande Western railroad. Miss Cleary, with Tory's arm still tucked into her own, set a pace toward the D&RGW platforms.

"Shall we walk a bit?" Miss Cleary suggested. "We shall be sitting for two hours and should take our exercise while we may."

"Of course," Tory murmured.

They walked to the end of the platform where steps led down to the tracks and rail yard, then retraced their steps. By then, Darrow had returned without Tory's bags.

"Allllll aboooooooard!"

"Shall we?" Miss Cleary asked. She led Tory toward steps leading up to a sumptuous private railcar and nodded at the conductor as they prepared to mount the steps. Tory thought the man's gaze narrowed as it swept over both of them, then stopped and fixed upon her.

"How are you this morning, miss?" the conductor asked. Something in his expression was careful. Guarded.

Concerned?

Tory's brows lifted. What was the man asking of her?

"I'm certain she is fine," Miss Cleary answered. The hard, clipped edge to her words startled Tory.

The conductor stood his ground. "I was speaking to the young lady," he replied. He asked again, "Are you all right, miss? Is anyone . . . forcing you to go with this . . . woman?"

That was when Darrow stepped forward. He reached around Tory and placed his ham-sized palm on the conductor's chest, pushing him back.

"This is a private car. Mind your own business," he growled.

Miss Cleary pulled Tory up the steps, but Tory's head swiveled to look back at the conductor. For a moment, before Darrow's hulking frame obstructed her view, she sought the conductor's eyes: They held a resigned sadness that she did not understand.

Miss Cleary drew her into the car and gestured to a velvet upholstered seat. "Please sit wherever you like, Tory. This is our employer's own personal car."

Tory wandered halfway through the car before sitting. Miss Cleary sat across from her while Darrow chose to stand near the door into the car. He said nothing, but Tory had the uncomfortable sensation that the man was there to see that she did not leave the car.

Moments later the train began to move. Tory, as nervous as she had ever been, gazed out the windows, hoping the scenery would calm her. Soon, the train cleared the station and began a sweeping turn toward the mountains to their west.

Tory had seen these mountains from her rooms at the Broadmoor. She was thrilled to see the train drawing closer to them.

"Could you be more specific regarding the nature of the work I shall do for you, Miss Cleary?"

The woman pursed her lips—as though what Tory had asked amused her—but she smothered the smile and answered, "Not for me, Miss Washington, but for our mutual employer. He lives in Denver, but keeps the two guest houses in Corinth. He has exclusive tastes, and wishes the houses to be managed in only the best manner."

"I see. But what, precisely, will my role be?"

Miss Cleary smiled again, this time a bit more openly. "As I said before, *hostess*, my dear. Our employer entertains frequently, and his hospitality is lavish. Your position will be in the larger of the two houses."

Tory digested the information. "Could you describe the house, please?"

"Certainly. A lovely, three-story mountain home with an expansive lawn. You will have your own room, of course, near the top of the house. I should prepare you, however. Although it is almost March and nearly spring here in Denver, up high in the mountains we are still subject to snow."

Miss Cleary's caution was needed. The train entered a steep, snow-crusted ravine and made slow turn after turn, inching higher. When they emerged from the ravine and drew near their destination, the sun glistened off new-fallen snow—a spring snow, Miss Cleary called it.

Corinth did not boast a station. All Tory saw as they disembarked were banks of snow everywhere, a little snow-bound siding, and a faded sign that read, *Corinth, Colorado. Altitude 7,586 feet.* Someone had shoveled a path through the siding, but the sign, fastened near the top of its post, poked out from a high drift.

A motorcar waited for them where a beaten track indicated an unpaved road. As Darrow and the car's driver transferred her bags to the car, Miss Cleary steered Tory to the rear seat.

In awe of the winter wonderland surrounding them, Tory looked around. When she saw not another person save the driver of the automobile, she shivered. In fact, the only sign of civilization anywhere was a wisp of smoke emerging from a stand of trees not far from the platform.

Tory, growing more nervous as Miss Cleary opened the door to the motorcar, asked, "What is over there, please?"

"Ah. That, my dear, is the home and workshop of Corinth's smithy. Not a lot of call for a smithy these days, but the railroad occasionally has need of him."

Perhaps the smoke is from his forge, Tory thought.

As she gave a final glance in that direction, she saw a man, no longer young, she deduced, based on his stooped posture and faded red hair. The man stared at her, a frown etched on his features.

Their eyes met—and Tory felt a sudden compulsion to run to him for shelter. She turned, but Darrow blocked her way. With reluctance, she joined Miss Cleary in the motorcar. Darrow climbed in after her and shut the door, sandwiching Tory between him and Miss Cleary.

Tory's heart pounded in her chest and she had difficulty breathing. *I am in trouble. Something is so wrong. Oh, why did I come with this woman?*

They did not drive far, and no one spoke; Tory noted a few scattered houses and then a small plaza surrounded by a small number of unassuming businesses. Not long after, the car entered a modest neighborhood, wound its way up a sweeping drive, and arrived at a magnificent house. Nearby, Tory saw a second house of similar grandeur.

Neither house seemed in keeping with the tiny village. They were both too large, too ostentatious, their grounds too pristine.

"This way, my dear," Miss Cleary murmured.

Tory's heart thudded and skipped as they mounted the steps to the house's grand entrance. Miss Cleary knocked, and a man in a shiny black suit opened to them.

"Welcome home, Miss Cleary."

Tory followed Miss Cleary into a wide foyer where the man began to take and hang their cloaks in a closet at the base of a wide staircase. The man nodded once to Tory.

Tory glanced at him, then toward the stairs. She thought she heard soft feminine voices from the floors above.

"Thank you, William. Please have Gretl serve tea in the parlor."

"Right away, miss."

Miss Cleary turned to Darrow. "Have Tory's things taken upstairs."

She beckoned to Tory. "Come with me, Tory. We will warm ourselves in the parlor while I acquaint you with your duties with us."

Miss Cleary led the way through an arched doorway into the largest, most luxurious parlor Tory had even seen: In size, it rivaled the lobby of the Broadmoor. Tory swept her eyes around the room, taking in a roaring fire in a marbled fireplace, thick carpets, the gleaming wood of fine furniture, and a large bar surrounded by mirrors and shelves of crystal glasses and stemware.

"You must be cold, Tory, as am I. Do warm yourself by the fire while our cook prepares tea. When she serves us, then we shall talk."

Tory walked to the fireplace and turned her back to it. She appreciated the heat radiating from the fire in more ways than one—for the chill she felt was not from the wintry weather outside. Tory had felt Miss Cleary's attitude shift subtly the moment they set foot within the house, and Tory's misgivings grew stronger. She could not stop clenching her hands together—she fought a wild urge to run to the front entrance, grab her cloak, and flee down the long drive.

Yes, it is cold outside, but I could walk back to the siding. Perhaps the smithy would let me wait with him for the next train?

Miss Cleary had taken an opulent, high-backed chair for her seat. She watched Tory, a soft smile playing on her lips, her fingers tapping gently against the chair's arm.

William, the man who had opened the front door for them, reappeared.

"Gretl will serve tea directly, Miss Cleary."

"Thank you, William."

Tory watched William take up a position near the arched doorway to the foyer, his hands folded before him. She had a terrifying apprehension that William was there to prevent her from leaving, should she try. So great were her apprehensions that she had to clench her jaws together to keep her teeth from chattering.

She stared at the rich carpet under her feet, visualizing the faded verse folded into the secret pocket in her corset: *For I know the thoughts that I think toward you, saith the Lord, thoughts of peace, and not of evil, to give you an expected end.*

Tory shivered all over. *I do not know what is happening. I sense such . . . evil—yes, evil!—in this place, and I am so scared!*

"Ah! Here we are."

Tory's head snapped up when Roxanne spoke. A plain, plump young woman, her expression carefully neutral, carried a tea tray into the parlor. She set it on the low table before Miss Cleary's chair, bobbed a curtsy, and disappeared as quietly as she had appeared.

"Come take tea with me, Tory."

Tory started to seat herself on the couch.

"Sit here, please." Miss Cleary indicated a narrow chair next to her, its back to the foyer. To William. Her tone broached no disagreement.

Tory glanced at the man before she sank onto the chair. She felt her chest would explode, so rapidly was her heart beating.

Miss Cleary busied herself pouring tea. "Cream or sugar, Tory?"

Tory licked her dry lips. "Sugar, please."

Miss Cleary handed her a cup and saucer. "There now. Isn't this cozy?" She sipped from her own cup and sighed. "Ah, I did need this. It has been a long day already."

Tory tasted her own tea. The hot, familiar sweetness was calming. "A long day already? Is . . . is there more of this day before you?"

Miss Cleary chuckled over her cup. "Oh, my. Yes, indeed. Our 'day' begins in earnest at six o'clock and it is already near three."

"Our day?" Again, Tory heard the sound of voices—women's voices—echoing faintly down the stairs. "Miss Cleary, who else is in the house? Are those guests I hear?"

"No, Tory. Our guests do not begin arriving until six each evening."

Tory swallowed more tea, her hand rattling the cup when she replaced it on the saucer. "Each evening? But I thought you said the guests came for the brisk mountain air? How do they not arrive earlier in the day? And do they not spend the night?"

"Our clients come up from the city every evening and return in the early morning hours, Tory."

Tory did not like the direction of the conversation. She sat her cup and saucer upon the table. "Miss Cleary, I confess that I am uncomfortable—and I have reconsidered my acceptance of your offer. I wish to return to Denver. Now. This evening, in fact, since you assure me that the trains run at night."

Miss Cleary finished her tea as if she had not heard Tory. "Tory, I took you to be a discerning young woman, knowledgeable of the ways of the world. Do you not yet understand what this house is? What we do here?"

Tory stared at Miss Cleary. Fearing her. Loathing her. "I do not care what this house is. I wish to leave, to go back to Denver. Now. Tonight."

Miss Cleary smiled a lazy smile. "Ah, Tory. This house and the one 'next door,' so to speak, are the most exclusive brothels in all Colorado. We service only the rich and the famous. In *this* house, our ladies are handsome, cultured, educated, and *talented*—if you take my meaning. You, my dear, will be a perfect addition to our selection of beauties."

Miss Cleary's words roared in Tory ears; the point of every qualm and reservation crystalized and became clear.

"Brothel? No. *No*, I will not!"

Tory lurched to her feet, disconcerted to feel William's presence behind her. He placed his hands on her shoulders and pressed her back into the chair. Held her there.

"Stop that! Let me go!" Tory tried to push his hands off, but William's fingers were strong, and she could not move them.

Miss Cleary leaned toward her. "Tory, compose yourself." It was not a request; it was a command.

Tory, her eyes wide, fixed them on the woman who was openly mocking her now. Her terror increased.

"I give my new girls a choice, Tory, always. I will put that choice to you also. You may choose to acquiesce to my expectations of you, or I shall have a few of my men 'convince' you to acquiesce."

"You want me to become a prostitute?" Tory moved her head back and forth. "No. I will never do that."

Miss Cleary stood and slowly inclined her head. "As you wish. William?"

William looped one arm about Tory's neck and grasped its wrist with his other hand. He began to squeeze, just enough to cut off Tory's air.

Frantic, Tory struggled, but she could not free herself. Her arms flailed, and her fingers scrabbled at his grip and could find no purchase. She kicked out at Miss Cleary, but the woman dodged Tory's boots and stepped to her side. The room whirled and spun, and darkness encroached. A sharp buzzing grew louder in her head until . . . she passed into darkness.

"You may take her," Miss Cleary directed.

William picked Tory up, slung her over his shoulder, and followed Miss Cleary up the broad staircase and around a corner to a second set of stairs. He carried Tory into a third-floor room at the end of the hall, a room that contained only a narrow bed, a wardrobe, and a small vanity.

He dropped Tory on the bed.

"I will send another man to join you, William—but you both know the rules. When she wakes, I want her suitably broken in. However, other than a few bruises, you must not mark her. Not this first time."

"I understand, Miss Cleary."

"Oh! And be mindful of the time. We have but a few hours until our guests arrive. You will be needed downstairs by dinner time. When you have finished with the girl, dose her with laudanum. I do not wish our guests to be disturbed by her cries or screams."

"Yes, Miss Cleary."

CHAPTER 24

Tory awoke to terror. All around her was darkness except the faint outline of narrow windows across the room. She fought against the weights that held her—until she realized she was hopelessly tangled in harmless sheets and blankets. Eventually, she disentangled herself and turned over—only to slide off the edge of an unfamiliar bed onto the floor.

Tory had to hold the edge of the bed as she picked herself up. She was weak and unsteady.

Disoriented.

Fearful.

Naked.

And in pain.

Where am I? What—

Like a fearsome wave, the remembrance of what had happened earlier when she woke in this room crashed over her: Two men had taken turns violating her.

Tory heaved and threw up on the floor. She retched again and again. When her body had purged itself, she fumbled for a corner of a sheet and wiped her mouth.

She was parched, but she did not care. *I must get away from this place!*

Tory staggered toward the dimly outlined windows and found them shrouded in heavy curtains. When she swept one panel aside, sunlight poured into the room. She covered her throbbing eyes until they could bear the brightness.

Tory gazed on the scene far below her—at high drifts and virgin powder untouched by human foot or conveyance, the sun's rays glancing off new-fallen snow. She shielded her eyes against the intense light, but everywhere she looked was snow and more snow.

She then spied other houses, smaller, more in keeping with the mountain hamlet, not far away. *I must be at the top of this house. Third floor? And I have been here longer than I thought, for the night has passed and it is fully morning.* Then she remembered. *They forced me to drink something . . . afterward. They drugged me.*

She listened . . . and heard nothing. Sweeping the rest of the drapes apart, she searched around the room, hoping to find her clothes and boots.

After I dress, perhaps I can sneak down the stairs and get away.

Tory saw nothing in the room that belonged to her. She rushed to the high wardrobe and flung open its doors. The lingerie she saw hanging within brought up her gorge. Again, she vomited, although only a little fluid came up.

Nothing. Not a single stitch of my own clothing in this room—only these ... trollop garments. Tory ran to the window a second time, gauging the distance to the ground and the depth of the drifts. *I do not know what lies beneath the snow. If I dropped naked from this window, would I survive?*

Smoke rose from the chimneys of the little houses so close but inaccessible. *Would the people take me in? Would they believe me?*

Tory heard voices outside her door and froze.

"She's awake, Miss Cleary. I hear her moving around."

A man—a guard—had been outside her door all along.

I am a prisoner!

The door opened. Tory grabbed at a drape and wrapped it about her.

Miss Cleary entered. Behind her were two men—Darrow and another she did not recognize.

"Ah, I see you are up, Tory. The rest of the girls are still abed, of course, and I hope we can allow them their sleep. They work hard each evening and must have their rest for their labors tonight."

Tory clung to the drape and did not answer, but Miss Cleary advanced toward her. The two men followed her.

Miss Cleary arranged her skirts to sit on the only chair in the room, a tiny seat in front of the room's vanity. She clasped her hands over her knees. "As I said yesterday, Tory, I operate two houses here in Corinth, two houses with distinctly different purposes to service our clients' varying needs."

She indicated the house they were in. "We proudly advertise this house as the 'Corinth Gentlemen's Club,' the more exclusive of my employer's houses. Nothing in Denver compares to the Corinth Gentlemen's Club, I assure you.

"We generally bring new girls to our "lower" house where our guests pay a high price for the experience of, shall we say, a younger girl. These girls are not talented, merely innocent. I assumed that you, as a more independent and womanly acquisition, could begin here where culture and accomplishments are our stock in trade.

"Last evening, in the most glowing of terms, I announced your addition to our stable of girls. You should have witnessed the enthusiasm!

"I described you as tall, graceful, and as regal as an African princess, accomplished, and fluent in French and Italian. You created quite a stir, I assure you."

She arched her brows at Tory. "This evening, I expect you to dress in the clothes I shall supply you, join the rest of the house for dinner, and present yourself in the parlor as our guests arrive. Several of our gentlemen have already reserved you."

"No."

Miss Cleary looked at her hands. "I understand your reticence; however, you seem like a level-headed young woman, Tory, able to grasp life as it is, rather than how you may wish it. Therefore, I must speak plainly. I do not know how to convey to you otherwise the gravity of this moment—*this single choice*—in terms you will both understand and, if you have the good sense I believe you have, will yield to. I can but do my best."

Miss Cleary crooked her finger. The two men stepped forward. Tory saw their repressed excitement.

"This is how it works, Tory. Last evening, I gave you to Michael and Thomas. I'm certain you remember the experience? Ah, I see that you do. We often break in our new girls in such a manner—but, aside from having their way with you, I did not permit Michael and Thomas to *harm* you. However, that is not how we will go on.

"At our club, we pride ourselves in providing the best girls money can buy—only the most beautiful and gifted conversationalists and musicians. This is where I attempt to convince you to join our merry band—or, if I fail, I allow these gentlemen to try their hand and their . . . convincing measures."

Tory's glance flicked from her to Darrow and his companion. Darrow's small, piggy eyes gleamed with appreciative avarice.

"Yes, that is right, Tory. You must decide *now* to accede to my wishes. If you do not, I will give you to Darrow and Jingo." Miss Cleary's eyes narrowed. "I really *prefer* not to resort to such barbaric measures, but they have my leave to enjoy themselves with you until they tire of you, and to employ their fists anywhere on your body they like—except your face. Unless necessary, we do not like to mar our girls' faces, do we, gentlemen?"

"No, ma'am," Darrow whispered. "Unless necessary."

"So, what will it be, Tory? You choose. A half-dozen well-mannered gentlemen this evening? Or Darrow and Jingo and whatever punishments they wish to dole out?"

Tory closed her eyes and saw the futility of her situation. Nothing could save her from what Miss Cleary described. Nothing.

Tory turned further inward. She pictured her mother before Bastiann Declouette; she saw Adeline capitulating to him—but only after Bastiann had threatened to violate her daughter.

Me. You were willing to forfeit yourself in this way for me, Maman, to protect me. I shall not lightly throw away what you were willing to sacrifice yourself to save. I will not give in to this woman and her threats. These men may break me, but I will not make it easy for them.

Her words quavering, giving lie to the decision of her will, Tory said quietly, "I will not be a whore for you."

Miss Cleary tilted her head, considering Tory. "I thought as much."

To Darrow and Jingo, she said, "I believe Tory to have exceptional strength of character. Rather than prolong her rebellion, I will forego my usual restrictions. You have my leave to use whatever means are necessary to force her capitulation."

"Yes, ma'am!"

Darrow's eager grin elicited a sharp rebuke. "I warn you, Mr. Darrow: Do not break any bones. She must heal and be ready to work five to seven days from now."

She stood, sighing. "As it is, I shall have several disappointed clients this evening."

~*~

"There, there. Do not struggle so, Tory."

The soft voice belonged to a young girl, not Miss Cleary. Tory moaned as a cold cloth dabbed at her mouth.

"I know it hurts, but I must clean it. I shall be as gentle as I can be."

Tory tried to open her eyes. She commanded her eyelids to rise, but one of them refused to respond; the other lifted only a little, affording Tory but a cloudy glimpse of the person who tended her.

A lamp near the bed glowed with low light, and a girl with a wealth of honey-brown hair soaked a rag in a basin. When she turned, Tory again recoiled.

"I promise not to intentionally hurt you, Tory, but I must get you cleaned up."

The girl hesitated, and Tory thought she frowned. "The blood has dried and crusted. It would be painful for me to keep dabbing at or rubbing your wounds, so I am going to place this wet cloth on your face and allow it to soften the dried blood."

She laid the cold rag across Tory's face. At first it stung like fire, but soon the cloth's coolness seeped into Tory's skin, soothing her. Without meaning to, Tory drifted off to sleep. She woke a while later when the cloth was lifted.

"Much better, I think. I'll try sponging you with a bit of warm water now." She returned with a warm cloth. "I am Helen, by the way. Helen Hawthorne."

She washed Tory's face, rinsing the rag many times, before applying an ointment. Tory kept her eyes closed and her body immobile. Her mind kept replaying what Darrow and Jingo had done to her—in addition to the hitting, slapping, and pinching—and she was afraid to move her body, was repulsed to acknowledge how they had used her. Had owned her.

She had never felt such deep shame.

"Tory, I must bathe the rest of you, now," Helen whispered.

"No . . . No, please . . ."

"I-I am so sorry, but Miss Cleary insists that I . . . clean you."

Another choice removed.

To escape the backdrop of last night's horror and the present invasion of her privacy, Tory willed herself to drift away. She returned to Sugar Tree, to the grassy orchard and the distant, shimmering river. She wandered toward the scent of lilacs and the sounds of Sassy singing to herself while frying catfish on the old cookstove.

Tory cried out as the pain jerked her back to reality.

"I am so sorry, Tory. You are torn; it will hurt until you heal."

Tory heard something in Helen's apology. She opened the one eye that would obey her. Yes, tears stood in Helen's eyes, even as she finished her ministrations and lifted the sheet to cover Tory.

Helen swiped away her tears. "I must get some food and water in you now. I have water and a bit of soup here. It is all Miss Cleary will allow you . . . until you join us at the table." She held a glass to Tory's mouth.

When the precious liquid reached Tory's throat, she coughed and choked. Helen lifted her up to sitting and held the glass to her lips again. Tory drank it all.

"More, please."

She downed another full glass. "More."

"I am sorry. You are not allowed any more. Take a spoonful of broth, instead."

Tory did, but the salt in the soup stung where fists had struck, cutting the inside of her mouth against her teeth. She refused more.

"I will come back later, Tory. Please rest now."

Helen placed her hand on Tory's forehead and caressed her. Tory focused on the gentle touch of the girl's fingers until she slept again.

When she awoke, she heard low, feminine voices prattling softly, and the swish of dress and footstep as they passed her door. Although her head pounded, she forced her eyes to open.

The nearby lamp still burned, and Tory could see enough to make out the furnishings. She needed to use the room's chamber pot most desperately, so she sat up, groaning as she did. Her fingers explored tender places on her chest, stomach, and legs, knowing they were bruised, remembering the blows that had inflicted so much agony.

Eventually, Tory swung her legs over the side of the bed and stood. When she had relieved herself, she checked the door to her room: locked from the outside.

She crawled back into the bed. Her mind drifted. She was back at the Broadmoor, choosing wallpaper for the grand suite, discussing carpet with Charles and—

Charles.

Charles had deceived her. He had betrayed her trust, had knowingly sent her to this hellhole. She wondered how it was that he could go to such lengths—*and such depths*—to rid himself of her . . . simply to please *Belinda Holmes*, all to save himself and his precious hotel.

Tears leaked from under Tory's swollen lids. "I trusted you. You said you cared for me like a father cares for a daughter, Charles, but you lied."

~*~

Helen returned hours later in the still-dark hours of morning to bring Tory a little more water and help her to the chamber pot. "I must go to my room and sleep now, but I have left a half-filled glass for you on the table. Please try to rest more, Tory."

Tory's mouth was sore and her tongue was thick, but she spoke anyway. "Th-thank you for . . . kindness."

Helen took Tory's hand. "It was not that long ago that I was the one lying in that bed, Tory. I am grieved you have come to this . . . place. I know what they did to you. All I can say is that if you set your mind to survive here, you can do it."

Tory managed to shake her head. "No. Want . . . die."

Helen bowed her head. "I understand. It would be a mercy."

It would be a mercy.

Helen's words repeated in Tory's mind, even as dreamless sleep sucked her down into insensibility.

~*~

Tory woke again to the stirring of the house, girls' whispers, shuffling feet, creaking floors, and closing doors. The door to her room opened. Helen peeked in.

"You are awake? Good. Miss Cleary has directed me to tend you as soon as breakfast is over. I will be back shortly."

A while later, Helen returned with a tray. She again washed Tory's wounds and applied ointment. Then she offered Tory a spoonful of broth.

The salty bouillon still stung the inside of Tory's mouth, but Tory sucked it down. Helen handed Tory the cup and spoon to feed herself. She was ravenous and drank down the broth in moments.

Helen saw the hunger for more in Tory's eyes. "I need to tell you something, Tory."

Wary, Tory waited.

"I need to tell you . . . that this place has rules. Strict rules. When we break a rule—any rule—the punishment is . . . severe."

Tory watched Helen's face, noting the sorrow and compassion on it.

"You are recovering from your first beating, but they will not hesitate to beat you again—any and every time you defy Miss Cleary or break a rule. This, what I am doing for you? Every girl here is, eventually, required to do the same for another new girl. I am helping you, but I am also 'putting you in the know,' apprising you of Miss Cleary's rules.

"One of her rules is that a girl who does not work, does not eat. You will receive nothing more than water and a twice-daily dish of broth until you begin to work for Miss Cleary. That is how she controls us: She withholds food and water, and she directs Darrow and his men to beat us and . . . use us."

Helen sighed. "When Miss Cleary speaks, the only acceptable answer is, 'Yes, Miss Cleary.' If we talk back, if we refuse, if we exhibit a 'bad' attitude? We are punished. We are not permitted to call her 'Roxanne'— although behind her back we often do. We are careful with our little rebellions, Tory, for if we are caught mocking her, we are punished.

"When you are nearly recovered and are entirely hungry, Miss Cleary will call you to her office. One of us girls will help you undress before her. She will examine you and determine whether you are well enough to work."

Helen gathered the rags and empty dishes onto the tray. "Miss Cleary has certain expectations of her girls: We must always be cheerful and willing, and we must not complain. The cardinal rule, the law above all others? We must never create a scene before our guests. Those who do so disappear, Tory. They are taken away immediately. We never see them again."

Tory began to tremble, then shake, and Helen clasped her hand.

"Listen to me, Tory. Your bruises will fade. In a few days, Miss Cleary will call you to her office." Taking a deep breath, Helen added, "Now that you understand the rules and the consequences of defying them, you need to consider carefully what your response to Miss Cleary will be."

Tory's breath was moving in and out so quickly that Helen squeezed her hand. Hard.

"Be careful, Tory. I do not want to see you hurt again."

With that, Helen picked up the tray and left.

Faint from her rapid, shallow breaths, Tory stared at the walls.

O God, if you exist? O God . . . I am calling on you. Please help me.

~*~

Three afternoons later, Tory stood stiff and mistrustful before Miss Cleary. A girl who said her name was Sarah had helped Tory into a robe and led her downstairs to Miss Cleary's office. Sarah stood by in passive silence while Miss Cleary examined Tory's naked body. Then, at the wave of Miss Cleary's hand, Sarah departed, as silent as she had arrived.

"You may don your robe, Tory. But tell me, how do you feel today?"

Tory managed to croak, "Better."

"Your bruises are quite faded now. Have you thought of what we discussed when you first arrived? Are you prepared to go to work this evening?"

Tory did not answer, but all the moisture in her mouth dried at the recollection of what Miss Cleary expected of her. She tried to swallow and began coughing.

"Dear me. Do take a little water, Tory." Miss Cleary stood and poured water from a crystal decanter into a glass. She put her arm about Tory and held the glass to Tory's mouth.

"Sip it. That's it. You have had a terrible time; you must be parched—and famished, too."

Tory *was* famished, something Miss Cleary knew full well. She had allowed Tory nothing in five days except a single cup of broth, morning and evening, and limited water.

While Tory obeyed Miss Cleary's injunction to sip at the glass the woman held, Tory was determining whether or not she could kill the woman. *I am taller and likely stronger than she is; if I grabbed the decanter, I could strike her over the head and . . .*

Tory could not get past "strike her over the head" for, in her mind, she continued to strike Miss Cleary—again and again and *again* and ***again***.

She did not realize she had gone still, her eyes fixed on the heavy decanter.

"You must not entertain such thoughts, Tory. Why, even if you were to succeed in harming me, do you know how many men surround this house? Do you comprehend what they would do—*will do*—to you should you attempt to run?"

Tory shifted her gaze to Miss Cleary's face. "I will not do what you ask," she whispered.

Miss Cleary sighed. "It distresses me to hear this, Tory." She returned to her desk and reached for the nearby silver bell. Her hand hovered just above it. "Shall I ring for Darrow and his men to escort you back upstairs?"

Tory felt her determination crumble. "No!" In a smaller voice she pleaded, "No, please do not."

"Then will you agree to dress for the evening and take up your responsibilities? Will you do this, or shall I ring for Darrow?"

"No—I mean . . . yes." Tory sobbed, just once. "Yes, I will . . . dress for the evening."

"And take up your responsibilities? I really must hear you submit to me, Tory."

"Yes . . . I will take up my . . . my responsibilities."

"Good. Now, be aware: Darrow will be your shadow this evening. If he perceives any but the most pleasing of behaviors, he will escort you from the room. However, if you charm our guests—as I am persuaded you are capable of doing—we shall have no difficulties and you will discover that life here is not terribly strenuous."

Miss Cleary folded her hands. "Our daily schedule begins thusly: My girls rise at ten each morning, partake of breakfast in the dining room, and perform their daily chores. I assign chores according to what must be done and who is best suited. Later, we have dinner and receive our guests."

She glanced at the clock on her desk. "Ah. It is half past three o'clock now. Dinner is at five; our guests begin arriving at six. You may go now to attend to your dress and appearance."

"Miss Cleary?" Tory had to know. She had to know if Charles had knowingly sent her to this place, to suffer a life of humiliation and shame. She had to know if, after all they had weathered together, he had chosen to sell her into slavery.

"Yes, Tory?"

"I wish to know, that is, could you tell me if . . . if Charles knew?"

The woman studied her. "Did Mr. Luchetti know who I was and what sort of 'employment' I was offering you?"

Tory blinked away tears of betrayal. "Yes. Did he . . . did he . . ."

Miss Cleary laughed softly. "No. Mr. Luchetti may be a fool, but he is innocent of that charge."

"But then, who? How?"

"Ah! Now, *that* is the right question! You wish to know whom to spend your nights hating? Is that what you are asking?"

Tory stared at her. "Yes."

Miss Cleary laughed again. "I apologize, but this truly is delicious, and I must explain. You see, my dear, at one time, some years ago now, a friend and I shared a room. It was a dirty little room, but it was all we could afford working together in a factory as we were.

"We were young and grew weary of the squalid life, and I suggested that we were suited to much better things. Soon, we began 'working' on the side, shall we say, at a *different*, more lucrative sort of job. Oh, I had the aptitude and ambition for it, but my friend, I fear, did not. When her brother's wife died unexpectedly, she moved in with him, but we kept in touch, even after I took up my position here in Corinth."

"You . . . are you describing Miss Visser?"

"You are insightful, Tory. My friend was Trudy Visser. She dislikes you, you know. You are beautiful, regal, and intelligent and, above all, you were a woman—and a black woman at that—in a man's world doing a man's job with authority and independence. I believe Trudy aspires to such independence.

"When the wealthy Miss Holmes arrived in Denver and set her cap on your Charles, Trudy saw an opportunity. You see, you were quite the impediment to Miss Holmes' aspirations, Tory. It seems Miss Holmes saw how Charles doted on you, but she desired *all* of Charles' attentions and affections. She wanted control of the hotel, too, and knew that as Charles' ally, you would withstand her. Oh, and yes—she could not abide the thought of a 'family' connection with someone of your inferior blood."

Tory's mouth opened as the pieces joined together.

"When Miss Holmes and Trudy realized they shared a common enemy—you—they became friends and confidants. Trudy suggested that I might have use for you, and dear, *sweet*, genteel little Belinda absolutely *adored* the idea."

Tory swore under her breath, using words she had heard Charles and his poker guests use when they forgot she was within earshot.

Miss Cleary's eyes glittered. "I did not agree to their scheme for the benefit of Miss Holmes, Tory. I did it for my old friend, Trudy. Miss Holmes has promised her your position in the hotel—to be advised and guided by Miss Holmes, of course, and by her impeccable élan."

Miss Cleary gave full voice to her laughter then. "I thought the décor of the Broadmoor's lobby to be exquisite—you have flawless taste, Tory. Sadly, I predict that, within the year, the Broadmoor will succumb to gold-painted furnishings and velveteen-flocked wallpaper. Really, it is too bad."

The ring of Miss Cleary's little bell startled Tory from her shock. Darrow entered the room.

"Darrow, Miss Tory will be joining us this evening. Please escort her to her new room so she may attend to her toilet. And send Helen to her to give her instructions."

Darrow showed Tory to a different room on the third floor. The room was narrow—as though the framers had built as many bedrooms onto the floor as space would allow—but the room was decorated much like the parlor—beautiful furniture, carpets, draperies, and bed linens. Helen arrived soon after.

"This is your room now," she said. "This is where you will entertain guests and sleep. When the evening ends, Darrow will give us a signal and we retire to our rooms. We are not permitted to leave our rooms until ten o'clock the following morning. They lock our doors after the club closes, in any event."

"Helen, I brought luggage with me when I came here. What became of my bag and trunk? Where are my things?"

"I am sorry, Tory. Miss Cleary does not allow us to have personal possessions unless we earn them."

"But, do you know where my clothes are?"

Helen chewed a nail. "I might—but I cannot bring them to you. You must understand, Tory. It would break a rule."

"I am only looking for one thing, Helen, something small but precious to me. It is . . . it is hidden in the corset I was wearing."

"Darrow and Jingo ruined that corset when they . . . you know. It may be in the scrap bag in the sewing room. We toss useful bits, such as buttons and stays, into the bag to replace ours when they break."

Tory's eyes implored Helen. "Can you . . . is there any way to retrieve it?"

Helen studied Tory for a long moment. "Come with me. And be quick about it."

She led Tory down a back flight of stairs to a small room on the second floor. Tory saw a sewing machine against one wall.

"Here is the scrap bag. Hurry."

The bag was deep and filled. Tory pawed through torn garments; she pressed and felt the folds of fabric, searching for whalebone stays.

"Hurry, Tory!"

Tory's fingers found the hard stays and pulled them toward her. "I have it." She undid the button on the hidden pocket and withdrew the locket. She nearly left the scrap of paper. At the last instant, she took it with her.

"Come on, Tory. We must wash and dress now."

Tory returned to her room and slipped the locket and bit of paper under her mattress. *I will find a better place to hide Maman's picture soon.* Then she turned herself to the unhappy task of preparing for the night ahead.

~*~

A few hours later, Tory stood in a corner of the parlor, surrounded by gentlemen who flattered her and, without disguising their lust, competed for her attention and time. Darrow was not far away, his piggy eyes daring Tory to fail.

"I understand that you and I have an engagement, Miss Tory," one portly man declared. He grinned around at the other guests, openly flaunting his victory. "Shall we withdraw upstairs?"

Tory nearly panicked, but one glance at Darrow returned her attention to the man who held out his hand to her. "Of course, Tobias. It is Tobias, *n'est-ce pas?*"

"Quite right, my dear!"

Her heart failing her, Tory led the way.

CHAPTER 25

Nights of agony dragged by. The "club" was closed only on Mondays, meaning the girls worked long hours, six nights a week. They had no time of their own and no interests of their own, for when they were not working or sleeping, Roxanne kept them busy. Roxanne stripped "her girls" of every vestige of freedom.

Tory had expected to feel guilt, indignation, humiliation, rage, and disgust, and she had—initially—but soon, she felt nothing. She moved through the evenings, smiling, conversing, "flirting," and "performing" in a deadened state, her emotions insensate and unresponsive. She did what she was told with a heart as frozen as an icefield—except when she pulled her locket from beneath her mattress and stared into her mother's loving eyes.

What she felt then was anxiety. Her locket was her sole connection with her past life, who she really was. She fretted over the locket, worried that someone would discover it—and her mother's irreplaceable photo— under her mattress. She understood that the discovery would result in the loss of both locket and photograph and some sort of punishment, and Tory did not relish additional punishment.

She agonized over where to best hide the locket: If she sewed it into the risqué corset she had been given, a guest might feel the slight lump of it and ask what it was, even ask to see it, and then mention it to Roxanne Cleary. In addition, where would she hide the locket when she laundered her corset?

Weighing her limited options, Tory chose what she felt was the safest course of action. Since the girls slept during the first morning hours, all the bedrooms had thick, darkening drapes. Tory stole a straight pin from the sewing room and picked open a seam in the corner hem of a heavy panel. The panel hung nearest the wall and was least often handled. She inserted the locket into the hem and, with the pin, closed it up.

She was content most days to know the locket was safe. She drew it out only in those darkest hours when despair raised its ugly head and she contemplated ending her life. She would gaze at the picture, close her eyes, and feel her mother's touch, her kiss upon Tory's cheek or forehead. Then Tory would close the locket and, rubbing her thumb across the now-cracked ivory rose, remember Miss Defoe, Mademoiselle Justine, and Madame Rousseau and the happiness she had found with them.

The scrap of paper with the enigmatic passage was different. Tory folded it and placed it under a leg of the armoire to keep it hidden and safe. She did not need to take it out to read it, for she had committed it to memory. She found herself thinking on the verse more often than her locket.

For I know the thoughts that I think toward you, saith the Lord, thoughts of peace, and not of evil, to give you an expected end. Then shall ye call upon me, and ye shall go and pray unto me, and I will hearken unto you. And ye shall seek me, and find me, when ye shall search for me with all your heart.

In a strictly literal way, the passage bothered her, particularly where the first line spoke of 'thoughts of peace, and not of evil.'

"I am imprisoned under Roxanne's thumb in this house of evil! No peace will ever be mine—not until I escape this hell upon earth. And even if I did escape, would I be free of the awful things I have done? *No.* And how could I flee, surrounded as I am by the many men who are paid to keep me a slave? There will be no peace for me; I must likely die to escape this life of whoredom."

However, before Tory could sleep each night, she needed to clear her mind—expunge the horrors she nightly endured. She would repeat the single Bible verse over and over, finding numbing comfort in it—although she did not understand why. She only knew that murmuring the words softly seemed to calm her and help her slip into the oblivion of sleep.

"Ye shall seek me, and find me, when ye shall search for me with all your heart." Tory often pondered this statement. "Who is this 'me' I must seek and find? And how do I search for him 'with all my heart'?"

Then she would sigh. "I have no heart. It is crushed and dead."

Tory's only other source of comfort was Helen, the girl who had cared for her after Darrow and Jingo beat her. Helen's simple kindness—and the tears she had shed for Tory—had bonded them. Tory and Helen watched out for each other and helped each other navigate the snares and pitfalls of Roxanne's stringent rules and expectations.

Although Tory believed there was no hope for her or Helen, she continued to ponder and repeat the words of the Bible passage because of the calming influence it held over her—perplexing as that soothing effect was.

~*~

Tory had been a prisoner and a whore for Roxanne Cleary for two months when a new girl was shifted from the "lower" house to Corinth Gentlemen's Club. The new girl had, according to the gossip, been in the lower house for a few weeks while she was being "broken in."

"Esther caught a glimpse of her," Sarah whispered as they dawdled in the hall, "says she is scarcely more than a child—would not put her above fourteen."

Tory's chest constricted. "Poor thing."

"I hear, too, that she is Chinese."

"Chinese!"

"Yes, and Esther says she is exquisite: heart-shaped face, perfect ivory skin. You know how Roxanne is. She'll paint and costume the child, then present her as some new and exotic delicacy for the 'guests' to fawn and squabble over." Sarah's mouth hardened. "Did I say guests? I meant filthy lechers. That's what men are—all of them."

Tory nodded and hurried on her way. She still needed to dress for dinner and the evening—and tardiness to the table earned a girl an empty plate while the others filled theirs.

It was at dinner that Roxanne introduced her most recent addition. "Corinth Gentlemen's Club has a new attraction. I think you will not find her lacking in refinement, charm, and eloquence. We shall call her Little Plum Blossom."

The girl, as tiny and fragile in appearance as a flower, acknowledged Roxanne's introduction with a graceful inclination of her head and took her seat; she stared straight ahead, a slight smile fixed on her otherwise expressionless face. Tory and Helen exchanged glances.

As Sarah had predicted, Roxanne painted the girl's face and dressed her in an elaborate, custom-made kimono. The Little Plum Blossom's debut was an instant success. Clients flooded the house, often reserving her weeks in advance.

The Little Plum Blossom's popularity did not diminish the demand for Tory's "favors," however. Club "members" regularly asked after her, and she considered herself lucky in that regard. Disfavor with the club's "clients" was to be feared, as was the passage of time.

No girl lasted at the Corinth Gentlemen's Club longer than a year or two, some only a few months. Girls whose attitudes and skills were not exemplary or whose popularity waned were sent either to the "lower," less exclusive house next door or were "sold" to cheap whorehouses down in the city.

The lower house had eleven girls, but the number and complement of the stable changed often. New girls were regularly lured to Denver through false employment opportunities. Once they were snared, they were taken to the lower house to be "broken in," assessed, and eventually (when their novelty wore thin) "sent down mountain."

Whether at the lower house or the Corinth Gentlemen's Club, the threat of being "sent down mountain" was another tactic Miss Cleary used to keep "her" girls in line. "You have plenty of food with me, lovely surroundings, and our guests are clean. Think on these benefits before you act foolishly and lose your position here."

At present, the club boasted a baker's dozen of such beauties: Esther, Molly, Sarah, Dotty, Crystal, Jess, Ava, Savannah, Dahlia, Helen, Mimi, Tory and, most recently, the Little Plum Blossom. Helen, who had the gift of a compassionate ear, got close to the Little Plum Blossom first and won the child's trust.

"Her real name is Mei-Xing," she reported to Tory, "but she will not say where she is from or how Roxanne tricked her into coming here."

Tory nodded. "You know the story of my phony employment offer. Weren't most of the girls here fooled by false employment advertisements in the newspapers?"

Helen sniffed. "Not all. Savannah and Esther were already skillful courtesans. Roxanne promised them a better situation and higher wages. Of course, they found out when they arrived that wages are nonexistent and leaving is not an option.

"As for me, I answered a newspaper listing to care for the two children of a widowed doctor. My new 'employer' sent me a letter with instructions and a train ticket to Denver. The instructions told me to call for a second ticket when I arrived at Union Station. That ticket took me to Corinth, where Darrow and two other men met me. The men threw me into the motorcar and brought me to the "lower" house where I was given to a man who pays to deflower virgins. Later, when Roxanne discovered I was classically trained on piano, she placed me here."

She sighed. "Yes, my tale of woe started with a newspaper advertisement—but I would think Mei-Xing unlikely to answer such an advertisement. She seems too young. Too fragile."

"Fragile? Perhaps."

The Little Plum Blossom was as much a puzzle as she was popular with the guests. Tory and Helen took the girl under their wings whenever they could—but Tory sensed a depth lurking under the girl's demure exterior, a strength and determination that Roxanne's methods must eventually crush.

Tory said nothing to Helen about her concern for Mei-Xing. What would be the point?

~*~

Tory's life in Corinth devolved into a predictable pattern, a soul-searing sameness: night after night of men and day after day of chores. Following breakfast late each morning, Miss Cleary assigned common household tasks to the girls: dusting, polishing, mopping, scrubbing, and never-ending laundry. With a steady stream of visitors to the house, the clearing up and preparing for the next night was ongoing.

When Roxanne discovered that Tory had been a seamstress, she consigned her personal mending to Tory, with the warning, "Take care that you do not misuse the sewing kit I have allowed you, Tory."

In reality, the kit had been rendered harmless: a single needle, thimble, darning egg, thin crochet hook, an assortment of threads, and a tiny, blunted pair of scissors for clipping threads.

"I suppose Roxanne doesn't wish any of us to drive a pair of shears into her or Darrow," Sarah muttered, "although I confess to fantasizing of such an opportunity."

The girls were kept so occupied that Tory was surprised to realize that spring had come and gone and summer had settled on the mountains. Once weekly, when weather permitted, Roxanne ordered that the girls, in controllable groups of three, be taken on walks along nearby mountain paths "for their health." Darrow and his men accompanied them, chasing off any Corinth villager who happened near them.

Tory and Helen managed to include Mei-Xing in their threesome on such walks. While Tory and Helen spoke in soft whispers over her head, Mei-Xing was quiet. She rarely said anything, but Tory noticed the girl's alert and observant manner. In fact, Tory worried that Mei-Xing was planning something.

It was July when Mei-Xing attempted to escape.

Apparently, Tory had not been the only one to sense that Mei-Xing had been biding her time, waiting for the opportune moment.

She was immediately recaptured.

I was right, Tory thought. *Mei-Xing was only pretending to have given in.* She suppressed a shudder. *And now she will pay the price.*

Mei-Xing's shrieks and screams echoed through the house that afternoon as Darrow and another man administered the requisite punishment. They then drugged her, so she would sleep through the evening without disturbing the club's guests.

The following morning, Tory was given the task of caring for Mei-Xing's wounds—just as Helen had cared for hers. When she opened the door to the punishment room, she shivered. It had not been that long since *she* had been the one in the bed, broken, torn, bleeding.

Tory cleaned Mei-Xing as best she could and gave her water, but the girl would not look at her or speak a word.

"They will send her down mountain now," Helen murmured, "yet she is so tiny and delicate. How long could she last in a cheap bordello?"

"She is stronger than we give her credit for," Tory insisted, "And perhaps Roxanne will make an exception? The Little Plum Blossom is a club favorite."

"No, Tory. Roxanne never keeps a girl who has tried to run."

At dinner, Miss Cleary—cold and harsh—addressed the assembled girls. "The Little Plum Blossom took advantage of her status in this house. Well, she has been punished—as will be any girl who makes such a foolish attempt. She will be given no food for five days—not a scrap. I guarantee she will not try such imprudence again."

Although Roxanne glared around the table, she said nothing more.

Tory bent her face toward her plate, avoiding eye contact with the woman, but she wondered, *Roxanne is not sending Mei-Xing away?*

"I think the man who owns these houses must have insisted that Roxanne keep Mei-Xing," Helen theorized. "She earns him a great deal of money, after all."

Tory exhaled, still anxious. "Perhaps, but as badly beaten as Mei-Xing is, she still seems . . . undaunted. Undeterred. Do you think she might try it again?"

"For her sake, I hope not."

In all outward appearances, Mei-Xing had learned her lesson. She settled in, applied herself to her "responsibilities" and gave no sign of rebellion, no indication she intended to attempt another escape. Summer passed by, and the Little Plum Blossom retained her prominent standing in the club.

Tory, however, kept a disquieted vigilance over Mei-Xing for, in the slightest turn of her head or lift of a brow, she sensed the girl's veiled defiance.

Charles taught me well; I am skilled at reading people.
Oh, Mei-Xing.

~*~

246

High in the mountains, cooler weather came more quickly to Corinth than to Denver and Colorado's eastern plains. While the city below them enjoyed balmy September days, in the village, brisk, chilling winds already forecast the change of seasons.

As the temperatures cooled, a more unsettling change came to Corinth and its two houses of ill-repute—an upheaval portended by the arrival of a young blonde woman in the village.

The girls of the Corinth Gentlemen's Club always found ways to eavesdrop on the business of the house. Whether hiding behind doors or affecting disinterest, the girls overheard discussions and heated arguments between Roxanne and Darrow regarding the mysterious woman. And, with so little to brighten their lives outside their "work," the girls in the house were quick to devour and share tidbits of news they gleaned.

In particular, they were keen to pass on all they gathered concerning "the blonde woman." Information may have been scarce, but the girls shared and commented on such scraps of gossip during quick, passing moments.

On a morning in late September, Tory and two other girls huddled in the third-floor hallway to revel in the latest uproar the blonde woman's presence in Corinth had provoked.

Savannah whispered, "Darrow told Roxanne that the woman's name is Joy Thoresen. I heard she is related to the wife of Corinth's minister. Cousins."

"Corinth has a church?" Tory was shocked.

"Yes, much good as it does us," Savannah sneered.

Dahlia leaned closer. "Well, I overheard Darrow say he went to Denver to pick up two girls who had answered newspaper advertisements, but this Thoresen woman would not let him have them. Imagine it: She defied him in public, in the midst of Union Station! She got the crowd to turn on him! And now Darrow is furious because it seems this Miss Thoresen brought those same girls to Corinth. They are here, in the village, right under his nose, and he has not been able to capture them."

"This Thoresen woman is a fool, as Darrow and his men will soon demonstrate," Savannah pronounced.

Savannah's warning ended the whispered conversation; the girls hurried about their respective chores, heavy-hearted for the naïve do-gooder, Miss Thoresen, who would, they were certain, feel the weight of Darrow's wrath before long.

Tory was as intrigued as she was concerned. Listening at doors or around corners carried a risk, but Tory's curiosity regarding "the blonde woman" was great.

A week later, Tory overheard Darrow complaining to Roxanne.

"You know that old house on the overlook near the siding we tried to buy? The house the owner refused to sell? Seems the owner has had a change of heart—and has sold it to this Thoresen woman."

"What! Why would she want such a large house—and here in this lifeless village?"

"She intends to turn it into a resort hotel and call it Corinth Mountain Lodge. What is worse, our two girls, the ones she stole from us, are helping her."

Darrow growled in frustration. "I think this Miss Thoresen fancies herself some sort of reformer, tryin' to rescue whores and help them 'find Jesus.' Well, if she thinks that, Morgan will have us fix her wagon, he surely will."

"She will not be finding any girls to help from *my* houses," Roxanne had replied.

Tory turned to scuttle away and nearly tripped over Mei-Xing who had also been listening behind her skirts. Neither girl said a word. They slipped away in silence.

Later, Tory repeated the conversation to Helen.

"Morgan? Who is Morgan?" Helen asked.

Tory shrugged. "Could he be the owner of these houses? Roxanne's boss?"

She asked another question, one that had ignited her hopes. "Darrow said Miss Thoresen might be trying to rescue whores. Do you think . . . do you think she might help us?"

"One woman against all Darrow's armed men? I doubt it."

"You are probably right." Tory mused on the overheard conversation and her dashed hopes. "I suppose, as bad as living here is, we are the lucky ones. We could be in a Market Street crib in Denver. We could be working in filth."

"I suppose," Helen answered.

Tory gave her friend a sharp look, dismayed that she did not appear as well as Tory thought she should.

"Are you all right, Helen?"

"Yes. Why do you ask?"

Tory shrugged, but she began watching Helen, noting subtle changes in her appearance. In her heart, she cried out, *Please do not let Helen get sick! She is my only friend—please do not let her get sick!*

She heard herself begging, but could not put a name to the one she begged.

Neither did she dare call it prayer.

As Sassy had said, *"Prayers be worthless in a house of sin."*

CHAPTER 26

November arrived, and with it greater numbers of guests, men who found the biddable companionship of Corinth preferable to the tedious and rigid social scene of Denver, men who frequented Corinth to escape the boredom of their spouses and the censure of society.

Floating among the girls of the house was the most recent rumor concerning Miss Thoresen—that she and her friends had received a shipment of furniture to fit up her Corinth Mountain Lodge.

"Gretl heard Darrow say that the lodge will be ready to receive guests soon," Dahlia reported.

Again, Tory's hopes lifted. "Do you . . . do you think it is possible that the people in Denver—I mean the good people—know nothing about us? About these houses?" she asked. "Could Miss Thoresen's lodgers intervene to help us?"

Dahlia was quick to shake her head. "Why, what could they do?" She jerked her chin in a gesture of disgust. "We must accept the facts, Tory: To the world we are but worthless whores. No one cares about us—and no one will do anything to help us."

~*~

Thanksgiving passed with no special observance, and the month drew to an end. On the last day of the month, Corinth received fresh snow. Colder temperatures arrived with the snow.

At breakfast the following morning, Tory nudged her friend. "Helen, you have eaten nothing."

"I am not hungry this morning, Tory."

Tory gazed down the table and, trying not to draw Roxanne's attention, studied Helen out of the corner of her eye. She did not like what she saw. Helen's usually thick, shining hair seemed thinner. Duller. Her face a pasty color.

Before dinner, as they finished their preparations for the evening, Tory pulled Helen into her room. "Let me look at you."

"Please, Tory. Just let me go. It will take me forever to get ready as it is. I-I am just so tired."

"Then let me help you. I want to."

Helen reached for Tory and hugged her, but Tory was dismayed to feel that Helen had lost weight.

"You are a good friend, Tory. I am grateful to have you in my life."

"This is not a life," Tory growled.

"Do not think such a thing. Do not say it."

Tory sighed. "All right, go. I will hurry, then come help you."

Tory was on her way to Helen's room when she came upon Mei-Xing. "Hello, Mei-Xing."

Instead of answering Tory, the girl sucked in her bottom lip and her eyes skittered away. A chill of alarm ran through Tory. Glancing both ways first to ensure they were not observed, she grabbed the tiny girl's wrist and whispered, "Mei-Xing! Please tell me you are not considering . . ."

Tory couldn't finish the statement. If Mei-Xing tried to run again, Darrow would—again—punish her. If Mei-Xing survived the punishment, Roxanne would certainly sell her down mountain.

Mei-Xing smoothed her expression and smiled sweetly. "You have a kind heart, Tory, but please do not concern yourself over me."

Mei-Xing had never opened herself to any of the girls, so what she murmured next terrified Tory. She had started to turn away, when Mei-Xing added, "What I do, I do with my eyes wide open. I choose to die a free person."

"Oh, Mei-Xing!"

But the girl had slipped into her room.

~*~

Late into the night, Tory felt that she had only fallen asleep when shouts and bellows jolted her awake.

"We got 'er. She didn't get far."

"Bring her here!"

Tory ran to her door; it was, as usual, locked. She placed an ear to the wood and listened. Someone was being dragged up the back stairs. Not carried, but dragged. She could hear the body thumping up the carpeted steps.

Darrow's unmistakable baritone swore; a girl's defiant voice answered, but with words screamed in a language Tory did not recognize.

Chinese?

Mei-Xing!

Tory clutched her nightgown in helpless dismay. Darrow was dragging Mei-Xing to the punishment room at the end of the hall. His shouting went on, even after the door to the room slammed shut, but Mei-Xing's voice went silent.

Tory knew every girl in the house had to be awake and dreading the screams that were sure to come. The worst part was that they could do nothing—nothing to prevent the violence to follow.

She stood at her door for a long time. She did not hear Mei-Xing crying out or begging for mercy. Not once.

Had Darrow or one of his men killed her? Was she unconscious? Tory waited, listening to the silence of the night, a silence punctuated occasionally by Darrow's occasional shouted slurs.

An hour passed without a sound from Mei-Xing. Fear for her little friend was like an oppressive weight on Tory's chest. Tory found herself praying for Mei-Xing and, for the first time, she put a name to her desperate pleas.

"Jesus, if you are the Lord, the same Lord who thinks thoughts of peace and not evil, please help Mei-Xing! If you really walked on water and made bread and fish to feed the crowd that came to listen to you, can you not help my friend?"

After a lengthy time, Tory heard the slam of a door and the thud of boots descending the back stairs, Darrow and his men leaving Mei-Xing alone in the punishment room. Tory twisted her doorknob in frustration. While the front and back doors of the house were key locked each night, the bedroom doors were bolted from the outside by the simple twist of a latch. Every night after the club closed, one of Darrow's men walked the halls of the second and third floors, the clack of latches turning and doorknobs rattling to test the locks intermixed with his footfalls.

Tory growled in frustration—and then went cold as an audacious idea came to her. She raced to her bureau and removed the bag of mending Roxanne foisted on her each week.

She yanked the stocking she had been darning from the bag and felt for the thin crochet hook she used to pull broken threads from the outside of the fabric to the inside. She slid the hook from the stocking, then fumbled a hairpin from her head. She straightened the hairpin and bent its end to a sharp right angle. Tory returned to the door, knowing full well that if she succeeded with what she planned but was found out, she, too, like Mei-Xing, would be punished.

"I do not care," she muttered over and over. The truth was, Tory did care. She was terrified—but she poked hook and hairpin into the keyhole anyway, feeling for the bolt's locking mechanism.

The bolt snapped open more quickly than Tory had anticipated.

She inhaled slowly and, for a long moment, did not move. Then she eased the door open an inch, listening.

All was quiet.

With crochet hook and hairpin still in her hand, Tory crept down the hall to the punishment room. Esther's bedroom shared an adjoining wall, so Tory was careful to make no noise when she turned the latch and entered Mei-Xing's dark room. Moments later, she crouched over Mei-Xing's bed.

The girl was turned on her side, her knees pulled to her chest. Tory bent closer. "Mei-Xing?"

Tory heard a single, soft sob.

"Mei-Xing? It is Tory."

Tory heard movement outside the door. She dropped to the floor and pushed herself under the bed—no mean feat, as the bed was low to the floor.

She heard a woman—Roxanne!—muttering, "How could they have been so derelict! Leaving her door unlocked. Why, even in her state . . ."

Roxanne took a moment to light the lamp, then stood over Mei-Xing, the toes of her shoes but inches from Tory's face. "Mei-Xing, turn over. I wish to speak to you."

When Mei-Xing did not respond, Roxanne added a threat. "If you do not obey me, I shall call Darrow back."

The bedsprings above Tory's head squeaked as Mei-Xing began the painful process of turning her body.

Roxanne held up the lamp. "Let me look at you."

Several moments passed before Roxanne sighed and said, "It is too bad, Mei-Xing, it really is. You could have had such a good life here."

Another pause was followed by, "Your nose is broken. Likely your looks are ruined. In any event, you are no good to us here anymore. We will make arrangements to have you moved in a few days."

Mei-Xing did not answer. Roxanne put out the lamp and left the room, locking the door behind her.

Tory wanted to make sure that Roxanne was gone before she crawled out from under the bed. She was amazed when the bedsprings creaked and Mei-Xing's tiny feet, one at a time, touched the floor. The girl, gasping at the effort, leaned on the edge of the bed.

Tory wriggled and crawled out from beneath the bed. "What . . . what are you doing?"

Mei-Xing, doubled over and breathing hard, did not answer. Sucking in another pain-filled breath, she pulled at the bedsheets.

Tory understood: Mei-Xing was not going to wait for Roxanne to send her down mountain. She placed one hand on Mei-Xing's shoulder. Gently. "Are you sure?"

Mei-Xing nodded once.

Tory saw the puddle of Mei-Xing's nightgown on the floor where Darrow had stripped it from her. *Mei-Xing left the house in only her nightgown? In the snow and cold?* Mei-Xing's shoes were nowhere to be seen. Darrow had probably left them downstairs where his men caught her.

"You are braver than I, Mei-Xing, but I will help you."

Tory picked up the nightgown and drew it down over Mei-Xing's nakedness, helping her lift her bruised arms and put them through the sleeves. Together the two young women stripped the bed and made a rope of the two sheets. Tory pulled with all her strength on the knot joining the sheets then looked to the window. How would they secure the rope of sheets so Mei-Xing could slide down it? And it was three floors to the ground! The two sheets would not be nearly long enough.

Mei-Xing was already at the window. As she slid it up, the swollen wood screed and stuck. Tory helped her push until the protesting window was half raised.

"Hold . . . sheet for me, Tory."

"But . . ."

"When I am down . . . tie it to a chair. Wedge . . . chair against window."

Tory looked from Mei-Xing to the chair. The girl could not weigh above eighty pounds. Theoretically, the chair could hold her weight.

"All right."

Mei-Xing, barefoot and dressed only in her nightgown, climbed over the window sill and, holding onto the upraised window frame, poised there. Tory handed her the sheet. She had knotted the end, too, and Mei-Xing grasped it. In the pale moonlight, Tory saw the devastation of Mei-Xing's face, the blood dripping from her battered nose onto the sheet's bleached muslin.

Tory reached her palm to the girl's face and, as gently as she could, cupped it. "I . . . I wish you well, Mei-Xing."

She sat on the floor and braced her feet against the wall beneath the window, taking up the slack in the twined sheet and tightening her grasp. "I am ready."

Mei-Xing was fearless. When the sheet went taut, she released her weight to it. Tory's arms strained with the pull, but she held tight and began to feed out the sheet. When she came to the end of the rope, she let Mei-Xing's weight pull her to standing until she could give the girl no more length without tumbling out the window behind her.

A moment later, the rope went limp. Tory leaned out and saw Mei-Xing's figure far below, crumpled in the snow behind the shrubs. Mei-Xing's head turned. She glanced up. Then she got up and, limping, hobbled across the snow-covered expanse of lawn.

Tory looked for the roving guard that should have been patrolling the circumference of the house at night. Did he think trudging through the wet snow too much effort? Perhaps he believed Mei-Xing's capture would discourage another escape attempt?

Tory pulled her head inside. She fastened the sheet to the small vanity chair and laid the chair on its side against the wall under the window.

Tory picked the lock to the punishment room and left, latching the bolt behind her.

Jesus? If you are there? Please give Mei-Xing enough time to get away? And please, Jesus . . . please let the blonde lady at the lodge help her?

~*~

The day began as usual. Tory had to mask her anxiety; regardless, Helen knew something was bothering Tory. Helen, however, was too savvy to do more than whisper a one-word question.

"What?"

Tory's chin lifted a fraction, and Helen dropped her eyes to her plate: Tory would tell her later.

After breakfast, before she apportioned tasks, Roxanne assumed a sad, reluctant expression. "I apologize for the disheartening news I must report, ladies. Last evening, shortly after closing, Mei-Xing chose to hide herself in a downstairs closet and sneak out the front door—in her nightgown, of all things!"

Roxanne wagged her head in mock sympathy. "She was, of course, immediately found, returned to the house, and punished—but this, her second attempt, I am afraid, will be her last."

Roxanne even managed a false sigh. "Mei-Xing will be confined to the, ah, discipline room on the third floor until I have made arrangements to send her down mountain. It pains me that such a gifted and accomplished girl has willfully chosen to waste her talents in a foul bawdy house servicing flea-ridden farmers and factory workers."

She leveled her gaze on the girls, studying each one's reaction, before adding, "Savannah, you will tend to Mei-Xing today, but she is to have nothing to eat—not even broth—and nothing to drink but water."

"Yes, Miss Cleary."

The girls, when they were dismissed from the table, whispered their consternation and regret over Mei-Xing's fall from grace. Tory said nothing and went about her business.

Not many minutes later, Savannah's excited shouts for Roxanne echoed down the stairs, and Mei-Xing's daring escape from the third floor became known.

The girls, drawn to the drama, clustered in the hallway as Roxanne examined the rope of sheets and Darrow issued directives to his men.

"She could not have gone far in this snow wearing nothing but a bloody nightgown," Roxanne ground out.

"We'll find her, Miss Cleary," Darrow promised.

Esther, not a particular friend of Tory's, sidled up and linked arms with her. "I could not *bear* to listen to Mei-Xing's screams last night, so I covered my head with my pillow," she confided.

Tory slid her eyes toward the beautiful blonde with midnight blue eyes. "I believe that once they got her into the punishment room, she was quiet. At least, I heard nothing more."

"Hmm. Well, as I said, I had my pillow over my head and heard *nothing*. Why, I was as amazed as anyone to hear the commotion just now." Esther cut a glance toward Tory.

Tory answered with the briefest of nods.

Esther had heard Mei-Xing's preparations; she had heard the window complain as Me-Xing raised it. Perhaps she had even heard whispers and recognized the second voice as Tory's. Maybe she knew that Tory had found a way out of her locked room and that she had helped Mei-Xing!

Esther could have reported Tory to Roxanne and earned a reward, but she kept silent. Tory pressed the hand Esther rested on her waist.

"I can only hope the best for Mei-Xing, Esther. She is not suited for this life."

"I agree. She is not like you or me."

Like you or me? Tory thought. *Oh, Esther. I am not like you. Not at all.*

CHAPTER 27

C ontrary to Darrow's promises, his men did not find Mei-Xing. Her trail led across the club's snow-covered lawn and onto the road but, from there, her tracks disappeared.

"What do you mean, you cannot find her? She was barefoot and bleeding on snowy ground! How could her trail vanish?" Roxanne shouted. "Have you asked around the village? The nearest houses? What about that woman and her lodge? The smithy? Someone had to have seen Mei-Xing. Someone is hiding her."

"We walked the perimeter of the lodge and the smithy and found no indication that she went there. Put my best man on it, and he says—"

"I don't care a fig what your 'best man' says! Get out there yourself—and don't come back until you bring the girl with you."

But, days later, when Darrow did return to the club, it was without Mei-Xing—and Roxanne's temper mounted. No one was exempt from the rough side of her tongue.

Tory had her own concerns. Helen was not at all well, and they both knew that it would not be long before Roxanne noticed. If Helen did not recover her looks and energy soon, Roxanne would send Helen down mountain.

Late in the night after the club closed, Tory helped an exhausted Helen to her room and into bed. Afterward, when she went to her own room, Tory could not sleep until she had pleaded with the Jesus she had read of in John, chapter 6.

"Jesus, I have no hope anymore. If they send Helen away, I will surely die! I do not know what to do, Jesus!"

Somehow, calling on Jesus brought a measure of peace to the landslide of troubles hanging over Helen and her. She recounted Sassy's promise to pray for her and the old woman's sorrow that she had not told Tory about Jesus.

"I, too, wish you had told me about Jesus, Sassy," Tory murmured to herself.

When winter set in fully, and more snow fell, Darrow offered a plausible rationalization for Mei-Xing's disappearance. "The boys and I figure the girl followed one of the paths 'long the side of the mountain. Not being able to see the path clearly 'cause of the snow, she stepped too close to an edge. Fell. New snow's covered her up. Find her in the spring."

Roxanne scowled. "That explanation may suit you, Darrow, but it will not satisfy Mr. Morgan. Mark my words."

Roxanne's warning hung in the air until mid-January when Darrow received notice to take the train to Denver for a meeting with the mysterious Mr. Morgan. When Darrow returned that afternoon, his face was set in barely contained belligerence—and he was not alone.

At dinner, Roxanne clapped her hands to capture the girls' attention. "Ladies, may I present Mr. Banner? Mr. Banner is now in charge of security for the club and, of course, our other house."

The girls schooled their expressions into docile, accepting lines and nodded in his direction, eyes downcast. For his part, the new head of security was soft-spoken—soft-spoken in the manner of someone whose mere whisper imparted fear.

"I am certain we shall get on well," Banner murmured, "and that no unpleasantness will be needed."

Tory chanced one look at the man and was horrified to see his appraising glance fall upon—and remain on—Helen.

Helen had been particularly ill the day before, vomiting all morning, unable to keep food or water down. Miss Cleary had granted her the evening off for Helen to recover from her intestinal distress.

"We cannot, of course, have you running to empty your stomach while we have guests—or passing on your illness to them."

Tory watched Banner catalogue Helen's lank hair, pale skin, and spiritless demeanor. When he nodded to himself, Tory's gorge rose. Banner must have felt Tory's eyes upon him, for he turned to her and, with a lazy smile, looked her up and down.

Tory was distracted all that evening, concerned for Helen, worried about Banner's first action as the club's head of security, struck with fear that Banner was planning something that involved Helen.

Her fears came home to roost late the following afternoon when Roxanne summoned Tory to her office. In the corner, lounging in a chair, sat Banner. He again eyed Tory and smiled in a hungry, way—a knowing inspection with which Tory was familiar.

"Tory, you are friends with Helen, are you not?"

"Yes, Miss Cleary."

"Can you help me understand the nature of her illness?"

"Not being a doctor, I cannot, Miss Cleary, but I am certain that, with a few days of rest, she will recover."

"Not a doctor but certain she will recover, are you? And yet she has lost a great deal of weight, has she not? I hardly think her illness to be as transitory as you assert."

Tory focused her eyes on the wall behind Roxanne. She did not answer. Nothing she said would change what Roxanne and Banner were deciding.

Roxanne glanced at Banner before dismissing Tory. "Thank you, Tory. You may go."

Tory left Roxanne's office and closed the door behind her—but not so it latched. She made a point of walking away, her footsteps deliberate and audible. When she reached the foot of the staircase, she crept back and listened at the door.

"I don't like it, Mr. Banner. We generally ship a girl down mountain when her usefulness comes to an end."

"And yet, I must insist, Miss Cleary. Following the outrageous loss of the Little Plum Blossom, Mr. Morgan has tasked *me* with restoring order to these houses—and I intend to do just that. We cannot allow an apparently successful escape to sow seeds of rebellion or spur similar attempts.

"I will, therefore, make an example of Helen and, in short order, establish the *proper* tone in this house. Helen is not long for this world anyway; my hands about her thin little neck will provide a pointed example."

"But, really, Mr. Banner—at the table? I shall have girls losing their breakfasts."

With stunned revulsion, Tory understood: *They mean to kill Helen?*

No, not 'they.' Banner.

Banner's chuckle set Tory's skin crawling. "Then, perhaps before breakfast would be more appropriate?"

Tory stole away, her heart racing, her mind declaring, *I cannot allow this evil man to harm Helen. I cannot.*

I will not.

~*~

Tory passed the evening in fearful trepidation, watching Banner every moment she could, frantic in her mind over the coming morning. *But what can I do? How could I get Helen away from this place? She is so weak already and is barely managing her work this evening.*

Later, after the club had closed and after the night guards had walked the third-floor hallway, locking each of the seven bedrooms as they went, Tory climbed from her bed and paced the length of her room, back and forth, crying out in muffled pleas, *O God! Are you there? I am seeking you with all my heart. You said if I sought you with all my heart I would find you—can you not help us? I am begging you!*

Tory vacillated in an agony of distress. *Should I try to escape and take Helen to safety? But if I try and we are caught? Banner will do to me what he plans to do to Helen.*

And perhaps worse. Tory had seen the licentious way Banner had studied her, had sensed the cruelty—a lust to hurt women, to torture them—lurking beneath his cool, composed manner.

For more than an hour, Tory paced and fretted over what to do, calling on the Lord from "her" Scripture verse, the one she had memorized. For more than an hour, Tory agonized over what to do. *O Jesus. If you are the Lord, please show me how to get Helen away from that monster, Banner.*

She stopped in shock when, in the back of her mind, she "heard" a voice. She knew she hadn't heard the voice with her ears; instead, it had rumbled somewhere within her.

Go, the Voice said. The Voice's power shook Tory harder than her fear had shaken her. *Go!* the Voice insisted.

Teeth chattering, Tory whispered, "Is that you, God? Are you . . . are you truly speaking to me?"

The Voice whispered this time: *I have set before thee an open door, and no man can shut it. Go.*

Tory vacillated only a moment more, but she knew the Voice would not speak again. It was now up to her to act. She nodded. "All right. Whether we live or die, I will attempt to get Helen away from here."

She stripped off her nightgown and buttoned herself into one of the plain housedresses she wore during the day while doing chores. She was no longer shaking: Her mind was clear and sharp, her body calm.

After she had donned stockings and shoes, she went to the draperies, unpinned the drape's hem containing her locket, slipped the locket into her dress pocket, and pinned it closed. She took up the crochet hook and the hairpin she had bent to her purposes.

Tory threw on her cloak and listened at the door to her room. She heard nothing. With unnaturally steady fingers, she picked the lock on her door. Seconds later, she stepped into the hall, noiselessly closed the door behind her, and turned the latch to reset the lock.

Helen's room was across the hall, on the opposite side of Esther's room from the punishment room. With as little noise as she could manage, Tory turned the latch on Helen's door and entered. She went directly to the window, drew back the drapes, and let what moonlight there was into the room. Then she went to Helen's bedside and placed her hand over Helen's mouth.

She need not have been so careful. Helen's eyes opened immediately. Tory whispered, "We are leaving, Helen. Now."

Helen neither protested nor asked questions. She allowed Tory to help her out of bed and stood passively as Tory dressed her and wrapped her cloak about her shoulders.

Tory put her mouth to Helen's ear. "Is there anything precious you wish to take with you?"

Helen patted Tory's steadying arm about her waist and waggled her head.

Now came the most treacherous moments. Mei-Xing had escaped through her window, but Tory and Helen could not: Helen did not possess the strength for such exertion. Tory would have to walk Helen out the front door. Between them and freedom lay two flights of stairs, a bolted door, and a guard.

At the top of the first staircase, Tory breathed into Helen's ear, "Rest your weight on me."

All down the stairs, Tory trod with care and concentration. She knew which steps creaked and where, which ones rang hollow. With Helen's arms about her neck, Tory leaned against the bannister and eased them to the second floor.

At the second-floor landing, Tory paused and listened. She heard nothing but a low snore coming from the room nearest the stairs—Miss Cleary's bedroom, larger than the other bedrooms and made sumptuous to suit her lavish tastes.

Afraid to linger long, Tory started Helen down the second flight. This final length of stairs terrified Tory. She knew a night guard wandered the grounds and, periodically, the house. She had also heard Gretl report that the guard—against his orders—spent most of the night in the kitchen where the gas-lit stove's pilot light kept the room warmer than the rest of the house, warmer, certainly, than the out-of-doors.

Jesus. If you are there . . .

Tory sat Helen on the bottom step, then listened for the guard. When she heard no sounds, she crossed the wide foyer to the door. She removed her tools from her pocket and went to work on a lock that was much more complex than the bedroom doors.

After three frustrating minutes, the lock gave way. Tory sighed with relief—and recoiled when she heard a man's footsteps approaching from the back of the house.

Tory shoved her picks into her pocket, grabbed Helen, and tiptoed across the foyer carpet to Roxanne's office. The door was locked, and she did not have enough time to unlock it.

Looking about in desperation, Tory saw the same closet Mei-Xing had hidden in. Seeing it was her only choice, Tory shoved Helen inside—and discovered that the closet (full of umbrellas and galoshes) had scarcely enough room for Helen. At the last possible moment, Tory grabbed a heavy-headed cane from the closet. She left the closet door ajar and edged into the foyer's corner, hardening her heart to what she must do.

Helen's terrified eyes blinked through the crack at Tory. Tory put her finger to her lips and pushed farther into the corner's shadow.

The sauntering footsteps drew closer.

Tory's pulse hammered at her throat. *Jesus? Are you there?*

"What the . . ." The night guard, a small man who went by "Slim," saw the closet's cracked-open door and reached for it.

Tory brought the head of the cane down on Slim's head. Once. Twice. When the guard crumpled, Tory hit him a third time for good measure.

She straightened and listened for any indication that her attack—or Slim's fall to the floor—had raised Miss Cleary from her bed.

Tory drew Helen from the closet and handed her the cane. She mimicked hitting Slim should he awaken. Helen swayed, but nodded. Tory glided to Miss Cleary's office and spent a full minute picking the lock, glancing every few seconds at Helen and Slim to ensure that both were as she wished them: Helen upright and Slim out cold.

When the office door gave way, Tory went inside to the windows and quietly removed the sheer panels under the heavier drapes. She returned to the unconscious guard and, winding the sheers into ropes, trussed him hand and foot.

Tory stifled a laugh when she saw that Helen had retrieved a mitten from the closet and was miming to Tory that she should stuff Slim's mouth with it. Tory took the mitten and did just that.

Leaving Helen leaning in the foyer corner, Tory dragged Slim into Miss Cleary's office. On her way out, she set the lock and pulled the door closed. Slim would not be discovered until Miss Cleary herself unlocked her office door.

Tory and Helen left the house together, closing the door behind them.

~*~

Tory urged Helen down the long, arching drive to the road. A mild wind rustled around them as they hurried, and Tory took only enough time to glance back a single time. The house behind them lay dark and undisturbed, but Tory knew what chaos would erupt when they did not appear for breakfast.

She pulled Helen faster until the girl's breath came in short, desperate gasps.

"I am unhappy to tax you so, dear Helen," Tory murmured, "but if we are seen, we will be captured and taken back. I must get you away before we are spotted."

She did not say what urgency burned within her—did not tell Helen that Banner planned to strangle her in front of the other girls in order to "establish the proper tone" in the house. Helen was already doing her best to put one foot ahead of the other.

Down the long road, past other homes, most plain and common, Tory cajoled, impelled, and dragged her friend. Wagon wheels and motorcar tires had cut the snow and softened it during the day; the night's lower temperatures had frozen the tracks to sharp, icy impediments for which their shoes were not designed.

Tory slipped and fell, dragging Helen down with her. Tory's knee took the worst of the fall. She got up, limping and in pain, but Helen made not a sound. Tory knew her friend was beyond her strength. Without Tory to compel her forward, Helen would have sunk to the icy road and laid there until she froze to death.

Tory pushed them forward, always moving in the direction of the rail siding. *Darrow said the blonde woman bought the large house on an overlook near the siding. I must find the siding, then the overlook.*

Tory had been at the siding but once and could not picture the house in question. She had been too distressed to notice more than the trail of smoke from the smithy's forge and the man who had watched her being taken away.

The house has to be there. I will find it. I will.

Helen faltered; Tory put her arm around her waist and dragged her forward.

I know Mei-Xing did not fall off the mountain. She fled to the woman at the lodge—Miss Thoresen. Mei-Xing is somewhere safe now. I know she is. We will go there, too. Miss Thoresen will help us.

Tory almost collapsed two more times. She could not feel her fingers or her feet. Every step now was by rote, by instinct, for she could not sense the ground beneath her shoes.

I cannot fall again. I will not be able to get up.

Tory gasped as the siding rose out of the night. She and Helen were closer than she had believed! Tory stopped and let her head fall to her breast, breathing hard, near the end of her strength. Turning her head, Tory thought the smithy to be through the trees on her right. Just enough moonlight confirmed her guess.

No, not moonlight. Morning was not far off. Morning, when Tory and Helen's flight could be seen by anyone.

Tory wobbled her head to the left. She glimpsed a shadow behind another stand of trees where a piece of the mountain jutted out over the valley. In the palest light, the shape took form: A roofline.

"Jesus . . . thank you."

Tory inched ahead, slowly, so slowly. She could not see where she was going; she could only point her leaden feet in what she supposed was the right direction.

Some time later—to Tory's benumbed mind it could have been minutes or hours—she ran into a wagon. Tory forced herself to look up. The house—a two-story log-built edifice—was but yards away.

"Come on, Helen." Tory rasped. "Come on."

She stumbled to the back door and fell against it. Helen slipped from her frozen hands onto the icy ground.

Tory, with her last strength, raised her hand and smacked the door with her open palm. Once. Again. And again. And again. Her best efforts were too soft to be heard.

Her legs failed her, and she started to slide. *I can do no more . . .*

Tory began to fall, not knowing that the door had slowly opened inward. She did not see the grizzled old gent who caught her or the younger man behind the elder who scooped Helen up in his arms.

CHAPTER 28

The door closed behind them. Fear sent energy to her cold limbs, and Tory jerked herself from the old man's grasp. She backed into a wall near the door, the wall of . . . a kitchen.

Helen! Tory saw her friend propped against the chest of a muscled youth. Her latent distrust of men—all men—caused her to grab Helen from the man and pull her into her arms. Helen sagged, and the young man made to catch her. Tory growled at him. "Stay back."

She addressed the two men with what little dignity she could muster. "Miss Thoresen. I wish to see Miss Thoresen."

The old gent jutted his chin at the younger. "Go on up, then, Billy. Fetch Miss Joy."

When the boy opened the door to a narrow staircase and started up, the older man reached for a lantern.

"No. Please," Tory asked. "Please do not . . . light a lamp." They waited in the dark kitchen until she heard footsteps shuffling down the stairs. Instinctively, she pulled herself up, pushed Helen behind her against the wall, knowing Helen would crumple if she stepped away. Fearing she would, herself, again collapse.

A tall woman with a wealth of blonde hair wound in a single, long braid, stepped into the kitchen. She looked from Tory to the old man and back.

Tory stood as upright as her fatigue would allow and whispered, "Please forgive me for waking you, miss. Would you be the lady who assisted Mei-Xing?"

The woman bit her lip. "I believe that if certain people knew we had assisted the girl who ran away from Miss Cleary's, it might lead to difficulties for us."

Tory began to shake. "Upon my soul, miss, I am no friend of theirs. We are in mortal trouble, miss, and must get off this mountain *soon* or . . ." Tory could not control her shaking; it controlled her, possessed her.

"Does this have something to do with the new boss in town? The man called Banner?"

"He is evil itself, miss—I-I beg your pardon." Tory's eyes teared. "Will you help us? I beg of you! He will kill Helen if he discovers us."

Helen whimpered. Tory reached her arm about her friend.

"What is your name?" The woman asked Tory.

"Tory, Miss Thoresen. Mei-Xing was a dear friend. We just want to come away from this place . . . as she did."

"She spoke well of you, Tory. She said you took care of her when they assaulted her."

"Yes, miss. I did." Tory laughed without mirth. "We are obliged to perform that service for another girl at some point. Then they return the favor when it is our turn. It is . . . It is different with Helen. It may be hard to see just now, but she was a great beauty only five weeks ago— she speaks French and Italian and even knows philosophy! But she has grown sickly . . . and has not been able to work.

"I overheard Banner tonight tell Roxanne he intends to make an example of her because . . . because he said he 'needs to set a proper tone' and 'she is not long for this world anyway.'" She glanced at Helen, saddened at what she saw.

"What? He means to *kill* her?"

"In front of the other girls, you see. That is why we had to leave straightaway. Please. You have to help us, miss. We are begging you!"

The woman nodded again. "Wait here."

Tory did not know what she was waiting for, but the young man had built up the fire and she was starting to warm, beginning to feel her fingers again.

Miss Thoresen returned; a small figure stepped out from behind her. "Mei-Xing? Mei-Xing!"

Tory reached her arms for Mei-Xing and the girl flew into her embrace. Tory held out an arm to Helen who joined them as they held each other.

An English gentleman—a lodger, Tory presumed—entered the kitchen just then. "What's the commotion?"

Tory paid little attention to him or others, but the woman she knew as Miss Thoresen and that others addressed as "Joy" or "Miss Joy" gave orders for her people and the Englishman to go out into the snow and hide Tory and Helen's tracks.

It was all Tory could do to hold on to Mei-Xing and Helen, while she rejoiced over and over, *We have made it. They will hide us.*

Miss Thoresen spoke softly. "Won't you please sit down? We will wait a little longer to put some lights on, but Mei-Xing, would you start some coffee?"

~*~

Later, Mei-Xing led Tory up two flights to an attic room; Billy carried Helen behind them. "Miss Joy says I am to put you both to bed, particularly Helen."

Mei-Xing frowned at Helen's vacant expression. She did not voice her concerns in words, but her eyes sought Tory's.

Tory only answered, "I will help you get Helen into bed."

Soon after, she was grateful herself to crawl into Joy's narrow bed built under the attic eaves. Mei-Xing tucked the quilt around her and sat close by in a chair. "I know how you are feeling, Tory" she said softly. "You are worried Banner and his men will track you here."

Tory nodded.

"Miss Joy and her friends are good people. They have guns. They will not allow you to be taken back *there*."

Tory wasn't sure how far she could trust Joy Thoresen, but she was exhausted and had no choice but to accept her kindness. Her eyes began to droop.

She heard the wind rising outside, softly moaning through the trees, crooning a forest lullaby . . .

~*~

Tory slept for hours before she awoke and crawled from the warmth of the bed clothes to relieve herself. She cocked her head: The weather had shifted, and winds that had sung such a comforting refrain as she fell asleep now blew at blizzard strength.

"Ah, you are up at last. You must be hungry."

"Yes, Miss Thoresen, but—"

"Please call me Joy? And Helen is just here." Joy led Tory into the next room.

Helen lay in deep sleep, seemingly undisturbed by the winds pounding the lodge and howling about the eaves.

"We are in the grip of a storm, Tory. I have to believe it is God's provision for you."

Tory glanced at Joy. "God's provision?"

"Banner, Darrow, and the others cannot track you in a storm, can they? The wind is tossing snow in every direction and piling on more. Flinty tells me he cannot see his hand in front of his face."

"Flinty?"

"A friend. He is the smithy who lives over across the siding. He tells us he saw you, nearly a year ago, when you arrived. I . . . I am sorry that no one was here then to prevent what happened to you."

Tory nodded. "I remember him. He seemed concerned."

"He has been 'concerned' for several years yet unable to do anything about it. The houses have too many armed gunmen. We are praying now . . . about how to help."

Tory looked away and then changed the subject. "Miss, I am worried about Helen. She needs a doctor."

"I agree, but there is no doctor in Corinth. She should go to Denver. Unfortunately, the train is the only way up and down the mountain in winter, and we shall see no trains until this storm subsides."

"Banner will be watching the trains, Miss Joy."

Joy nodded. "I know. We are seeking God for a plan to remove you and Helen from Corinth."

Tory studied the woman's face. *She seems so confident in God—not like me. I do not even know who he is. Who Jesus is.*

~*~

Days later, crews running steam-powered snowplows cleared the train tracks between Denver and Corinth. The British lodger, a Mr. O'Dell, went down to Denver in the morning and returned in the evening.

At the end of the week, a few days after the plows had cleared the tracks, three finely dressed women disembarked at the Corinth siding. Banner's men noted the visitors, and saw the conductor set their luggage on the platform. The carriage from Corinth Mountain Lodge met the three passengers and whisked them away.

As soon as her guests stepped into the lodge's great room, Joy drew them into the kitchen and introduced them to Tory. "Ladies, this is Victoria Washington. Tory, may I present Emily Van der Pol and her good friends, Viola Lind and Grace Minton?"

Tory nodded. "I am pleased to make your acquaintance."

"And we, yours, Tory—or do you prefer Victoria?"

"Tory is fine, Mrs. Van der Pol. Thank you."

"Tory, I understand from Mei-Xing that you have an eye for fashion," Joy began.

"That was kind of her." Tory thought Joy's statement an odd segue after the introductions.

"I mention fashion for a purpose," Joy continued—and a smiled played on her lips. "You are quite tall, but I believe Viola to be closest to your height? Will you tell me what you think of her taste in hats?"

Viola, still wearing the broad-brimmed concoction, reached up both hands and brought down the hat's veil. The thick, dusky fabric covered her face and neck and draped against her fur stole.

"It is a lovely hat, Mrs. Lind, and the veil, in addition to protecting your skin against a chilling breeze, is an elegant touch."

"I think so, too," Joy answered. "In fact, I believe this hat and veil would be stunning on *you*, do you not agree, ladies?"

"Ah, yes, I do!" Emily answered, smiling wide. "It is perfect."

Joy continued, "Emily, Viola, and Grace will be our guests tonight and tomorrow, but on Sunday, Emily will return to Denver *with her two friends.* However, Viola and Grace will not depart until Tuesday. Do you take my meaning, Tory?"

Tory looked from face to face until the scheme dawned on her. "You mean for us, for Helen and me, to—"

"To accompany me down to Denver," Emily finished. "Three women arrived, the same three will depart."

"You saw how we transported our guests the short distance from the siding to the front entrance of the lodge?" Joy asked. "We shall do the same in reverse Sunday afternoon, delivering Emily, Helen, and you to the siding. The only difficulty may be Helen's ability to walk from the carriage onto the train. Billy can, of course, help her down from the carriage, but you may need to support her across the siding and up the steps to your car without being too obvious."

"I am certain Helen will understand the hazard of the situation and do her best—but what of Mei-Xing?"

"Ah, yes. Unfortunately, Mei-Xing presents a difficulty this scheme cannot overcome. She is altogether too small to pose as either Viola or Grace—or as any of Emily's friends. We must keep her here a little longer and find another way to take her off the mountain."

"And where . . . where will we go, Helen and I, when we arrive in Denver?"

Here Emily spoke up. "I have many friends far from Denver, Tory. We think it best to remove you from the city—and quickly, do you not agree?"

"I do agree. I cannot . . . I do not care to return to Denver at this time."

Joy patted Tory's hand. "Then it is settled. If you will explain the details to Helen, perhaps she can prepare herself for the exertions she will be called upon to make come Sunday."

~*~

On Sunday afternoon, the men assigned by Banner to watch the siding for signs of Tory and Helen, observed the lodge's three guests depart for Denver. The women were dressed against the winter cold much as they had been when they arrived—full-length coats, furs, and gloves—and wide, veiled hats.

Helen leaned on Tory's arm as she moved across the platform with regal grace, Emily on her other side. When the women reached the steps up into their car, Tory murmured to the conductor, "Will you kindly assist my friend? She has been ill and is somewhat weak."

The conductor took Helen's arm and bore her weight as she struggled up the steps. Tory, directly behind her, placed a discreet hand on Helen's belt and, with the view obstructed by Emily, helped lift Helen.

Banner's men saw nothing other than three wealthy women returning down mountain from a weekend of relaxation.

Part 4:
Philadelphia,
Pennsylvania

CHAPTER 29

FEBRUARY 1909

After a four-day secret stay in Denver and a flurry of trunk calls made by Emily Van der Pol, Tory and Helen left for the city of Philadelphia. Three days later, they were met by the Misses Eloise and Eugenia Wright, Emily's trusted friends. The sisters, both in their seventies and as thin as two lengths of lath, waved their hankies in unison to attract Tory's attention.

After introductions, Tory expressed her concern regarding Helen. "My friend was growing ill before we left Colorado, and I am afraid that the stress and exertion of travel have further weakened her to the point of collapse. I do not think she can disembark under her own power."

The spinsters immediately took command of the situation, directing their chauffeur to carry Helen down from the train car and lay her in their vehicle, a covered Austin Touring automobile. The chauffeur, Benson, settled Helen across the rear seat with her head in Tory's lap while Miss Eloise and Miss Eugenia perched on the car's forward seat beside their driver.

"We shall call our personal physician as soon as we are home," Miss Eugenia declared.

"As soon as we are home!" Miss Eloise repeated.

Tory thanked them and murmured, "You are most kind."

The doctor, after examining Helen, met with Tory and the Misses Wright in their parlor. His pronouncement devastated Tory.

"Ladies, as I cannot announce good news, I shall not mince words. My diagnosis is that Miss Hawthorne has a cancer in her abdomen. Such a cancer, particularly in an advanced stage such as this, has no treatment. I shall do what I can to make her comfortable; however, you should not expect her to linger above a month."

"A month!" Tory could not believe the prognosis. "So soon? Is there no hope for her at all?"

"My dear Miss Washington, as her friend, you do not wish her to suffer, do you? For suffering she is, although she may not complain much. A month of suffering? We should pray for a quicker release than that."

The doctor left a large bottle of brown liquid to be administered "for temporary respite from pain" and promised to secure the services of a nurse. "Miss Hawthorne will require around-the-clock care."

The elderly women Tory had only just met both put their arms around her. "We comprehend how dear Helen is to you, Tory. We shall do all we can to comfort her—and you—during this difficult time," one of them said.

"Yes, all we can do. All we can do," echoed the other.

Tory did not know how to respond. It had been so long since anyone had shown her kindness or compassion. And now that she and Helen were free, after all they had borne, Helen was dying?

Tory crumpled in the Misses Wright's arms, sobbing.

"There, there," Miss Eugenia whispered on one side. "Do not despair. You are not alone. We will not forsake you."

"We will walk with both of you through this dark valley," Miss Eloise whispered on the other, "and entrust Helen to our Savior's lovingkindness."

Beginning that evening, the two women demonstrated what they had promised.

"It is not as though we do not have full faith in Dr. Pritchard. We do—he has been our physician for nigh on twenty years, after all—" began Miss Eloise.

"But in a situation as dire as this, we must explore every option," interrupted Miss Eugenia.

"Yes, every option! So, tomorrow we will seek a second opinion—"

"From a surgeon who comes to us highly recommended—"

"By good friends," finished Miss Eloise.

Tory's head had swiveled between the sisters as they finished each other's statements. She began to perceive that conversations with the Misses Wright would often proceed in similar fashion.

"In the meantime—"

"Yes, in the meantime!"

"We have ordered Cook to prepare a nourishing broth for Helen—"

"And a hot meal for you, my dear. Why, you must be fatigued from your travels—"

"While we, ourselves, generally do not eat more than a bite of soup in the evening—"

"Because we take our main meal of the day at half past noon."

They sat Tory down in the dining room and fussed over her and her dinner until she had consumed every bite they placed before her. Then they escorted Tory to her bedroom "to settle in."

The room the Misses Wright assigned to Tory was palatial in size and lavish in furnishings when compared to the narrow confines of Tory's room in the Corinth Gentlemen's Club. The sisters had ensconced Helen in the next room over.

After Tory unpacked her pitifully few possessions—two hand-me-down dresses and a few toiletries provided by Emily Van der Pol—she sought out her friend. She found Miss Eugenia seated beside Helen's bed, holding her hand, and singing softly. Tory watched as the elderly woman stroked Helen's brow, marveling at the sweetness in the woman's touch.

"Ah, there you are, Tory. Would you care to sit with Helen for a bit?"

Tory sat all night with her friend, often nodding off herself. When the pain roused Helen and she began to toss or moan, Tory would spoon a dose of the medicine into her mouth. Eventually, the drug would cause Helen to doze, but for a space of a quarter hour or more, while the medication worked to dull her pain, Helen and Tory would talk.

"What did the doctor say, Tory?"

Tory's throat was so tight she was unable to answer.

"I have felt a growth in my belly for some time. Is it that?"

"Y-yes."

"I see. May I have a sip of water, Tory?"

"Of course."

When Helen had taken a sip, she asked, "How long shall I linger, does the doctor think?"

Tory hunched over, tears sliding from her eyes. She felt her chest would burst from the pressure in it.

Miss Eugenia appeared at Helen's side. "We have another doctor coming tomorrow, dear. Shall we wait and see what he says?"

"Thank you, Miss Eugenia." Helen moved with discomfort. "You and Miss Eloise . . . I am sorry to be such a burden."

"Ah, but how can you be a burden, my dear, when you are our little sister?"

The joyful smile that bloomed on Helen's face broke Tory's heart.

"Why, I have never been a little sister!"

~*~

The highly esteemed surgeon came and went, leaving behind a report no better than the first doctor's. The nurse arrived in the afternoon and assumed Helen's care.

Then Miss Eloise took Tory in hand and, against her initial wishes, had Benson drive them into town where they first purchased nightgowns and toiletries for Helen and then a small wardrobe of ready-made wear for Tory.

When they returned, Tory again found Miss Eugenia seated beside Helen. Helen appeared to be sleeping. Tory drew up a chair near the door and sat down to listen to Eugenia's song.

> *What a friend we have in Jesus,*
> *All our sins and griefs to bear.*
> *What a privilege to carry*
> *Everything to God in prayer!*
>
> *Oh, what peace we often forfeit,*
> *Oh, what needless pain we bear,*
> *All because we do not carry*
> *Everything to God in prayer!*

For an elderly woman, Eugenia's voice was steady, clear, and pleasing. Tory soaked in the lyrics of the hymn, not having heard it before or even knowing to call it a hymn, but attracted by the joyful reverence of the songwriter's profession.

Then Miss Eugenia sang about heaven, and Tory was transported to a place of glory, a kingdom of majesty.

> *In heaven above, in heaven above,*
> *Where God our Father dwells;*
> *How boundless there the blessedness!*
> *No tongue its greatness tells.*
> *There face to face, and full and free,*
> *The ever-living God we see,*
> *Our God, the Lord of hosts!*

She was taken aback when Miss Eugenia spoke to Helen. "You know, Helen, heaven is the most wonderful place. Our heavenly Father is there, seated on his throne, surrounded by angelic hosts singing his praises. Oh! And Jesus is waiting for you, waiting to take you by the hand and bring you into the Father's presence. He even promises to wipe every tear from your eyes and heal every wound in your heart."

Helen whispered something Tory could not hear. Even Miss Eugenia had to bend close to catch her words.

The woman listened and nodded, then answered, "Ah, but you are not the only sinner in this world, Helen. We have all done awful things, even shameful things, myself included. No, you are not alone in your sinful state."

"And to be sure, God must already know about your sins, mustn't he? He is God, after all. He sees and knows all things—every detail of every sin we have committed and every aspect of our wicked hearts.

"And to think he loves us anyway? He loves us so much, in fact, that he sent Jesus to die and pay the penalty for our sin. Why, it is beyond our comprehension, don't you agree? What a great, incomprehensible sacrifice he made for us!"

When Helen did not answer, Miss Eugenia sang another song, and its haunting refrain pulled at Tory's heart.

> *At the cross, at the cross where I first saw the light,*
> *And the burden of my heart rolled away,*
> *It was there by faith I received my sight,*
> *And now I am happy all the day!*

Miss Eugenia sang several verses, from memory, afterward repeating the same tender chorus.

As Tory listened, the line, "and the burden of my heart rolled away," spoke to a place deep inside her. She found her face wet with tears of longing. *What would I not give to have the burdens of my heart lifted and rolled away? To know what happiness was?*

Helen struggled through the next days and weeks. She grew weaker and was racked with pain. The nurse cared for her physical needs, but it was Miss Eugenia who cared for Helen's heart. As Helen's body declined, Miss Eugenia comforted her and sang.

> *I must tell Jesus all of my trials,*
> *I cannot bear these burdens alone;*
> *In my distress He kindly will help me,*
> *He ever loves and cares for His own.*

> *Tempted and tried I need a great Savior,*
> *One who can help my burdens to bear;*
> *I must tell Jesus, I must tell Jesus:*
> *He all my cares and sorrows will share.*

By the close of their third week in Philadelphia, Helen's body refused food. Knowing the end could not be far away, Tory rarely left Helen's side. She assisted the nurse, turning Helen, cleaning her, changing linens often, taking her turn sitting with Helen, sleeping on a little cot in the corner of the room.

The nurse, Miss Eugenia, Miss Eloise, and Tory pressed water on Helen with every opportunity. During one such attempt, Helen pushed the glass Miss Eugenia offered her away and rasped, "How . . . how can Jesus want . . . me? So . . . so many awful things . . ."

Miss Eugenia put the glass to the side and took Helen's hand again. "Child, Jesus has been waiting for you all your life. If you will go to him right now, he will certainly receive you. Will you confess your sins to him and ask his forgiveness? Will you proclaim Jesus as your Lord and Master?"

Tory edged closer, sensing something so holy that she trembled in its presence.

Pain gripped Helen, and she writhed until the spasm eased. "How . . . How?"

"Will you allow me to lead you in prayer, Helen?"

Helen nodded.

Miss Eugenia spoke with confidence, "Lord God, I am a sinner. I am lost without you. Will you forgive me of my sins? Will you cleanse my heart and soul? I surrender to you. I surrender everything—all that I am—to you."

As much as she was able, Helen repeated Miss Eugenia's words.

The elderly woman finished with, "Jesus, I receive your gift of grace. Jesus, I welcome you into my spirit as my Savior, my Lord, and my King."

Helen struggled to say the words; Miss Eugenia had to spoon water into her mouth and reiterate her prayer so Helen could respond.

After several attempts, Helen, at last whispered, "Jesus . . . please be my Savior, my Lord, and my King."

Silence filled the room—no, not silence, but a palpable hush. And something more.

Tory stood behind Miss Eugenia's chair, staring down at Helen. Helen blinked, curiosity and surprise on her face followed by . . . wonder.

"Oh!"

Tory leaned closer, not believing what she saw: The pain had etched deep lines around Helen's eyes and mouth, but those lines seemed to fade, to smooth away. Peace washed over her countenance; grief departed from her thin, pinched cheeks.

Miss Eugenia, still clasping Helen's hand, began to sing.

'Tis so sweet to trust in Jesus,
Just to take Him at His Word;
Just to rest upon His promise,
And to know, "Thus saith the Lord!"
Jesus, Jesus, how I trust Him!
How I've proved Him o'er and o'er;
Jesus, Jesus, precious Jesus!
Oh, for grace to trust Him more!

Helen sank into a peaceful slumber and did not wake for hours. When she did rouse, her wasted body rebelled even against water.

"It will not be long now," the nurse murmured.

Helen lay still, unable to move, but with her eyes wide open. She stared straight ahead, her expression tranquil. Helen's face relaxed and grew soft and lovely again, even though the disease had wasted her.

Tory, hovering over her bed, gasped. "Miss Eugenia? Do you see?"

"Yes, oh, yes! It is the presence of God resting upon her, Tory."

The nurse left Helen's room to fetch Miss Eloise. She joined her voice with her sister and they sang in tender harmony,

My Jesus, I love Thee, I know Thou art mine;
For Thee all the follies of sin I resign;
My gracious Redeemer, my Savior art Thou;
If ever I loved Thee, my Jesus, 'tis now.

I love Thee because Thou hast first loved me,
And purchased my pardon on Calvary's tree;
I love Thee for wearing the thorns on Thy brow;
If ever I loved Thee, my Jesus, 'tis now.

I'll love Thee in life, I will love Thee in death,
And praise Thee as long as Thou lendest me breath;
And say when the death dew lies cold on my brow,
If ever I loved Thee, my Jesus, 'tis now.

Helen's eyes remained open, but her breaths came in quick and shallow pants. Miss Eloise and Miss Eugenia continued to sing softly,

In mansions of glory and endless delight,
I'll ever adore Thee in heaven so bright;
I'll sing with the glittering crown on my brow,

If ever I loved Thee, my Jesus, 'tis now.

They sang the last two lines a second time in a whisper, *I'll sing with the glittering crown upon my brow, If ever I loved Thee, my Jesus, 'tis now*. When they finished, Helen's chest fell once more . . . and did not rise.

Tory saw the moment her friend passed. She pressed her clenched fist against her mouth, but it could not prevent the sob that ripped through her. Her legs failed; she dropped to her knees, a keening wail of anguish pouring from her.

Miss Eugenia and Miss Eloise knelt beside Tory and held her, rocked her, laid their soft, papery cheeks against hers.

"There, there, Tory. It is all right," Miss Eugenia murmured. "Helen is all right. She is safe now."

"Yes. She is safe now," Miss Eloise repeated. "Safe with Jesus. No more sorrow. No more pain. Safe."

Tory dropped her face into her hands and wept. *I cannot bear this. I cannot! O Jesus! Are you there? I am so lost. I do not know what to do!*

Miss Eugenia placed her hand upon Tory's cheek. "Jesus will help you, Tory. Will you surrender your burdens to him? Will you give him your life, all of it? The good, the evil, your pain-filled past?"

"Yes, I want to!" Tory sobbed. "I want to!"

"Then let us go to him now."

Miss Eugenia led Tory in prayer as she had led Helen; she prayed and Tory prayed with her. Every word was an agony, a relinquishment, a little death.

Then, death became life.

Tory opened her tear-stained eyes. "Wh-what has happened to me?"

"You have passed, Tory, from the kingdom of darkness into the kingdom of light," Miss Eloise whispered. "You are no longer a slave to the ruler of that evil realm."

"You are no longer a slave," Miss Eugenia repeated. "Because now you are a child of God Most High, and he has made you free."

"Free?" Tory felt the shackles of sin and bondage shatter, felt the weight of shame and guilt fall from her shoulders.

"Free? Free! Oh, thank you, Jesus!"

❧ ✺ ❧

CHAPTER 30

When Tory's tears subsided, the Misses Wright tried to pull her from the room, but she would not go until she had said goodbye to Helen. She knelt by the bed and took Helen's lifeless hand in hers. Shaking her head, she marveled at the sweet repose on Helen's face.

"Dear, dear Helen, my sweet and dearest friend! How glad I am that we got away from Corinth. I had hoped, with time and rest, that you would recover. I had hoped we could find our way in life together, supporting each other in much the same manner as Miss Eugenia and Miss Eloise do.

"But, if it was not to be, then I am thankful to God for bringing us here to these sisters. I am grateful beyond measure that you were able to die in their home, at peace, surrounded by those who loved and cared for you. And, oh! I am so grateful that we found Jesus together, Helen! But . . . I confess that I shall miss you horribly. I do not know what I shall do now you are gone."

Miss Eugenia touched Tory's shoulder. "Will you come away now, Tory? We must allow Nurse to tend to Helen."

With a last glance at Helen's lifeless form, Tory permitted the sisters to lead her downstairs and into their dining room. The cook had laid out a light meal for her.

"I cannot eat," Tory protested.

"Sit, Tory, and try a bite or two. You have not eaten properly for days."

With Miss Eugenia on her right and Miss Eloise on her left, Tory tasted the food before her. Within moments of the first bite passing her lips, Tory's appetite awoke. She went from picking at her plate to shoveling omelet and toast into her mouth, trying to fill a gaping hole in her belly.

When she finished, she glanced from Eloise to Eugenia. "I did not know I was hungry. I could not feel it."

"Worry and grief do that," Miss Eloise murmured.

Tory nodded. "Thank you for taking such loving care of Helen. And of me."

"How could we not?" Miss Eugenia patted Tory's hand. "The Lord gave you to us. You are ours."

Tory bent her head, more tears close to the surface. "What will become of Helen? I do not know how to make arrangements, and I . . . have no money."

"Did Helen have family, Tory?"

"Not that I know of. She did not speak of any nor do I know where she was from."

"Ah. Then do not worry; we shall make the arrangements."

"Yes, we shall make all the arrangements," Miss Eloise echoed. "Do not worry."

"I-I cannot thank you enough."

"We shall bury Helen's body, Tory; at the same time, we shall rejoice that her spirit has gone into the presence of the Lord. So, while we prepare to lay her body in the ground, we will comfort ourselves—and you—by reading the many promises concerning heaven and eternal life found in God's word."

"I do not know any of them. I scarcely know who Jesus is!"

The two sisters smiled in complete accord.

"Today you have met him, but we shall be happy to make you better acquainted with him in the days to come," Miss Eugenia promised

"Better acquainted!" Eloise agreed.

~*~

They buried Helen two days later in the Wright family plot. Miss Eloise and Miss Eugenia's household staff turned out to honor Helen, as did the nurse who had taken great pains with Helen's comfort during her decline. Reverend Mallory, the Misses Wright's pastor, oversaw the graveside service.

Tory smiled through her tears. *Jesus? I do not need to ask if you are real now. You have come to live within me. I can even feel you! Thank you for saving Helen and me from that place in Corinth. I know it was you who spoke to me that night. Thank you for bringing us to Miss Eugenia and Miss Eloise, and thank you for taking Helen home to live with you. I have, at last, found your peace—the peace you spoke of in the Scripture verse I memorized.*

As the cemetery's men lowered Helen's coffin into the ground, Reverend Mallory read from his Bible,

> *"Then said Martha unto Jesus,*
> *Lord, if thou hadst been here,*
> *my brother had not died.*

But I know, that even now,
whatsoever thou wilt ask of God,
God will give it thee.
Jesus saith unto her,
Thy brother shall rise again.
Martha saith unto him,
I know that he shall rise again
in the resurrection at the last day.
Jesus said unto her,
I am the resurrection, and the life:
he that believeth in me,
though he were dead,
yet shall he live:
And whosoever liveth and believeth in me
shall never die."

Tory walked away from Helen's grave with the sure promises of God echoing in her heart. *I am the resurrection, and the life: he that believeth in me, though he were dead, yet shall he live.*

"I do believe in you, Jesus. I do. I am yours."

~*~

Miss Eugenia and Miss Eloise's household mourned Helen for another five days, but it was not the kind of mourning Tory expected. The sisters encouraged Tory to talk about Helen, to share little memories of her. As Tory's acquaintance with Helen was short, most of those memories were intertwined with their life in the Corinth Gentlemen's Club, the horrors they endured together, the comfort they were to each other.

The Misses Wright listened, sometimes asking discreet questions, their lips often clamped together in quivering umbrage. They comforted Tory when she wept; they hugged her, fussed over her, plied her with food, and took her on long walks twice daily to ensure she took proper exercise.

And always, when opportunity presented itself, the sisters read aloud from their Bibles and prayed over Tory. At first, the passages they read were overwhelming and confusing, so the sisters would pause, break the verses into smaller phrases, talk them over, then reread the passage in whole.

In this manner, the verses they read began to sort themselves out and make sense. Tory started to comprehend the Scriptures in her heart. When she woke to grief in the night, she was amazed to "hear" the voices of Miss Eugenia and Miss Eloise and a recently read verse speaking to her need.

A week after Helen died, Misses Eugenia and Eloise sat Tory down and presented her with her own Bible. As Tory held the precious book in her hand, she stroked its leather cover with wonder.

"My own Bible!"

"Yes, Tory. Your very own," from Miss Eugenia.

"Your own, Tory!" from Miss Eloise. "Think of it: God's word right there in your hands."

The Misses Wright then looked at each other and hesitated.

"What is it?" Tory asked. "Do . . . do you wish me to go now?"

"Go? Oh, no, child," Miss Eugenia remonstrated. "You will have a home with us as long as you wish. However, we think it best if you begin to think to your future. Do you have plans? Ideas?"

"None," Tory confessed. "I . . . do not feel adrift as I first did when Helen died, but I have no sense of what to do next."

Miss Eloise glanced at her sister, who nodded. "Would you permit us to guide you, Tory? Would you be disposed to accept direction from us?"

Tory looked from one sister to the other. "How could I not be? I owe my life to you."

The sisters, again exchanging glances, nodded in unison.

"Very well," Miss Eugenia pronounced, "then we wish to take you out this afternoon. Would you please dress for a formal call and be ready at half past four o'clock?"

"Where shall we be going?"

The hint of a mischievous smile lit Miss Eloise's mouth. "No, we shall not say. Some things are better *felt* than '*telt*.'"

The sisters clasped hands and giggled at their little joke, but Tory could only wonder what they were up to.

When she came down the stairs at half past four, she wore the best dress she owned—which was not saying much, since her wardrobe consisted of five ready-made dresses. Finding the Misses Wright in full regalia—exquisite dove-gray day dresses, elegant hats, and complementary walking boots and gloves—did not increase Tory's confidence.

Oh, dear. I am the poor, backwards country mouse to their sophisticated city mouse, she realized.

The sisters, however, said nothing. They sailed through the front entrance of their house and into their motorcar. Tory sat silently between their smug, smiling faces for the thirty-minute drive into the city proper.

When Benson parked the motorcar and opened their door, Tory's gaze sought some marker to indicate where they were. She spotted a sign that read,

Parisian Mode O Day
Monsieur Pierre LeBlanc, Proprietor

Tory sucked in her breath. "W-we are not going there, are we?"

"Monsieur LeBlanc is our good friend, Tory," Miss Eloise answered. "We wish for you to meet him."

"He really is *the* most sought-after designer in all Philadelphia," Miss Eugenia added.

"The *most* sought-after!" Miss Eloise gushed.

"But-but . . ." Tory could not articulate her reticence without casting aspersions on the clothing she wore—the clothing the Misses Wright had paid for out of their own pockets.

They were, perhaps, not as oblivious as Tory assumed. "As it is now five o'clock, the shop is closed to customers, Tory. Monsieur LeBlanc has graciously agreed to meet you after hours. Shall we go in?"

With Miss Eloise and Miss Eugenia already trotting up to the shop's entrance, Tory was stymied. *I cannot sit here while Monsieur LeBlanc is expecting me!*

With no little reluctance, Tory followed her patrons.

A maid held the door of the shop while the Misses Wright sailed through. The maid curtsied with deference to the sisters and offered the same respectful bob to Tory—while at the same time, flicking her eyes over Tory's ready-made wear, one brow quirking in disdain.

The maid's quick perusal did not escape Tory, and her face burned. *Oh, how well I perceive and understand your derision. I have not been so long from haute couture to mistake your contempt.*

Under the memory of Charles' recurrent chastisements, Tory straightened to her full height and lifted her chin. *Stand tall. Walk as a queen*, she lectured herself. *Make the best showing you can for Miss Eugenia and Miss Eloise's sake. Do not, by your manner, disappoint them.*

"Monsieur, may we present Miss Victoria Washington?"

Tory had to lower her chin—for Monsieur Pierre Monsieur LeBlanc was, at two inches above five feet, less in height than the Misses Wright—and far shorter than Tory! He was, however, dressed in impeccable style, his face wreathed in smiling goodwill.

"Ah, Mademoiselle Washington! I am so glad to make your acquaintance at last." His English was heavily accented.

Tory instinctively sank into a deep curtsy and responded in French. *"C'est un honneur de vous rencontrer, Monsieur."* It is an honor to meet you, sir.

"Regal! Stunning! Flawless!" He smoothed the little mustache above his upper lip and turned to the Misses Wright. "You did not exaggerate, my dear ladies. Mademoiselle Washington is a perfect model."

Tory glanced at her friends. They were beaming with pride.

"We knew so the moment we laid eyes upon her," Miss Eugenia murmured.

"The very moment," Miss Eloise concurred.

Tory looked between them and to Monsieur LeBlanc. "Model?"

"Yes—should you be seeking gainful employment, Mademoiselle Washington," he added.

Something wild and ecstatic leapt in Tory's breast. "You wish to offer me employment, sir?"

"Most certainly. I wish you to model my designs for my clients here, in my humble shop, and in my spring and fall fashion parades. When might you be available to start?"

Tory forgot her ready-made wardrobe—she would be modeling the most sought-after designs in the city?

"Je suis entièrement à votre disposition, Monsieur." I am entirely at your disposal, sir.

"Bon! Would tomorrow be too much of an imposition?"

"Non, Monsieur. Please name the time."

~*~

The Misses Wright had—again—proven their wisdom. Tory's new workday, from eight in the morning until half past five in the evening, kept her so completely occupied that she had little time to dwell on her grief. Yes, she mourned, but her new employment kept her busy all day, and Tory was grateful for the distraction. In the evenings following dinner, she and the Misses Wright continued their Bible study; when they finished, Tory's fatigue drove her to bed where she slept deeply, only to wake in the morning and repeat the same pattern.

The work was demanding.

It was exhilarating.

Tory had no modeling experience but, in addition to Charles' many admonishments to sit, stand, and walk tall, Roxanne had required all the girls of Corinth Gentlemen's Club to carry themselves with confidence and elegance.

Appearing before the elite of Philadelphia was little different—with this important distinction: Monsieur LeBlanc's "living mannequins" were not to make eye contact or conversation with his clients or attempt to please them in any manner save turning or walking as Monsieur or his assistant directed.

This suited Tory entirely: She adopted a serene and detached air and found appearing this way before wealthy women liberating. As for her emergence as a model for Monsieur LeBlanc's designs, she was soon his clients' favored choice, asked for so often that she was engaged all day.

Before long, Tory had developed an easy rapport with Miss Champlain, Monsieur LeBlanc's assistant, often selecting accessories for the gowns she modeled that proved a better complement than those the dressers, Miss Pearsall and Miss Fields, provided.

"You have an excellent eye, Miss Washington," Miss Champlain stated, "and, if I am not mistaken, some experience also? Have you previously worked in a house of couture?"

Tory sighed. "I did when I was younger, for the space of a year and three months."

"You have a future in fashion, if you wish it."

"Thank you. At present, I am content to be a simple mannequin."

Tory's suggested improvements held the potential to upset the shop's status quo—the employee pecking order and competitive jockeying for position—but her deferential manner defused such feelings before they took hold. She was not seeking promotion; in her heart, she had no desire to "climb." She was content to live free of Roxanne's control and work in an industry she loved. She dedicated herself to making Monsieur LeBlanc successful, and her efforts elevated those around her, for she took no credit for her recommendations.

"I hardly know what to think of this young woman," Miss Champlain said to her employer.

"She is a jewel, is she not?" he answered, "but, perhaps, a fragile one? We must not allow the sharp tongues of certain clients to wound her."

"I shall watch closely, Monsieur."

"Please do."

CHAPTER 31

Six weeks after Tory began her work for Monsieur LeBlanc, she entered the shop and found it in chaos. Miss Pearsall, Monsieur LeBlanc's principal dresser, was wringing her hands; his fitters and maids were in tears.

"What has happened?"

"Not thirty minutes ago, Miss Champlain was struck by a motorcar as we left the trolley—right in front of the shop," the distraught dresser exclaimed. "Stupid fool! He was driving entirely too fast, and he raced away leaving poor Miss Champlain lying in the street. I ran to Monsieur for help. He and some passing gentlemen lifted her into his automobile and Monsieur has, himself, taken her to the hospital."

"Oh, no! Is she badly hurt?"

"A broken leg for certain. Perhaps her arm, as well. Fie! I cannot wipe the horrible images from my head!"

Another maid appeared. "Miss? We have customers outside waiting for the doors to open."

Miss Pearsall and Tory looked at each other, and Tory nodded at the older woman. "We must, somehow, carry on in Monsieur and Miss Champlain's absence, of course. What do the appointments look like today, Miss Pearsall?"

Miss Pearsall dabbed at her eyes. "Oh, dear. We have the Mayfair bridal party arriving first thing this morning—that must be them, waiting. Monsieur has completed the sketches of Miss Mayfair's wedding gown and her bridal party's dresses, but should Miss Mayfair or her mother dislike them, I would not know what to say to them. I am a dresser, not a designer! Please, Miss Tory, could you present the sketches?"

Tory's eyes widened. "What? Why, I—"

"Oh, you must, Miss Tory, for I cannot possibly present the designs; these women terrify me. Please say you will take charge—I promise I can assist you!"

Tory had seen the designs. She exhaled and straightened.

When Monsieur LeBlanc returned from the hospital near noon, he gathered his staff and reported that the doctor had splinted Miss Champlain's leg and wrapped her arm. "Her forearm is badly bruised but, mercifully, it is not broken. Ah, but her leg? It is fractured. She must remain in hospital, with her leg immobile, for two weeks, to be followed by four weeks of careful rest at home."

He bowed his head, the worried expression on his face out of character for him, "Miss Champlain's misfortune is a great blow to me and to my house, but we must, somehow, weather this storm."

He lifted his eyes and sought Miss Pearsall. "Have we lost the Mayfair wedding, Miss Pearsall?"

"No, Monsieur. Miss Mayfair and her mother are pleased, sir. They have approved the designs—with one or two modifications as suggested by Miss Washington."

Monsieur LeBlanc turned his gaze upon Tory. "You presented the designs, Mademoiselle Tory?"

"I-I apologize, sir, but . . . no one else was willing."

"No apology is needed, my dear; you have my thanks. You have saved a large account, for which I am grateful." His thumb and forefinger smoothed his little mustache, and his features lost some of their tension. "I think . . . yes. Until Miss Champlain is able to return, it is my wish that you assume her duties."

"What? I, sir?"

He spun on his heel. "Miss Pearsall. How did Miss Mayfair and her mother receive Mademoiselle Tory's assistance?"

"They were delighted, sir. And, if I may say so, sir," Miss Pearsall slanted a look at Tory, "Miss Washington was superb."

"*Bon!* Just so! The matter, it is settled. The showing of my spring collection is but weeks away, and I must have an assistant."

"But . . ."

Monsieur LeBlanc waved his staff away. "Back to work everyone, if you please. We have much to do this day."

He gestured to Tory. "Please show me Miss Mayfair's approved designs and the requested modifications. We must now set my seamstresses to work."

~*~

That evening when Tory returned home, Miss Eugenia handed her an envelope.

"A letter? For me?" Tory opened the envelope and unfolded the fragrant stationery. She glanced at the signature. "From Emily Van der Pol!"

Tory read the short missive, exclaiming over its contents twice, going back to read it again, then lifting her gaze to the sisters and their open curiosity. "Miss Eloise, Miss Eugenia—I must read this news to you."

"Please do," Miss Eloise murmured. "We are on pins and needles."

"Tenterhooks, my dear," Miss Eugenia corrected. "Tenterhooks!"

Tory smothered a smile. "This is what Emily writes."

My dear Miss Washington,

I have received momentous news, which I hasten to write to you, as I know you will be rejoicing as much—and likely more— than I at its reception.

Only days ago, U.S. Marshals and men of the Pinkerton Agency entered Corinth en masse in the hours prior to dawn. They arrived in time to save our dear Miss Thoresen from the man who purportedly owns those abominations, Corinth's two houses of evil doings. The marshals arrested a Mr. Morgan as well as Banner, Darrow, and their men. They also arrested Roxanne Cleary.

"To God be the glory," Miss Eugenia breathed.

"God be praised!" exclaimed Miss Eloise.

"I can scarcely comprehend it," Tory whispered. "How just. Roxanne! Arrested! In jail!"

"Pray continue, Tory."

"Yes, do, please!"

"Certainly."

The marshals were not in time to save the Corinth Mountain Lodge. I am saddened to report that Banner and his men burned it to the ground. I am further saddened to say that Miss Thoresen herself was scandalously mishandled and suffered broken and bruised ribs. She is in much pain, but I am assured that she shall recover with time. She is in the care of her cousin in Corinth's church parsonage.

As the lodge had burned and they had nowhere else to go, Joy's widowed mother, Rose Thoresen (who recently joined her daughter at the lodge), and others from the lodge have taken up residence in the one of the houses—in point of fact, the very house of your own unhappy acquaintance.

Mrs. Thoresen informed the girls of both houses that they were free to go and offered train tickets to any girl who had a home to go to. Some, but not all, of the girls took advantage of the offer and have departed Corinth.

I cannot, at present, say what will become of the remainder of the young women. Miss Thoresen and her mother wish to remove themselves to Denver, acquire a suitable house, and take with them those girls who have no homes and who need a loving environment while they acclimate to their freedom.

We must wait to see what God will do in that direction, but I did not wish to delay this letter and its happy news any longer: Your friends in Corinth are safe, including your dear Mei-Xing.

In the name of the One who loves us,
Emily Van der Pol

Reading the letter aloud made the news more real, and Tory broke down, sobbing, "Thank you, Jesus! Thank you!"

"Yes, Lord, we thank you and praise you," the two sisters echoed.

Six more weeks flew by. Monsieur LeBlanc's spring show was a success; with the show behind them, his entire staff sighed with collective relief. Orders resulting from the show assured staff employment for some weeks. In addition, Miss Champlain's doctor released her to resume her work the following week.

"Mademoiselle Tory, I wish to speak with you." Monsieur LeBlanc rocked back on his heels, a smile playing about his mouth.

"Yes, sir?"

"Come into my office, if you please."

Tory entered and took the seat he held for her.

"Mademoiselle Tory, I am most pleased with your work in Miss Champlain's absence."

"Thank you, sir."

"And I have reaped the benefits of your design modifications and improvements. Indeed, I have taken a great liberty and have peeked at that sketch pad you carry with you at all times."

Tory blushed. "My inadequate attempts, sir."

"*Non.* The emergence of a true designer."

Her heart pounding in her throat, Tory stared at the little man. "Sir?"

"Miss Champlain returns next week, *non?* She must not do too much at first. We must be careful of her."

"Yes, sir."

"You will continue to assist me when Miss Champlain tires. You will also select two of your designs and work with our seamstresses to bring them to completion. I wish to see you model them."

"Sir?" Tory was astounded—and more excited at the prospect than she let on.

"Just as I said. We shall proceed and see where this road takes us, eh? However, I have prayed, and I believe I have God's mind in this."

"Y-yes, sir."

Tory, between her work supplementing Miss Champlain's duties, presented her two best designs to Monsieur LeBlanc's head seamstress. Together, they brought the gowns to life.

"This one I well like, Mademoiselle Tory." Monsieur LeBlanc fingered the fabric of one of the finished gowns. "The other not as much—but what do I know? You have an eye for what is ahead, while I, perhaps, look too much to the past."

He put his hands upon his hips. "I wish you to present both gowns at my fall fashion parade in October. We shall discover then if my clients like your designs."

He changed subjects. "In the meantime, you will continue to assist me as my apprentice."

"Your—I beg your pardon, sir?"

"I offer you an apprenticeship, Mademoiselle Tory. Five years at my side to perfect every aspect of this profession. I shall supply the knowledge you are lacking and help you refine your technique. However, you must stay true to your own unique style. You see, while you will continue with me for the foreseeable future, I predict that you will someday establish your own house."

Tory's head reeled at the possibilities—the unprecedented opportunity—Monsieur LeBlanc offered her. "I am most grateful, sir!"

With little fanfare, Tory became Monsieur LeBlanc's apprentice and second in command. She spent half of her time at his side, listening, observing, asking questions, contributing her opinion when requested. The other half of her time she spent designing and working with the seamstresses to birth her creations.

The labor was demanding, for Monsieur LeBlanc oversaw and checked every detail of her work. He pointed out her design flaws with the precision of a surgeon: "*Non*, Mademoiselle! One cannot simply drop a waistline without considering the effect upon the décolletage. Harmony! Design must harmonize on every point, every aspect. And what are you thinking to shorten sleeves on a winter dress? Do you also wish to lengthen gloves? Think!"

She accompanied the little gentleman when he visited cloth merchants and placed his orders—discovering him to be a shrewd bargainer. She peered over his shoulders as he scrutinized finished dresses, appraising every stitch, every line, the cut of the fabric, identifying flaws Tory had not known existed.

She observed his interactions with his clients, and learned how to convince a woman that a style did not become her *without* saying, "Madame, your posterior is already large enough without accentuating it" or "Mademoiselle, since you have not the ability to fill the bodice, a ruffle is required to render the illusion of fullness."

Monsieur LeBlanc also insisted she review his accounts—then demanded she manage them. After handling the books of the Broadmoor Hotel, the transition was not a difficult one. However, to her chagrin, Tory had to often stay late to balance the books and send out payments to Monsieur's creditors.

This is not at all what I envisioned as Monsieur LeBlanc's apprentice, she laughed to herself with wry humor. *I must again call Miss Eugenia and ask forgiveness for missing dinner.*

By the end of summer, Tory had found her footing. Tasks that had seemed overwhelming fell into place. Vast details became daily trifles, keeping the books routine. Her sketches took on a more professional patina and her line of clothing an elegant simplicity that the dressers—and Monsieur LeBlanc's clients—applauded.

~*~

In late August, Tory received a second letter from Emily Van der Pol. "Miss Eloise? Miss Eugenia?"

"Yes, dear. We are in the drawing room."

Tory was flushed with excitement. She held an opened letter in her hand. "I have received a second letter from Mrs. Van der Pol. May I read a portion to you?"

"But of course, Tory! What does the dear woman say that is of such great import?"

Tory scanned down the letter to the right place. "Here it is."

A precious (but entirely unpredictable) friend, Martha Palmer, has astounded us all. This godly elder woman has given her old house to your dear acquaintance, Miss Thoresen, and her mother, Rose. The house is quite large but has been closed up for years and is in a sad and neglected state.

Miss and Mrs. Thoresen have now taken up residence in Denver with the girls from the mountain who elected to come with them. Joy and her mother intend to make the house into a home for these young women who have nowhere else to go. They have christened the establishment Palmer House in Martha Palmer's honor.

Of course, each young lady must find work, a difficult proposition given their previous occupation. (I write plainly to you, Tory, knowing you will take no offence.) To that end, Joy and her mother hope to train the girls in various vocations. Joy feels that they should teach some of the girls to sew, in particular how to run the newest of electric-powered sewing machines. Joy has declared herself unfit for such a task, so, of course, I thought of you.

Miss Eugenia sat up straight. "She thought of you, Tory?"

"Well, of course she did, Eugenia. Tory must be one of the few girls from *that place* equipped to make her own way in the world."

"But, Eloise, why would she say, 'Of course, I thought of you'?"

"I think it is because I know enough to teach others to sew, and I know how to run a hotel and am learning to run a dressmaking shop."

The two spinsters stared at Tory until Miss Eugenia said, "You have not been long with Monsieur LeBlanc, Tory, and your period of apprenticeship is five years. It will not be complete for some time."

Eugenia had not an unkind bone in her body; she was merely stating facts.

"That is true, and Monsieur LeBlanc has already been too good to me. I would never presume to dishonor my agreement with him."

"But?" This from Eloise.

Tory shrugged. "I can only say that my heart leapt in my chest when I read Mrs. Van der Pol's words. I can think of no better service to God than to dedicate my life to helping those who have been misused as I was. It is true that five years is a long time to wait. However," and here she smiled, "God's timing is always perfect, is it not?"

"Indeed, it is," Eugenia murmured. She slid her eyes toward her sister.

"Yes, I quite agree," Eloise echoed.

But Eugenia was not fooled. She recognized the contemplative expression on her sister's face. After Tory had left the room, she lifted her chin. "I know you, Eloise. What are you thinking?"

"What am I thinking? I am thinking we should pray. God did not rescue Tory from a life of hopeless depravity merely to clothe the idle rich."

Eugenia clasped her sister's hand. "How insightful, Eloise. Just so. We will pray."

❧ ✳ ❦

CHAPTER 32

October arrived and, with it, Monsieur's fall showing—his autumn fashion parade. "Think of it, *ma chère!*" her mentor enthused. "You shall introduce yourself to all Philadelphia at this showing. I wish you to have, at a minimum, six dresses and three gowns on the parade circuit. We must hire more models to accommodate your line."

The showing was deemed a grand success—and so was Tory. At the reception afterward, Monsieur LeBlanc spoke of nothing but Tory's future. "Mark my words," he told his clients, "Mademoiselle Tory will outshine us all."

His words were captured in the fashion pages of the city's newspapers—as were photographs of Tory herself when she took her bow at the end of the show and while greeting the show's attendees at the reception. For weeks following the show, Monsieur's clients came to the shop asking for Tory. Monsieur LeBlanc soon set aside two showrooms specifically for her and assigned Miss Fields as her permanent assistant.

Tory was overcome by Monsieur LeBlanc's generous spirit. She had never known such an unselfish and giving heart—honest in his dealings, genuinely concerned for his employees' well-being, and proud that Tory had begun to make a name for herself.

As November passed into December Tory realized that, for the first time in her life, she was happy and content. "This is what you meant, isn't it Lord?" she prayed. "*For I know the thoughts that I think toward you, saith the Lord, thoughts of peace, and not of evil, to give you an expected end.* You did not leave me hopeless in Corinth! You made a way out—and prepared this new life for me."

Tory rejoiced in her situation, convinced that God himself had brought her to this place. "I do not ever wish to take for granted what you have given me, Lord. I see Monsieur LeBlanc and his heart—he enriches all who come into his circle—and I know it is you, living through him."

Tory's contemplation ran deeper. "I want to emulate this godly man, Lord. I want my life to count for something more than my own success. Whatever you decide, Lord. I wish to be a testimony of your goodness and mercy."

~*~

December arrived and colder weather with it. Tory, like many of Monsieur LeBlanc's employees, took the trolley to and from work. She never tired of riding the car across town. She enjoyed the sights of the city— even as the weather turned and more riders employed the trolley as shelter on their daily journeys. True, the cars did become crowded, particularly when winds howled. On such blustery days, the overfilled trolleys required many passengers to bunch together in the center aisle, holding to poles, overhead handles, or the edges of nearby seats.

It was the end of a long week, the second week of the month, and Tory, already fatigued, gripped the overhead strap and swayed to the trolley's rhythmic ride. *Oh, how I am ready for Sunday rest, Lord. I long to worship at our church and spend the afternoon quietly at home. Perhaps I can talk Miss Eugenia into—*

The trolley's sharp turn caught several passengers unprepared, including Tory. She lost her grip and fell backward onto a fellow passenger's chest.

"I am terribly sorry," Tory apologized as she found her footing. *Well, that was humiliating.* she thought.

The gentleman nodded to her, but looked away, seemingly as embarrassed as she.

Tory thought no more of it until another week had passed. She left the shop at a reasonable hour, intending to get off the trolley at a little candy shop to purchase a box of chocolates for Monsieur LeBlanc's employees. She stepped off the trolley in the center of the road, watched for traffic to clear, and walked briskly across to the cheerful little store.

She perused the many confections offered before deciding on her selections. She had turned toward the front of the store when her eye caught a glimpse of a man peering through the door's window glass—a glimpse only, because the man withdrew the moment she turned.

Tory blinked, thinking the man had looked familiar.

Was that the man I fell onto last week on the trolley? She blinked slowly. *No, I am likely mistaken.*

Tory paid the shopkeeper to box up her candies and wrap the box in festive paper. She was eager to catch the next trolley home. *How I shall enjoy exchanging these shoes for my soft slippers.*

But outside the candy shop, Tory felt a prickle on her skin. She stared around, convinced someone was watching her, but saw no one.

~*~

Christmas came and went—a holy, happy time for Tory. She and the Misses Wright had such fun together. For elderly spinsters, Tory thought them less set in their ways—and a great deal more energetic—than many folks decades younger.

"It is such a pleasure to have a youngster in this house," Miss Eloise murmured. "We haven't done much Christmas baking in recent years. Why bother if there is no one to eat it all?"

Tory was more than happy to eat her share and Miss Eloise's, too.

"And why decorate when there is no one but us to look at it?" Miss Eugenia explained.

"Oh, please, may we have a tree?" Tory begged.

The two sisters grinned and answered together, "Yes!"

After they put up the tree, Tory served tea and they made inroads on the mountain of cookies they had baked and decorated.

"I love Christmas," Tory sighed.

The sisters looked with fondness on Tory.

"Ah, but we love *you*, dear Tory. You have made our lives so much brighter," Miss Eugenia said.

Miss Eloise nodded her agreement. "So much brighter."

On Tory's return to work after New Year's Day, she spotted the same man who had been peering at her through the window of the candy shop. He was standing at the corner where she usually got off the trolley. Although he leaned against a lamppost and held an open newspaper before his face, Tory was positive it was the same man. He was the right height and the same coloring—dark-haired, cut short.

Determined to confront the mysterious individual, Tory altered her course toward him. She was close enough to catch the dismay in his eyes— light brown—as he peered over the newspaper and realized she was nearly on him. The man spun away from the lamppost and raced off.

"So, he *was* following me!"

Now Tory was truly alarmed, and she told the Misses Wright about the man. They, too, expressed concern, but could offer no possible explanation for the man's unwanted attention.

"We shall have Benson drive you from now on, Tory," Miss Eloise declared. "One can never be too careful these days—and you have become somewhat of a celebrity, you know, with your picture in the fashion pages of all the newspapers. No, I shall not rest at night thinking someone has developed an unhealthy regard for you. Benson must drive you."

"Can never be too careful. Benson must drive you henceforth," confirmed Miss Eugenia.

Benson did drive her for the remainder of the week. He not only drove her to and from Monsieur LeBlanc's shop but, on Miss Eugenia and Miss Eloise's express orders, he escorted Tory into the shop and called for her at the door each evening. However, although Tory, during the drive to and from work, vigilantly scanned the streets and corners, hoping to glimpse the man again, she saw no sign of him.

"Good riddance," she sniffed, "whomever you are."

~*~

A week later, Monsieur LeBlanc called Tory into his office. His expression was grim.

His barely repressed anger unnerved Tory. She had never seen him disturbed in this manner, not even when Miss Champlain had been struck by the speeding motorist.

"Yes, sir?"

"Please sit down, Mademoiselle."

As Tory sat, a weight settled on her chest. "What is wrong?"

"Rumors, Mademoiselle Tory. Horrible, ghastly rumors."

Tory's eyes widened. "W-what rumors?"

"Rumors, I am most regretful to say, *ma chère*, which concern you. They speak of . . . your past."

"W-what?" Then Tory could not speak because a churning fear took over.

If word were to get out about my life in Corinth, if the wealthy of the city were to hear that I worked as a whore, Monsieur LeBlanc would be ruined. He cannot employ or promote a tainted woman without tainting himself.

"Who, Monsieur? Who is saying these things?"

"I have not ascertained the source. One rarely can, you know. An old and dear friend of mine, a wealthy dowager—also an *émigré* from France—came to me privately this morning to tell me. She says the rumors began over the holidays and have spread like what you Americans call 'wildfire.'"

Tory's careening thoughts supplied a suspicion. "Could it be that man? The one who was following me?" She quickly scotched her own idea. "No; how could it be? How could anyone in Philadelphia know about my past?"

"I cannot say, mademoiselle. However, we must be prepared to combat such baseless accusations for, according to my friend, they have already taken hold. I shall refute them myself, *certainement*. You are an honorable, chaste woman. I will attest to it!"

Tory stared at the floor. "But you know the rumors are not baseless accusations, Monsieur LeBlanc. Miss Eugenia and Miss Eloise told you of my past before I met you."

"You are not culpable for what you were forced to do, mademoiselle, and your behavior in this city has been nothing but praiseworthy. We shall, of course, refute such talk wherever it rises. I shall speak to the staff and—"

Tory's harsh laugh interrupted him. "Will it matter? No. It will not change the outcome one whit."

Monsieur LeBlanc sank into his own chair. "Nevertheless, we must try, no? You and I must explain. Surely our most loyal patrons will understand and defend you. And we must pray, Mademoiselle Tory. The wickedness of these stories and their intent to defame you are not of God."

Tory nodded, but, as the significance of the rumors—the magnitude of their consequences—began to sink in, she gasped, then doubled over. She felt as though she had been kicked in the stomach. The pain! It was like Darrow and Jingo attacking her—their fists punching and striking her, their hands clawing at her, their bodies holding her down, violating her.

Again.

And again.

And again.

Tory scrabbled at her bodice and the neck of her dress, her entire body overwhelmed with panic. She could not catch her breath.

"Mademoiselle Tory? Mademoiselle Tory!"

Tory slid from her chair. She sank, unconscious, onto the floor of Monsieur LeBlanc's office.

~*~

Much later, when Tory revived and could stand on her own, Monsieur LeBlanc helped her to his automobile and drove her home. He allowed her the silence she craved. When they arrived at the Misses Wrights' home, Tory left Monsieur's motorcar and, ignoring the sisters' questions, walked to her room in silence. She closed and locked the door and remained alone until morning, worrying over all Monsieur LeBlanc had told her.

Nevertheless, we must try. You and I must explain. Surely our most loyal patrons will defend you. And we must pray, Mademoiselle Tory. The wickedness of these stories and their intent to defame you are not of God.

Out of respect for Monsieur's wishes, Tory returned to work. No smile lit her face; no greeting passed her lips. She nodded to the staff members she encountered on her way to her office. There she waited for Miss Fields to announce her first client of the morning.

Fifteen minutes after Tory's first scheduled appointment, Miss Fields appeared to whisper that Tory's client had not arrived nor had the woman called to cancel. Her second appointment, a kindly matron, Mrs. Helmsworthy, arrived early. Miss Fields escorted the solemn-faced woman to one of Tory's private showrooms, then notified Tory of her arrival.

When Tory entered the showroom, Mrs. Helmsworthy waved Miss Fields away. "I wish a personal word with Miss Washington, if you please."

Here it is, Tory thought. *You must stand tall, Tory.* Aloud, she said evenly, "Good morning, Mrs. Helmsworthy."

The woman hesitated only a moment. "Miss Washington, are you aware of the gossip circulating throughout the city concerning you?"

"Yes, ma'am."

"Well, what have you to say for yourself?"

Tory glanced at the floor, then at the woman's anxious face. She was surprised at what she saw. *Why, I believe she is genuinely worried for me.*

The older woman's show of concern touched Tory. It did not, however, deter Tory from speaking facts that would confirm her client's worst fears.

"Mrs. Helmsworthy, nearly two years ago I accepted an offer of employment not far from Denver. However, when I arrived to take up my post, I discovered that the offer was fraudulent—a lie. Instead of honest work, I was forced into . . . prostitution. Eleven months later, by the grace of God, I escaped from those who held me captive."

Mrs. Helmsworthy's mouth tightened. "Held captive? Forced? Forced how?"

"I was beaten. Raped repeatedly by two men. Starved until I complied."

The woman stumbled backward and dropped into a chair. "No."

Tory tipped her head to one side. "Sadly, it is the truth. I was told I would be raped and beaten again and again until I submitted to their demands."

Tory realized her client was crying. Tory looked away, then offered her handkerchief. "I did not choose such an occupation, Mrs. Helmsworthy, and I can do nothing to alter what happened to me." She shrugged. "I moved here, to Philadelphia, and began a new life—yet now, as I have gained a little success, someone has chosen to whisper into society the details of my past. After all my efforts to live an upright life, this individual has ruined me."

Mrs. Helmsworthy dabbed at her streaming eyes. "I cannot say . . . how very, very sorry I am, Miss Washington."

Tory twitched her shoulders. "But you will be taking your custom elsewhere?"

The woman wagged her head. "What else can I do?"

Tory did not answer, but inside, she burned. *You could stand up for what is right, rather than bow to what is convenient.*

"Shall I see you out, Mrs. Helmsworthy?"

"I . . . yes, thank you."

Three of Tory's clients that day either canceled or did not show. To the two clients who did keep their appointments, Tory made the same explanation she had offered Mrs. Helmsworthy. With similar outcomes.

The last client of the day used her appointment to soundly condemn Tory and promise that neither she nor her friends would employ Tory's services in future.

The client was not interested in Tory's explanation.

By midday, all of Monsieur LeBlanc's employees had heard the rumors, so Monsieur took them aside, a few at a time, and shared the facts. In view of Tory's stony demeanor, however, not one employee spoke to her that day—with the exception of Miss Champlain.

The woman was not unkind, but she was blunt. "I have worked for Monsieur LeBlanc for fifteen years, Miss Washington, through good times and bad. If you were compelled against your will to do . . . those *things*, as Monsieur insists you were, then I lay no fault at your door for the present public outrage against you.

"You have been good to Monsieur and also kind to me and all Monsieur's staff, Miss Washington, so I am sorry to be the bearer of an unhappy observation. You see, facts seldom alter public opinion once it is settled—and Monsieur depends upon his good name and upright reputation to remain in business. The reality, then, is that if you do not resign, you shall ruin Monsieur—and not only him, but the rest of us also.

"Monsieur is entirely too devoted to those he loves: He will never ask you to go. However, if *you* care for *him*, then you must leave of your own accord—or bear responsibility for the downfall of this house."

Tory nodded. "Thank you for your honesty, Miss Champlain, for helping me to see my duty."

She sat in the solitude of her office a little longer.

Lord? Why? Why did you allow this to happen?

CHAPTER 33

Tory wrote a letter of resignation and placed it on Monsieur LeBlanc's desk when the shop closed in the evening and Benson arrived to drive her home. She again bypassed the Misses Wright and shut herself up in her room. When she did not appear for dinner, Miss Eloise and Miss Eugenia knocked at her door. When she did not answer, they spoke to Tory through the keyhole.

"Tory, dear? Are you all right?"

"Yes, Tory, dear—are you all right?"

She did not answer.

Three days went by. Each day, the good ladies tried to reach Tory, but she refused to respond or come out to eat.

"She must be out of water by now."

"No water."

"She has taken no food."

"No food."

"If she does not come down by tomorrow, I shall have Benson force the door."

"Force the door. Yes."

"Perhaps we should call Monsieur LeBlanc, first?"

"Oh, yes. Quite right. Call him immediately."

Their small friend with the giant heart abandoned his clients and came at once. He and the two sisters cloistered themselves in the parlor for more than an hour. They discussed all options, prayed, and reached a decision.

Monsieur LeBlanc stood outside Tory's bedroom with Miss Eugenia and Miss Eloise hovering in the hallway. Benson, nearby, awaited the order to break the door's lock.

"Mademoiselle Tory, *ouvre la porte*. I must insist: Open the door. I wish to speak to you, and I will not leave until you have heard me," Monsieur LeBlanc began.

He received no reply, so he added, "I give you but one minute to open to me, Mademoiselle Tory. If you do not open the door to me within that minute, Benson will release it by force."

After a sustained silence, Tory whispered, "Please go away."

"*Non*, Mademoiselle Tory. I will not go. You have but a few seconds remaining before I give Benson leave to break the lock."

He thought he heard a sigh, then Tory answered, "Send them all away, and I will open the door to you."

Monsieur LeBlanc whisked the sisters and Benson out of the hall. "Go now. All will be well."

The Misses Wright and their chauffeur departed.

"They are gone, now, Mademoiselle Tory."

The door slowly turned on its hinges, and he stepped inside, shutting the door behind him. He found the stuffy darkness of the room oppressive. Before greeting Tory, he went to her windows, swept the curtains aside, and threw open a window. A brisk winter breeze soon chased the stagnant air from the room.

"Ah! In the same manner as I have opened a window to cleanse this room from what is old and unhealthy, now you and I must do the same for you, my dear young woman," Monsieur declared. "Come sit with me, and we shall welcome the breath of God's Spirit together."

Tory, however, was uncooperative. The conversation proceeded in short, stilted sentences before it petered to an end.

"If you will not share your pain with me, Mademoiselle, how can I help you?"

"You cannot help," Tory whispered. "I have nothing left. This person—this gossip, whoever it is—has taken everything from me. What can anyone do to help? Nothing. Nothing can be done. It is all gone now. I may not even look to the happiness a woman hopes for. A husband. A family. I am ruined."

"Ah, *ma chère*, I comprehend your pain so much more than you know. First, your innocence was taken, *non?* I, too, could make the same claim. Your childhood was stolen—as was mine." He coughed politely into his hand, but Tory saw it for what Charles had taught her: a gesture of discomfort. A means to delay, to gather his composure, to find the right words.

"I hesitate to speak of such indelicate issues," he began again, "but I feel I must overcome my natural reticence and say what is in my heart, or you may never recover from the wounds you have suffered."

He patted and clasped her hands, and his gentle brown eyes captured and held Tory's as she, with reluctance, gave him her complete attention.

"You see, mademoiselle, the innocence of a boy may be stolen in the same manner as a young woman who is forced."

As his meaning came clear, Tory's lips parted in anguish. "No. You do not mean that!"

"Ah, but I do mean it, Mademoiselle Tory."

"Then . . . then you-you . . ."

"*Oui*. I am, sadly, by virtue of my own experience, in possession of the intimate details of your anguish and, more to our conversation today, the longevity of that agony, the residue of cruel misuse at the hands of another human being and the shame such misuse engenders. But I wish to ask you a question, dear woman, if I may?"

"Whatever you ask, Monsieur LeBlanc. I-I owe you so much."

"We shall not frame our conversation in terms of 'owing,' shall we? As two creatures made in the image of God Almighty, let us share the fellowship we have in him, eh?"

"As you say, sir. What did you wish to ask me?"

"*Trés bien*. My question to you is, do you observe in my manner— my attitude and day-to-day state of disposition—a defeat of mind and spirit? Do you sense, in my word or deed, the pain of which we speak?"

Tory's brow creased a little. "No, Monsieur. You are a gentleman of invariably steady and cheerful temperament."

"*Bon*. And do you distinguish in my mood or outlook that which is disingenuous or, as they say, 'put on'?"

"Not at all, sir. I find your joy to be authentic; it is an example I admire and would seek to emulate . . . if but I could."

"You humble me, mademoiselle. However, if you give me leave to ask, if you admire and desire to emulate my joy, will you receive a word of advice from one whose concern is only for your happiness?"

Tory's eyes stung and began to water. "You are too kind, Monsieur LeBlanc, but—"

"But you do not wish to recover and live a full and happy life?"

"Well, certainly, I do, but my future here is at an end. I shall never live down these reports."

"Forgive me, Mademoiselle Tory, *mais oui ou non*—the answer is either yes or no: Do you or do you not wish to leave the past forever in its grave and look to your future with hope and joy?"

"I-I do wish it."

"Then you must no longer be the victim."

Shocked, Tory stood and stepped away. "*The victim!* Must no longer be *the victim*? Monsieur LeBlanc, I *am* the victim!"

She stared at the floor, the tips of her shoes, the legs of her bed, her bureau, the clothes she had left scattered on the floor and saw none of those things, only the parade of men—beginning with Drake but extending through her eleven months in Corinth—men who had degraded her, had made her laugh and smile while she pleasured them, had forced her to pretend to enjoy their attentions and lustful behaviors.

And then the man who had dogged her steps filled the ears of the whole city with her shame. Tears filled and overflowed her eyes.

"Mademoiselle Tory, please to look at me."

"I-I cannot."

"I do not force you, mademoiselle; I ask, most humbly. I beg your leave: Please to look at me."

Tory sniffed back her tears, patted her cheeks, and pinched the bridge of her nose. When she felt in sufficient control of herself, she lifted her eyes and looked at him. Her chin trembled when she admitted to the compassion she saw in his expression.

"Please. Please to answer my questions?" he asked. "Yes or no only: Do you wish to recover? Can you answer me?"

"Yes," Tory whispered.

His small smile was kind. "Tell me, have Mademoiselle Eloise and Mademoiselle Miss Eugenia shared the Good News of Jesus with you?"

"Yes, they have."

"And have you surrendered your heart to the *Seigneur Jésus?*"

"I . . . I have."

"And have you felt the miracle of the new birth, the new heart?"

Tory nodded. "Yes."

"*Bon.* The Scripture, it tells us many things about our new life in Christ. When we are first born, we are like God's little children, *oui?* But soon, our heavenly Father calls us higher, and we must grow up into maturity. The Scriptures, in the Epistle to the Ephesians, says we must 'henceforth be no more children.' But each one must decide if he will grow or remain a child. It is a choice—do you see?"

"I . . . yes."

"The process of maturation, of growing, is not *un mystère*, a mysterious thing. It is not veiled or hidden. The Scripture tells us,

> *But speaking the truth in love,*
> *[we] may grow up into him in all things,*
> *which is the head, even Christ*

"Truth, then, is required for growth. Truth, *oui?*"

Tory nodded.

"The passage continues thus:

> *This I say therefore, and testify in the Lord,*
> *that ye henceforth walk not as other Gentiles walk,*
> *in the vanity of their mind.*

"We, the redeemed of the Lord, are not to walk in vain, fruitless, futile, unproductive thinking, like those of the unregenerate. We are to, the Holy Book tells us, *Put off the old man, and be renewed in the spirit of our minds*. Our minds, it seems, have many problems. We must wash our minds with the truth—but what is truth? Is this not the age-old question?"

He turned and stared out across her room before he spoke again. "Here is truth, mademoiselle: Everyone has suffered wrong. This is the fact, is it not? I have in my acquaintance many people, some of poor means, some of wealth. I know of no man or woman, great or small, who has not been wronged, who does not carry a burden of suffering in one manner or another.

"My dear woman, if you have suffered more wrong than I have, I promise you, someone has suffered deeper wrong than you. And if that man or woman's pain is greater than yours, another has suffered even more.

"You must admit to this truth, *this fact of life*, that you are not alone in your pain, mademoiselle, nor are you unique in your suffering. This does not lessen the trespass you have suffered nor does it diminish the anger of God at such sinners. But we are not talking of justice at this moment, eh? We are speaking of your future. It is *your future* at stake. For your future's sake, you must commit these wrongs into the hand of God."

"But someone has ruined my life in Philadelphia! If I stay here, your life's work will be tarred with the same stain! And will no one ever be punished for these wrongs, Monsieur LeBlanc? Will they escape justice? It is not fair! It is not right!"

"No, mademoiselle, it is neither fair nor right; however, no one escapes justice. Indeed, justice comes to all people, whether in this life or the next."

He bent his chin to his chest. "But to live free now? In this life? Ah, that is the conundrum—and that is why, *for the sake of your freedom*, Scripture commands that we are not to avenge ourselves but leave room for God's wrath. Of this you may be sure, mademoiselle: The justice of God will find its way. Wait for it. It is coming."

"Wait? Shall I wait here, in this room, forever dependent upon the kindness of Miss Eloise and Miss Eugenia? No work, no future, no hope?"

"*Non*, mademoiselle. You must go."

Tory stopped. Her mouth worked. "You . . . Miss Eugenia and Miss Eloise are casting me out?"

"Only in the meaning of the Scripture that commands us, 'Cast thy bread upon the waters: for thou shalt find it after many days.' The Misses Wright and I have concluded that we must cast our bread upon the waters of Denver. You are our bread, and you shall go, Mademoiselle Tory, and open a fashion salon—and also a sewing school for the girls of this Palmer House the Misses Wright speak of.

"You shall be our seed in that city to raise up strong, independent women of these 'girls from the mountain.' Where Satan has harmed and broken, Jesus shall heal and make whole."

Tory blinked and stammered. "Y-you will s-send me to Denver?"

"With our full backing, mademoiselle. You shall locate the right building for the establishment of your salon and sewing school. The Misses Wright and I shall pay to furbish the sewing room, reception area, and showrooms. We shall purchase machines. From my own stock, I shall send fabric, notions, and every necessary supply. And I shall ask of my best seamstresses, 'Who of you wishes to become Mademoiselle Tory's head seamstress and the teacher of those she hires?' All will be done, Mademoiselle Tory, to give you a successful start."

Tory's response was whispered. "But . . . surely, Denver . . . someone, some man will recognize me. Remember me. The rumors will fly again."

"Ah, but the Misses Wright assure me that you have many friends in Denver—powerful, wealthy, and influential friends—whose custom and open support will sustain you. Is this not so?

"Also, and this is most important: *You must never again play the victim*, Mademoiselle Tory: It is *fact* that men injured and abused you, but it is *truth* that Christ has redeemed you. And before all of heaven and earth, *Christ's truth has defeated fact*."

Monsieur LeBlanc stood to take his leave. He placed gentle hands upon Tory's arms. "Your work will be for the Lord of Heaven. As Scripture declares of the Lord, *He is the glory and the lifter up of mine head*. When you arrive in Denver, mademoiselle, you must stand tall, lift your head high, and walk as a queen."

Tory reeled at his directive—at the words already so familiar to her. "I must . . . stand tall . . . and walk as a queen?"

"*Oui*, mademoiselle—because you are no longer a child of shame. You are a daughter of the Most High King. For no other reason, you must behave as such."

~*~

Tory, Miss Eugenia, and Miss Eloise sat together late into the evening. Tory bared her heart to the sisters, weeping and confessing her anger toward the gossips who had ruined her blossoming career in Philadelphia. Tory apologized to the sisters for her hurtful behavior toward them. Then they prayed together, asking the Lord to fulfill his will in Tory's life.

"Of course, we do not wish you to leave, Tory," Miss Eloise whispered. "You are as dear as life to us. And yet it seems evident that you must go."

"Yes, you must go," Miss Eugenia echoed, "but please remember that not one iota of this turmoil is a surprise to our great God. He knows the end from the beginning—"

"The end from the beginning," her sister interjected.

"—and no act of man can prevent the Lord's will from being accomplished in your life—if you are careful to obey him."

Tory slowly nodded her understanding. "This move will be difficult for me, but I have purposed to obey him. Months ago, when Emily's letter arrived describing Palmer House and the need for the women there to have respectable employment, my heart yearned to help. I suppose I would never have answered his call as long as I was content here."

"Ah, yes. Contentment. Contentment can be a great stumbling block," Miss Eloise murmured. "While it is accurate that those vicious rumors wounded and shamed you, they also served to push you out of your contentment and into God's call upon your life."

"Into God's will!" echoed Miss Eugenia. "Just so. Now let us ask the Lord for his guidance and direction as we make our plans, shall we?"

~*~

Tory returned to Monsieur LeBlanc's shop that week—not as designer, dressmaker, or model, but as a lowly seamstress, unseen by the public that had so lately adored and sought after her. Monsieur LeBlanc's responses to all inquiries into Tory's past or her role in his shop were, "Mademoiselle Washington is no longer available." And, although Monsieur's shop experienced a temporary decline in orders, his loyal clients soon returned.

Through many frank discussions, Tory and Monsieur determined that Tory's last weeks in Philadelphia would be spent honing and perfecting her basic sewing skills: patternmaking and cutting, the operation and maintenance of the machines she would be taking with her, and every aspect of dressmaking, from concept through completion, so she would be prepared to oversee those tasks.

Monsieur LeBlanc spoke to his sewing staff, extending the offer to move someone to Denver and take up the position of Tory's head seamstress. One accomplished woman, Mrs. Bellows, accepted.

"I am a widow. I have but one daughter who has married and moved away. I am secure in my position with Monsieur LeBlanc; however, I am too far down in seniority to advance here. I wish the opportunity to oversee your sewing shop, Miss Washington."

Tory liked the woman's spirit, but she needed to be sure that Mrs. Bellows understood the challenges ahead. "You have heard the reports about my past, Mrs. Bellows?"

"Aye."

"The, er, house I lived in was not far from Denver. It is possible that my past will come out in that city, just as it has come out here. My reputation and that of my salon—and those who work for me—will face censure because of it."

"I am a Christian woman, Miss Washington. I believe in forgiveness and redemption, and I would like my life to count for more than just earning my daily bread." She raised her plain face. "And frankly, I have seen nothing but chaste, godly behavior in you. That is good enough for me to cast my lot with yours."

Tory worked to stem the moisture that threatened to fill her eyes. "Thank you, Mrs. Bellows." When she could speak without choking, she said, "In the beginning we shall hire experienced seamstresses and a few novices to train. The untrained girls will come from Palmer House—and you will have your hands full with them. Some will be rough, coarse, and vulgar. Patience and a firm hand will be required to mold their character as well as their skills."

"Aye. You may count on me to polish them up, Miss Washington."

Tory smiled. She already liked Mrs. Bellows.

From late January through the first week of April, Tory worked and prepared. She and Monsieur LeBlanc formulated lists of equipment and supplies. Tory wrote to Emily Van der Pol and told her of her plans. The letter she received in reply read,

My dear Miss Washington,

I cannot tell you how delighted I was to receive your news. I have shared it with my good friends, Viola and Grace; however, at your request, I have not informed Mrs. Thoresen or the others at Palmer House of your plans. I understand your desire to make yourself known to them after you have arrived in Denver.

Please consider my home open to you and Mrs. Bellows until you have found suitable lodgings.

In God's grace,

Emily Van der Pol

When April arrived, the equipment and supplies for Tory's shop were crated up. They would be shipped to Tory after she located and leased a proper location. Mrs. Bellows would not leave Philadelphia to join Tory until that time.

The Misses Wright had been busy during this preparation period also. They had insisted upon buying Tory a wardrobe appropriate for the proprietor of Denver's first house of *haute couture*. Tory's new clothes were a compilation of Monsieur LeBlanc's and Tory's best designs—everything she would need to show herself to Denver society as a woman of outstanding taste and distinction.

At the beginning of the third full week in April, Tory said her goodbyes, first to Monsieur LeBlanc. With her voice quavering, she told him, "I thank God for you, Monsieur. You have seen me at my best and at my worst. I shall never forget your kindness."

When she took her leave of Monsieur, he kissed her upon both cheeks. "I shall pray for you every day, Mademoiselle."

Benson drove her to the train station early the following morning. Tory sat on the rear seat, Miss Eloise and Miss Eugenia on either side, holding her hands. At the final moment of parting, Tory could not speak.

"We are confident of one thing, Tory," Miss Eugenia whispered, "that our God who began his good work in you is not finished. He will complete it until the day of Jesus Christ."

"He will complete it," Miss Eloise repeated.

As the train steamed away, a curtain of tears hid the station and her dear friends from Tory.

PART 5:
HE RESTORES
ALL THINGS

CHAPTER 34

APRIL 1910

Tory gaped. *Palmer House.* She had visualized the house through Emily's descriptions, but still she gawked. "It is so . . . big!" To call it palatial would not be overstating the fact: The three-story Victorian splendor sat far back on the corner lot surrounded by a tall iron fence. The second, third, and attic floors boasted pediment-topped dormer windows and gables; from the third floor, three octagonal turrets stretched toward the sky. Palmer House was even larger than the Corinth Gentlemen's Club had been—it was a house of impressive and enduring character.

Tory looked closer. As imposing as the house was, it was aging and had not been kept in the best of conditions. She noted mismatched shingles and flaking paint, although the yard showed signs of recent tending.

She unlatched the iron gate and started up the walk—taking care not to trip on paving stones that tree roots had lifted. The steps up to the front door led to a wraparound porch that crossed the breadth of the house and terminated at a gazebo at one end. The porch was clean and swept, even if the paint was chipped and faded.

Tory knocked on the heavy wooden door. She soon heard the sound of footsteps coming toward her. When the door groaned open, an older woman, slight in stature, with faded ash-blonde hair and solemn gray eyes set in a sweet expression, greeted her.

"Yes, may I help you?"

"Good afternoon. Is this the residence of Miss Thoresen? Miss Joy Thoresen?"

"It is, but she is away at present. I am her mother, Mrs. Thoresen. May I be of help?"

Tory smiled. "Mrs. Van der Pol speaks highly of you, Mrs. Thoresen. But I apologize. May I introduce myself?"

She offered Rose her card. The stiff ivory paper had a gold border around the engraved words *Miss Victoria Washington.*

"How may I be of service to you, Miss Washington?" Mrs. Thoresen asked.

"I have only arrived in Denver, just last evening, and I am staying with Mrs. Van der Pol for the present. However, I came back to Denver to offer my services."

Before Mrs. Thoresen could respond, the front gate opened behind them. Tory and Mrs. Thoresen turned toward the sound of voices coming up the walk.

Tory saw a tall blonde woman and a gentleman. She recognized the woman, but restrained the urge to rush to her.

Joy stopped, puzzled when she saw the visitor. Then her confusion cleared. "Tory?"

"Yes, miss!"

"My goodness!" Now it was Joy who rushed to embrace her. "Oh, my dear, but I am so happy to see you!" She pulled back and gazed in Tory's face. "You look so well, so *lovely!*"

Tory blushed under Joy's praise. "I am equally happy to see you, miss."

Joy turned to her mother. "Mama, this is Tory. She is one of the first girls we helped to escape from Corinth. Tory, this is my mother, Rose Thoresen."

They moved into the house and seated themselves in the parlor, and for more than an hour, Joy and Rose explained all that had happened in the 15 months since that bitterly cold January when Tory and Helen had arrived at the lodge in the dark hours of the night.

Tory listened intently, her brow creasing in fear and sorrow, as Joy and Rose told of Banner and his men burning the lodge and taking Joy and the lodge's other occupants prisoner.

"Emily wrote to tell me how the U.S. Marshals and Pinkerton agents saved you, Miss Joy. How they arrested Morgan, Banner, Darrow, and the rest. I would love to have seen it all," she whispered, breathing hard. "I would love to have seen Banner and Darrow and Roxanne taken away in handcuffs."

She dashed away a few tears. "I would have given anything for Helen to have seen it."

Joy touched Tory's hand gently. "I am so sorry about Helen, Tory."

Tory nodded. "Thank you. Thank you for everything you did for us, Miss Joy. *For everything.* Mrs. Van der Pol sent us to the Misses Wright—Miss Eloise and Miss Eugenia Wright—precious women in Philadelphia. They cared for Helen until the end. She had the finest doctors, but they all said . . . they said they could do nothing for her."

She was quiet for a moment, lost in her thoughts. "Miss Eugenia spent the most time with Helen. She sang to her. Sang for hours. She sang the most beautiful hymns to her. Then she described heaven to Helen, how beautiful it would be, and how much Jesus loved her and how he would be waiting for her."

Tory choked and had to stop speaking.

"It is all right, Tory," Joy soothed her.

"I gave my heart to Jesus when Helen passed," Tory said, sniffling through her tears. "And I am determined to serve him however he leads me. The Misses Wright apprenticed me to Monsieur Pierre LeBlanc, and I have been working for him for more than a year."

Joy gave Tory a sharp look. "Monsieur LeBlanc is well known, even in Europe, for his designs."

"Yes, miss. When I showed him some of my sketches, he assigned seamstresses to make two of my designs." She ducked her head modestly. "The dresses were well received, and Monsieur LeBlanc moved me permanently to my own design table with my own seamstresses."

Joy and Rose murmured their compliments and congratulations. Tory watched Rose's hand stray to her heart and a flush climb into her face.

"Many months back I received a letter from Mrs. Van der Pol about this house, the girls you have living here, and some of your plans," Tory continued. "I have been praying for you and wishing I might help in some way. Of course, since I was apprenticed to Monsieur LeBlanc, I could not come to help, although I felt the desire to do so.

"Monsieur LeBlanc is a good man, a man who loves the Lord. He knew who I was—what I had been—when he took me on, but he had compassion on me. We had agreed that it was best for his business to keep my past in confidence, but . . ." here her voice trailed off, "my designs were beginning to bring me recognition, and we were both somewhat concerned that eventually my past would come out."

Tory did not disclose what had happened in January, how the vindictive report had spread through the city's elite society revealing her past. She skipped over the painful details and the three months spent preparing to leave Philadelphia.

"Citing the letter from Mrs. Van der Pol, the Misses Wright explained to Monsieur LeBlanc that I was needed in Denver. They expressed their confidence that the Lord would make a way. And he has.

"Monsieur LeBlanc has released me from my apprenticeship. He and the Misses Wright decided to anonymously establish me in my own shop here in Denver. Monsieur LeBlanc is sending a large selection of fabrics and notions and several machines here, while the Misses Wright have provided funds to rent space for the first year. They will be silent partners in my endeavor, and I will share the profits with them. All I need is a suitable building to begin."

Instinctively, she turned to Rose. "Mrs. Thoresen, that is why I am here. I want to train your girls to design and sew."

"Merciful heavens above!" Rose exclaimed.

Joy gasped. "Mama!"

"B-but . . . you do not understand—I was praying about this very thing not twenty minutes before Tory knocked on the door!"

~*~

NOVEMBER 1910

The clock in the reception area chimed half past eight. The grand opening of *Victoria's House of Fashion* was only thirty minutes away. Mrs. Bellows, Tory's head seamstress, and Miss Tobin, the shop's principal dresser, followed Tory on her final inspection of their preparations.

The past months had overflowed with grueling work. Nothing, of course, had gone precisely as planned, and every step—from selecting the right storefront, remodeling it to accommodate the shop's needs, installing electricity and the machines, and hiring and training staff—had taken longer than anticipated or desired.

And the cost?

In Tory's estimation, the depth of Monsieur LeBlanc and the Misses Wright's financial investment was breathtaking. And yet, they had not hesitated or held back. Miss Eloise had written, *We have purposed this money for the increase of God's Kingdom. We have faith that you will not lose sight of this goal.*

"Lord," Tory prayed with fervor, "please make me worthy of this great trust!"

As Denver had changed some in the three years since she and Charles had arrived, Tory had first sought out her competition. She walked up and down Fifteenth Street, Sixteenth Street, and Larimer, identifying department stores that had expanded into women's wear. She explored the women's departments within going concerns the likes of *Joslin Dry Goods Company*, *M. Philipsborn & Co.*, *J. C. Bloom & Co.*, *Gano Clothing Company*, and *Daniels & Fisher* to see what they offered.

With rising excitement, she realized that most Denver stores were owned and managed by men—and none of them provided the *haute couture* experience she would.

Finding a suitable building in a competitive location had taken six weeks—and the building had not been available for their occupancy for six weeks after that. When she had secured the storefront and attached workspace, Tory had hired four Palmer House girls to clean up behind the laborers as they performed plumbing and carpentry work and connected the electrical wiring. The painting, papering, and carpeting had come next. The installation of the sewing machines, furnishings, and telephones had followed.

Even before the machines were installed, Mrs. Bellows had begun training the selected Palmer House girls, teaching them how to take proper measurements, use a wire mannequin to create patterns, lay and cut those patterns, and properly baste the pieces together. Later, she added three experienced seamstresses to the workroom.

Tory took two Palmer House girls, Marion and Alice, under her wing to train as maids for the shop. Just as Mademoiselle Justine had instructed her, Tory taught them. "Your role is to answer the telephone, schedule appointments, welcome our clientele, make them comfortable, serve tea, and alert me to any problems or difficulties." The girls had been answering the telephone for a week, and the appointment book was filling nicely.

The window dressings were resplendent with a lovely winter wardrobe Tory had designed and Mrs. Bellows had sewn to entice new customers. Tory had discovered a clever local milliner, a young woman selling her hats out of her home. Tory had persuaded the milliner to bring her talents to *Victoria's House of Fashion*. A selection of her creations enhanced the window's winter lineup.

More effective publicity than the window dressings were the gowns and ensembles Emily Van der Pol, Viola Lind, and Grace Minton wore and proudly proclaimed as Tory's creations. Tory and Mrs. Bellows had even fashioned two sets of day attire for the formidable Martha Palmer, the woman after whom Palmer House was named.

The white-haired old lady, bent nearly double over her cane had, at first introduction, terrified Tory. She knew that one word from Martha Palmer could make or break *Victoria's House of Fashion*. What Tory had not known was that Martha Palmer was a lifelong friend to the Misses Wright.

Martha Palmer, her head turned at an impossible angle so she could look up at Tory, proclaimed, "God has brought you back to Denver at precisely the right time, missy." She stamped her cane on the floor for emphasis. "Do not doubt God's guidance, even when difficulties come— and they will come, mark my words."

Today, the many preparations were complete, and the anticipation of Denver's elite for the opening of Tory's shop—minutes away—was at a fever pitch. Women who had secured appointments on the shop's first day dropped that tidbit of information wherever they took tea—to the envy of their friends.

Tory walked the reception area. The furnishings were pristine, the carpets thick and lush. Marion and Alice were garbed in black worsted dresses and starched aprons. With their hands folded before their aprons, they curtsied.

Tory nodded. "Excellent, ladies." She glanced down. "Marion, your stocking is pooling about the top of your shoe."

Marion's face flamed. She bobbed and raced to the back to secure the offending stocking.

Tory, shadowed by Mrs. Bellows and Miss Tobin, entered the first of two private showrooms. She checked the dressing area, the carpets, the chairs, the tea tables.

"Excellent." It was all Tory could manage for, despite her calm exterior, her heart was in her throat.

The next stop was the sewing floor. As Tory entered, the seamstresses stood. "Good morning, Miss Victoria."

"Good morning to you all, ladies. Please continue your work."

An entire wall of the sewing floor was stocked with bolt after bolt of fabrics and notions. On the floor, five machines whirred and rattled. Mrs. Bellows had set the seamstresses to stitching ready-made undergarments of every size from fine-spun silk. Two experienced hand sewers were adding exquisite embroidery and lace touches. The undergarments would be stocked on shelves in the showrooms where clients could browse them in private.

"It is almost time," Miss Tobin whispered to Tory.

Tory nodded. In front of her staff, with not a whit of self-consciousness, she bowed her head and prayed, "Lord God, this house is yours. All we do here is yours. May this work glorify you in every way."

Mrs. Bellows whispered, "Amen," while a startled Miss Tobin looked on.

~*~

Nine hours later, Tory dismissed the staff for the day, all but Mrs. Bellows and Miss Tobin. They sat around a small table in Tory's office, exhausted but elated. Tory served the tea herself.

"Ladies, I salute you and our staff. We have acquitted ourselves well today, the first of many good days at this endeavor, God willing."

Both women beamed with the pride of success as they accepted their cups from Tory's hand.

"Now to do this all over again tomorrow," Tory laughed.

"Aye. And the day after," Mrs. Bellows grinned.

Miss Tobin smiled in the spirit of their camaraderie. "And for many days to come!"

"Yes, by the grace of God," Tory whispered.

CHAPTER 35

November passed into December, and the shop's pace continued unabated. If Tory had thought failure would be difficult, she had no idea how stressful success could be. From morning until evening, every day but Sunday, the shop's staff ran full out. To accommodate the influx of holiday and winter season orders, Tory added two more experienced seamstresses and an assistant for Miss Tobin.

And Tory met with Mrs. Bellows and Miss Tobin to plan for her first public showing.

"It is called a 'fashion parade,' a gala event with refreshments followed by a reception," Tory explained to Miss Tobin. "While the guests are seated and enjoying themselves, a line of live mannequins or models, dressed in my spring lineup, will walk a circuit among the tables, pausing briefly to turn and pose along the way. During the reception afterward, we shall provide opportunity for our guests to book appointments."

"It is a brilliant idea, Miss Washington," Miss Tobin responded. "I have read of such events. I believe you shall have the distinction of holding Denver's first fashion parade."

"Thank you, Miss Tobin. Now, to choose a date."

She huddled over the calendar with Mrs. Bellows and Miss Tobin. "I realize February is early for a spring fashion parade, but I fear if we wait until March, many of our clients will have booked travel to New York to order their spring and summer wardrobes."

Miss Tobin—a mature woman with a strong mind and outstanding taste in her own right—tapped the end of a pencil on her chin and replied, "You raise a valid point. The winter season is still running strong in February, but by the end of the month, society has sickened of wintry weather and the endless stream of débutante balls, cotillions, and parties."

"A February show would deliver them from their winter doldrums," Mrs. Bellows suggested.

"That is my thinking. The end of February, then?" Tory asked. "Are we agreed?"

"Yes," answered Miss Tobin.

"Aye," from Mrs. Bellows.

Tory drew a circle about the last Saturday in February. "I shall hire a hotel ballroom to accommodate the showing and a reception after."

Tory asked Miss Tobin and her assistant to see the majority of the shop's clients while she secluded herself in her office and dove into sketching a spring lineup. Humming to herself as she flipped through the latest fashion magazines, Tory made a few notes for herself. *Hems are rising to show off a little ankle; skirts are multi-layered but narrow at the hem; the parasol has made a comeback . . . and hats are even more outrageous.*

Through Christmas and into the new year, Tory focused on her spring line, asking Miss Tobin to interrupt her only for particularly important clients. When the shop closed and her staff went home, Tory remained behind to review new orders and bring the shop's books up to date.

"You must hire someone to do the books," Mrs. Bellows admonished her. "You are wearing yourself to a nub, trying to do everything yourself. And it is not wise for you to carry the deposits to the bank yourself— even during the day."

"Perhaps you are right, Mrs. Bellows," Tory sighed.

She left the shop an hour later. Although early evenings in January were dark, the area around her shop had been deemed relatively safe by neighboring shopkeepers. Tory felt at ease as she walked to her rooms, and she was not alone on her short trek. Many other Denverites passed her as they hurried from their own labors to their respective homes and dinners. Tory's heart and mind were content, filled with the day's victories and tomorrow's tasks; she allowed her thoughts to drift to the work ahead of her.

A passing gentleman jostled her shoulder and jarred Tory from her thoughts. She paused and pivoted toward him. He did not stop, however, even to apologize. But he did glance back.

Tory's heart stuttered in recognition.

She knew him.

It was the man who had stalked her in Philadelphia.

When Tory reached her rooms, she could not eat or rest. She shivered and could not sit or stand still. Her thoughts were in turmoil.

What does this man want of me? Who is he? How does he know me? Why is he following me? Was it he who started the rumors in Philadelphia? But why?

The recurring "why" pounded at Tory's heart with every step she took.

After an hour of frantic (and fruitless) pacing, Tory realized how fear and confusion had stolen the joy of her shop's successes. Worse, the tumult had shifted her focus away from God.

Tory knelt by her bed, opened her Bible on her coverlet and, with her hand on 2 Timothy 1:7, began to pray. "Lord, you have not given me a spirit of fear. You have given me the Holy Spirit. He is the Spirit of power, love, and a sound mind. You have given me sanity, Lord! Therefore, I refuse to be driven daft by this man—whoever he is. He has, for some reason, followed me here to Denver, but I will not allow him to intimidate or move me. I choose to trust you, Lord."

Having cleared her mind, Tory began to worship. "Thank you, Lord God! Thank you for bringing *Victoria's House of Fashion* into reality. Thank you for the godly employment we are providing for many Denver women, not just women of Palmer House. Lord, I praise you for every obstacle you have helped us to navigate. I thank you for the orders placed today—and I thank you for the many more to come. How I love you, Lord! How I love the glory and joy of your presence!"

She prayed late into the evening. When she climbed into bed, she fell into an exhausted, dreamless sleep and woke refreshed.

Refreshed and ravenous.

"It was silly of me to allow my emotions to run out of control," she muttered as she buttered a slice of toast. "And, more than likely, I was mistaken in the first place. Yes, a rude individual jostled me on the street last evening, but I doubt it was the same man who dogged my steps in Philadelphia. How could it have been? Lord, please help me to keep my imagination in proper check."

~*~

Another week passed. If nothing further untoward had happened, the jostling incident would have faded from Tory's concerns.

"A word, Miss Washington?"

"Yes, Miss Tobin?" Tory pored over her spring folio, studying her notes and instructions for Mrs. Bellows. The next seven weeks—filling existing orders and preparing for Tory's fashion parade—would test the mettle of her shop.

Her principal dresser, generally unflappable, seemed flustered. Tense. "I-I hesitate to sound the alarmist; however, I must apprise you of a most disturbing trend."

"Oh?" Tory glanced up and gestured to a chair. "Please sit down, Miss Tobin. What is the problem?"

"Today alone, we have received two cancellations."

"Appointment cancellations?"

"No, miss; we manage schedule adjustments in an ongoing manner. What I mean is that we have received two *order* cancellations—large orders."

Tory sat back. "How large?"

"A total of five walking ensembles and three evening gowns."

"Did the client give a reason?"

"No . . . but that is not all."

With a sinking feeling, Tory asked, "What else?"

"We received a similar call yesterday—the cancellation of a walking suit, three morning dresses, and a gown. The client gave no explanation."

"Three order cancellations in two days?"

"Yes. Quite unprecedented." Miss Tobin's shoulders moved uneasily. "I cannot but wonder what is happening."

Tory whispered, "Thank you for bringing this to my attention, Miss Tobin. Please carry on."

As soon as Miss Tobin left the room, Tory reached for her telephone and had the operator connect her with Emily Van der Pol. Tory was relieved when her friend answered.

"Emily, good morning. This is Tory calling. I beg your indulgence for my abrupt question, but I was wondering if any . . . gossip concerning my shop had reached your ears?"

"Oh, Tory! I have just been praying over that very thing. Three close friends have called me in the last two days, the latest this morning." Emily sighed. "My dear, you should prepare yourself."

With rising anxiety, Tory asked, "What did they say?"

"They said . . . they said they had heard that you were a . . . former prostitute, passing yourself off as a respectable couturière, that you had been driven from Philadelphia by similar accusations."

Tory bowed her head, cringing over what was coming.

"We knew this was a possibility. You understood the risks of returning to Denver, particularly since it was so near to Corinth."

Tory swallowed. "Yes, I understood the risks. But this time I will not let them drive me away. I will stand up to the gossip and speak the truth. W-will you and your friends stand by me?"

"Yes; we are committed to you and your work, Tory."

Tory told Emily about the cancellations. "We had, of course, already begun work on these orders. It is money spent that I cannot recoup. But . . ."

Her voice dropped off as she recognized a deeper concern: The details of the rumors were stunningly similar to those that had swept the social scene in Philadelphia. Too similar *not* to be the work of the same individual.

The man who jostled me. I did not imagine it. It has to be the same man who stalked me in Philadelphia—he is here.

"Tory, I do not wish to wound you further, but my friends shared one other bit of gossip. If we are to combat these lies, then we must be forearmed."

Tory could not imagine anything worse. "What is it?"

"They . . . the report said that you are the illegitimate daughter of a negro woman and a white man. A married white man."

Tory turned that word over in her mind: Illegitimate.

It meant spurious. Unlawful. A bastard.

The shameful offspring of a shameful liaison.

A sudden wave of condemnation roared over Tory, swamping her confidence.

I will not be able to stand up under these accusations. The truth will not matter, what was done to me will make no difference—the gossips will break me and break my business. I will be forced to close my doors.

Everything I have worked for will be snatched from my hands. All my workers will lose their livelihood, including the girls from Palmer House. I will have wasted Monsieur LeBlanc and the Misses Wright's investment.

I will never have a home. I will be forced to leave Denver in shame— to go where?

It is happening again.

"Th-thank you, Emily. G-goodbye." She hung up on her friend's protests. She began to tremble, to shake.

"O God! Please help me! If you do not speak to me, I shall fail!"

Immediately she felt Monsieur LeBlanc's hands upon her arms, heard his last words to her reverberating through her being.

As Scripture declares of the Lord, He is the glory and the lifter up of mine head. When you arrive in Denver, mademoiselle, you must stand tall, lift your head high, and walk as a queen.

*You are no longer a child of shame. You are a daughter of the Most High King. **For no other reason**, you must behave as such.*

"I am not a child of shame," Tory whispered. "I am not a child of shame."

She sat up in her chair. "*God* is my Father. I cannot—*I will not*—walk in shame. I will not walk in shame for my parents' sin, not for the color of my skin, not for what was done to me, not for any choice I have repented of."

She folded her hands on her desk and prayed. "Lord Jesus, I am yours—all of me—my past and future. This business? *It is yours*. My reputation? *It is yours*. My safety? *I am in your hands*. Lord, I resist the obvious courses of action and lean all I am and all I have upon you.

"For the battles before me, for the war I *must* win—and for the welfare of the many women who now depend upon me for their livelihood, I ask your wisdom and guidance. Please show me what to do."

For a long time, Tory remained as she was. Waiting. Listening. Worshipping. Finding and holding fast to the peace that passes all understanding.

She stayed still and calm, deep in her Father's presence, until something began to intrude. Tory opened her eyes and listened. There it was again—a commotion coming from the reception area—strident voices raised in anger.

"I will stand tall. Lift my head. Walk as a queen," she murmured. "Thou, O Lord, art a shield for me; my glory and the lifter up of mine head."

Tory stood, left her office, and made her way to the front of her shop. She entered silently and took in the scene before her.

Miss Tobin, her patience at a breaking point, stood toe to toe with an angry client; Marion and Alice, the shop's two maids, hung back in wide-eyed apprehension. The client's maid, too, had pressed herself into a corner by the door. Another customer—caught up in the contentious dispute—looked on with curious interest.

The angry client pointed to a heap of clothing piled on the reception area's carpet. "I said I have returned these filthy rags, and I wish my money refunded—immediately!"

"As I have explained three times, madam," Miss Tobin replied, "these garments were custom tailored to you and have been worn. It is not our policy to accept worn returns."

"Mrs. Elliston, I believe?" Tory asked.

The irate woman swiveled toward Tory. "You! Y-you are a soiled woman! A fraud!"

Tory ignored the insult. "You wished to return these garments, I believe?"

"Indeed, I do! And I do not care if you *are* Martha Palmer's so-called protégé—she is protecting a disreputable woman just as she protects that horrid, so-called Palmer House. Well, I, for one, shall never shop here again."

"Marion, take Mrs. Elliston's returns into the first showroom. Miss Tobin, please make a detailed inventory of Mrs. Elliston's returns."

Miss Tobin slid her eyes toward Tory. "But—"

"We shall make an exception in this instance."

"As you wish, Miss Washington."

Tory turned to her erstwhile client. "Would you care to sit while we issue your refund, Mrs. Elliston?"

The woman sneered at Tory. "I would not dream of defiling myself further."

Tory inclined her head. "As you wish."

Tory left the woman gawking at her back and went to the showroom where Miss Tobin and Marion were sorting the returned clothing.

"I will write a check for Mrs. Elliston as soon as you have a total for me, Miss Tobin. I shall be in my office."

Tory shut the door of her office and leaned against it. "This is likely the first wave of such a backlash, Lord, but I shall refuse to contend with those who cast insults upon me. No, I shall not answer them back."

Tory's chin dropped to her breast. "But, oh, how I need to talk to someone older and wiser than myself, Lord! If I were in Philadelphia, I would pour my heart out to Miss Eugenia and Miss Eloise and they would pray with me, but here in Denver? Who can I turn to?"

Tory cast about in her mind. Then it came to her. Joy's mother— Rose Thoresen!

Tory slid into the chair behind her desk and asked the operator to place the call. Rose Thoresen herself answered the phone.

"Palmer House," the woman said.

"Mrs. Thoresen? This is Victoria Washington calling."

"Tory! How lovely to hear from you. What can I do for you?"

"Mrs. Thoresen, would you . . . that is, may I call upon you? I . . . I need the counsel of a mature woman in the Lord."

After a brief pause, the answer came back. "Would you care to take tea with me this afternoon?"

"Yes. Yes, thank you."

~*~

"I knew it was a risk, coming back to Denver," Tory confessed, "but the Lord spoke so powerfully to my heart to bring you help in the form of training and employment for the girls of Palmer House. We have made a beginning, but I had hoped to hire more of them in the future."

"Where the Lord leads us, we often encounter opposition," Rose observed. "The devil despises the advancement of God's work. He will enlist those who belong to him and look for means and opportunity to oppose God's people. Conversely, God is not far from us and often sends us help at just the right time."

"Well, I must have help," Tory admitted. "Someone is determined to ruin me and my business, and I do not know to whom I might turn for aid."

"If I may? I believe you made the acquaintance of a Mr. O'Dell in the few days you spent at Corinth Mountain Lodge?"

"The English gentleman staying at the lodge?"

"The same—although you may be surprised to learn that Mr. O'Dell is as American as you or I."

Tory *was* surprised. "You must have more to tell me?"

"Oh, yes. Mr. O'Dell is actually a detective with the Pinkerton Agency."

"What?"

"He was, at the time you met him, 'working undercover,' as he calls it, on several kidnapping cases. He spent months at Joy's lodge and was instrumental in convincing the U.S. Marshals to break up the horrors of those houses in Corinth."

"Oh, my!"

"Indeed. Mr. O'Dell usually works out of the Chicago Pinkerton office, but he is in town at present. If you are looking for help, my dear Miss Washington, my recommendation is that you consult with Mr. O'Dell and the Pinkertons."

CHAPTER 36

Tory stepped down from the trolley, glanced around her, then walked with quick, determined steps to her destination. She took in the simple signage painted on the window as she entered: Pinkerton Detective Agency.

She approached the reception desk. "Good morning. I am here to see Mr. O'Dell."

"Do you have an appointment, miss?"

"Yes, he is expecting me." She handed him her card.

The man read her card and nodded. "One moment, please." He strode down the hallway to an office near the end.

Moments later, he returned. "This way, miss."

O'Dell greeted her. "Miss Washington. I am delighted to see you looking so well. Please, will you have a seat?"

After exchanging pleasantries, Tory folded her hands and came to the point of her visit. "Mr. O'Dell, as you may have surmised, I am in need of your assistance."

"The Pinkerton sort of assistance?"

"Yes. I am experiencing some . . . difficulties, Mr. O'Dell, and do not know what to do. Mrs. Thoresen suggested that you might advise me."

"Can you tell me what is happening? I will do what I can."

"Thank you. Perhaps you know that I recently opened a dress shop? With the high recommendations of Emily Van der Pol, Martha Palmer, and others, the shop began well, and we stood every chance of success. However, a few days back, it came to my attention that someone is spreading rumors, rumors injurious to my business."

O'Dell thought he understood but needed to be sure. "What kind of rumors, Miss Washington?"

Tory's face flamed. "Whispers that I had . . . that in my past life I had been . . ." Tory was too mortified to finish.

"You need not elaborate. I was there when you fled from that house in Corinth to Joy Thoresen's lodge. I know what you escaped."

"You are kind, Mr. O'Dell. Thank you." Tory sighed. "But, perhaps you can imagine the reaction to these tales? Many of my clients have canceled their appointments—have even cancelled orders already in progress. The flow of new customers to my shop has dried up and, to be frank, my fledgling business is in jeopardy."

Tory paused, then added. "If that were not bad enough, Mr. O'Dell, I believe that someone—someone unknown to me—is watching and following me. They must have tracked me from Philadelphia to Denver. In any case," She looked into O'Dell's face, "I-I am beginning to fear for my safety."

That caused O'Dell to sit up. "Wait. Someone followed you here from Philadelphia? What do you mean?"

Tory's fingers fidgeted with her handbag. "When I lived in there, I worked for Monsieur Pierre LeBlanc, a leading couturier of the city. He offered me an apprenticeship that began in May of last year. However, about nine months later, strange rumors surfaced."

"The same type of rumors that are plaguing you here in Denver?"

Tory looked down. "Yes. Monsieur LeBlanc heard them first from a most devoted friend and client. He vouched for my morals, of course, and insisted that I lived a spotless life—as did the Misses Wright. However, many of Monsieur LeBlanc's clients left him and took their custom to other modistes."

O'Dell frowned. "I see."

"It was a difficult period but, in a way, the situation proved a blessing. I had felt called to return to Denver and begin a sewing school for the girls of Palmer House but had completed less than a year of my apprenticeship. Unbeknownst to me, the Misses Wright were praying about my desire to return to Denver and how best to facilitate such a return.

"When my continued presence in Philadelphia became untenable, the Misses Wright and Monsieur LeBlanc determined to send me here to not only establish a sewing shop but also a design house in my own name—with their backing. I returned in April and opened my doors in November."

"And all was well here in Denver until when?"

"Until recent weeks." Tory outlined the shove on the sidewalk, her recognition of the man, followed immediately by the strange rumors that bore so much resemblance to those in Philadelphia.

"Mind you, I determined before I left Philadelphia that I would stand up to accusations and reply with the truth that I was forced into such a life and that my business was dedicated to helping other women who were similarly misused. As I said earlier, I have friends here in Denver, influential friends who would vouch for me."

"But?"

"But if appointment and order cancellations continue, my shop will soon be in dire financial straits. And Mr. O'Dell? I have scheduled a public fashion parade for next month to display my spring line. I have invested a significant amount of money in the show's success. If these rumors are not quashed, my showing will end in public humiliation and my business will fail."

O'Dell's mind was racing as he processed Tory's situation. "Tell me, Miss Washington: When you compare the rumors in Philadelphia and those here in Denver, what similarities do you see?"

"That is what is so concerning, Mr. O'Dell. The tales spread in Philadelphia and the ones circulating here are too much alike not to have come from the same source. As for the sense that I am being followed— I do not have a word for it—it, too, is remarkably like what I experienced in Philadelphia. And I am certain the man who shoved me is the same man who was following me in Philadelphia."

"The word you are searching for, Miss Washington, is 'stalking.' Someone—likely an individual holding personal animosity against you—has set his sights on you."

"Personal animosity? I cannot fathom who it might be, but whoever it is, they are perilously close to ruining my business!"

"Forgive me if I believe that someone stalking you poses a greater danger," O'Dell answered.

He took a notepad from his desk drawer. "Since I am only visiting in Denver at present, I would ordinarily recommend your case to a capable detective; however, I wish to handle your case personally. What I need is for you to tell me everywhere you have lived and everything you have done. No stone unturned. I will cancel my engagements this afternoon while you dictate these details to me. I hope to gain a sense of who may hold a grudge against you."

Tory's heart plummeted. "Everywhere I have lived? Everything I have done?"

O'Dell smiled. "Come, come. You are not that old. How much can it be? Now, where were you born?"

Tory squirmed and stalled.

"I assure you, Miss Washington, I have seen and heard it all. Nothing you say can shock me—nor will an iota of what you have spoken in confidence leave this office. You have my word."

Tory nodded. "Well ... I suppose I might tell you I was born in Jefferson Parish, Louisiana."

It was nearly evening when they finished. O'Dell sat back, both enlightened and saddened by what Tory had recounted.

"Do you have any hope to offer me, Mr. O'Dell?"

"In Christ there is always hope, Miss Washington."

She smiled. "Thank you. I suppose I needed to hear that."

"You are welcome. More to the point of your question, the answer is yes: I have hope. You have lived in five towns: New Orleans, St. Louis, Denver, Corinth, and Philadelphia—although we would be prudent to count Denver twice. What of New Orleans?

"My problems cannot arise from New Orleans," Tory protested. "I was . . . quite young when I left that city, not old enough to have earned anyone's enmity."

Tory almost said, "I was only a child when I left that city." Then she stopped herself.

I will not speak of Bastiann Declouette or how I fled his pursuit. I am of age now, and he can have no legal hold on me or any purpose in hounding me. He can have no bearing on my present troubles.

"St. Louis, then? From what you have told me, Charles kept you too cloistered for you to have made personal enemies there, except for this Mitchell Waring?"

"He has already extracted his pound of flesh from me," Tory murmured.

O'Dell nodded. "You say you had no conflicts you know of with anyone in Philadelphia? Corinth? The men who held you captive are, themselves, in prison—with the exception of Dean Morgan, whom you have never met. I might, therefore, surmise that your problems arise from someone here in *Denver*—but that does muddle the question of who was spreading rumors about you in *Philadelphia*."

He thought a moment. "I shall contact Pinkerton offices in the cities where you have lived. They will make inquiries to ensure we have not missed something important."

O'Dell added a note, then addressed Tory. "We shall leave no stone unturned, Miss Washington. You have been back in Denver since April last year?"

"Yes."

"So, ten months. In that time, have you had any unpleasant or tense encounters?"

"I do not think so."

"Have you encountered anyone you knew from your previous stay in Denver?"

"Only Emily Van der Pol, her friends, or Joy Thoresen. I hardly count them dangerous."

"Any dissatisfied customers?"

"That is part of what is curious, Mr. O'Dell. I know of no dissatisfied customers prior to the onset of the rumors. If a client *had* expressed displeasure, I would have expended the greatest of efforts to assuage the situation. Nothing is worse for business than a discontented client who, whenever the subject of *Victoria's House of Fashion* arises, will talk of nothing but her unpleasant experience with us."

"Hmm. That leaves your time at the Broadmoor Hotel." O'Dell stared at Tory. "I know the hotel, and I know of Charles Luchetti. Now it is time for you to trust me to do my job. Can you do that?"

"I-I suppose so."

"Then I will contact you when I have unearthed anything of note. In the meantime, I wish you to exercise great care. Do not walk outside alone and do not travel alone. Did you come by trolley?"

"Yes."

"I shall see you home myself."

"If-if you think it necessary."

"I think it more than necessary—I insist. Mind my advice, Miss Washington, if you please."

~*~

The following morning, O'Dell reviewed his notes, amazed at Tory's story, astounded at the evident thread of God's grace running through her life, even during the months she suffered under Roxanne Cleary's control. He made many notations in the margins, then stopped to think over his plan of action. It had come to him in the night, after he had spent an hour praying for Tory Washington.

"Lord, please guide my steps and my tongue today," he prayed. "According to 2 Corinthians 5:9, I make it my goal to please you in all things—knowing that you have Miss Washington's best interests at heart, rather than my sense of justice. Please help me to remain true to *your* goals at all times."

His first step was to place trunk calls to Pinkerton associates in Louisiana, Missouri, and Pennsylvania. When he finished his calls, he told the agent at the front desk, "I will be out for a while."

O'Dell hailed a cab. "Broadmoor Hotel, please."

Minutes later he strode into the lobby and to the front desk. "I would like to see Mr. Luchetti."

"May I help you?" The lean, angular woman hovering near the front desk interrupted him with an air of authority.

"As I said to your desk clerk, I wish to see Mr. Luchetti."

"I am Miss Visser, the Broadmoor's hostess. May I be of assistance?"

Having learned of Miss Visser's role in Tory's suffering, O'Dell recognized her—and was not in the most charitable frame of mind toward her.

"Only if you are Mr. Luchetti."

The woman stiffened under his gaze. "I shall see if Mr. Luchetti is available. Whom shall I say is calling?"

O'Dell, without taking his eyes from her, removed a card from his pocket. "Edmund O'Dell. Pinkerton Detective Agency."

Miss Visser shifted in discomfort. "I see. One moment, please."

She returned moments later, still discomposed. "This way, Mr. O'Dell."

She showed him into an office where a man of weary demeanor slumped behind a desk. The man lumbered to his feet and extended his hand. "Mr. O'Dell? I am Charles Luchetti. How may I be of assistance?"

O'Dell turned and looked at Miss Visser, who had remained in the room. "I would prefer to conduct my business with you in privacy."

Charles nodded. "That will be all, Miss Visser. Mr. O'Dell, please have a seat."

As Miss Visser departed, she left the door ajar. O'Dell smiled at Luchetti, walked to the door, peered around the threshold, and encountered Miss Visser.

"As I said, Miss Visser, I prefer privacy." O'Dell closed the door on her startled expression.

"Why, you make yourself quite free with my staff, Mr. O'Dell! What is this all about?" Luchetti demanded.

"It's about Victoria Washington."

Charles Luchetti sank into his chair. "Tory! Do you have news of her? Is she all right?"

Lord, set a watch on my mouth today, O'Dell prayed. He took a seat and answered, "She has recently returned to Denver."

"The devil you say! Tory is here? In the city? But why has she not contacted me? Sh-she left here nearly three years ago without even saying goodbye. I have not had a line from her in all that time!"

When O'Dell did not answer, Charles whispered, "May I see her?"

"I do not think it wise at present."

Luchetti breathed heavily, his face awash with sorrow and . . . regret? "Mr. O'Dell, I love Tory. I-I did not realize how much so until she disappeared. I care for her as though she were my own daughter."

He studied his hands. "I acknowledge that I allowed my determination to marry well—all to save this blasted hotel!—to shunt Tory aside. I wounded her deeply—and that is why she left without a word. Please. Would you speak to her for me? Would you tell her I would like to see her? That I wish to ask for her forgiveness?"

O'Dell studied the man across from him. He may have once been a card sharp and a charlatan, but no longer. What O'Dell saw was discouragement and defeat.

"Mr. Luchetti, I had heard that you were a savvy gentleman, and I would have thought you smart enough to have figured out a few things by now. Namely, that if your foster daughter left without saying goodbye—contrary to her normal behavior—she did not do so willingly."

Charles paled. "What do you mean?"

"What I mean is that the charming Miss Visser told Tory that you had no wish to ever see her again. That Miss Visser and *your wife* saw Tory as a threat and conspired to rid themselves of her—and destroy her into the bargain. Shall I tell you how?"

Charles' head moved slowly side to side. "I do not think I can bear to hear it."

"For heaven's sake, be a man, Luchetti!" O'Dell jeered. "For once in your miserable marriage, *be a man.*"

Charles stared at his hands again. "You are right, of course. I-I have allowed Belinda to take over this hotel, to promote that harridan Trudy Visser above my wishes, to manipulate me and run me into the ground—because she controls the purse strings." He blinked and set his jaw. "What did they do to Tory? Please. I-I must know."

O'Dell told him. He left nothing unsaid that needed saying. He did not blunt the truth nor couch it in language less horrifying than the truth demanded.

When he finished, Luchetti was shaking in revulsion and rage, and O'Dell had surmised two things: *one*, that Charles Luchetti had nothing to do with Tory's present troubles and, *two*, that Belinda Luchetti could expect a taxing conversation with her husband in the near future.

O'Dell frowned. What he still needed to ascertain was Mrs. Luchetti or Miss Visser's culpability in the nasty rumors hounding Tory and the mysterious man stalking her.

The door to Charles Luchetti's office swung open.

A woman considerably less delicate and less blonde than Tory had described, stood with hands fisted upon her hips. "What is the meaning of this, Charles? Who is this man and what does he want?"

"Ah, you must be the ineffable and lovely Mrs. Luchetti. I was just telling Charles how inventive you and Miss Visser are."

The woman pulled her bottom lip under her top teeth. "Whatever do you mean? Of course, Trudy and I work together to, ah, manage certain aspects of the hotel."

"I wasn't referring to the hotel. I was referring to Victoria Washington. How you and Miss Visser conspired to get her out of your way."

Belinda Luchetti's mouth went slack. "Wh-what did you say? Such utter nonsense!"

Her words lacked conviction of any sort.

"Mrs. Luchetti, have you or Miss Visser been spreading ugly rumors across the city regarding Miss Washington?"

"W-what? I have not seen or heard from the woman since she left Denver three years ago."

"Yes, three years ago—when you *sold* her to Roxanne Cleary. However, Miss Washington has returned to Denver. And, Mrs. Luchetti? She has told me everything."

Belinda Luchetti's eyes bulged. She swung her head back and forth. "No. Whatever she has said, it is a lie."

Charles Luchetti stood. He fingered O'Dell's card. "I may reach you at this location, Mr. O'Dell?"

"Yes."

Luchetti extended his hand and then looked down at it. "Given what you have told me, I do not expect you to shake my hand, sir, but I offer it in humble gratitude of the difficult deed you have performed this day—confronting me with my own culpability in Tory's humiliation and suffering. I am a cad and a coward, but you have my heartfelt appreciation for ripping the blinders from my eyes, for showing me how far I have fallen—and for exposing the woman I married for the unconscionable shrew that she is."

"Charles Luchetti! Do not dare to use such tone or langu—"

"Shut up, Belinda."

He had started to withdraw the hand he extended to O'Dell when O'Dell reached across the desk and took it in his. "It is never too late to begin again, Mr. Luchetti . . . or to make amends."

"I . . . I shall think on how to do both, Mr. O'Dell."

O'Dell picked up his hat and tipped it to Mrs. Luchetti. "Have a pleasant evening, ma'am."

He was certain she would have anything but.

O'Dell was not finished at the Broadmoor. He left Charles Luchetti's office in search of the sharp-tongued Miss Visser.

There. O'Dell saw her skittering across the lobby, away from him.

"Miss Visser!" O'Dell did not shout, but his voice boomed in the high-ceilinged lobby.

Miss Visser walked faster. She broke into a trot.

O'Dell bellowed, "Miss Visser! If you do not stop, I shall tell the world who you truly are and what you have done—beginning with your relationship with Roxanne Cleary."

At least a dozen pairs of eyes in the wide lobby fastened themselves first on O'Dell and then on Miss Visser.

O'Dell tapped his derby against his thigh and growled, "Come to me, Miss Visser, or I shall recite your follies right here, before the Broadmoor's guests."

Miss Visser, considering the spectacle she was embroiled in and fearing the scene growing even worse, changed course. She crossed the lobby and approached O'Dell.

"What is it you want?"

O'Dell knew fear when he saw it, and the woman was oozing with it. "I am not here today about your past sins, Miss Visser, but about your present ones: Are you spreading gossip about Victoria Washington around Denver?"

Relief mixed with guilt washed the woman's face. "Victoria Washington? Is she in Denver?"

O'Dell did not buy her feigned ignorance: The fashion pages of Denver's newspapers had acknowledged Tory's emergence as a Denver couturière. Luchetti might not read the fashion rags, but his wife and Trudy Visser likely did.

"I asked if you have been spreading gossip about her."

She wagged her head with indignation. "No, I have not. I swear it."

When she did not drop her eyes under O'Dell's penetrating scrutiny, he believed that she was telling the truth. However, O'Dell had the disturbing sensation that she knew more than she was saying, that he had not asked the *right* question.

He placed his hat on his head. "We shall discuss what you did to Victoria Washington another time, Miss Visser. You shall answer for your crimes. You have my word on that."

❧ ✺ ❧

CHAPTER 37

Preparations for Tory's fashion parade went forward. Every employee of *Victoria's House of Fashion* labored from early morning to late evening every day but Sunday in the weeks leading up to the showing.

Tory, who scarcely saw her own bed during the race to complete her spring lineup, called Miss Tobin to her side midmorning. "I really must run to the bank this afternoon; please manage in my absence."

"Yes, miss."

Tory left the shop while the staff were having their lunch and crossed the distance to her bank in short order. The skies were leaden and drizzly and the temperatures bitter, so she carried the deposit under her cloak, hugged close to her person where it was unseen. She reached the bank without incident.

Relieved to have completed her task, Tory started back to the shop. The sidewalks were clogged with pedestrians shivering and hurrying to get out of the cold, and Tory did not see who shoved her: One moment she was at the outside edge of the crowded sidewalk—and the next moment she was sprawling in the street with an automobile bearing down on her.

Just as quickly, a strong arm grabbed onto hers and yanked her from the cobblestones into the gutter—a hairsbreadth from being run over. As the motorcar sped past her, its churning wheels splattered her with mud.

Not that the spray mattered much—considering that Tory was sitting in a gutter rank with running mud and trash.

Tory's first thought was, *I shall have to go home, bathe, and dress again before I can return to work—and I have so much to do.*

"Oh, bother."

"Is that all you have to say?"

Tory glanced up at the stranger leaning over her. "I beg your pardon?"

"You were nearly run down! I pulled you from beneath the tires of that car, and all you can say is, 'oh, bother'?"

A small crowd was gathering, men and women concerned and murmuring.

"I say, is the lady all right?"

"She was almost killed!"

"Why, I believe that is Victoria Washington—I saw her photograph in the Post."

"I think you are right—it *is* her. My, but did you hear what is being said about her?"

As the comments reached her, Tory's face burned.

"Don't listen to the old crows."

Tory lifted her eyes toward her knight in shining . . . wool. Combed, charcoal-gray wool, a nice weight for this bitter day. Her gaze went higher and discovered a pair of concerned green-flecked hazel eyes under a head of wavy brown hair.

"Dear me! I am . . ." Tory eyed the gutter with distaste. "Would you mind?"

"Not at all. You have been sitting in the gutter far too long."

Tory frowned. Did his comment hint at humor?

He pulled her to standing, and Tory stepped onto the sidewalk, sore and disheveled but otherwise unharmed.

"Are you all right?" her rescuer asked.

"I shall be. I do not . . ." she looked around. "I do not know how I fell into the street."

"You did not fall. You were pushed. I saw it happen."

Tory started. "Yes. I remember now!" She stared at the crowed that was now breaking up. "Who? Who pushed me?"

"I did not get a good look at him—I was too busy pulling you from certain death. But come, you need to run home and clean up, yes?"

Tory examined her suit. "Ugh. Most certainly. I do not live far."

"I shall escort you."

"No, that is not necessary," Tory protested. *And I do not know you,* she thought, recalling too late Mr. O'Dell's stern warnings and how she had ignored them.

The man reached into his breast pocket and withdrew a card. He handed the card to Tory who read, *Jack Monroe, Attorney at Law.*

"Mr. Monroe, I thank you for your timely assistance, but I—"

"I comprehend your reluctance to accept the services of a stranger, miss; however, someone pushed you—deliberately pushed you—into oncoming traffic. I will not leave you to a second attempt. If you will not accept my company, I shall follow along behind at a discreet distance to ensure that you arrive home safely."

A second attempt? The words struck a note of terror in Tory's heart.

She cleared her throat. "Very well. I shall . . . accept your offer, Mr. Monroe."

"A wise choice." He did not offer Tory his arm, but gestured for her to provide direction.

She nodded and set off for the corner. They crossed together and walked in silent companionship to her rooms. When Tory turned to thank him, he forestalled her.

"Will you return to work after you change?"

"Why, yes. I must."

"I shall wait for you," he pointed at a bench under an awning, "just there and make sure you reach your shop intact, Miss Washington."

It was only after they had arrived at Tory's shop and he had left her that she realized, *I never gave him my name, and he knew I worked in a shop. How could he have known?*

Then she remembered. *He must have heard the comments of the crowd while I sat in the gutter.*

Nevertheless, she was not reassured.

~*~

O'Dell called at the rear entrance of *Victoria's House of Fashion*, so that his presence in the shop was unseen by her clients. However, the girl who opened the door to him lived at Palmer House and recognized him.

"Mr. O'Dell, sir!"

"You are Marion, are you not?"

She curtsied. "Yes, sir—and glad I am to see you, sir. Are you here because of what happened?"

"What do you mean? What has happened?"

Marion looked around, then whispered, "Miss Washington went out to the bank at lunch. A man pushed her into the street, and she was nearly run over."

"What? Is she all right?"

"Yes, sir. A passing gentleman pulled her out from under the wheels of a motorcar, he did." She looked around again. "Please do not say I told you. I overheard her telling Miss Tobin."

O'Dell frowned. "Please tell Miss Washington that I am here. I must speak to her."

"Right away, sir."

She returned to escort him to an office where Tory rose from behind a desk to greet him. She turned hopeful eyes on him. "Have you news already?"

"No. I have ruled out Charles and Belinda Luchetti and Miss Visser, but I am no further along than that." Tory's expression was stoic as he related his visit to the Broadmoor.

"Roxanne Cleary told me Charles did not know, that he was not part of the plan to . . . to send me to Corinth. I suppose I had my doubts."

"Charles had no idea. He was shocked."

"Was he?" Tory was wary.

"I can only say that when I asked him about you, he appeared genuinely distressed that he had not heard from you in three years. He kept saying he did not understand why you left without saying goodbye."

Tory dropped her face to her hands. "Miss Visser. She lied to me. She told me Charles refused to see me before I left."

"All the lies will come out, Tory, if you are willing to confront them; however, it is more important that we deal with the present dangers first." He allowed his displeasure to show. "You ignored my advice, Miss Washington. You left my office and straightaway ignored my advice."

Tory sighed. "Who told you?"

"Who told me is not important. Someone tried to harm or even kill you, Miss Washington. The stalking and attempts to ruin you have become a frank attempt upon your life. These actions suggest personal animus at their core but, perhaps, also a more tangible purpose."

Tory searched O'Dell's face. "But what could that be?"

"I cannot say at present, but it is certain that you must take proper care for your safety."

"My spring showing is but a week away. I and much of my staff are here day and night, working to complete our preparations. I am hardly alone or vulnerable."

O'Dell's ferocity intimidated her. "You are, as I have said, at your most vulnerable when you walk in public—whether day or night. If you do not have an escort, call a cab—particularly after dark."

Tory winced. "I shall heed your admonitions, Mr. O'Dell."

"See that you do. And I also cannot help but think that your upcoming fashion parade provides an opening for whomever is behind these attempts to discredit you."

"What? How?"

"It is a public occasion. It presents a favorable time and opportunity for a bold and motivated individual to call you out before your friends and clients—to finish the job he began of ruining you. Or, if he has a more devilish goal, to attempt another assault on your person."

Tory swallowed as she absorbed O'Dell's "attempt another assault on your person." "And yet the rationale eludes me. Why? What could motivate anyone to hate me so?"

"That is the missing piece, Miss Washington. The missing piece I must uncover. Please report any fresh faces or acquaintances to me in a timely manner."

"I . . . I suppose I should mention that the gentleman who pulled me from the street just as I was about to be struck insisted on seeing me home to clean up."

O'Dell's expression hardened. "You accepted the escort of a stranger?"

"Certainly not—but he said he would follow me from a distance if I did not allow him to see me home safely. He waited outside while I cleaned up, then walked me to my shop."

"Who is this man?" O'Dell demanded.

"Here is his card."

O'Dell took the card. "Jack Monroe. I will set men to locate him immediately. In the meanwhile, I caution you to exercise the highest level of care, Miss Washington, and I will arrange suitable security at your fashion event next week."

O'Dell tipped his hat. "I pray all will be resolved then."

CHAPTER 38

T ory entered the ballroom to enthusiastic acclaim. She wore a gown of her own design for the event—a lovely, beaded creation that sparkled and shimmered along her slim figure as she moved. The light glinting from the amber beads infused her gleaming caramel skin with rich fire. The mahogany fox stole draped about her arms was the perfect accent. Golden pearls, courtesy of Grace Minton, adorned Tory's neck and dangled from her ears.

Denver's elite might not be present at Tory's fashion parade in the numbers she had initially hoped for—but neither had as many stayed away as she had feared. The influence of Martha Palmer, Emily Van der Pol, her friends, and other godly women of Denver's society had wrung a credible success from what could have been a resounding disaster.

While Tory's entire spring lineup traveled the parade route, the models wending their way among the tables and posing before the seated guests, the hotel's staff served hors d'oeuvres and beverages. When the models had twice walked the circuit, the popping of celebratory champagne corks signaled the beginning of the reception.

Tory was gratified to see a line forming at a side table where Miss Tobin was taking appointments. She circulated among her guests and thanked them for coming to view her spring lineup; she accepted their accolades at her success.

"Miss Washington, I simply adore your designs! I shall be making an appointment and placing an order as soon as you can accommodate me."

"Thank you, Mrs. Lerner; you are too kind. I look forward to seeing you in my shop."

Near the end of the reception, Tory retired from the crowd and stood near a watermarked silk curtain overhanging a cozy nook. She sipped on a champagne flute filled, at her request, with ordinary mineral water. *As Charles would say, I do not wish my senses dulled.*

From her vantage point in the room, Tory studied her guests and patrons—the wealthy and pampered of Denver. She kept a small smile at all times, one she knew projected confidence and satisfaction, but it was a smile that gave nothing away. Particularly her fear.

Without turning her head, Tory swept her eyes across the room, searching. Searching for that one individual in the crowd Mr. O'Dell had insisted would attend her event: the unknown someone who had proven himself determined to destroy her reputation and her business.

I am poised on the brink of success in this city while this man plots to harm me—but why? I do not understand. And will the reasons matter if he succeeds in ruining me?

Tory exhaled to calm her nerves. The "why" was unimportant at the moment and must wait for an answer. *Mr. O'Dell believes this man— whomever he is—will be here, that my event presents him with a favorable time and opportunity to strike, neither of which he will pass over.*

"He is likely here already," Tory breathed, "waiting, biding his time."

Tory nodded at Emily Van der Pol and Viola Lind to her far right. *They are praising my designs to the heavens, Lord,* she thought. *Oh, please bless them for their love and support. I will never be able to thank them enough.*

Her smile tightened in response to a nod from far across the room. The handsome gentleman raising a glass to her was also suspect: Jack Monroe. Tory did not believe Monroe to be the man who had dogged her steps from Philadelphia to Denver. She had caught glimpses of her stalker—and he was not Jack Monroe.

But Mr. O'Dell cautioned me to trust no one he has not personally cleared—and Mr. Monroe remains a cypher. An unknown entity.

She spied Edmund O'Dell moving among the guests. Tory trusted few individuals without limit—life had shown her how rare were those she could rely upon implicitly, but Edmund O'Dell was one such rarity. She knew he had placed three additional Pinkerton men in the room, one who stood his post mere feet behind Tory's shoulder. O'Dell had assured her that the man would not leave her side.

Tory exhaled to calm her nerves. *Mr. O'Dell is convinced my enemy will act this evening.* She blinked as a thought occurred to her. *Enemy? Or enemies? Could more than one man be stalking me? Is it possible?*

She observed Jack Monroe edging his way through the reception throng. He was moving in her direction. As he moved closer, she saw his expression shift. Harden.

Tory's pulse quickened in response. She looked around for O'Dell, hoping to catch his eye, hoping he was close by, but she had lost sight of him.

When she looked again at Monroe, his mouth had twisted; he began to run toward her. As he bore down on her, Tory panicked and dropped her champagne flute. She heard it shatter, but she had already turned toward Emily and Grace and the safety of their presence.

The Pinkerton agent assigned to protect her touched her elbow. "Miss Washington, Mr. O'Dell has ordered me to take you to safety. Come with me."

Tory glanced back at Jack Monroe—he was running all out and shouting. The Pinkerton man, tugging on her arm, opened a service door that had been hidden behind the curtain. Tory was relieved to pass with him into the safety of the dark hallway.

~*~

O'Dell saw the suspect's headlong sprint toward Tory. He bulled his way through the crowd and launched himself at the man, catching him about the knees. They fell to the floor together—amid the shocked screams of nearby attendees. O'Dell got to his feet first, grabbed the collar of the man's jacket, jerked him to standing, and pulled his arms behind his back. O'Dell's two Pinkerton agents arrived; one of them grabbed the suspect from O'Dell.

"Not me, you fool!" the suspect shouted. He struggled, but could not free himself. "It's not me—it's him! He took her! He is going to kill her!"

O'Dell's eyes jinked about the room, looking for Tory, but not seeing her; looking for her guard and not seeing him, either. Then he heard a faint, muffled scream. So did the man he held.

"Look—my name is Jack Monroe. I am not a threat to Miss Washington. Let me go—we can save her!"

One glance at the suspect's expression told O'Dell what he needed to know. He nodded to his agent to release Monroe. "You saw where they went?"

"Yes. Follow me." Monroe ran toward the service door.

O'Dell and his men followed close behind—nearly tripping over an unconscious form half hidden by trailing drapery. It was O'Dell's Pinkerton agent, the detective assigned to guard Tory.

O'Dell clamped his jaws together. "Ignore him for now; Miss Washington is our first concern." He and his two remaining agents followed Monroe through the service door into a dark corridor.

Monroe had stopped; he was listening, unsure of which way to go. Then he heard scuffling to their left and was off like a shot. The thudding, scraping grew louder—and then they saw.

The man had Tory pressed against a wall; his hands were about her neck, his fingers digging into her throat. Tory's feet were flailing against the floor, kicking against the wall.

"Stop!" Monroe roared. He was on the man a second later—but instead of attempting to pry the attacker's fingers from Tory's neck, Monroe clouted the attacker's ears with his open palms.

Howling with pain, Tory's attacker released her—and collided with Monroe's bunched fist. O'Dell arrived next and threw the man to the floor.

O'Dell and Monroe turned to Tory at the same time. She was barely conscious; her breathing was faint.

"Tend to her; I'll be back directly," Monroe hissed. He turned and sprinted down the hall toward the ballroom. One of O'Dell's men, not fully trusting Monroe's abrupt departure, raced after him. He found him at a serving table tossing crushed ice into a napkin.

"Do not get in my way," Monroe commanded. "In fact, stay here and assure this crowd that Miss Washington will be all right—and have someone summon an ambulance."

The Pinkerton man noted the pandemonium sweeping the ballroom. "Got it." He raised his voice and announced, "May I have your attention, please! The, er, situation is under control. We have apprehended a man who, um, intended to disrupt the event. We have taken him into custody. Please do not be alarmed."

"What about Miss Washington?" a man shouted.

"Yes! Is she safe? We heard her scream," another voice chimed in.

"She is with friends. I, er, I *believe* she will be fine."

Grace Minton challenged him. "Then why do you need an ambulance?"

"Yes, why?" Emily Van der Pol demanded. She drew herself up. "You will take us to her at once."

~*~

When Monroe returned to the corridor, Tory was slumped against the wall, only semi-conscious. O'Dell was holding her hand and chafing it. Monroe removed and unfolded his pocket square, laid crushed ice into it, and rolled the kerchief into a poultice.

"Move," he gestured to O'Dell. "I must place this ice on her throat to reduce the swelling."

O'Dell, sensing only good intentions from Monroe, stood and stepped away.

Emily Van der Pol, strain and concern etched in her features, arrived seconds later, accompanied by Grace Minton.

"Do not worry," O'Dell reassured them, "Our friend here has things in hand."

"Our friend? Just who is he? And who is *that* man?" She pointed at the unconscious form not far from where they stood over Tory.

"I do not know, but I believe Tory's champion here," O'Dell jerked his chin at Jack Monroe, "will be able to answer our questions in due time."

~*~

Hours later, Tory reclined on the sofa in Emily Van der Pol's parlor, a cool cloth about her swollen, bruised neck. Emily hovered nearby with an ice-filled beverage the doctor had insisted Tory sip on for the rest of the evening. Also in the room were Grace Minton and the quick-thinking Monroe. O'Dell had taken a chair near Tory, and placed the stranger on the other side of the room where he could study the man.

The doctor had departed. Tory's attacker was in police custody.

It was time for answers.

O'Dell leveled his first question at Monroe. "Mr. Monroe, would you care to tell us the identity of the man who attacked Tory?"

"Certainly, but please let me formally introduce myself. As I told you earlier, my name is Jack Monroe—John Monroe, actually, although I go by Jack."

"We will accept your introduction at face value, Mr. Monroe—for the moment. Now, you saw the attacker take down my agent and that is why you ran toward Miss Washington, is that correct?"

"Something like that. I already knew that you were Pinkerton, Mr. O'Dell, so I familiarized myself with your men, particularly the one guarding Miss Washington. When I realized the guard was missing and saw who had taken his place? That was when I rushed to help."

"You knew I was Pinkerton? And you just happened to be at her event? A complete stranger who had already saved Miss Washington once before? I don't think so."

O'Dell's gaze hardened. "It is time you came clean with us, Mr. Monroe: How is it you know Miss Washington—and just how do you figure into her affairs?"

"Ah, yes—but, of course, I did *not* 'just happen' upon her event, Mr. O'Dell. I was present quite on purpose."

"Why? You are unknown to Miss Washington and, I wager, you are not from around here."

"Correct on both points. Before last week, I had never laid eyes on Miss Washington or set foot in your fair city. I am an attorney from New Orleans, Louisiana, as was my uncle, my mother's brother, before me. As to how I figure into Miss Washington's affairs," Monroe nodded at Tory, "my uncle, Richard Follinger, handled your father's estate."

"My father?" Tory's voice was not much more than a croak.

"Henri Declouette was your father, yes?"

Tory swallowed before she breathed her answer. "Yes."

O'Dell touched Tory's shoulder, and he whispered in her ear, "Courage, Miss Washington. I think we shall know everything soon, and your troubles shall be at an end."

Monroe continued. "You may be unaware, Miss Washington, but your father made provision for you in his will."

"H-he w-what?"

He nodded. "I shall not, at this time, go into the specifics of the will's provisions. However, if I am to explain tonight's events, we must look first to the year 1902, the year Henri Declouette died. To our knowledge, you, Miss Washington, disappeared from your home in Louisiana the same month—May of 1902. By 1909, you had been missing seven years, and a certain individual petitioned the courts of Orleans Parish to declare you dead *in absentia*.

"Oh!"

"I, as the standing attorney for your father's estate and the trustee of your inheritance, placed new notices in newspapers across the South asking for information as to your whereabouts. My uncle and I had done so many times to no avail, but this time a Miss Defoe and a Madame Rousseau saw and answered those notices. Their sworn statements declared that you had appeared upon the doorstep of Madame Rousseau's establishment in May 1902 and that you had remained in their care for fifteen months, until August of 1903.

"Now I must backtrack a little. According to court records, your father's brother, Bastiann Declouette, petitioned the courts for your guardianship in 1902 and had been granted custody of you. However, he did not discover your whereabouts—at *Madame Rousseau's Haute Couture*—until August 1903. When he came to claim you, Miss Defoe and Madame Rousseau attest that you immediately fled, and no one had heard from you since."

Her voice rough from more than her injured throat, Tory interrupted, "Miss Defoe . . . Madame Rousseau. Are they . . . are they well?"

Jack smiled. "They are. If I do not mistake the fervor with which they asked after you, I believe they would give anything to see you again, Miss Washington."

Tory's breath caught on a sob.

"Shall I continue?"

Tory nodded.

"Although Miss Defoe and Madame Rousseau's account did not lead us to you, their testimony did provide a last-known sighting—in August 1903, not May 1902—six years past, not seven. And so, I was able to delay the petition to declare you dead in absentia and intensify my search for you."

Jack Monroe's eyes were sympathetic. "The man remanded to police custody is the same man who petitioned the courts to declare you dead. He is also the man who pushed you into the street last week and tried to strangle you tonight. His name is Devereaux Declouette. Your half-brother."

"M-my half-brother?"

Monroe nodded. "Your half-brother frittered away much of his inheritance and, having never been required to work a day in his life, sought to wrest what remained of his father's estate to himself before he went broke. It is my understanding that his mother had often railed at the injustice of his father leaving anything to you . . . his illegitimate and mixed-blood daughter."

Tory sighed. *Marguerite Declouette.*

"When the court delayed the petition to have you declared dead, Declouette hired detectives to search for you—not so he could restore you to the bosom of your friends and family. Not so you could receive your rightful inheritance. My sense is that he wanted to find you before anyone else did and ensure that your untimely and, er, unexplained demise ended any possibility of your ever inheriting from your father. You see, in the event of your death without spouse or posterity, what was meant to be yours would flow back to him.

"Declouette's detectives traced you first to St. Louis, where you were said to be in the company of one Charles Luchetti. From there, they traced Luchetti and, presumably, *you*, to Denver. Declouette traveled to Denver and took up rooms at the Broadmoor Hotel, believing he would find you there—only to discover that you had taken employment elsewhere and your present location was unknown.

"At the outset of his short and frustrating sojourn in Denver, Declouette struck up an acquaintance with an employee of the hotel, one Trudy Visser, who hinted that she knew more than she was saying. Using flattery and feigned attentions to gain her confidence, Declouette became convinced that Miss Visser knew where you had gone.

"In the end, he bribed Miss Visser—whose greed was as strong as her desire for a beau—to tell him exactly what had become of you. For the right price, she told him why he need never fear that you would resurface."

Monroe offered half of a smile. "I apologize if my recounting of these things distresses you."

Tory bowed her head. It was too painful for her to talk, physically or emotionally.

"But how did Declouette get from Denver to Philadelphia?" O'Dell asked. "Miss Washington's location after her escape from Corinth was a closely held secret at the time."

"Actually, when Declouette left Denver in September 1909, he returned home to New Orleans, confident that all he need do was wait another year and renew his petition to declare Miss Washington dead *in absentia*. The seven years would expire in August of 1910, with no one in Louisiana—save Declouette—any the wiser that Miss Washington was known to be alive less than two years previously."

"Go on," O'Dell urged.

"You are familiar with the saying, 'The best laid plans of mice and men'? A month later, in October 1909, now seventeen months ago, Declouette's detectives spotted articles and photographs of Miss Washington in the fashion pages of Philadelphia papers—and reported this information to Declouette. Can you imagine his chagrin? He was expecting, in a matter of ten months, to renew his petition to have Miss Washington declared dead.

"As you and I might surmise, the news of Miss Washington's whereabouts threw Declouette into a fit of action. He left for Philadelphia forthwith and, over a few weeks' time, ingratiated himself into the city's polite society and, when he found opportunity, began a campaign of insidious rumors based on the information he had gained from Miss Visser."

"The incomparable Miss Visser," O'Dell drawled. "She and I have an appointment with her soon-to-be *former* employer at a not-too-distant date."

"Good," Monroe declared.

O'Dell frowned. "How is it that you are in possession of these facts, Mr. Monroe?"

"Ah. This is where Providence truly comes in, Mr. O'Dell. Only weeks ago, you called the Pinkerton office in New Orleans, asking them to look into Miss Washington's childhood. Two of *their* agents were the very detectives Declouette had hired to locate Miss Washington. With a little digging in Orleans Parish records, those detectives found the petition to declare Miss Washington dead *in absentia*—and, knowing her to be verifiably alive, realized that Declouette's interests in "locating" Miss Washington were nefarious, to say the least.

"My name as the attorney for Henri Declouette's estate was on the petition to declare Miss Washington deceased, and I soon after received a visit from them."

Monroe's eyes swept the room, ending with Tory. "I believe that when Declouette located Tory in Philadelphia, she was too sheltered and inaccessible for him to do her the harm he intended. He soon devised a smear campaign designed to ostracize Miss Washington and drive her from The City of Brotherly Love, far from the friends who protected her.

"In a new locale where she was unknown, Declouette felt he could more easily arrange an 'accident.' He never dreamed Miss Washington's friends would send her *back to Denver* with ample funding to establish herself—and where even more powerful friends surrounded her. By this time, Declouette was, himself, strapped for money and, I presume, growing desperate."

"We are beginning to comprehend the direction of your story, Mr. Monroe," O'Dell said. "Please continue."

"Declouette's dwindling resources made it impossible for him to enter Denver society with the same flair and style by which he had entered Philadelphia society. Thus, he found inciting a smear campaign against Miss Washington to be harder going than in Philadelphia. Eventually, however, his rumors gained some traction."

"That 'traction' must not have met his expectations since he attempted to kill Miss Washington last week," O'Dell growled. "And I find it quite fortuitous that *you* happened to be there, as they say, 'in the nick of time.'"

"I don't believe in fortune or luck, Mr. O'Dell. I believe in God. *He* put me in the right place at the right time. However, while I saw her shoved into the street and was able to pull her to safety, I did not see the face of the man who pushed her—although I had strong suspicions."

"You say you knew who I was, that I was Pinkerton. Why did you not come to the Denver Pinkerton office and tell me everything you had uncovered?"

Monroe growled, "Should I have trusted you, Mr. O'Dell, given that the Pinkertons had—unwittingly, I admit—led Declouette to Miss Washington in the first place? Could I have known you were not in Declouette's pocket?"

O'Dell nodded. "I take your point." He was beginning to like the man in spite of his initial instinct to disbelieve him.

Beginning to like him—but not trust him. Not yet.

"What of this inheritance?" he asked.

"It is, of course, a private matter, for Miss Washington's ears only."

"You will forgive all of us in this room if we refuse to allow Miss Washington to meet with *anyone* 'privately' for some time to come."

"I suppose I cannot fault you on that count," Monroe answered.

Tory signaled Monroe. "Tell," she rasped.

"You give me leave to speak of your inheritance before these people?"

Tory nodded, and Emily handed Tory the glass so she could sip the icy water. "Yes," she managed.

"As you wish." But he ran a hand through his hair, not entirely at ease with the idea.

"Mr. Monroe?" O'Dell asked.

"Yes?"

"May I alleviate your discomfort? We cherish Miss Washington and are concerned only for her welfare. None of us want or need her inheritance."

"I see. Very well." He looked at Tory again and sighed. "Your father left you five thousand dollars, Miss Washington, in a trust over which my uncle was, and I am at present, the sole trustee. He also left one thousand dollars to your mother, who died before she could receive Henri Declouette's bequest. Both sums of money have sat, untouched, for nine years. The interest on them has accrued nicely."

Tory swallowed the lump in her throat—one unrelated to the bruises on her neck.

"A second, specific bequest was for the painting, *Joseph Reveals Himself to His Brothers*, by Groote van Nierop. Van Nierop was a talented Renaissance painter, the apprentice of a great Dutch master. His work has come into its own in recent years. This single painting is valuable, should you ever wish to sell it. And, of course, you own Sugar Tree."

Tory's eyes widened and her lips formed the word, "no,"—but not a sound emerged.

"Yes, you do," Monroe repeated.

"How does one inherit a tree?" Grace Minton asked, as puzzled as Emily and O'Dell were.

"Not a tree, madam, but an estate removed some ten miles from New Orleans and so named 'Sugar Tree.' It is where Miss Washington was born and spent her childhood. It is where her mother, Adeline Washington, is buried in the orchard."

Tory was weeping now, overcome with Monroe's sweeping revelations.

"When you are fully restored to health, Miss Washington, you must accompany me to New Orleans and present yourself to the court to disprove the assertion that you are dead. You will then receive your inheritance."

Straining, Tory whispered, "I cannot. I . . . business to run; fashion parade . . . some success, but reputation . . . ruined. Must . . . work."

Emily spoke up. "My dear Tory, an inheritance is just what is needed to shore up your flagging 'reputation.'" She half smiled, and her voice took on a biting edge of cynicism. "Nothing inspires Denver's vain, *nouveau riche* society quite like the scent of money. Most of them have their own closet skeletons and will ignore both scandal and humble beginnings—if you possess an adequate bank account. Why, just ask Margaret Brown—although most of Denver calls her Molly."

Emily laughed a little. "Tory, if I were you, I would instruct my entire staff to remark to the public in general that I am returning to Louisiana to receive my father's fortune."

Grace laughed with her. "Oh, yes, my dear. Why, the clients will positively flood in!"

Monroe grinned; O'Dell grinned, too. Emily and Grace giggled.

And no one had anything to add.

CHAPTER 39

MARCH 1911

Jack was familiar with their destination and insisted upon driving Tory her first morning back in the city she had left as child of twelve years. Her breath caught when the familiar plaza came into view. As Jack navigated the plaza's circumference, skirting the grassy park, Tory's eyes followed the iron fence to the ornate benches edging the brick-paved circle.

In the center of the circle she spied the pump—still in use—the pump she had drunk from the day the beggar boy had brought her out of the grimy slums of New Orleans in exchange for a share of her sweet rolls.

We licked the icing from the paper. How well I remember its sweet taste.

Tory tore her eyes away to stare at the covered boardwalk and the sign attached to the balcony railing over the shop.

Haute Couture
Madame Charlotte Rousseau, Modiste.

O Jesus! Please let them be there. Please let them be just as they were.

Jack pulled his motorcar alongside the boardwalk and came around to assist her down. He took Tory's arm and they started up the steps.

"I bid you good morning, sir."

Jack and Tory found the owner of the greeting, a police officer, standing above them.

"Yes, officer?"

"Begging your pardon, sir, but coloreds are not allowed in the plaza. That means you, girlie." His eyes looked Tory up and down. "Don't matter how you dress a darky, they's still a darky."

Jack's face flamed as red as a fire engine. "Does that injunction include me?"

"You, sir?" The policeman scrutinized him. "You look white enough to me."

"White *enough?* My great-grandmother on my mother's side was negro. Guess that makes me octoroon."

The officer's affable expression hardened. "Then get along afore I makes you sorry you bothered me."

Tory tugged discreetly on Jack's arm and they returned to his motorcar. "I take it things have not improved since I was here last," she murmured.

"Hardly. The laws and attitudes have worsened. I am 'white enough' to not often be questioned, but I suppose I did not think through the likelihood of your being affronted, Miss Washington. I apologize most profusely for my thoughtlessness."

Tory shrugged. "Jack, if you will drive around that corner—which is out of the plaza—you will find an alley behind these shops."

"You wish to enter through the alley?"

Tory nodded. *I suppose it is fitting that I return the same way I left.*

He parked in the alley and helped Tory down. "Do you wish me to go in with you?"

Tory smiled. "Thank you for offering, but no. I wish to do this alone."

He smiled in return. "I shall wait for you, but do not hurry on my account."

She took a breath, nodded again, opened the back door to the shop, and stepped inside.

Tory closed the door behind her, conscious at once of the scent of spicy tea and shortbread biscuits. She squeezed her eyes closed, again the hungry child so grateful for a cup of hot, sweet tea and three sugary biscuits.

"May I help you, miss?"

Tory sniffed and cleared her throat. "I beg your pardon. Is . . . is Miss Defoe at work today?"

The girl studied Tory, twisting a tea towel in her hands. "Miss, this is the worker's kitchen. We do not, of a rule, receive customers here . . . or negro customers at all, for that matter."

Tory exhaled slowly. "Well, I am not a customer. Would you kindly inform Miss Defoe that . . . an old friend is calling?"

"An old friend, miss? Would you give me your name?"

"Just say, 'an old friend,' please."

Armed with wary curiosity, the girl marched away.

Several minutes went by. Tory grew nervous. Then anxious. She walked the length of the kitchen, her back to the passageway.

"This is most unusual, miss. May I ask your business?"

Tory turned. There stood her beloved Miss Defoe, arms crossed, imperious frown in place. Her hair was grayer and thinner perhaps, yet all else was the same.

Tory tried to smile; she could not.

Her heart was too full.

It overflowed her eyes.

She could only sob, "Miss Defoe . . . I have come back."

The frown dropped from Miss Defoe's face; incredulity replaced it. "V-victoria?"

Tory stepped toward her. She was now many inches taller than Miss Defoe, but that woman's arms wrapped themselves about her and pressed Tory's face to her shoulder.

"Oh, dear God in heaven! You have brought my child home! Dear God! Thank you!"

Then, somehow, they were seated on a bench at the table, arms twined about each other, weeping in complete accord. When Tory could lift her head, she found Miss Defoe, her tears unabated, studying her.

"You have grown into such a beautiful woman, Victoria," she managed. "I always knew you would, but how I have missed you! How I have prayed that God would have mercy upon me and bring you back to me."

"He did! It was God! He brought me home to you."

"What is this? What is going on?"

Tory would have known that voice anywhere.

On shaky legs, she stood. Curtsied as low as her trembling knees would take her. "*Bonjour,* Madame."

The folds of Madame Rousseau's powdered cheeks drooped with shock and disbelief. "No. It cannot be." She looked to Miss Defoe. "Patrice?"

"It is our Victoria, Charlotte. She has come home to us!"

Madame swept Tory into an embrace, and muttering, "Thank you, God! Thank you, God!" she wept upon Tory's shoulder.

When they had spent their tears, Madame Rousseau and Tory pulled apart to search each other's eyes. Then they joined Miss Defoe at the table, Miss Defoe and Madame clutching Tory's hands, still incredulous and thanking God for her return.

After many minutes, Tory had to ask the question, the question that would explain the profound change of heart she witnessed in both Miss Defoe and Madame Rousseau.

"I hear you thanking God. Are you . . . are you followers of Jesus, now? How is this possible?"

"It was Miss Sarasses," Miss Defoe answered. "When you ran—when I shouted to you not to come back—we were profoundly grateful you had escaped that monster, Bastiann Declouette, but we were distraught for ourselves. Brokenhearted. Miss Sarasses, who has long lived her life for Christ before us, spoke hope into our sorrow. We had forbidden her to talk about her faith for years but, when you left, we were desperate, and she was very brave—brave enough to risk our wrath many times to tell us about Jesus. Eventually, we listened."

Miss Defoe turned to the girl Tory had sent to fetch her—the same girl who had run to Madame Rousseau to report strange happenings in the kitchen. She had looked on, boggle-eyed, as Madame and Miss Defoe alternately wept and caressed the stranger.

"Go quickly, Danielle. Help Miss Sarasses bring Mademoiselle Justine here."

"Help her?"

Madame Rousseau clasped Tory's hand more tightly. "Our Mademoiselle Justine has had a stroke, Tory," she whispered.

"Oh, no!"

Madame Rousseau patted the hand she held. "Do not worry. We have cared for her and shall continue to. Patrice and I found a place for the three of us to live together. It is small, but we make do. We bring her to work with us in a wheeled chair and she spends the day in the workroom, happy among those who love her."

"The three of us," Miss Defoe said with a sigh, "have been together a long time. We were in the same workhouse as children, although Charlotte and Annette-Francoise were a few years older than I. We were hungry together and suffered abuse and neglect together. We . . . wandered down some terrible paths together, too, before we landed in a factory and learned a few useful skills."

"It was Patrice who dreamed up our grand scheme, who showed us how we might escape poverty and drudgery," Madame Rousseau whispered. "I am ashamed of the many things we did to break free in order to better ourselves. We started a small sewing shop in a sordid New Orleans ward, working twelve hours a day to keep a roof over our heads and food on the table—and using our feminine charms at night to add bit by bit to our nest egg, until we had the seed money we needed."

Miss Defoe nodded. "With that seed money, we left our old haunts and established ourselves in a better neighborhood, teaching ourselves to speak and act as women of distinction while saving every spare penny until we had enough to rent space in this plaza.

"Then we created new personas and assumed false airs—Charlotte was best at pretending to be a French *émigré*—and established this shop and our new lives. But, years later, you showed us, Tory, that we had gained only material security and acceptance. We had given up on love."

"Yes, love," Madame repeated. "When you fled Bastiann Declouette, you shattered our hearts and took the fragments with you. Miss Sarasses showed us a God who cared about our wounded hearts. We surrendered our lives to him—"

"And he has brought you back to us," Miss Defoe finished.

At that moment, Miss Sarasses, pushing a chair on wheels, entered from the passageway. Her face lit with joy when she recognized Tory. "God be praised! You have come back!"

Mademoiselle Justine, too, realized who the tall stranger was. She waved a curled fist at Tory, and one side of her face smiled.

The other side sagged and did not move.

Tory knelt and embraced the woman who had, with great patience, trained her to be a maid in a house of couture, whose lessons Tory employed as she built her own house of fashion.

Madame Rousseau stood and announced, "Miss Sarasses, the shop is closed."

"Madame?"

"Please inform the staff in the workroom that I give them a holiday— *with pay*. I shall inform our clients in the front that we are closing early, shoo them out the door, and lock it behind them."

Her powdered face quivered with exultation. "Our daughter has come home, and we shall praise God and celebrate."

Many hours later, only Tory, Miss Defoe, and Madame Rousseau remained in the shop's kitchen. Tory had sent Jack on his way with her thanks; Mademoiselle Justine had grown fatigued so Miss Sarasses had taken her to the house shared by Miss Defoe, Madame Rousseau, and the crippled Mademoiselle Justine.

"I, too, found the Savior," Tory whispered. She tugged at a chain about her neck and drew out the locket that hung on it. The crack in the ivory rose on the locket's face had given way, and half the flower had fallen off, but Tory wore it near her heart, day and night.

She flicked open the locket with practiced ease and stared at her mother's faded photograph. "This locket, the image of my dear *Maman*, and the memories I had of you kept me from giving up through many difficulties—as did a scrap I tore from a Gospel tract:

"For I know the thoughts that I think toward you, saith the Lord, thoughts of peace, and not of evil, to give you an expected end. Then shall ye call upon me, and ye shall go and pray unto me, and I will hearken unto you. And ye shall seek me, and find me, when ye shall search for me with all your heart.

"I did not understand the words, but they held a power over me that kept me wondering, 'Is God real? Does he care for me? Does he see me? Will I find him if I search for him with all my heart, as he promises?'

"And I did. I found the Savior," Tory whispered, "or should I say, he found me? But the road to him was . . . difficult."

Tory spoke of the nine years since she had seen them last, beginning with the hours after she fled her uncle and Charles Luchetti took her under his wing, to those harrowing moments at her Denver fashion parade. At times, she spoke dispassionately; at other junctures, her throat closed on the words she tried to speak.

Madame Rousseau was tearfully attentive throughout Tory's telling. Miss Defoe asked many questions. By the end of Tory's account, the three of them were spent and silent in their own thoughts.

Finally, Miss Defoe broke the hush. "You say you have a shop and . . . friends in Colorado. Does this mean you have not come back to stay, Victoria?"

Tory sighed. "In many ways, I had forgotten what the South is like. When Jack—Mr. Monroe—drove me here, a policeman forbade me from setting foot on the boardwalk. Because I am 'colored.'"

Madame Rousseau's fist struck the table. "Unconscionable! If I owned this plaza, why, I—"

"The laws have become stricter in recent years," Miss Defoe interjected, "the prejudices more engrained, the color lines more defined and separate."

Tory shrugged. "I am a woman of mixed blood. I accept that fact . . . but things are better for me in Denver. I am not saying the city is without its faults and sins—not at all. Among other faults, Denver is a bastion of prostitution and vice. But I . . . that is why God has called me to live there. I have a work to do for him in Denver, helping other women such as myself."

Her friends nodded, their expressions accepting but bleak.

Tory, to break the silence, exclaimed, "Oh! How could I have forgotten? I have learned that my father left me a bit of money. Could you . . . could you think of joining me in Denver? We could buy a house, a nice one, large enough for us all to live together.

"We could hire a nurse to care for Mademoiselle Justine. You could help me in my shop, but relax a little, too."

Miss Defoe and Madame Rousseau locked eyes in unspoken communication. Madame shook her head once, and Miss Defoe folded her hands before she answered.

"This place, this Denver, is considerably different from Louisiana, is it not? Mountains instead of bayous? Snow and ice in winter? Freezing temperatures? We do not feel Annette-Francoise could make such an adjustment. Her condition is fragile, her mind often confused. She requires routine and familiar surroundings. She is our friend, and we are all she has. You understand."

"I do understand, but . . . how long can the two of you continue to work so hard? Will you not retire at some point?"

The women did not respond at first, and Tory observed a dogged stubbornness creep onto Madame Rousseau's features. Tory glanced at Miss Defoe and glimpsed . . . sorrow? Defeat?

"What is it? What are you not telling me?"

Miss Defoe reached for Tory's hand again. "Ah, child. The fact is, we cannot stop working. We spent nearly all we had saved when Annette-Francoise fell ill. If we do not work, we have nothing to live on. And, sadly, this shop does not make as much as it once did. Ready-made clothing has improved and costs much less, as you know."

Tory sat back, humbled by Miss Defoe and Madame Rousseau's great love for their friend but distraught that, after a lifetime of toil, they had nothing to sustain them during their sunset years.

Miss Defoe, however, sat up straight and grew animated, as though recalling an item of import. "Victoria! You must come home with us. Now. This evening."

"I-I have a hotel room. My things are there."

"Yes, yes. I do not mean come and spend the night—but you must walk home with us. Will you?"

"Yes. Certainly."

~*~

The house the women rented was not in the best neighborhood, nor was it adequate for their needs, but it was clean, and they kept the minuscule yard tidy and pleasant. Mademoiselle Justine slept in one bedroom, while Madame Rousseau and Miss Defoe shared the second.

As soon as they entered the house, they went to the kitchen where Madame Rousseau put on the kettle. Miss Defoe disappeared. She returned minutes later and placed a bulky bundle tied up in a scarf in Tory's hands.

"Open it," Miss Defoe commanded.

Tory laid the bundle on the table and undid the knot that bound it. The scarf fell open, disclosing a matching mirror, brush, and comb. And a familiar velvet bag.

Tory touched the ornate back of the mirror. "Why, this . . . these are *Maman's* things!"

"Yes, they are. Now, open the bag, Victoria."

She undid the bag's drawstring, and poured out a handful of jewelry, a few dollar bills, and some change.

"*Maman's* jewels!"

"Do you remember when you came to live with me and we hid your mother's jewels in the floor of my apartment? I assured you then that you had nothing to fear from me. For nine years I have kept them for you."

Tory picked them up, piece by piece, each one a treasure trove of memory—she saw her beautiful mother brushing back her sleek, raven hair and fastening diamonds to her ears. Only the pearl earrings were missing.

Beneath the bag of jewelry lay a square of stiff, faded brocade, folded in two. Tory knew what was inside, but her fingers trembled as she lifted the brocade and slid the photograph from its protective embrace.

She stared at the full image of her mother for a long time, tears dripping down her cheeks, then turned it over, knowing what she would find written there: *For Henri, my only love and the father of Victoria, my greatest joy.*

~*~

Jack Monroe arrived at Tory's hotel in the morning to drive her to Sugar Tree. It had been a restive night for Tory, as she grappled with her emotions and the difficult decisions before her.

While Jack steered his motorcar down the road leading out of town, Tory tried to picture herself, at age eleven, walking the same graveled road. *O Lord, I believed I would never return to Sugar Tree, yet you have brought me full circle. Your love and faithfulness humble me.*

"I hope your expectations are not too high, Miss Washington. The house at Sugar Tree was neglected under Bastiann Declouette's short 'guardianship,' then vandalized when he was killed.

"After his death, my uncle took possession of the estate, to preserve it for you. We closed up the house and appointed a caretaker, someone to live here and keep an eye on the house for us. We hired a crew to work the orchard and maintain the grounds."

Tory nodded. She didn't want to talk; she only wanted to breathe in the moist air of spring, redolent with lilac, honeysuckle, and wild wisteria. *This morning is not unlike the morning I discovered that Henri Declouette was my father, the day that put in motion so many heartaches,* she realized.

Jack seemed to understand, for he said no more until they turned onto the winding drive. The Southern sugar maples lining the drive had leafed out, their new-green foliage bright and bold.

"It is never cold enough in Louisiana to tap the trees for their sap," Tory murmured. "I think naming the land Sugar Tree spoke to the sweetness of life here. And it *was* sweet for my early childhood."

They continued up the drive until the house came into view. It looked no different to Tory, except a little smaller than she remembered, and her heart lurched in her chest. *Oh, Maman! How I wish you were here, still mistress of this house!*

"As you can see, the ground floor windows are boarded up. I have a key, but perhaps you wish to look around the grounds first?"

Tory nodded. She knew the way and did not wait for him. She found the path and started around the house. And she knew what pulled her, that she would not stop until she reached the orchard.

The trees had been pruned and the tall grass among the trees had been mowed. Many trees were in bloom: A riot of blossoms and the hum of bees sipping nectar greeted Tory. She wandered through the trees until . . .

She saw a bench, a lovely wrought iron bench in the shade of a peach tree. Close by was a headstone. Tory stumbled toward it. Upon the stone, in plain-carved letters, she read,

Adeline Thérèse Washington
1873–1902
Loving Mother

Tory dropped to her knees before the gravestone and leaned her cheek against its cool surface. She traced the year of her mother's birth, realizing, for the first time, that her mother had been only seventeen when she gave birth—three years younger than Tory was on this day.

"*Maman!* I am here. I have come back," Tory whispered.

"Bin a-prayin' ye would find your way," a rough voice whispered.

Tory raised her head slowly. Bent, thinner and frailer, her black face creased more deeply with years, there stood Sassy Brown.

Tory rose from her mother's grave. "You came back, too!"

"Aye. Couldn't abide Venus' shack or her man. Sleep behind th' kitchen, I do, same's before."

Tory drew closer. "Is it really you?"

"Come give this ol' woman the hug she bin yearnin' for, child."

Tory drew Sassy into her arms, half afraid she would break Sassy's bones, as fragile as she looked and felt. "Dear Sassy! Seeing you again makes me believe *Maman* is just inside the house, reading in the parlor, and soon I shall join her for tea."

"Many's th' time I've thought th' same, child."

"But what are you doing here?"

"What am I doin' here? Why, I's th' caretaker—din't yer lawyer tell ye that?"

"You!"

"Aye. Naught t' do but walk th' land once, twice a day, weed th' garden, eat, and sleep. Th' groundsmen come an' go, but I stay." Sassy stared up at Tory. "Can ye kneel, child, and let this old woman look in your face?"

Tory knelt, which put them nearly eye to eye. Sassy laid a thin hand on Tory's cheek and studied her.

"S'much of your mother. But as much of your father, too, I 'spect. A child o' two peoples."

"A child of the King of Kings, Sassy. That is what matters."

"Is so? Is so? Glory t' God, my prayers be answered!"

"I remembered you saying you would pray for me, Sassy. I wondered, for the longest time, who was this Jesus you had wished to tell me of. Then I found him for myself."

"Glory t' God, Miss Tory. And now ye are grown—and grown more beautiful than your *mère*. Din't think it possible, but 'tis true."

Tory shook her head, unable to believe Sassy.

"I see you have met the caretaker, Miss Washington."

Tory rose to her feet and turned to Jack. "A better choice you could not have made." She looked toward her mother's grave. "Who did this?"

"Sassy showed my uncle where your mother was buried. We agreed her grave needed a permanent marker."

"Thank you. From the deepest place in my heart, I thank you."

~*~

"What will you do now, Miss Washington?" Jack asked. They were walking the grounds of Sugar Tree in comfortable companionship. "What will you do now that Sugar Tree is yours, you have the means to restore the house, and you are reunited with your somewhat unconventional family?"

"I wanted to discuss the house and grounds with you . . . and my wishes regarding them."

He stopped and drew away a bit where he could study her. "You do not intend to stay?"

"No, I cannot. God called me to Denver to help other women who have suffered abuses similar to mine, the cruelties of forced prostitution. My soul's desire for these women—some not much older than school girls— is for God to heal them of their wounds and show them how to live strong, independent lives, full of grace and dignity, free from every shame—even the ones others will, either intentionally or without malice, heap upon them. That is what God has called me to; it is what I shall do."

It was the first time Tory had used such blunt language in front of Jack. She looked sideways to see him first flinch, then nod in acceptance.

Tory continued, "Of course, a part of my heart will always live here, and I hope to visit at least once a year."

"So, you will not be selling Sugar Tree?"

"No, I could never sell Sugar Tree, but neither will it sit empty and wasted." She drew a deep breath. "What I wish, Mr. Monroe—"

"Will you call me Jack, Miss Washington? We have been through a great deal together, have we not? I was hoping you might consider me . . . a friend?"

Tory blushed. "I do consider you a friend . . . Jack. Thank you."

"You were saying? Before I so rudely interrupted?" He grinned, making Tory laugh.

"Yes, I was saying that I wish to make Sugar Tree into a home for my friends, a safe and beautiful place for them to live out their lives in peace and with a measure of comfort. I want for Miss Defoe, Madame Rousseau, Mademoiselle Justine, Miss Sarasses, and Sassy Brown to live in the house, and I want to provide them with an annual allowance for necessities. Do I have the money to do this, Jack?"

He was already nodding, slowly. "Yours is a modest inheritance but, with care and restraint, yes, you have the money. For some time, at least." He looked up, admiration in his eyes. "It is a worthy gesture of your love for them, Miss Washington."

Tory smiled. "I am glad you feel so." She released a long breath, relieved her plan would be possible to implement.

"There is another woman at Madame's shop—her name is Marie. I did not know she still worked there until Madame told me. Marie is an unmarried and desperately unhappy individual, but she is still young and vigorous. I wish you to offer her a position at Sugar Tree—companion to my friends. Housekeeper, if you will, for as long as she likes. If she accepts, perhaps . . . perhaps she will find happiness at Sugar Tree."

"As you wish. Of course, the orchards do provide the estate with some income and a green garden would go a long way toward feeding six or more mouths."

Tory laughed, remembering the long hours of canning in the summer heat. "It fed us—my mother, Sassy Brown, and me—quite well."

"Anything else?"

"I think not. I will stay on another week to work out the minutiae. My friends must be amenable to this scheme, of course, and Madame Rousseau would need to consent to selling her shop—although I believe she actually shares joint ownership with Miss Defoe and Mademoiselle Justine. I hope the shop's sale will also give them a bit of padding for their retirement."

They had returned to the front of the house. Tory took a last look, fixing her eyes on the boarded drawing room window where she had, many times, waited for Henri Declouette to canter up the lane on his magnificent *Victorieux*.

I never called you Father or Papa, Tory thought. *I despised you and swore to hate you forever. But, you gave Sugar Tree to Maman and to me and, when you were close to your death, you acknowledged me as your daughter. Today I am grateful. For both.*

"I forgive you . . . *Papa*."

$\mathscr{P}$OSTSCRIPT

A week later, Jack saw her to the train. They had spent many hours together, going over the details of how Tory wanted Sugar Tree and its grounds to be maintained. A comfortable rapport and fellowship had grown between them, and Tory wondered if it might be a seedling, the tender sprout of something more to come.

At the moment Tory was to board the train, Jack captured her hand. "May I write to you, Miss Washington?"

Tory stared into Jack's soft hazel eyes. "I would like that."

He fumbled in his pocket. "I almost forgot." He held something in his hand. "I don't know if you will recognize these or know to whom they once belonged."

"Allllll abooooooard!"

Jack shot the conductor a frown of irritation, then opened his hand, palm up. "They are a matched pair. Quite valuable. Possibly an heirloom."

Tory started and stared, first in astonishment, then with incredulity. Her shaking fingers touched one lustrous pearl drop on a silver hook. "*Maman's* earrings? How? How!"

Jack shrugged. "After Bastiann Declouette died and the court appointed us caretakers of Sugar Tree in your absence, we removed everything of value from the house for safekeeping. As the workers were taking down your great-grandmother's portrait hanging in the drawing room, something rattled. We removed the portrait's backing and found the earrings."

"But . . . but I pawned them in the city—years ago when I was only a child. To keep from starving. How could they—"

"Allllll abooooooard! Last call!"

"We may never know all the answers in this life, Tory, but I do know this: Our God delights in showing us just how much he loves us."

Tory blinked, trying to grasp the unexpected, incomparable goodness of God in this moment.

"Miss! Are you boarding this train or not?" The conductor's patience was at an end.

"She is coming." Jack closed Tory's hand around the earrings. "Go now, Tory. And God be with you."

Tory smiled. "Goodbye . . . Jack. Until we meet again."

"Goodbye, Tory. I pray it will not be too long."

Jack held her arm and assisted her as she mounted the steps onto the train. Tory turned into the nearest car and found a seat where she could see Jack. He was searching for her. She leaned toward the window and waved. His face lit, and he waved back.

The train lurched and began to slowly move out of the station. Jack followed—weaving in and out among others on the platform, waving and keeping Tory's face before him—until he reached the end of the platform and could follow no more.

Tory flushed, then smiled again. She opened her hand and caressed the glowing pearls nestled in her palm. "I cannot thank you enough, my Lord. You truly do restore all things."

Sniffing back tears of joy, Tory fastened the earrings to her earlobes. *I shall wear these in your memory, dear Maman.*

"Miss?" The conductor stood by Tory's seat.

"Ah, my ticket. One moment." Tory found it and presented it to the waiting man.

He punched it, then hesitated.

"Yes?" Tory asked. Over his shoulder she noticed a woman staring at her. When the woman realized Tory had caught her staring, her expression hardened.

Tory returned her gaze to the conductor. "Was there something else?"

He shifted in discomfort. "I am obliged to tell you, miss, that the cars for coloreds are that way—behind us."

"The cars for . . ."

The conductor leaned a little closer. "The woman over there complained, miss. She says you are colored and, well, it is the law. I can do nothing about it."

"I see."

"Thank you, miss."

Tory began gathering her things, and the conductor moved on.

Lord? Tory stood in the aisle, indecisive. Then, instead of heading toward the cars designated for "colored," she walked toward the woman who had complained.

The woman lurched to her feet and drew back. "Do not touch me!" she hissed, both angry and a little fearful.

"Of course not," Tory answered. "I merely wished to say something to you."

"W-what?" She had to look up, because Tory towered over her.

"I wished to say that I forgive you."

"You *w-what?*"

"I forgive you, ma'am. Because God in Christ Jesus has forgiven me, I can forgive you."

"Oh!"

Tory turned and began her trek toward the back of the train. She exhaled with freedom in her heart—the freedom no person, no law, and no insult could steal.

"Stand tall, Tory. Your Father is the Most High King. He is the Glory and the Lifter of your head."

She raised her chin. "Walk like the queen you are."

THE END

Read more about Tory, Tabitha,
Rose and Joy Thoresen,
and the girls of Palmer House
in the series, **A Prairie Heritage**,
available in print and eBook format
from most online book retailers.

What a Friend We Have in Jesus

Lyrics, Joseph M. Scriven, 1855
Music, Charles C. Converse, 1868
Public Domain

In Heaven Above

Lyrics, Laurentius L. Laurinus, 1622
Norwegian Folk Melody
Revised, John Astrom
Public Domain

Alas! And Did My Savior Bleed (At the Cross)

Lyrics, Isaac Watts, 1707
Music and Refrain, Ralph E. Hudson, 1885
Public Domain

I Must Tell Jesus

Lyrics and Music, Elisha Hoffman, 1893
Public Domain

'Tis So Sweet to Trust in Jesus

Lyrics, Louisa M.R. Stead, 1882
Music, William J. Kirkpatrick, 1882
Public Domain

My Jesus, I Love Thee

Lyrics, William R. Featherston, 1864
Music, Adoniram J. Gordon, 1876
Public Domain

ABOUT THE AUTHOR

Vikki Kestell's passion for people and their stories is evident in her readers' affection for her characters and unusual plotlines. Two often-repeated sentiments are, "I feel like I know these people" and "I'm right there, in the book, experiencing what the characters experience."

Vikki holds a Ph.D. in Organizational Learning and Instructional Technologies. She left a career of twenty-plus years in government, academia, and corporate life to pursue writing full time. "Writing is the best job ever," she admits, "and the most demanding."

Also an accomplished speaker and teacher, Vikki and her husband Conrad Smith make their home in Albuquerque, New Mexico.

To keep abreast of new book releases, visit her website at **http://www.vikkikestell.com/** or connect with her on Facebook at **http://www.facebook.com/TheWritingOfVikkiKestell**.

Faith-Filled
Fiction™

www.faith-filledfiction.com | www.vikkikestell.com